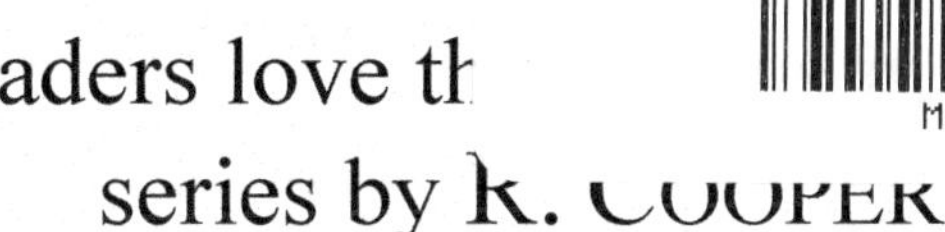

Readers love th
series by R. COOPER

Some Kind of Magic

"R. Cooper will leave you with a smile on your face as you immerse yourself in *Some Kind of Magic*, a tempting delicious tale."

—Sensual Reads

"*Some Kind of Magic* is some kind of charming… Vivid descriptions, wonderful characterizations, and terrific world building, it's all here."

—Scattered Thoughts and Rogue Words

A Boy and His Dragon

"*A Boy and His Dragon* was a surprisingly sweet romance."

—Elisa - My Reviews and Ramblings

"This is one of the loveliest romances that I have read in a while… Highly recommended if you're looking for a beautiful romance."

—Reviews by Jessewave

A Beginner's Guide to Wooing Your Mate

"…sweet, charming… I loved the magic and the baked goods in the story; they added a whimsical touch and kept things light."

—Prism Book Alliance

Little Wolf

"Expect to be wowed by this book, and expect to smile for weeks after reading it when a phrase or scene pops into your head. I can't wait to see what is coming from this author next."

—The Novel Approach

By R. COOPER

Animal Magnetism (Dreamspinner Anthology)
Let There Be Light
Medium, Sweet, Extra Shot of Geek
Play It Again, Charlie
A Wealth of Unsaid Words
Wicklow's Odyssey
Winner Takes It All

BEING(S) IN LOVE
Some Kind of Magic
A Boy and His Dragon
A Beginner's Guide to Wooing Your Mate
Little Wolf
The Firebird and Other Stories

Published by DREAMSPINNER PRESS
/www.dreamspinnerpress.com

THE Firebird and OTHER STORIES

R. Cooper

Published by
DREAMSPINNER PRESS

5032 Capital Circle SW, Suite 2, PMB# 279, Tallahassee, FL 32305-7886 USA
www.dreamspinnerpress.com/

The Firebird and Other Stories

Cover Art

http://www.paulrichmondstudio.com
Cover content is for illustrative purposes only and any person depicted on the cover is a model.

ISBN: 978-1-63476-402-5
Digital ISBN: 978-1-63476-403-2
Library of Congress Control Number: 2015945838
First Edition September 2015

Printed in the United States of America
∞
This paper meets the requirements of
ANSI/NISO Z39.48-1992 (Permanence of Paper).

For Debbie (you deserve love *and* jewelry) and for Kristi, who made Walter and Hyacinth happen.

“Of course I know the story!” the kid squawked. “Everybody’s heard it. They came fleeing down from the Ardennes in the summer heat, running from the guns. All of them naked and afraid. All of them like angels, like angels with shimmering wings.” The private’s voice grew soft there, making him sound even younger than he was. A boy like the rest of the boys here, except this one didn’t know why anyone would want to hear the story again. He didn’t know yet that there was boredom and terror and death to come, again and again and always, until gray, monotonous fear was all there was. There was nothing for men down here to do but talk and dream. Telling tales about them, those things that everyone and no one had seen, that was chatter to keep you from thinking. Stories of the creatures made me wish I’d seen one of those things instead of hearing about them. They made me afraid I wouldn’t live long enough to see anything as beautiful as a fairy with my own eyes.

I hoped I’d get the chance. A chance was worth trying for.

Excerpt from *Pavot the Fairy* by Talfryn Graves
From *The Lost Ones*
Editor J Rifkin

The Firebird

1934

KAZIMIR LICKED the lingering taste of vodka from his mouth and tried to draw strength from it as he passed his guests. On the sofas arranged before his fireplace was a group of what looked like scholars. Josephine sat among the dusty, bespectacled professors as though her provocative gown and radiant beauty did not have them stuttering. She held them at bay with experienced grace and help from both the big cat curled at her feet and Rennet seated on her lap. Josephine, braver than Kazimir, had found and raised the friendless imp child without fear of the consequences. Kazimir was fond of the boy as well, but with his head aching, he turned before the child's red eyes could meet his.

The flowing folds of Kazimir's silk kimono made not a whisper on the lush carpeting of his flat as he drifted through the sea of Parisian café society on pointed Turkish slippers. Human and magical beings alike dripped with jewels, but even those who wore no finery and lounged in his chairs with gin at their lips, speaking angrily of the suffering of the masses, sparkled as brightly as those who did. Journalists and actors and aristocrats grew tipsy as they debated the fascists in Italy and the troubles in Austria and Poland. Everyone seemed to glow, not only Kazimir and the fairy in Trudy's entourage.

The doubled-up rope of pearls at his neck felt heavy, and he regretted the impulse to wear them. But he moved through his flat without stopping. His kitchen, hidden behind closed doors, would be full of hungry, drunken revelers, or worse, poets in need of an audience, and Kazimir had no patience for that. There had been weariness in his bones from the moment he had applied his thick stage makeup tonight, and now that he was home and had removed most of it, the feeling of exhaustion had not gone away.

At Kazimir's other side were women in fur coats and men in tuxedos, as well as men in fur coats and women in tuxedos. He did not know them, but at the sight of starched white shirtfronts and tails, he turned in a new direction, away from the fire, away from the mass of bodies and curling cigarette smoke, toward the doors to the enclosed balcony.

The steady rush of rain against the glass ceiling was instant relief from the noise of so many voices, though he could still hear the child, Rennet, loudly full of impish certainty as he announced that trouble was coming, big, big trouble. In the way of imps and children, Rennet could be certain without being able to explain why.

Kazimir put his hands to his temples to rub away the lingering tension and slipped among the overgrown flowers and ferns that made his balcony a jungle. A few others were out there with him, murmuring voices somewhere out of his vision, but Kazimir brought in light to their dark place, so they either quieted or left him alone to stare out the glass.

Here it was finally cool, though the blur of the rain and his aura of fiery gold denied him a view of the streets below. He pulled his robe closed over his bare chest, though it would only fall open again, and stared at his shimmering reflection, his messy, light, short hair, his kohl-smudged eyelids. He looked tired, though of course, still beautiful. To think in such an arrogant manner was to invite a curse, but a firebird knew all there was to know of curses. The people he drew to him did not. Firebirds were creatures of tragedy, so he had been told, from his first owner to his last. Kazimir would have disagreed and told them their own greed and lust had been their undoing, but truthfully he knew nothing about firebirds. Humans had told the only stories he had heard of firebirds, and he had never met another of his kind.

Humans tended to blame the bird, and after a while, Kazimir had found that useful. He had brought about the destruction of more than one man by using the man's own desires against him. He'd been free for years, but he hadn't forgotten the skill.

Another figure appeared behind him in the glass. Kazimir frowned and felt his pulse quicken when a hand landed on his shoulder to forcibly pull him around. He swallowed hard, as though the weight of his old collar once again compressed his throat, and then he remembered himself.

He lifted his chin to a high angle and regretted his lack of a tiara, though his pearls had probably once graced the neck of a grand duchess or two. Against his luminous skin they seemed a vanity now able to be used as a weapon, easily wound tight to render him helpless. Every shiny bauble drew attention to the length of his neck, the bare lines of his collarbone. His robe, dark and embroidered with dragons, was again open nearly to his navel. Decked in black and white, his golden skin looked warm to the touch, as indeed it was, though he had given no one permission to touch him.

Light spilled in from the doorway, but most of the illumination in the darkened room came from Kazimir himself. He considered the man who had dared lay a hand on him, letting his large eyes of dark blue glitter before he lowered his eyelids to covertly look over this barbarian. The man wore a tuxedo, well tailored and new, doing all it could to flatter his figure with an eye to deny his very human middle age. He did not seem ashamed that he had lost control of himself, though he wore the slightly repentant expression of a scolded child. He also smiled, playing at being charming.

From his clothing, he clearly had money and possibly the brains to take the power that went with it. Kazimir let his robe fall open more, exposing a hint of hip bone and more golden skin. He titled his chin that much higher when the man licked his lips.

"I did not give you permission to touch me." Kazimir's voice was rough from the night's performance. The man flinched. Color suffused his cheeks, but he held out the glass in his hand, as if Kazimir had said nothing.

"I brought you some champagne." As though it were all a joke, he took Kazimir's hand and pressed the stem of the glass into it. He let his touch linger.

"I did not ask for it." Kazimir could not drain the melody from his voice any more than he could leech the color from his skin, and he could see the effect it had. Even chastened, the man flushed anew; perhaps he'd consumed several glasses of champagne before he had followed Kazimir to where he might find him unprotected. Kazimir steeled himself and tried again to penetrate the fog of drink. "I came here to be alone."

"Out here?" The man's American accent made his French as clumsy as his manners, and he could not hold his liquor. "With the rain close, you will get sick."

Most of the magical creatures Kazimir had met in his lifetime did not get sick. If this human did not know that, then he had not encountered many of them. More than seventeen years had passed since the fairies had first chosen to step back into the human world. With human expansion and human wars destroying their homes, other beings of magic had little choice but to follow. Seventeen years was enough time to learn about anything, but to many humans, magic remained forbidden, evil, or a curiosity. Seventeen years of living among them, and humans still knew nothing. They—meaning men like this one—did not even know each other, and refused to listen when they were told.

Kazimir angled his head back, feeling pearls slide invitingly against his skin, then smiled and moved away. He went a few steps along the window, then stopped at the lock on the little opening in the glass wall where a bird might fly free. The man followed him. Kazimir could have met him before, or the man could have been any other pale, frightened man with excited, lust-filled eyes, who held on with grasping fingers yet still felt Kazimir slip away.

Kazimir twisted to glance at him, aware of what his sapphire gaze did, the challenge it presented. He let his lips part. "Do you think me delicate? In need of protection?"

Perhaps the man had a wife. He recognized the tone of the words this time, frowning in confused displeasure at being mocked. "Aren't you in a good humor, pretty bird?" Something of a whine crept into his voice. "I brought you champagne."

"So you said." Kazimir turned away again, offering a glimpse of shoulder as he readjusted his robe. To the side, he saw motion, as if they had a witness. Kazimir allowed his robe to dip as he crept away from the hungry American. He moved toward whoever else was on the balcony with them.

The man ignored the hint and stepped back into Kazimir's line of sight. His flush seemed deeper, even in the dim light. "If I didn't know any better, I would say you were avoiding me, and all I've done is bring you a drink. I wanted to compliment your performance tonight. I have never heard anything like that."

"Truly?" Kazimir did not affect boredom, did not have to, but he did not turn away again. "What do you think of my necklace?" he asked coolly, displaying the pearls in his palm by rolling a few between his fingers.

"Lovely." The man swayed in toward him, his expression too eager. "Do you like those? I can get you more if only—"

"If only?" Kazimir drew him in, recognizing the man at last. He had seen him outside his dressing room, been caught alone by him before. The man had offered Kazimir roses the first time, then orchids when Kazimir had told him no. Kazimir vaguely recalled the fact of a wife, an angry woman with a lined face, with a tiara Kazimir would have taken if only to spare her the humiliation of it and the reasons her husband had given it to her. It would have looked beautiful on him, for he was beautiful, and he would have worn it without shame.

Those who were shamed were never the ones who should have been. Kazimir looked at the man, watching his eyes consider the value of the pearls around his neck and then calculate the value of Kazimir himself.

"If only you would be mine," the man finished, gulping as if his own lust shocked him.

Kazimir did not smile, though he shivered at a frisson of fear. He stared without speaking, without breathing, then turned his back on the man. His blood in his ears deafened him.

"Have I displeased you?" The man would still talk, meaningless words steeped in frustration and a growing awareness of his failure, though he did not yet consciously know he had failed. Kazimir knew who the man would blame when he did, and tensed when he was again spun around by his shoulder. The man had returned to English, assuming Kazimir would know it, or not caring if he didn't. "What do you want, then? If not pearls, what? Pearls would do for dragons, they told me. Fairies require nothing—they are so desperate for affection. All of you desperate things, out in the cold without us, especially you." The man's face twisted, growing ugly for the first time. "You magic émigrés are like every other useless royal in Paris. You think you are above it all, but you would be nowhere without men like me. We are the ones who pay for your apartments and your jewels. Those pearls weren't cheap."

For a moment the man breathed harshly in and out. Then he leaned in, and Kazimir could not help wanting to fall back. "I will be generous. Only tell me what you want."

Kazimir tightened his hold on his necklace. He shuddered visibly at the hot breath on his skin but swept the fear away enough to raise his chin and roll a shoulder. His robe slipped farther, but he swallowed and spoke in English, his voice like crystal.

"Do nothing, for I want nothing." Kazimir gathered his strength and yanked at the necklace until the thread snapped, sending pearls out across the floor. Two remained in his palm, and he clutched them tighter at the burning pain at his neck. "To hell with you."

"The cost of those…." The man had lost control again, arguing cost in cracking words. "Those were valuable."

"To some." Kazimir glanced away. He looked back a moment later, noticing that their audience had remained for the denouement. For the benefit of that audience, Kazimir took the glass of champagne and tossed its contents into the nearest plant. The glass itself he threw over his shoulder and did not care where it landed.

The sound of breaking glass was drowned out by screams from his living room, accompanied by laughter. Kazimir wondered if Rennet had freed the cheetah again, mere seconds before the cheetah's sleek, spotted form dashed into the room, a cackling devil-child hot on its heels. For a moment only, boy and beast were illuminated by the outside light, and then Kazimir's view was blocked by the man, who shouted to see the big cat on the loose, and ran from the balcony.

Kazimir blinked, turning to follow the two wild creatures playing tag among his plants, before imp and cat slipped out the same way they had come in. More screams preceded them as people saw them coming. His guests might be leaving Kazimir's flat sooner than he had expected. As a reward he should give Rennet all the pearls he could find to play with.

"That was quite a show," remarked someone from the shadows. Kazimir's head ached, but he kept his chin up while the witness came forward until the toes of his shoes were on the edge of Kazimir's soft circle of light.

His audience was a man of average height, with a stubborn jaw, though part of his face was hidden by an unfashionable short growth of beard and a small mustache. It didn't seem deliberate, but more as though the man had forgotten to shave for a few days. Curls of brown fell into his face where they were not tucked behind his ears, and glasses hid his eye color, but his clothes were plain—a shirt and pants, with braces, or suspenders as Americans called them. The man was American too, though his French accent was better. Kazimir had the impression of a direct gaze before the man glanced away again. His lips were full and pliant.

"Do you mean at the theater tonight or what occurred here?" Kazimir stared at him, waiting for the man to look at him again, wondering why he would look anywhere else with Kazimir in the room.

"*Here.*" The emphasis on the word was almost amusing. "What just took place. Though I also thought your performance tonight was incredible. Not everyone gets an opera written for them. Not everyone deserves it."

He implied that Kazimir did, which Kazimir already knew. But Kazimir nodded, and the man took a drink from his own glass. It held something brown, with ice. The man swallowed with evident pleasure and then said nothing, continuing to keep his eyes from Kazimir.

"You should not capture a firebird," Kazimir addressed the topic at hand, and watched soft lips open on what could have been a silent laugh. His glow was flattering to the man's cheekbones, the light olive tone to his cheeks.

"Should not?" The stranger moved, and Kazimir got a hint of dark eyes narrowed in thought. "Was that act for his benefit, then?"

"If not his, then for the next creature he tries to buy." Kazimir shrugged and sighed loudly at the stillness from the man opposite him. "You have more to say? You think I was cruel? That he did not deserve rejection?"

The man considered him over the wire rim of his glasses. Kazimir knew he was being studied, and yet could not catch the man's gaze. The strange, somewhat insolent human took another drink of his brown booze. "You didn't have much respect for his feelings."

Kazimir surprised himself by letting out a short, icy laugh. "He should have had respect for mine."

"Were yours clear?" If possible, the man seemed equally amused, though Kazimir did not understand why he should be, unless he found Kazimir himself funny. The human could have been one of those men who showed disgust at things like magic or the blended world that magical creatures lived in, where human morals and customs did not apply. He barely looked over thirty, but it was not only old men who regarded fairies and demons with hatred and loathing. Lately many seemed to, as if the problems of the world were to be laid at their door. Beings of magic had not been the ones destroying banks and dividing countries into arbitrary pieces.

Kazimir drew himself up and curled one hand into a fist, the two remaining pearls hard in his palm. "What responsibility is it of mine to make my feelings clear? My feelings are *mine*." His voice rang out; the little American would not argue. Kazimir kept on. "He was told no. It's not my fault he did not listen."

He let out a puff of air and wished for more vodka. It was a long time before he thought of speaking again, but when the American did not say a word, he chose to answer with silence, and so they stood. Then the American shifted forward again, coming farther into Kazimir's light but stopping before Kazimir had to step back. Kazimir wondered if this human had seen him shudder away from a touch earlier, or if he had simply been raised with better manners.

The man finally inclined his head.

"A no should be clear enough for anyone." He granted Kazimir the point. "I'm sorry."

Kazimir felt something, not altogether fear, slide down his spine. He frowned and made his smile cold. "Human men in general usually do not give ground until forced to," he pronounced, bitter and unsurprised, and wondered if a mere glimpse of his neck would be enough to undo this one, or if more would be required.

The American stared to the side for a moment longer, then took another drink. He gave Kazimir a short look, then snorted and spoke in English. "Fucking true enough," he remarked. "We will defend to the last man slivers of ground of no value for the sake of appearing to avoid retreat."

Kazimir was not entirely sure he translated the confusing statement correctly. Before he could ask, the American went on, growing warmer at the subject, or from his liquor. "Not to say you have no value, or that you are a piece of land. Merely agreeing with you. It's difficult to let go. It *can* be difficult." He scowled at his glass.

"You are drunk." Kazimir was neither amused nor shocked, although he was not certain why he bothered commenting. Most of his guests were currently swimming in gin.

"Usually." The American hummed a little, a piece from the opera tonight. "I usually am, when not working. May I ask you something?" He paused. "Did you not like the pearls? The gesture was beautifully executed, and I applauded, but outside of this apartment, people are hungry."

"And the inhuman creature throws away pearls while the bread lines grow." Kazimir glanced down as he straightened his robe, and when he raised his eyes, the American was staring right at him. It took Kazimir too long to speak again. "Perhaps I prefer diamonds." He held the man's gaze even with the touch of electricity along his spine and the ache in his bones. "Do you have diamonds?" He ducked his head to inhale greedily and then glanced up, an unrivalled courtesan. He swept a look over the American's clothes, noting the lack of starch in the shirt, as if it had been worn a few times since its last cleaning. It might be the man's sole dress shirt. Kazimir clucked his tongue pityingly and straightened. "I don't think you do." He sighed as if bored, and waited. When insulted, some dogs licked your hand, others bit.

This dog tilted his head to one side. "You want diamonds? Common diamonds?" He seemed unwilling to admit the possibility that anyone would see a diamond as anything other than a shiny stone, though he returned the same intense study Kazimir had given him.

Kazimir felt himself go still. The human pretended not to see, though he must have.

"No, rubies surely. You must have been offered rubies too," the American went on, then wrinkled his nose and gave Kazimir another of his brief, searching glances. "Forgive me, but as much as I can see you in jewels, your own natural beauty would render them redundant. You're handsome, yes, your jaw, your shoulders, your tapered waist and straight nose, but mostly… beautiful. Beautiful is the word that best suits you, or, I should say, it is the only word that comes to mind that wouldn't embarrass me."

"So you offer me no jewels at all?" Kazimir could have played coy, accepted the compliment and whatever money the man did have. He intended to, but the words escaped him in a sad lilt when there should have been a scornful blast of sound.

"Flowers. Those I could give you, if I had the money to, which I don't." The American nodded and took another drink. Kazimir could not tell if he meant it; the man looked at Kazimir in the same manner as before—direct and then from the side, strangely shy. He was a schoolboy until he spoke.

"Roses?" Kazimir angled his chin up and let out a pointed, light yawn. His heart would not slow. "Orchids?"

"Mere weeds!" the American scoffed, serious or playful, Kazimir could not determine and did not allow himself to react, though the American went on. He was ridiculous and had to be teasing. "Painted blooms in paper coffins, cut and wrapped and stuffed into a vase for display. No, not those. Not for you."

"What, then?" Kazimir leaned back against a wrought-iron stand, velvety fern fronds tickling his bare skin. He put his wrist to his forehead dramatically, like a film actress. The American's breath seemed to leave him in a rush, and when Kazimir looked, the man was watching him, earnestly now, if he had not been before.

"Wildflowers, the kind I have only ever seen in fields in Belgium, the kinds that grow on this continent no matter what is done to the land. Cascading colors so bright they're obscene. Blooms so beautiful they make you forget that even flowers fight for survival. Wildflowers, hardier than anything grown in a nursery. I'd make you a necklace—or perhaps a crown of them, like the fairies do."

"Free flowers, then?" Kazimir countered. His hand fell to his throat, though the weight of the pearls was long gone.

The American threw his head back and laughed. He was too loud from drink, but his laugh was still a rich, pleased sound that drew attention. A few people stopped at the doorway to peek at them.

"No jewels and no flowers will please you, Monsieur Firebird?" He was charming now suddenly, this American, leaving Kazimir to stare and wonder where the shyness had gone. One moment they had been jesting back and forth, and now Kazimir was warm, as if he were being seduced.

People usually did not seduce something they thought to buy. Kazimir struggled to remember the American's question about jewels and flowers.

"I have never asked for them," Kazimir insisted, still with his hand at his throat, and the man dropped his crooked smile before Kazimir had fully realized it was there.

"So you throw them away as though they are nothing? Or do you scorn them because they are lures in a trap?" He was gruff but quiet, and once again Kazimir could not tell if he was joking. He could not ask any more than he could ask for stories of these fields where wildflowers grew. Kazimir had traveled by train many years ago, but had never stopped to look out at farmland turned gray with trenches and rain.

Kazimir took a breath. "That is no way to talk, Monsieur L'Américain, not if you wish to win a firebird." He was not drunk, but he sang it out, so sweetly it seemed a mockery of his intention. For some reason a biting tone escaped him and his words emerged soft and curious.

The American frowned. "You said I should not—" he started, but was cut off by the arrival of Michel, who turned on the lights as he strode in. The American shut his eyes for a moment and swore, in the crude manner that seemed his habit. "Fuck."

Kazimir took a moment to study him in the light, from the shine in his brown curls to the dull scuff of his shoes. His trousers were recently ironed, but frayed, and a tarnished watch was ready to fall from his pocket. His lips were indeed yielding and pink, but held lines at the corners that spoke of pain. He was no schoolboy, but older than thirty, though not much. He was thin, and his skin had a tint of its own, as if good food and sun were all that were needed to make him beautiful. That, and perhaps a shave. He was not a picture of health. His skin was dotted with sweat despite the chill, like a tipsy human without much money who had not eaten a solid meal in some time.

Kazimir's kitchen held plenty of food, although Kazimir himself subsisted mostly on bread and tea and vodka. He thought of offering this American food from his pantry and then wondered why he should bother. But an hors d'oeuvre held out in one slender, golden hand might bring that gaze up to meet his. Two, and the American might say what he meant instead of hinting. Three, and he might never leave.

Many were starving in the world outside the flat, that was true. But a certain kind lived the way this man did, living on ideals instead of practicality. That made him an artist or musician or writer, someone who others thought was brilliant, and who might actually be. But there was no paint on his strong, well-shaped hands, only ink and faint white lines, crisscrossing between his fingers and at the edge of his palms.

"One of yours?" Kazimir raised his head and looked to Michel. He found it hard to do and did not care for the feeling. This was not the first drunk human to offer him flowers. Kazimir had no need to keep staring at him.

Michel stroked his delicate mustache and shook his head to indicate the American was not his lover. "Found another diamond in the rough, Kaz?" he inquired merrily, seemingly unaware of Kazimir's irritation at the name and at the stream of people now following Michel onto the balcony.

The American opened his eyes, only to immediately avert his gaze from Kazimir. He faced Michel. “I thought he did not care for diamonds.” The people entering the room were tripping on the scattered pearls, spilling clumsily onto each other and giggling. The American finally darted a glance to Kazimir, revealing lustrous eyes of amber brown. “I feel as though I should make a comment about pearls before swine.” He quirked his lips. Kazimir stared back and denied his urge to return the smile until the man’s gaze returned to his glass.

“Don’t talk nonsense.” Michel pooh-poohed the American with a wave of his hand, and continued in effortless English. “This is our Kazimir, generous benefactor to the desperate and deserving. He’s a lot like you, Rifkin, spotting genius before the geniuses do. In the stories I have heard, firebirds and their like are creatures of inspiration, leading men to greatness or ruin. I think Kaz’s ability to spot talent has something to do with what he is, but he won’t tell me. He enjoys the mystery.”

Kazimir affected a pout at Michel for lavishing such praise on the stranger in front of him, and knew the American, Rifkin, was watching him again.

“You’re wrong. There is no one like him,” Rifkin offered abruptly, lifting his head for another direct look, one aimed at Michel. Michel seemed taken aback, though not for long, and then he grinned and poked Kazimir in the ribs.

“You’ve made another conquest, Kaz! You will not rest until the hearts of Paris are under your feet. But take care with this one.” He poked Kazimir again, harder, as if this time he was truly cross. “We need him a whole man. Perhaps then he will create for us again.”

“What is it he does, Michel, that the world needs him whole?” Kazimir put his head up to watch the lightning in Rifkin’s eyes. Rifkin did not seem to like being discussed and made no effort to hide it; Michel was simply oblivious as he explained Rifkin spent much of his time editing. “Editing?” Kazimir tutted. He kept his eyes on Rifkin’s face. “How dull.” The flash of lightning was directed at him now, full and fearless, and yet the man made no move. Kazimir lifted a hand and held it out in a lazy, placating gesture. “But I’m sure it’s exciting when *you* do it.”

Rifkin gave Kazimir's hand a hot look, appearing as though he would rather bite than kiss it, but when he met Kazimir's eyes, he stilled. A moment later he smiled. The glimpse of teeth was rueful. "You are good, Firebird. You are very good." He let Kazimir's hand stay in the air between them. "Am I supposed to rise to the challenge and try to prove you wrong? What if I do? Will you throw that in my face too, or sigh in disappointment and claim you never asked me to do it? Your ability to inspire used as a weapon… that is… that is truly frightening, Firebird, if it's real."

"Kazimir," Kazimir corrected him, dropping his hand and feeling something burn through his skin at being so denied. "My name is Kazimir, not Firebird, and you would have to accept the challenge to find out."

"I…." Michel coughed uncertainly, then tossed his head with a nervous laugh. "Oh la la, what have I done?"

"We are putting out a book soon. You will have to wait until then to discover how good I am." Rifkin's glasses reflected Kazimir's golden glow, but his skin seemed to absorb it, rendering him in diffused, soft light, at odds with the nature of his words. He sighed suddenly and glanced away again. "If we ever get the damn thing out."

"The stories I have seen so far have been wonderful!" Michel interjected, with some desperation. He turned to Kazimir and gestured between them. "Kazimir," he began in that tone he was so fond of using, the one that said he had someone Kazimir simply *must* meet, and wouldn't Kazimir *please* help him in supporting them with generous amounts of money. "Kazimir, this is the man I told you about all those weeks ago." Michel had mentioned no Rifkin that Kazimir remembered. Kazimir gave Michel an unforgiving glare, and Michel promptly swung toward Rifkin to gesture at him for Kazimir's benefit. "Kaz, do you know what it took to get him here?"

"A great deal of whisky?" Kazimir guessed dryly, and Rifkin snorted.

"Tickets to your opera!" Michel corrected, nearly twitching. "I had to bribe him and then force him here. The man never stops working. I thought if you met him, if you beheld him with your very eyes, you would want to read what they have done." Kazimir gave him a cutting look, but Michel, the idiot, did not see it. Kazimir did not think Rifkin would be so blind, not even when drunk. Kazimir imagined, somehow, impossibly, that Rifkin might even understand Kazimir's true nature if Kazimir gave him the chance to. It could not be true, and yet Kazimir wanted to make those eyes meet his, more than he had wanted anything in a long time.

"Kazimir." Michel was almost swooning now. "Kazimir, speak to him and you will want to help get it published! He and his friends, such brilliance!" As though he had just eaten a delicious meal, Michel kissed his own fingers in excitement. Michel was not the sort to praise lightly.

"Brilliance," Kazimir repeated dryly, despite quaking inside to know that it was true. He raised an eyebrow at Rifkin. "And you write as well?"

"No," Rifkin said curtly, then hesitated and seemed to change his mind. "Not for others to read." He finished his drink in a gulp and appeared sorry to see it gone. He swiped a martini from a tipsy man who had bumped into him and knocked over one of Kazimir's plants. Rifkin pulled the onion out of the glass with his fingers and flicked it at the man when the fellow protested. "Be more careful with other people's things," Rifkin instructed him, then licked his thumb with a shrug when the man moved on without further argument.

Kazimir's lips parted. He had to tear his eyes away to face Michel while he wondered what kind of creature Michel had brought him. Whatever Kazimir's expression, it made Michel thrust his half-drunk cocktail at him and start in with an explanation of the book Rifkin had edited, and his work with a circle of writers. He stopped when Kazimir pushed the drink back at him, untouched.

Kazimir turned to Rifkin when Michel nodded encouragingly. Rifkin let their eyes meet this time. Perhaps the stolen martini made him brave, but he made a small, soft sound of pain when Kazimir faced him.

People wanted Kaz. They sometimes hated him. They did not stare at him with hurt in their pretty eyes.

Kazimir fought the need to offer apologies or to stroke a hand over shining brown curls. "A secret writer? Shouldn't you be starving in a garret, living in sin, as humans say, and suffering for art and beauty?"

His American took a sip from his martini, the old wounds on his hands clearly visible. He winced as he swallowed, as if he did not care for either gin or the sweetness of the vermouth, but kept his gaze steady, for a time.

"Not all art is beautiful." He tipped his head back to finish the drink, then thrust the glass at Michel, who took it and said nothing when Rifkin helped himself to Michel's cocktail too.

Kazimir briefly closed his eyes at the memory of the strong column of Rifkin's throat as he swallowed. "Perhaps we have different definitions of beautiful," he argued, breathing hard, as though he had just finished singing. For a moment he forgot where he was, who he was, and stepped forward, shivering when Rifkin raised his eyes to meet his.

Rifkin again made a quiet noise of pain. "You are beautiful," Rifkin told him, his mouth still wet and his cheeks flushed. "Creature of goddamn magic." He spoke like he couldn't fully credit magic as real, as many humans did, even now. They wanted magic to be the thing from their fairy tales. Magic to do everything, or nothing, to fix entire broken nations when it had not even been able to free Kazimir from the single room where his first master had kept him locked away. For all his power, Kazimir's mind had been his salvation. *Magic* was simply a word for the many things humans did not understand. "Beautiful," Rifkin repeated himself, but the wording was changed now. "Creature of magic."

"Is that all I am?" Kazimir heard his voice go too high and knew Michel noticed, but Rifkin had done something, and he could not look away. He did not think it was a human spell, but it took Kazimir's words from him. He straightened his robe onto his shoulders and frowned when he caught himself doing it.

"No, there is more," Rifkin announced at last, dropping his gaze again. "I have heard you sing. Magic might make your voice what it is, but *how* you sang, that was you, I think." He exhaled, long and slow, and closed his eyes. Kazimir wondered if he was thinking of a far-off field of flowers, but when he opened his eyes, Rifkin chose to focus on his glass. "I believe you know precisely what it means to create, don't you? You use it as a weapon, one of many, for all that you appear delicate. You are familiar with pain, and fear, but you are not hindered by them, and it's that which elevates you above other singers."

Kazimir nearly put his hands over his ears. Artists could be worse than seers when it came to the truth. Artists could challenge imps in acts of destruction and creation, and could leave footsteps behind them that lasted longer than the oldest fairy. The creators among the humans were the strongest and weakest of them. Most of them wanted Kazimir, and he used that. This one was shaking his head.

"You are very beautiful, but not for me," Rifkin informed him, continuing in the dreamy tone of a witch over a pool of water. "I will not chase you in order to capture you, and I could never woo you with what little I have to offer. I am but one of the swine." He spoke in a whisper, almost at Michel, and curved his mouth into an unhappy smile. A moment later he inclined his head in farewell, and Kazimir realized the man truly intended to leave, without money, or inspiration, or Kazimir himself.

Kazimir squared his shoulders, sending his robe down to his elbows, baring enough skin to light the room and make Rifkin's eyes widen.

"*Writers*," Kazimir hissed. He raised himself up, fire in his blood. "Am I not worth winning?" he demanded, sending the words out to frost the windows and turn all heads in their direction. Rifkin's lovely mouth went slack, and yet for all that his eyes were large and his throat delectable, Kazimir did not see what about this man should have driven those words from him. He clenched his hand tight and felt the pearls against his palm. Michel made a startled sound next to him that pushed Kazimir's chin farther up into the air, so high that a crown would have fallen to the floor if he had been wearing one. "*You* will not decide the worth of anything," he declared, swaying forward until he could curl his fingers around Rifkin's hand. "*I* will decide."

He pulled the martini toward him slowly, keeping Rifkin's gaze on him as he lifted his other hand and dropped his two remaining pearls into the mix of gin and vermouth. The glass was cold; his American's hands were hot. Kazimir felt heat in his fingertips when he released him and grew confused when Rifkin looked at him with that shining gaze before bowing his head once more.

The small show of respect was acceptable for the sacrifice of the pearls. They were nothing to Kazimir, and Rifkin knew that. Yet Kazimir kept his chin up for another moment longer, thinking of sirens and ships crashing into rocks, of ruin and approaching trouble, and a vast, open field blanketed in flowers. He had passed those fields and knew what those flowers had grown over. Rifkin was one of them, like Michel, one of the lost ones.

He stared, they both did, scarcely blinking, and then Michel coughed anxiously.

"For your book," Kazimir whispered with his American's unwavering gaze on him. The sentence made no sense to him. Kazimir supported nearly as many artists as Michel, but he had never before given them money in such a manner. He had as good as thrown the pearls away *and* stolen a gesture from Cleopatra. He thought perhaps he was piqued by Rifkin's refusal to worship him, and yet Rifkin already admitted he found Kazimir worthy of awe.

Kazimir's confusion rendered him mute. He could not breathe to say another word and fluttered against Michel at the realization. Rifkin's eyes seemed to tighten, and Kazimir put a hand on Michel to draw himself up to a graceful pose. He was Firebird Kazimir, he fell before no man, but it took another step before he could breathe easily again.

The look in Rifkin's eyes softened, but he didn't glance away. "You give me a gift?" he asked, with strain in his voice.

Too late, Kazimir realized he had done exactly that. He looked to Michel, astonishment leaving him silent. Michel seemed equally stunned, although when a slow smile began to curve his mouth, Kazimir quickly turned to Rifkin.

"In that case…." Rifkin paused. "In that case, I can hardly refuse, can I?" There was such pain in his eyes. Kazimir had not meant to create that, and he clucked his tongue.

"You can." Kazimir heard himself speaking gently. He shook as much as the drunken human he had chosen to chase after and felt his headache begin to pound in earnest. "You *may*. I hold no one captive."

He did not know if it was his tone or his words, but Rifkin blinked and then tightened his hold on the glass. He boldly drained the martini and poured out the pearls into his palm. He stared at them for some time before bringing his gaze up to Kazimir. Kazimir surprised himself by immediately glancing away.

"What have you done?" Michel wondered, at Kazimir's side. "You did not curse him? Tell me you did not."

Firebirds, or at least Kazimir, did not curse in the manner of human sorcerers and witches. They gave gifts. They granted inspiration and showed the path to greatness. Most people could not bear these things, and it led to their ruin. But for some the gift was truly that—a gift.

Kazimir shook his aching head while keeping a careful eye on Rifkin. He had not cursed him, but it felt as if he had, and he could not say why.

Rifkin saluted both of them with the empty glass before stumbling from the room. He appeared dazed. Kazimir was light-headed as well and had no liquor to blame.

"He will write for me." Kazimir had inspired many men. This should mean nothing. But Kazimir had asked. He had *given*. And in return… that was the difference. Kazimir had asked for something in return. "He will write for me, and it will hurt. Has it always hurt them?" The question was foolish. Of course the act of creation hurt. But most *wanted* it. Men had imprisoned Kazimir for the chance to suffer for their art. This one hadn't wanted the gift but then had taken it, and Kazimir didn't know why, or why it mattered.

Kazimir drew in a shaky breath. *Something* had transpired on this balcony. Not for the first time he wished he'd known another of his kind, perhaps his parents, who could have explained to him why he was trembling. Everything around them was now quiet enough for Rennet's words to echo back to him from earlier—trouble was coming.

Kazimir suddenly couldn't stand the silence and spun away. He hurried from the balcony, through the rapidly emptying blankness of his flat. There was no sign of Rifkin, or of anyone else, save a few lingering scholars, and Josephine, and her big cat, and Rennet.

Rennet smiled at him.

THE DIN of voices kept Kazimir behind his screen for a longer time than he needed to slip out of parts of his costume. So many people were in his dressing room that his dresser was out dealing with them, so Kazimir had to tangle with the orange and yellow feathers of his headpiece by himself. Long plumes, dyed in vibrant colors, spotted with sequins and crystals meant to catch the light and emulate the spectacle of a fully transformed firebird—a sight he was certain no one involved with the opera had ever witnessed. Similar feathers were attached to the arm pieces, which Kazimir always removed the moment he was off stage. Only the tail feathers and the chest piece didn't bother him, perhaps because the tail feathers weren't nearly as long as his own, and he found them amusing.

He had little patience for them tonight, however, and let them fall to the floor. He removed the chest piece too, leaving himself in the opera house's version of a *kosovorotka* and *shavovary*, a very shiny tunic shirt and trousers. The costume was surprisingly light, but tonight feathers seemed to fall off as if shaken, and stuck in glass beads as they tried to float free. The headpiece caught on the net holding his hair down, and he yanked them both from him. It left his hair ruffled.

The elaborate costume followed the story of his opera, one written for his voice as well as for what he was. Humans had taken an interest in the old stories in the past decades, reclaiming ancient myths and ignoring the facts in front of them. They used fairy stories and magic to make human heroes seem stronger in the face of an increasingly violent and confusing world. His opera was about a seductive firebird offering to help an innocent peasant boy, only to lead him to ruin. Kazimir ruined no innocents, but that did not matter. The public loved tales of humans led astray by wicked magic, and when the firebird died at the end, repentant and realizing too late the love he had destroyed, they both wept and cheered.

Their cheering had carried over into his dressing room, where he could hear them praising the energy in his performance. Many in the group were his friends, and yet not one of them could see how he might detest the opera that had brought him even greater fame. The songs were written for his range, and beautiful, but none of them praised the way he chose to sing, and the one who had was nowhere to be seen.

Kazimir had issued a challenge that should have had someone tripping over his feet to prove himself. Instead he was alone, and had been alone, for a week. There had been no word from Michel's newest genius. Of itself, that might mean Kazimir had frightened away the American after all, or that Rifkin was drunk again and had forgotten him. Kazimir was older than he looked, and experienced in the ways of men in ways that Rifkin would likely never understand. The loss of one drunken, failed writer should not bother him.

But the lights were turned up too brightly in a room filled by his natural brilliance, and the chatter around him was deafening. The sole thing in his stomach was a bite of chocolate from a box left on his makeup table by an admirer. Eating the chocolate was tantamount to inviting the unknown gift giver to reveal himself, but Kazimir had popped it into his mouth with a short, furious look around the crowded room before disappearing behind his changing screens.

He did not want to be a part of a crowd tonight. He wanted the solitude of his room, and the city lights through his window. A weight was on his chest, holding him down, and though he didn't understand it, he fell asleep every night curled protectively around it until morning. The feeling was stronger than waiting. He thought it was yearning, and shivered for the realization. If so little contact could create this, it was better that Rifkin had not returned. He had no obligation to. This was not a fairy tale where gifts came with strings and hidden promises.

But Kazimir winced as he stepped out into the main room and poured himself a glass of water. He was immediately surrounded as he drank it. The giver of the chocolates was the first to make himself known. A boy, barely a man, who introduced himself as Jean Drumont, and dressed with the confidence of old money. His name had been in the newspapers of late, which Kazimir would have remembered, even if the boy hadn't felt the need to remind him. The right-wing parties numbered many youth among them, boys too young or too sheltered to know what the world really was, and who thought the answer to all problems was more control.

Kazimir felt no surprise to find someone who would condemn the licentious ways of beings and homosexuals in his dressing room. That too, had happened before. But the age of the boy startled him, and for a moment Kazimir felt like one of the humans complaining the world was going to hell while every previously known fact slipped through his fingers.

The boy was only a few years older than Rifkin would have been when he'd first entered the trenches, but he was clean and untouched by the hardships of the world. Kazimir stopped him the second Drumont placed a hand on his arm. "I took of a gift freely given. In doing so, I have promised you nothing, but I will offer you my thanks." He added a cool smile simply for the expression of shock on the boy's face. "Thank you. It was fair enough, for chocolate."

The boy held champagne in his other hand. Kazimir tipped his empty water glass at him in farewell and turned away.

The boy followed. "It wasn't your thanks I was after." His tone was hot, insistent, but Kazimir moved away. He glided over to his dresser to hand off the glass and then draped his travel coat around himself so the feathers at the collar hid part of his face.

"You were trying to win me?" Kazimir yawned and languidly petted some of the feathers away from his mouth, although his heart was pounding. "My answer is no."

Again, Drumont grabbed his arm. "That isn't the way this works."

The room did not go silent, although it felt as though some of the crowd stepped away. Too many of the rich and well-mannered were here, people who liked the glamour of the opera and felt exotic to know a being, but when they went home, they would be back among the Drumonts, and those like them.

Kazimir flicked the boy a look of boredom and busied his nervous hands. "Didn't you and your fascist friends set some buildings afire last week during one of your riots?" He didn't wait for an answer or for the boy to argue for his cause. "Then I know how you think this goes. But I assure you, it does not. I will not be there in the background to support your rise to glory. Unless, of course, you wanted to take me home with you as your guest. Shall I meet your parents? Walk into church on your arm?"

He shook his head before smoothing down the feathers at his collar once more, knowing the boy's gaze followed the sweep of his hands. "No? Then go away. I am no one's caged bird."

"Perhaps it's your opera that makes him think you are." The quiet voice was familiar enough to make Kazimir too warm for his coat. He did not know what expression crossed his face, but as he turned to meet Rifkin, he glimpsed Drumont's wide-eyed shock.

Rifkin was there, with Michel, the best of men. Rifkin was pale and unsteady on his feet, with deep, dark shadows beneath his eyes and fingerprints on his glasses. He wore the same suit, his one good suit, perhaps his only suit, and appeared even thinner than he had the last time. But there was color in his cheeks and his eyes were bright. As if he had no time for shyness tonight, or simply to confuse Kazimir, he did not look away.

"The opera is beautiful," Kazimir told him, despite the rush of air into his lungs as the weight lifted from his chest. Rifkin—no, Jacob, Michel had told him his first name was Jacob—was a starving, handsome, foolish man, and he had come at last. Kazimir could not settle, and ruffled his feathers in barely concealed excitement. "Several people have told me so. You among them." Kazimir tried to pull back but ended up clutching at the coat he no longer wanted to wear. He deliberately raked his eyes over Jacob's body, noting his empty hands. "I see no offerings for me."

Jacob's soft lips twisted into a smile Kazimir didn't understand. "You will be my death, but I will die happy."

He didn't seem upset at his own statement. Michel, on the other hand, took him seriously. "Please, no talk of death," he begged, and put his hands out in a silent plea for a new subject.

Kazimir kept his attention on Jacob Rifkin, drunkard and editor and theater critic. "What is wrong with my opera?" he demanded icily, pulling himself up, although his anger was strangely absent.

"You don't have a problem with it?" Jacob was surprised. "I'll admit, distracted by you the first time, I overlooked a lot. But now that I've met you, everything felt wrong. The firebird was beautiful, *you* were beautiful, your voice… but you existed in the story only to be tragic. No, to be tragic for the human boy, which is all I have seen in these new stories of magical creatures. All of you living and dying to make a human look better, instead of living for yourselves!" Jacob's voice was rising, but he didn't seem aware. "Even the love didn't ring true! If he loved you, he shouldn't have asked anything from you. He should have offered you something of himself. Maybe that's nothing to someone like you, with your talent and beauty, but it would have been a sign of something real. You gain with love, but you lose something too. Or it becomes something else formed from the two parts, or…."

There Jacob paused and blinked as though the emotion in his words startled him. Then he twisted his mouth in another bittersweet smile. "After everything the firebird did for him, he should have been the one giving himself away piece by piece to help you, not demanding more and more from you and calling it love. And then there was that ending. That fucking ending, Kazimir." He blinked. "There has never been beauty like you in that final moment in which you realize that you love the one keeping you captive, so you die for him. But—" Jacob snorted. "Fuck that."

Kazimir held himself motionless for a single moment, perhaps two, and then exhaled. "Jacob Rifkin, you have come to me at last, and sober."

He got a squint, and then Jacob returned to his shy ways. He glanced to the side, and their audience. "I didn't mean to be sober. Michel insisted." Jacob had the sound of a chastened boy, but only briefly. "You wanted me here? I wasn't sure. The other night I was very…. I was good and lit from all the drinks I had. I have a tendency to be direct at the best of times. Perhaps I was rude?"

Kazimir wondered if he was smiling. He felt like frowning and smiling both and couldn't tell which had won out. The feeling was unfamiliar. "Our first meeting, and you do not recall it?" He forced himself to pout. It earned him another squint. Then Jacob grinned crookedly at him, young and handsome.

"Now you're teasing me again, Firebird. Kazimir." Jacob paused as a thought seemed to occur to him. "Who told you my name?"

Michel flapped his hands as though to absolve himself of any guilt.

"I've invested in you," Kazimir defended himself, though it was a clumsy excuse at best for asking about Jacob after their meeting. Which was something Jacob had not mentioned, and now Kazimir was twice the fool for admitting it.

He put a hand to his cheek and frowned at Michel, uncertain what was wrong with him. Jacob opened his mouth, then closed it.

"Who is this?" Drumont pushed his way into the conversation. He gestured at Jacob, who turned to him with that lazy, considering manner that Kazimir had first seen on him before he'd stolen a man's drink and challenged him to a fight. It seemed a natural part of him, even when sober.

Jacob finished his study of Drumont, then angled away from him and continued addressing Kazimir as if Drumont weren't there. "Yet another persistent admirer who does not understand polite rejection—or *were* you polite this time? Not that it matters. A no is a no is a no. Oh." He took a moment. "Or perhaps they aren't all this annoying." He sighed heavily. "And I am one of them, am I not? In the clear light of day, I must be quite irksome. I don't know anything about firebirds or opera. I shouldn't have offered my opinions if they weren't welcome."

"You apologize for seeing my opera as what it is?" Kazimir longed for more water and made do with licking his lips. It drew attention, but he ignored it. "You say men don't give ground, and then you grant me everything. You are the strangest man. One moment you are charging forward, the next you quiver and run." Kazimir tugged at his coat. He wanted to wrap Jacob in it. Jacob was so thin a winter in Paris might break him.

"Situational bravery is the kind of thing that keeps men alive," Jacob offered, making Michel, at least, nod and smile.

Drumont was overly loud. "A coward, then, like all his kind."

Michel made a *tch* noise. "A boy who has never fought should learn to close his mouth around those who have."

Kazimir looked at Jacob and felt his cheeks heat for a reason that Drumont would never have suspected. According to humans, magical beings were not supposed to feel shame, but shame was rich in the air around Kazimir now. He shouldn't have tolerated the boy this long.

He made his tone even colder. "And what kind is that?" There were any number of reasons for the son of an aristocrat to sneer at someone, but most would still have feigned politeness.

Jacob's mouth quirked. "Judging from what Drumont and his friends were chanting when they tried to spark a coup d'état, does it really matter? His party hates everyone." It was a little startling to realize Jacob paid more attention to the newspapers than Kazimir did, unless he had been there. In which case, he was more than a drunken editor, although Kazimir did not know what exactly he was. A correspondent for some American news service was possible, or an interested observer, or some sort of Communist agitator.

Michel was likely to blame. Michel was just the sort of aristo to rub elbows with revolutionaries and troublemakers—and magical beings, lest Kazimir fail to include himself.

Kazimir shrugged his coat from his shoulders, letting it pool at his feet. "Was this the riot where they blamed the bank collapse on the Jews and the fairies and the leftists? Perhaps the queers or the ones who love the fairies? Tut." He pursed his lips. "Are you sure you want a firebird, then, boy? You may think yourself entitled to my magic, but you have no idea what my magic can do. You don't even know what I am. I am not the wire and crystal bird from my opera. I am no longer a creature subservient."

"He's more dangerous than your mind can comprehend." Jacob spoke slowly, with the same lazy care he had taken when stealing a man's martini. "The firebird is ideas, and he can't be controlled, certainly not by a *shegetz* like you."

"*Jacob.*" Kazimir had lived with a weight in his chest for a week. Then Jacob had lifted it, without a clue of what he'd done. He would not even have come here if not for Michel. Despite all of that, Kazimir reached for him. "You fool," Kazimir whispered, mad with hunger or a headache or the light, fiery glow inside him that shone out of his skin. He was getting brighter and putting color in Jacob's cheeks. "You know what I am? And you came to me regardless? You came to me sober? You told me—" Jacob had said he stayed drunk when he wasn't working, hinting that it was to avoid his thoughts, or dreams—the things he didn't want to write about. Kazimir hadn't wanted to believe it after daring Jacob to write anyway. He'd foolishly felt guilty and wandered his bedroom alone for a week as a result. Now Jacob was telling him he'd known and accepted the challenge. "You know what I am," Kazimir said again, with enough wonder and apology in his voice to embarrass him.

Jacob blinked in exhausted confusion. "You are Kazimir, the most exquisite person in the world. I haven't been able to sleep for thoughts of you, for any of the thoughts you gave me." He blinked again, and Kazimir realized Jacob was not lying; he had not been sleeping. That was true exhaustion making him pale and weak. "I walked the streets, all night one night, but the ideas wouldn't stop coming. Even in my sleep, in my dreams. Even wine could not stop them. It's terrible. I feel like a man again. Of course I came to you."

"*Yasha.*" Kazimir stepped closer to Jacob and put a hand to his face. Jacob was unshaven, and the short growth of beard was rough to the touch. But Jacob allowed it, nearly swallowing his tongue as Kazimir petted him. Kazimir could not tell if Jacob liked the touch, and the thought of being tolerated instead of desired made him shake. "Is this good?" The care and feeding of humans was foreign to him. They liked praise and lavish attention. They liked Kazimir's body and his mouth. They liked the appearance of what they thought was love. But none of his past lovers, the wanted or unwanted, had ever needed his care, and he had never wanted to offer it like this. "Yakov, you must eat and rest."

"You challenged me," Jacob argued. "You gave me a gift. I did not take it lightly. Even if…." He shuddered. "The dreams are not easy ones. I need a drink."

"No." Kazimir swept Jacob's hair from his eyes and ignored Michel's expression of disbelief. The gesture had been clumsy, but

Jacob did not seem to mind. His eyes dipped closed, as if he had liked it. He appeared trusting, which made him an even greater fool, since he had already stated that Kazimir was dangerous. Yet he allowed every silly pass of Kazimir's hands through his hair.

Kazimir clucked his tongue, striving to seem less concerned than he was. "No, you do not need a drink. You will have your stories now." Of course, the stories might be no comfort. Jacob had been trying to avoid them with liquor, and Kazimir had taken that from him. "Ah," Kazimir murmured, and pulled his hands from Jacob. He ducked his head and wondered what it meant that he did not want to look Jacob in the eye. He tried, but after a moment, he had to glance away. Speaking was even more difficult. "I did not mean to make you suffer. You do not have to give me anything. When I gave you the pearls, it was only because most *want* me—" Hearing the pleading tone coming from his mouth made him stop.

"I want you, Golden Bird." Jacob slid his thumb under Kazimir's chin but pulled his hand away before Kazimir raised his head.

"Do you?" Kazimir meant it as another dare and tried to harden his voice, as he would have with any other man. "Then prove it."

Jacob lifted his gaze, blinking as though adjusting to light after darkness. He made a soft, hurt noise Kazimir had heard before, and Kazimir thought he understood at last why Jacob sometimes could not look at him. He reached out with a quiet noise of his own. "Jacob. Don't. I'm sorry."

"*Now* Kazimir finds his heart," Michel realized out loud, on a small groan. Kazimir spun toward him and stumbled on his own abandoned coat. He did not lack grace; he was a firebird. He was a creature of *goddamn magic*, and yet he tripped. He must be cursed.

His face was warm, and he put his hands over his cheeks. Jacob continued to stare in astonishment, his eyes those of a witch—no, a seer, one who hadn't wanted to use his gift. Kazimir wouldn't have done it if he'd known. He was not a cruel creature, whatever humans might write in their operas. This man did not deserve the tragedy of Kazimir for a lover. But he had let Kazimir reach out to try to soothe him and didn't care that Kazimir hadn't known how.

"Ridiculous!" Drumont spat. Kazimir had forgotten him entirely until that second and glanced at him in irritation. Drumont sneered. "If this is what you choose, you and *le Juif* deserve each other. Filthy being." He spat more hateful words, this time at Kazimir, although from the way he used it, he also thought *being* was an insult. The word had recently trickled over from England or America. Kazimir had thought it a sweet nickname, but perhaps it had been a slur all along.

Jacob reached out, took Drumont's glass of champagne from the boy's hand, and let it fall to the floor. Then, while Drumont stared after it in confused hesitation, Jacob pulled back and struck him in the eye.

Drumont staggered into a few people behind him and raised a hand to his face. Jacob curled and uncurled his fist as if checking his knuckles. He was smaller than Drumont and already weakened with lack of food and sleep. Nonetheless, he offered Drumont a grin and stepped up again. "This is better than the dreams," he remarked, more reckless than brave, and let Drumont fling himself at him.

The boy's face was red with fury, his eye swelling shut even as he moved. The others around them were gasping and screaming. Drumont swung his fist, and this time Jacob stumbled back. He could not win this fight, even if he got Drumont down. Kazimir imagined him beaten, or worse, arrested if it continued, but Jacob did not seem to care. He threw himself forward, surprising Drumont enough to knock him off his feet, and then he was over him, snarling like a were and striking him in the face again.

Kazimir caught a glimpse of blood. He moved to intervene, but Michel was faster. Jacob bloodied his knuckles twice more, and then Michel pulled him off and shoved him toward Kazimir. Michel yelled something, his harsh tone so different from his usual mild voice that Kazimir couldn't seem to recognize what he said. Michel was an officer again, and Jacob the soldier shrugged and listened and fell forward to Kazimir.

"Been a while since I've fought anyone," Jacob remarked regretfully, and attempted a smile, as if anything about this was funny. He couldn't catch his breath.

Blood not only stained his hands, but his mouth, where his teeth had cut his lip. Kazimir could see Michel and a few other men stepping in now to pick up the boy and coddle his wounded pride and convince him to leave. The boy was an ass but with a powerful family. Jacob was a fool. Already he was shaking from his exertions.

Kazimir felt cold but knew his flush was still there, making the room glow in strange warm colors. Jacob remained untouched by them, or perhaps Kazimir was distracted by the red staining Jacob's teeth. "Men have fought over me, but never for me." The gentle words were tricked from him. Too much truth surrounded Jacob to allow a person to think clearly. Everything felt like a revelation, and Kazimir had nothing but his glow and some thin satin to shield himself from it.

Jacob rolled a shoulder without raising his head. He dabbed at his mouth with the sleeves of his one coat.

Kazimir made a noise and forgot his silly notions about truth. "Don't fight for me, you foolish thing. You… you mad idiot! Once you start, you will never be allowed to stop."

Jacob winced as he pulled at his cut lip, then licked at the fresh blood. He fixed Kazimir with a serious look despite that. "If not for you, then who?"

"You…." Kazimir took hold of Jacob's shoulder, distantly aware he had now touched Jacob several times without permission, and Jacob had not protested. Jacob wasn't like him, and probably didn't mind. Kazimir was conscious of his faux pas all the same. All his graces had been stripped from him. He tripped on his coat again. "You are so stupid you make my chest hurt," he exhaled shakily. Something had been done to him to turn him into this screeching, plucked bird.

"Best not sully your feathers with me, then," Jacob told him quietly, and again Kazimir could not bear to meet his eyes. They saw too much. It was no wonder Jacob could hardly stand to look at the world around him without the haze of liquor in his mind.

"They are my feathers. Mine to do with as I please, though I don't know why I—" Kazimir stopped himself there and pulled at Jacob's coat. "Come." It was a whisper, so he lifted his chin and tried again, making it sharp. "Come." He made himself release Jacob and then turned and headed toward the wash closet beyond his changing screens. He passed his dresser, and from her expression knew that Jacob followed. The knowledge did not ease Kazimir's tension.

He'd wanted Jacob to worship and obey him. Now he didn't. He slipped into the wash closet, a small room with a sink and mirror and toilet, and closed the door when Jacob stepped inside.

Jacob began to protest. "I don't need—"

"Shut your mouth, Yasha." Kazimir didn't know himself, couldn't trust himself to glance in the mirror to see his own panic and fear. He wet a cloth with cold water and arched an eyebrow when he was done. Gratifyingly, Jacob remembered his place and sat. Kazimir could only glance at him for seconds at a time, but now Jacob's gaze was direct and strong. He was pretty, or handsome, whichever word worked best in English, even with his swollen, bleeding bottom lip. But he should eat; he should sleep. He should write before it drove him mad.

Kazimir squeezed the cloth until his fingers were wet, then handed it over. Jacob took it and held it to his mouth.

"Ice will make it feel better." Kazimir broke the silence first. He didn't explain how he knew that from his own experiences. Jacob did not ask, though he scowled. Kazimir sniffed. "Don't do that again. That boy was not the first to hate me, and I have been owned before. There is no honor here for you to defend."

"Wrong." Jacob wiped at the blood and folded the cloth instead of holding it still. Kazimir reached out to do it for him. Jacob's eyebrows went up. "Anyway, I should think you'd be used to inciting violence."

He thought he was amusing. Kazimir applied more pressure to make Jacob wince. Then he pursed his lips to relay what should have been obvious. "I can incite anything I want to."

Jacob lowered his eyes. "I know." He shuddered as the air left him. "Believe me."

Kazimir had not lied; his chest hurt. He pulled away the cloth to examine the damage. There would be a bruise later, and a scab, but Jacob would live. Yet Kazimir couldn't breathe. Once he had gained his freedom and fled to Paris, he had taken many lovers, most to teach himself how to choose and what he liked, as opposed to what his masters wanted. Jacob could have been one among them. And yet Kazimir couldn't breathe near him. He found himself panting. "Yasha, look at me."

Clearly startled by the request, Jacob lifted his head. Kazimir slid a hand under his chin, bent down, and kissed him. He wanted to be gentle. He did not want to do it at all, but it felt as necessary as the air he could no longer take in. He kissed Jacob, softly, and Jacob put his hand out but let it fall before it could wrinkle Kazimir's shirt.

That was something Kazimir could not take, and he drifted down onto Jacob's lap and lightly held Jacob's bruised face in both hands as he kissed him again. The kiss was slow, pressing them together as Kazimir learned Jacob's lips and the taste of his blood. Jacob breathed harder and tipped his chin up, offering his exquisite mouth for another kiss, and then another, all without kissing back.

"I did not mean for the gift to hurt you." Kazimir kissed the untouched corner of Jacob's mouth and enjoyed the feel of his unshaven jaw on his palms. Jacob made a blissfully confused sound and allowed himself to be kissed again. Kazimir felt like the most honored creature in France, and bestowed kiss after kiss against soft, parted lips. He was aroused but didn't move to take the kisses further, another new sensation for him to explore. This was Jacob's mouth, and he wanted to learn it. He wanted to honor it so Jacob could know what he felt.

Michel had said this was love, but it couldn't be. Love was supposed to cause pain. "I only wanted you to come to me." Kazimir knew he weighed almost nothing, and yet he wished Jacob would take hold of him, keep him in place. He could feel Jacob's fingertips through the satin of his shirt, touching him, not touching him, grazing the fabric, but Jacob would not hold him. Kazimir pulled his mouth from Jacob's at last. Fear cooled his skin and made him shut his eyes. "You said you wanted me."

"Anyone in his right mind would…" Jacob began, then settled his hands lightly at Kazimir's waist without finishing his first thought. "I am not that boy out there. I've given you no gifts. I haven't done anything to make you want me."

But he could. Kazimir could feel the strength in his hands and wondered briefly how long Jacob had denied it, and the toll it had taken on him. This was what Jacob was truly afraid of, but the denial had been killing him anyway. Like all of the lost ones, part of Jacob was still in a distant field, buried by mud and flowers.

This was the man Michel had wanted Kazimir to help, although Michel hadn't intended for Kazimir to desire him or to want to care for him as deeply as he did.

"Jacob." Kazimir knew better than to show a weakness, but a seer would find it anyway, wouldn't he? "Jacob, I want… I want you here. Selfishly, I want you for mine."

"You make me want to do anything, and think I can," Jacob countered, with an inelegant snort. "I'm afraid I'll disappoint you there. As an editor, I'm equipped, but as a writer, I'm not much."

"So you say." Kazimir opened his eyes and tossed his head haughtily. "I have no evidence to disprove this."

Jacob flicked a glance to the side, then smiled before returning to his study of Kazimir. The smile might have pulled at his split lip, but he licked at it without acknowledging the pain he must be in. Then he tipped back his head, making as tempting a sight as Kazimir had ever seen. Kazimir could not tell if Jacob meant to seduce him or if Kazimir would have been charmed regardless of what Jacob had done. He thought it the latter and felt younger than he had ever felt, even as a child in his first master's house.

Kazimir dragged a light touch down Jacob's throat and frowned harder for how Jacob smiled again. "You are beautiful," Jacob offered, as if Kazimir was not learning to worship him. Men had probably worshipped Jacob before. There was something in him, or about him. To a fairy he might have been as bright as the sun, as bright as Kazimir to human eyes. Kazimir wanted to know everything about him. He thought if he knew enough, it would banish the fear that this human would not want Kazimir in the same way as Kazimir wanted him.

"You are maddening," Kazimir informed him, sweeping a small trail of blood with his thumb. "Where do you come from?"

"New York," Jacob answered easily. "Where do you come from? I don't know about firebirds, although I have heard stories from all over about different creatures, legends of flaming, bejeweled birds, birds that were also a man. The bennu, the phoenix. And the firebird. I'd heard of you long before I saw you, Kazimir the Great. A firebird is supposed to signal change. Change is a frightening, often destructive force. Beautiful too. And here you are, all that but also more. You're a scared, lovely man in my lap."

Kazimir turned his face to the side, and then, when he could feel Jacob growing more curious, he stood up. Jacob protested wordlessly when Kazimir left his arms.

Kazimir rinsed out the cloth and then pressed it back to Jacob's mouth. With the distance, the weight returned to his chest. It made him speak slowly.

"There is a reason I am scared. This is…. Do you know where imps come from?" Few did, so Kazimir was unsurprised when Jacob shook his head. "They are fairies." From the corner of his eye, he watched Jacob give a start. "Oh yes," Kazimir assured him. "The fairies deny it, and the imps themselves—should you ever meet one allowed to survive into adulthood—do not seem to know. The imps think themselves related to fairies, but they don't realize what they are."

"And that is?" Jacob dropped the pink-stained cloth in the sink.

Kazimir met that incredible stare. "Imps are fairies that the fairies didn't want, anomalies in the fairy blood. Wherever they come from, they are born different—ugly, to fairies, with magic that isn't under conscious control, as the fairies' magic is. So most fairies leave them, abandon them to humans, who more often than not thought they were evil. Changelings are not entirely the myth fairies would have us believe."

"That imp at your party." Jacob's eyes did not only see all, they reflected far too much feeling. "That was just a child."

"And a sweet one." Kazimir sighed.

After a moment Jacob nodded. "Why are you telling me this?"

Kazimir gave the kind of shrug he had learned in his time in France. "Where I come from is also unknown to me. There was an egg. My first owner, a peasant who found me, had it in his possession." Without thinking, Kazimir leaned down to smooth the offended frown from Jacob's brow. He was very old to feel this fragile protectiveness for the first time. Perhaps he hadn't wanted to, or perhaps firebirds, phoenixes, a roc, whatever he was, experienced something like the werewolves did when they met their mates, and no one had been around to warn Kazimir it would happen.

All this time, convincing men who had captured him that they should revere him, do anything for him, driving them mad, and he had been undone in moments by a little drunk American.

"It was a very pretty egg," he added. "Like nothing else I've ever seen that wasn't created by men to entertain royalty. I think something unusual must create my kind. Something not easy or simple. Something once in a lifetime. We are linked to dragons in many cultures, and often to lightning or fire or thunder. Perhaps we are to dragons what imps are to fairies. Perhaps not. In some countries, as you said, birds of fire signal the start of a new era and die when it has ended. Perhaps that is true. In my years of life, I have already witnessed things that no one, not even the most gifted seer, could have imagined. But where do we come from?" Kazimir gave another Gallic shrug. "I know of no others, only stories I've learned since I gained my freedom. Perhaps I am purely magic, as even dragons are not."

A hand on his hip stopped him. He could feel Jacob's heat, as Jacob must feel his. Jacob was stern. "Not purely magic," he pointed out, quiet and true. "Magic is a force without feeling on its own, or so I've been led to understand. You are more than magic. I'm sorry if I ever implied otherwise." Jacob licked at his cut lip. "You are more than a legend."

"I have never felt as solidly and weakly human as I do at this moment." Kazimir admitted that and all the rest of his confusion. "You want me, you say, but you left. You haven't tried to capture me. You came for me, but at Michel's insistence."

The truth was out, and Kazimir was a desperate fool. He had survived on cunning and deception and his beauty. He had risen to fame and fortune with his talents. Now he was in a toilet of all places, and none of that mattered.

Jacob exhaled softly and tilted back his head even farther, until Kazimir needed to touch it to keep him there—his mouth, his cheeks, his glasses, and his brow. "You didn't come for me either," Jacob pointed out, making Kazimir huff in indignation at the very idea. Then Jacob ran the backs of his fingers across Kazimir's cheekbone, and Kazimir was compelled to close his eyes and shiver closer. "You are"—Jacob brushed Kazimir's golden eyelashes and his ears and the short length of his hair—"quite something."

His words were not poetry, but Kazimir was heated to his toes. "Something?" he scoffed, regardless of his pounding heart, and angled his head in a not-subtle direction for where Jacob ought to touch him next. Jacob obeyed him, careful and gentle for a man who had been brawling on the floor minutes before.

"You are a fearsome beast and a prima donna." Jacob surprised him with a shivery kiss beneath his ear. "If you tell me a rare event must have created you, then I think it must have been so. It must have been an event rare and wondrous. God, you're beautiful. It's a miracle you let me touch you."

"Have you thought about touching me?" Kazimir could not be smug when he had spent nights staring at the Parisian skyline and imagining Jacob in his bed. "You have not touched me much, if that is true."

Jacob gave a rude snort, and Kazimir opened his eyes.

"You could be playing with me as you have played with many others, yet I find I don't care," Jacob remarked. "I still want to win you, or I should say, win your favor."

"I haven't asked for anything," Kazimir insisted.

"Haven't you?" Jacob's tone was not without bitterness, but his gaze was warm and steady on Kazimir again. His hands and face were no doubt stinging and throbbing with pain. He had not slept. He had never been lovelier. "I won't give you an opera. Anything I create won't be pretty."

"That, I will decide." Kazimir tossed his head defiantly but tightened his hands into anxious fists.

"I am certain you will." Jacob accepted this with a nod, then got to his feet. He wiped his hands on the wet cloth while Kazimir was fluttering back to block the door.

"Aren't you angry?" Kazimir demanded. "You have challenged two men for less than nothing in the time that I've known you, and yet you accept this? I grant this… this inspiration, this gift. But I don't know how to care for you. I can't give you anything real. If this were my opera, I would grant you wishes, but it isn't. I have nothing for you, Jacob, except the suffering I have already caused."

Jacob turned toward him. The room was small. When he took a step, they were nearly pressed together. Kazimir heard himself make a noise. Jacob put his hands on him, tightening his fingers around satin before tugging Kazimir forward. Their mouths were close.

"You want me to tell you that you will be my everything, or do you mean that?" Uncertainty was as cruel and cold to Jacob as it was to Kazimir. If that was love, Kazimir didn't want it, but he did want Jacob close, and he leaned toward him with a hungry sound. Jacob inhaled sharply. The desire to kiss was all over his face, but he did not move. "You will be the death of me," he murmured at last. "I will give you everything or nothing, I suppose, if it turns out there is nothing in me. Is that real enough?"

He was not empty. Kazimir could feel it in his fingertips. Nonetheless, he made himself sniff in weak disdain. "And what am I to do with you?" he sneered, but it lacked force. He was too breathless, so he shut his eyes when Jacob took his hand and turned it to kiss his palm. "Jacob." Kazimir thought he knew what this was, and it was too much. Yet he opened his eyes and wouldn't move from the door. "You know what I am and you still want me?"

"Do you think I'm a prize?" Jacob gestured vaguely toward himself. "I can't even promise you a good story."

What a sad pair they were. Kazimir slid a hand to Jacob's chest to clutch at his poor excuse for a coat. He yanked it straight and flattened the lapels, ignoring the startled, then amused, expression on Jacob's face. "You are handsome, but there is no reason for me to find you intriguing," Kazimir conceded at last.

"Handsome?" The smirk on Jacob's face was not becoming.

Kazimir pushed his palm against Jacob's chest to put space between them. "You said I was dangerous. Look to yourself, Monsieur Rifkin." His tone mimicked every displeased wife he'd ever overheard.

"I'm hardly a good bet, but dangerous?" Jacob frowned at him, then fell silent when Kazimir held his stare. "To everyone or to you? Men like that, that boy out there, they are the dangerous ones. I *had* to challenge him. But I wasn't hurt, not much." Jacob held up his hands to show his scars. "I've had worse. There's nothing to worry about."

Jacob could not see the truth about himself, it seemed. When Kazimir's voice remained lost to him and he still could not speak, Jacob shook his head and leaned in to smooth Kazimir's hair down. His thumbs brushed Kazimir's neck before he urged Kazimir's face down to nearer his level. "I never thought someone like you would worry about someone like me," he remarked. "Why?"

"A firebird is supposed to break hearts. I can bring greatness and destroy a soul at the same time. That is what I have been told my entire life." Kazimir swallowed. "Michel, Josephine, even little Rennet, they see something else in me. Something more. It is not only that you heard the pain in my voice and saw me as a man. It's not only that you desire me or that you are handsome or fought for me or joked with me." Kazimir shuddered against the door. "I tell you this knowing it is equal to the pain I may yet cause you. I want… I want you, but as you said. I can only offer this." He held out his hands.

Jacob took a long time to answer. "Your heart for a story of mine? You set a low price for yourself."

"No." The men Kazimir had broken had deserved their fate. The artists he had helped had deserved that too. Jacob was someone else.

Someone neither simple nor easy. He was a good man, possibly a great man. Perhaps Michel was better, if equally damaged. But Michel was not for Kazimir to call his own. "No, I set a high price for myself. You will create greatness for me, won't you, Jacob? We will create it together."

Jacob steadied himself with a deep breath. "You fucking beauty," he whispered, compelling Kazimir to lift his head.

"You are terrible with compliments." A scornful tone was out of his reach. Breathless anxiety was all that was left to him. Love, it seemed, was a terror after all.

"And you choose me anyway." Jacob became very still at his own words. He put his shoulders back and lifted his chin. "So I will prove myself, then," he said, and had not been so fierce when about to punch Drumont. He stared into Kazimir's eyes. "You are toying with me, but I will leap right up over the top for you anyway." He set his jaw, although the action must have hurt, and then pulled back. "Okay. I will always be that same, foolish boy who wanted to face the guns, but face them I will, and worse. Because someone has to rewrite that ending, that useless, stupid ending. Of course…." He paused and quirked a rueful smile. "That may take a while."

Kazimir reached for him. "Am I expected to wait?" He scowled for the very idea. He didn't even know where Jacob lived.

"We all must suffer for art," Jacob told him, crueler than any master, but kissed him then, at last, strong and furious, with his arms around Kazimir and his strength holding him from the floor. His hands were hot, and Kazimir shivered for him and felt shame again for the weakness in his limbs, the need. This kiss made him strain forward to curl himself into Jacob's arms. He was alive, and Jacob was kissing him, murmuring, "Kazimir," against his lips and, "Golden Bird," against his cheek, and he shifted his thighs apart to feel the man's hard arousal and moan for it. He clung to Jacob until the room was blinding because of him, until he was faint against the wall and Jacob panted hungrily against his shoulder.

Then Jacob was gone, before Kazimir could realize he had been moved out of the way. Without glancing up, he touched two fingers to his mouth and frowned when they came away red with Jacob's blood.

He trembled and looked at himself in the mirror.

If there had been another of his kind, he might have asked what to do next. But there was nothing to do but wait and try to understand what Jacob had meant.

KAZIMIR SHOULD have known not to accept Michel's invitation. Michel, who had survived the Marne and lost a lover at Verdun, and who held a spot in his heart for soldiers and madmen and the lovelorn. Michel could have been a fairy, if not for the martinis sometimes required to keep the sorrow from his eyes.

There was drink at his house, too much drink, even for Kazimir, who sipped vodka without fear. Humans were slouched over couches that had once held courtiers and dancing around on floors walked by revolutionaries. They laughed and fought in loud groups throughout the many stories of Michel's house, many of them too stoned to pay much attention even to a firebird. Fairies of every imaginable color glittered obscenely under electric lights. As with Kazimir, wine would not affect them, but they laughed and danced too, and shied away from the displays of human anger.

He could not tell their ages from this distance, but their crazed laughter made him long for quiet. Perhaps he was aging too. If so, he almost welcomed it. Youth to him was remembered fear. Age was nothing. He would remain the same as he grew old, forever beautiful until the moment of his death, or so myth told him. He might even rise again like a phoenix at the dawn of a new age.

The thought of his uncertain fate pushed him forward, away from the great doors leading out to Michel's garden and toward the staircase. Someone called his name, begging him to sing, but he pretended not to hear and continued on. If the first floor was too much music and dancing, the second floor was liquor and heroin and dull faces turning toward him with interest. He found conversation and friends on the third floor, and walked into what must have once been a bedroom to find a mix of humans around a table, smoking and tossing ideas about the state of affairs in Italy back and forth over cards. A single elf was among them—female, with a mannish haircut and a cigar in her mouth—who did not look up when he entered, though the humans invited him over.

The humans were both finely and plainly dressed, and they spoke of their ideals with gin-soaked conviction, but Kazimir barely looked at them. He nodded to them as he slipped around their group and continued toward the darkened corner of the room and the enormous gilded sofa that had been turned to face the wall at the expense of the rug beneath it.

This was why Michel had invited him here. It was of course also why Kazimir had come, though his heart thundered in his chest and his black polo-neck sweater could not stop his shivers. He had dressed plainly, sternly, to leave all of himself covered but his face and hands, yet he remained naked and cold. He lifted his chin as he came to a stop and looked down at the resting figure stretched out on his back over faded pink damask.

Jacob had borrowed or stolen a new coat from someone, though he was down to his shirt and suspenders, with his collar open, and his necktie undone and shoved into a pocket. His hands were knitted together on his stomach, and his eyes were closed. His breathing was even, but the glow Kazimir brought to the corner revealed the shadows under his eyes and the hollowness of his cheeks. The wound at his mouth had not vanished completely in their time apart.

On the floor beside Jacob were a bottle and a glass, along with a worn leather satchel. Kazimir pushed his sleeves down over his hands and pulled at the cuffs. For a long moment he glared at Jacob's sleeping face and let his heart do what it would, and then he smoothed his expression and lifted his chin.

"You did not return to me," he announced in English, chipping at the words to force them from the ice. Jacob's eyes opened immediately, though he took a few moments to blink the sleep from them, and he went obviously still when he saw Kazimir standing over him.

"I had work yet to do," Jacob murmured after he seemed to recover, then narrowed his eyes when Kazimir answered that with silence. "I may have taken too long," Jacob admitted after another pause, but he lifted his glasses to scrub at his face, then took another few moments to study Kazimir. When he was done, he wiped at his face again. "Were I less tired, I would slide to my knees to beg forgiveness. If not granted, at least you would have an easier time removing my head."

Kazimir glanced to the bottle on the floor, then back to Jacob's face. Jacob looked at him with intoxicated eyes. The flush on his cheeks was nearly the color of his mouth. If he had not been with Kazimir, he should have been writing. But the sight of that bottle could have meant he had given up. With any other man, Kazimir would have expressed quiet displeasure or indifference. With Jacob he was frozen.

Jacob appeared to be trying to focus. "You weren't here," he announced unexpectedly. "I was told you would be here, but you weren't when I arrived, and I thought… I thought you had forgotten me." A few words from him, and Kazimir's heart was light again. "You are here now. Perhaps you were late too. Kazimir," Jacob called to him, as if his voice alone were enough to bring Kazimir forward to perch next to him. "Kazimir, I had a dream where you loved me. I had a dream where you came to rest on my lap, and instead of keeping you there, I vowed to tilt at windmills for you. I think perhaps I have finally gone mad."

"Jacob," Kazimir answered, although he trembled to think of Jacob so delirious that he could doubt the force that had brought Kazimir here. "It has been three days. If I kept you waiting here long enough for you to find drink, then you have kept me waiting longer. Did you find your windmills?"

"No dream, then?" Jacob opened and closed his mouth, then blinked several times in Kazimir's direction. He shook his head and seemed unconvinced he wasn't still asleep. "Three days? Has it been three days? I did not mean to be so tardy." Jacob spoke sincerely but did not move to his knees as offered. He stretched his arms before putting his back against the sofa and leaving more room at the edge of the cushions. He frowned with sleepy thoughtfulness. "Did you seek me out?"

Kazimir felt a touch of heat across his cheeks but said nothing. Jacob pushed his body up into something closer to a sitting position.

Jacob had held three names in the time Kazimir had known him, making Kazimir think of spells and their reliance on names. Kazimir had no other name, no father's or mother's name to link to his own. He was as alone as young Rennet, though far more wanted, with Kazimir being the name given to him as a curse by the first master he had destroyed. Before then he had been only Firebird. Jacob had given him another name, Golden Bird, a fleeting nickname, but he had made it teasing and tender.

"Yasha." Kazimir had given Jacob a name as well. Jacob did not seem to mind. They were a queer pair.

Jacob peered around Kazimir to whatever he could see of the rest of the room, then studied Kazimir's clothes. They were simple and undecorated. Kazimir wore no jewelry tonight.

"You look severe and beautiful," Jacob observed. "Exactly as I have imagined you every other time I thought of you in the past few days—except for when you were naked, or wearing the silk robe you wore when I met you before I removed it with your vigorous consent. These visions of you are getting to be a problem. Luckily I am rarely in polite company." He then leaned over to pour himself a drink, which he swallowed down before leaning back again. "Would you like one, dream Kazimir? I have no champagne for you, but then we have no plants to water either."

Kazimir gave him a carefully annoyed look. "I cannot feed the masses with champagne any more than I could water a tree with a sandwich." He thought it had been some time since Jacob had laid eyes on a sandwich, but did not think it was a lack of opportunity. Michel would have fed him if it came to that. "In any case it does not matter. I hate champagne."

"You don't appreciate it." Jacob gestured dramatically, taking on the voice of someone else. "But it costs a great deal. Don't you see how great it is? How great they are for offering it to you?" His little smile was mocking, but he wasn't looking at Kazimir. "It should work. It should dazzle you. Blind you to the hatred in their hearts for you and everything you are. Or at least, remind you that life can be sweet, with the right company. It can, can't it? I want your life to be sweet. Champagne is a better offering than a few pages."

Kazimir pulled harder at his sleeves, then swallowed. "My dangerous American," he began lightly, and waited to smile until Jacob's eyes were on him and sharp with sudden wakefulness. "They may offer me all the champagne they like. They may spend until their bank accounts are empty and their stocks are gone. Some have." He shrugged without any innocence. "But I hate champagne. And if you wish my life to be sweet…." The world was so cold. Kazimir was cold too. He did not deserve happiness, but he was greedy for it. "Then you must be in it."

Jacob made a shocked noise, the kind of sound a sober man might have made. He pushed himself up in a slightly better sitting position. His slow smile was as warming as his liquor. "I have no sandwich, and if I did, I think I would eat the half I didn't offer to you. But I have room on this sofa, if you would care to sit with me and prove to me that you are real and not another dream."

"Room to sit?" Kazimir tossed his head. Jacob's mood was affecting him. "You do not ask the bird to sing?"

The sigh from Jacob was music of its own. "You know I find your singing beautiful." He shut his eyes and slipped down against the cushions, as if dreaming again.

"However," Kazimir prompted, "do not deny the bird its praise."

"*However*." Jacob remained in his reverie. "The bird will sing if it wants to. No one can force that. No one should try. Anyone that does will answer to me."

Kazimir gave a start and nearly blushed for it, though Jacob's eyes were still closed. He stared at Jacob with his mouth open and his breath dry in his throat until a frustrated warning about uniforms and riots from the group at the table startled him anew. Jacob dreamed on. Kazimir was right before him, and yet he dreamed.

"I have seen that shirt before," Kazimir began again, his voice sharp, at least bringing Jacob's attention back to him. "Do you own no others?"

"You remembered?" Jacob's soft mouth indicated pleasure, as did his warm voice. The whisky had left it husky. But he frowned a second later. "I was in the middle of a sentence, and I was dragged to this place. They're lucky I dressed at all. I don't know why I bothered."

"For me?" Kazimir angled his head down, and Jacob's little smile grew larger.

"Yes," he admitted on an exhale, "for you. For Kazimir." He went still when Kazimir gracefully descended to the sofa and arranged himself next to him.

"Yet you did not approach me." Kazimir could hear the whine in his own voice, and looked away so he would not see Jacob's face as Jacob heard it. Jacob's body was hot, and his breath came faster as Kazimir stretched himself out on his side next to him. He put his hand over Jacob's chest to feel the beat of his heart and then laid his head against his shoulder. "It has been days, Yakov. You must be kind to me, even when you are writing. Artists forget the world when the ideas take hold of them, but you must remember me. I have never… felt like this. You must be kind. Unless…." This was something Kazimir had not thought of. "Do I scare you? When you didn't find me, did you retreat into that?" He didn't bother to indicate the bottle.

"There isn't much that scares me." Jacob took his time to reply, his words changing volume as Kazimir settled against him, but he shifted to make more room for him and swore quietly when Kazimir took over that space as well, and wriggled against him in a way that made the rest of Jacob wake up too. "Fuck. Are you punishing me for leaving you? Now *you* be kind. I've done what you asked."

This was not a direct answer, but Kazimir took it for one and watched Jacob's hand come up to scratch at his beard. He studied Jacob's scars.

"The fields of flowers you spoke of…." Kazimir inhaled. Jacob smelled of sweat and whisky, likely still wasn't sure that he wasn't imagining everything, but Kazimir asked a question anyway. "You are one of the returning soldiers, aren't you? Did you visit those fields?" He had already learned the answer from Michel. Some of the men who had fought all those years ago came back to see the monuments built, or to visit at graveyards. Whatever they expected to find, some stayed instead of returning home.

Jacob held up his hand. Time had smoothed out much of his palm, but this close Kazimir could see where the scar tissue was tight at the back of his hand. "Barbed wire," Jacob remarked, then put his hand down at his side. Kazimir frowned, picked it up, and pulled it to his hip. Jacob's breathing grew harsh again. He knew it was no dream now.

Kazimir rather liked the hand where it was. Jacob's touch was firm but not heavy. It did not take him long to spread out his fingers and warm Kazimir through his sweater. Kazimir wanted to let his eyes close.

"I know I haven't eaten or slept in far too long, but I must confess to some confusion." Jacob did not seem to notice Kazimir was trembling against him. A kiss might have made him stop talking, but Kazimir could not lift his head for one.

"It is very hard to hold on to a firebird," Kazimir told him, despite how Jacob knew he had never met another of his kind. He had heard once that the czars had kept them, to their peril. Persian kings had taken them and worn their feathers, courting disaster in their pride. Egypt was said to have honored them, but the pharaohs were still gone. "Those who try often live to regret it. I might.... Yasha, I might destroy you without ever meaning to." Jacob was a man half-gone already, furious and stupid and challenging everything with no care for himself.

Kazimir was so close to him that he could hear Jacob swallow. "Do you warn all men this way?"

"I could demand the impossible from you," Kazimir continued, feeling Jacob's hand tighten on him and curving his body even closer, "watch you throw yourself after what cannot be caught."

"Yesterday I would have said *this* was impossible," Jacob mused. "Try again, Golden Bird."

Kazimir, on the verge of asking for the moon, closed his mouth. There was little use in warning a drunkard from drink, or a man in lust—in love—from the object of his passion. He pressed his palm to Jacob's chest, surprised at the insistent thrum of Jacob's heart, the strength of the breath Jacob drew in. He smoothed out the wrinkles in the old shirt, taking his time and wondering when Jacob would speak again.

Jacob was strong for a man who worked with paper, his palms rough, as though physical labor was not far in his past. Kazimir pushed closer to brush Jacob's throat with his mouth and surprised himself by humming. This was lust, but unlike anything else. Once again he thought he could touch Jacob for hours without demanding more. He wondered if Jacob felt the same, and tested him by wriggling to get more comfortable.

"Need a sleep, do you?" Jacob inquired breathlessly, too tense for his mockery to be anything but gentle. "All worn out from your other conquests?"

"Would that upset you?" Kazimir asked with artificial calm, and resumed moving his lips over Jacob's skin. He went hot when Jacob shuddered in obvious pleasure.

"Oh, I like a good fuck as much as anyone," Jacob assured him, stubbornly unmoving. Piqued, Kazimir pulled his mouth away, but left his head at Jacob's shoulder. After a few moments of silence, Jacob snorted a laugh. "You want me to be jealous? I know you aren't fucking them."

Kazimir pushed himself up onto his elbow to scowl down at him. "How do you know that?"

Jacob put up a hand in apology, bringing it close to Kazimir's cheek. "They are still trying to win you," he observed, then directed his stare at Kazimir's shoulder. "As I am." His cheeks were very dark now. "If you don't want me, say so. When you read—when you see what pathetic bits I've got to offer, you can say no. You should be with someone handsome and strong and whole. That's who the firebird should love. Someone smart enough not to challenge everything like I do. A man with sense enough to keep quiet. Someone to share that strength with you, not take yours."

"Some of my admirers are powerful. Some are very rich men." Kazimir took his time saying the words, pleased with how Jacob's eyes came to him. "Why should I not have them all?"

"Then I would understand how you would be tired," Jacob tossed back, only to immediately appear pained. He pulled at Kazimir's sleeve, his fingers toying with the marks where Kazimir had stretched the fabric. "I would be jealous," he bit out, unexpectedly fierce, and released Kazimir's sleeve. "I would think of you kissing them the way you kissed me with my jaw banged up and my glasses crooked, and I would hurt. Would that make you happy? I could suffer that to make Kazimir happy."

Kazimir realized he was staring at Jacob's face. Jacob was so beautiful, stark and honest, whether drunk or sober. He was various shades of brown and red, and stubborn enough to have crawled out of a trench.

When Kazimir attempted to speak, the words were slow to come, and his frown was more real than he liked. "What does my happiness matter?" Kazimir had thought about this question too in the last several days. Jacob might have the answer. "Does my happiness truly matter to you, Yasha?"

"What does…?" Jacob's eyes searched Kazimir's face while lightning again came and went in his expression. Then he wrapped his hand around Kazimir's sleeve and tugged. "The world is a troubled and cruel place. Shouldn't we embrace happiness when we find it, no matter the odds on it lasting or the world interfering? When you look at me, I see greatness. When you touch me I feel great, though that is a lie. I think… I think you feel the same. Isn't that remarkable, that you should look at me at all, much less be pleased by the picture I make? Why shouldn't we want to hang on to that, as long as we can? There is, no, there *will* be a cost for that. There is always a cost, but it is worth anything, I think. I would give anything to have you feel what I feel right now."

"Jacob," Kazimir breathed the name. His voice cracked when he tried to say more.

Jacob stroked his hair. "Sleep with me," he suggested quietly, his mouth curved in the sad, happy smile Kazimir was starting to like very much. "Let's fall asleep together and wake up together too. We can't be expected to be brilliant every moment of every day, can we? Surely even the firebird needs a rest. Damn, I'm tired. I have suffered mightily for you, I'll have you know. But Kazimir wished me to write, so I wrote. I strung together a few thousand measly words I detest and which ripped my heart out anyway. It's down there for you, if you still want it. A heart for a heart, if I didn't dream that too."

Kazimir watched Jacob shut his eyes and wriggle in place until he was comfortable again, expecting him to laugh and yet unsurprised when he did not. Jacob was tense despite his light words.

The people at the table behind them were arguing now, some furious, some indifferent, voices raised over a discussion of legal provisions in other countries. It might come to a fight soon, but though Jacob had to hear them, he wanted to rest for a few hours with Kazimir in his arms. That he wanted to sleep when men had offered to kill for more from Kazimir was another puzzle among many.

"Don't be offended," Jacob remarked, as if reading his thoughts. "I would gladly take you to bed, but I'm too exhausted and drunk right now to be any good at it. You'll have to wait, Golden Bird."

"Are you seducing me, or am I seducing you?" Kazimir remarked in a high voice, hardly recognizing himself, and wrinkled his nose at Jacob's relaxed, handsome face.

"You think I could seduce you? Hmm." Jacob considered it, or pretended to, to drive Kazimir mad. He snorted when Kazimir poked him. "Are you seduced by sleep?" Jacob made a pleased noise when Kazimir lay back down beside him. "Other men may demand the famous singer, or the mythical beast, or the jewel of a man pleasing them in their bed, but I would also like the fellow with bony elbows, snoring next to me."

"I do not snore. And only a drunk man would demand sleep from me." Kazimir put a hand over Jacob's chest. "Other men…."

"What would they demand? Your body? Your voice?" Jacob put his chin atop Kazimir's head. Kazimir dug his chin into Jacob's collarbone until Jacob moved.

Other men would demand everything except the simple pleasure of Kazimir's company, but Kazimir kept that to himself. He shrugged, but then he found a spot where Jacob's shoulder finally made a good pillow. He was not bony. "Tomorrow I will be insulted that you have not," he finally responded. "But tonight there is nothing that will make me happier than resting in Yasha's arms." He shut his eyes at the slow touch of fingertips along his jaw, tensing again when Jacob's fingers explored his neck. "Except perhaps if you were to kiss me," he couldn't resist adding.

Jacob stopped petting him for a short while, then spoke without any real anger. "Give me a break. I was working. I haven't even seen a bed in about thirty-six hours, and before that was only a few moments rest. If I'm to kiss you, I want to do it right. Sober and righteous and all that, not wrung out and stoned out of my mind on whisky I drank because I was afraid you weren't coming." He ignored Kazimir curling into him in pleasure at the confession. "I have worked nonstop for you."

"Surely no book is that urgent. You do not even have a publisher." Michel had told Kazimir that, and much more, when dropping by with the invitation. The stories in the book Jacob had been editing, it seemed, were about love, or trying to find love, and mostly involved the magical beings that had come out into the human world after the Great War. The subject alone made them obscene. To humans those pairings, like other pairings even among their own, were forbidden. This was one of the reasons so many had flocked to Paris and America, where, if they were not welcomed with open arms, at least so far they were not attacked in their homes or held up as the reasons for society's decadence. At least not yet, but from the raised voices at the card table, Kazimir was no longer certain of anything.

"Cowards." Jacob's voice rose at the mention of publishers, then sank back down to intimacy. "This wasn't… I wasn't editing. Not the whole time. You know I wasn't."

Kazimir hesitated, thinking of the satchel on the floor. "I have not seen these stories you are editing." He curled his hand against Jacob's other shoulder in order to get comfortable. He did not want to think about the rest of the world. "*Michel* has seen these stories," he pointed out, and was startled at Jacob's laugh.

"You *will* take all I have!" His awestruck voice was loud, silencing the people at the card table at last. "You fucking beauty. If the goddamned government censors aren't the death of me, it'll be you."

"I am a firebird," Kazimir reminded him. His tone held a lightness, a brand-new contentment. He had found this creature he wanted, who wanted him, and he got to stay with him.

"A once in a lifetime creature," Jacob agreed happily. "With love enough to drive a man to madness and ruin, and make him smile as he goes."

"I have asked for nothing," Kazimir corrected him once more. He realized he was holding on to Jacob's shirt with a tight fist and forced himself to release it. "But if you have a gift for me, I will consider it." He was splayed out over Jacob with no intention of moving, and he feared Jacob knew it. It should have been frightening. Instead, he could feel Jacob's heart racing.

"It is for you. They will all be for you. Every story I have and then some." Jacob's breath stirred Kazimir's hair. His hand was warm at his side. "You should not have to ask. In lieu of roses or diamonds or champagne, or even a sandwich, I will bring them to you, one by one, until every story is gone from me and I can rest again. Would that make you happy?" He stroked carefully across Kazimir's ribs and then down over his shoulder, making Kazimir tense with expectation. "Or is the plan to leave me empty? When you are around, I cannot seem to make myself care either way, except to hope you will like them."

"But you will come to me, with these stories? Without them? You will still come to me?" Kazimir had no song in his voice, except one too sweet and sad to be teasing. "You will stay in bed and grant me the right to feed you and keep you warm as I take your stories from you, one by one?"

Jacob now knew the stories of firebirds, the destruction and creation they left behind. But he breathed evenly in and out, and after a moment, sighed. "I am not afraid of death," he whispered, and put his chin back atop Kazimir's head.

"I do not want you to die," Kazimir answered, as though musing upon a new necklace or pair of slippers. "I think I will keep you instead."

"I'm beginning to think you mean that." Jacob snorted in amusement.

"When you are sober, perhaps you will finally believe me." Kazimir poked him in the chest, then pressed his mouth over the spot.

"Sorry. Nature of the writing business. I'm a god one moment, worthless the next." Jacob breathed harder at every kiss Kazimir bestowed on him. Kazimir kissed him through his shirt, over the place where his heart had been.

Kazimir couldn't leave it on the floor. He twisted his body to pick up the satchel and hefted it between them as he returned to Jacob's arms. He held it in the crook of his arm, draped over Jacob, and stared at Jacob's face until Jacob opened his eyes.

"I will accept a kiss instead, if this hurts you." Kazimir made the offer quietly, but for the second time.

"It hurts to even look at you, but I can't seem to look anywhere else. Keep my heart. Do what you will with it," Jacob responded, as gallant as any courtier when he chose to be. But his tension did not leave him until Kazimir lay down once again and left the satchel unopened between them. He had already warned Kazimir his heart was not a pretty thing, but Kazimir felt it warm and alive enough for a heartless bird of fire.

"Jacob." Saying the name made him smile. He slid his mouth across Jacob's, making Jacob whimper and part his lips. Jacob pushed up, for a single, perfect moment, and then Kazimir dragged himself away.

Jacob slid a hand into Kazimir's hair and did nothing this time about Kazimir's chin at his collarbone. "Yes?" He was so quiet and dazed that the rising argument at the table behind them nearly drowned him out.

"The flowers you like." Kazimir stretched and let Jacob kick a foot over his ankle. "The simple ones. The kind that grow in the fields in the country. I would like to see flowers like that someday, to see them as you see them." Not now. For now Kazimir was content to stay where he was, settled and happy with no other view but faded pink damask and Jacob as he fell asleep.

"Finally," Jacob sighed, "you ask me for something." He was not mocking. He held Kazimir tighter, as though Kazimir were not curled over him to keep him there. Kazimir had found his heart. Nothing could take it from him now.

The Warrior's Sacrifice

1947

WITHOUT OPENING his eyes, Teo knew he was someplace unfamiliar and cold. He wasn't safe in his own bed, and he wasn't curled up on his small balcony to watch the night sky above Los Cerros. His shoulders were pressed against something as hard as stone, his eyes were heavy, and he *hurt*. His wrists throbbed, although his hands felt numb and distant, and when he moved his head, terrible lightning flashed behind his eyes.

He let out a small, soft noise of pain, not wanting to disturb his grandmother. But then he remembered she wasn't there, that she was dead and he was alone. He made the sound again. He recognized it as a whimper as warmth crept over his feet and spread to his knees, then to his lap and chest, as if someone else were close.

He had a flash of memory, of being moved, and experienced a dizzying moment of panic at the possibility he'd been pushed out of the neighborhood altogether. Not just from his grandmother's apartment, but out into the parts of the city where they spoke English and had pale faces. During the war he'd dared to venture that far on his own and had ended up running from a pack of drunken sailors on leave. Teo had run all the way back to the neighborhood, not stopping until he had passed the old house and the newspaper stand. Even then, he had not felt completely safe, not with the house empty.

A fearful sound tore out of him.

A rough voice said, "Teo," a moment before a hand pushed at Teo's shoulder. "Teo," the voice repeated, gruff and hoarse. Teo felt something light stir his hair, like a shallow breath from someone leaning over him. Then his shoulder was prodded again.

"Stop it," Teo instructed, and hoped he was frowning. "It hurts."

He was nudged again, down at his side, only with more strength. Teo realized he was being urged up to a position where his shoulders were no longer taking all of his weight. It felt good, and then it hurt too as blood raced back through his body. So he hissed and held very still. He did not say thank you.

"Teo," the voice insisted, as gruffly as before. But when Teo opened his mouth to breathe harshly in and out, it gentled. "Mateo," the voice pleaded, "wake up."

At the sound of his full name, Teo opened his eyes.

Handsome and naked and bloodied, the *tehuantl*—the jaguar—was crouched over him. The neighborhood had few working streetlights, but the outline of him in the moonlight was unmistakable. Teo had watched for him many times, had seen him as a cat and as a man, but he had never been this close. For one moment he stared into the jaguar's eyes, and then his gaze dropped to follow the gleaming dark trails along the jaguar's arms. Blood, Teo somehow recognized, but felt nothing except curiosity as he studied the jaguar's bared arms and shoulders. He could almost make out spots in the skin, like a jaguar's pelt, but they were already fading.

Teo's vision blurred, and his head hurt. He was probably dreaming. He clenched his jaw and tried to focus despite that, then gave up when a wave of sickness roiled in his stomach. He swallowed and quickly closed his eyes.

"Teo." He had never thought to hear the jaguar's voice again, and couldn't remember if it had always been so low and hoarse. "*Teo*."

"No," Teo protested weakly. "It hurts."

A part of him recognized it was silly to whine about pain when he was probably about to die. This was the guardian himself he was speaking to; he should try to be brave and stoic, not small and miserable. Or he should be afraid. But he couldn't seem to feel anything but a desire to sleep, next to the jaguar's warm presence if possible.

That made him pause, uncertain he wasn't being very obvious. He didn't know how long he had been silent, or if the jaguar was still there, until he felt the presence grow closer, and a delicate touch along his forehead. The jaguar exhaled over the side of his head, behind Teo's ear, where it hurt the most. Teo tried to flinch, but the jaguar held him easily. Teo couldn't have fought him, even if he'd had the use of his hands.

The jaguar was a warrior. Some other old men and women in the neighborhood, those who had grown up in other parts of Mexico than Teo's grandmother before coming to America, said the jaguars were like the naguals, tricksters, magic users with their own desires and agendas. They said the jaguars helped, but to never turn your back on them. But others remembered, or had heard stories going back generations, to before the Spanish, to before even the Mexica that the white people renamed the Aztecs. The fiercest warriors of the Mexica had honored the power of the jaguar by taking their name, and the people before them had sat on jaguar thrones, but beasts who were both cat and man had existed before even them, and they were more than men wearing the coats of the jaguar. They *were* jaguar.

All the old had stories of them, and Teo had listened to every single one. The jaguar were protectors, but they were to be respected, and appeased… and also feared by those who had done wrong.

Teo had always respected them, although he'd never seemed to feel the fear the others did. He had tried to catch glimpses of their jaguar, especially since Japan had surrendered and he had come back from the war. Their jaguar had been drafted along with all the other powerful creatures who had once been gods but were now only called beings, with a sneer.

The jaguar had been sent to the Pacific and had come home to his last relative still in the house, the old man, his grandfather, dead. He had not left the house since then, at least not during daylight. Not that Teo had seen. The jaguar chose to hunt in the dark.

Teo abruptly recalled the blood shining wetly on the jaguar's hands. Someone had met a fate they deserved. Teo didn't deserve his, but he was about to meet it anyway. He tried to make the sign of the cross, then remembered his hands were tied behind his back.

He swallowed down more sickness. His hands were bound because Francisco and his friends must have tied them after they'd beaten him. Teo couldn't remember being beaten. He could remember arguing now, that he'd yelled defiantly that he would do what he pleased, and then Francisco had gone around into the house and burst into his room to drag Teo down the stairs into the street.

He realized he was shaking, and that the jaguar was still touching him.

"Teo." The jaguar held him up and spoke urgently. "Teo, open your eyes."

"You know my name." Teo looked at the jaguar in amazement. He was close, wide-eyed and frowning. Teo could see the strength in his jaw that he remembered, and the fierce crooks of his eyebrows, and the strange, inhuman yellow-gold of his eyes.

He gave a small sigh and let the darkness come again.

A startled huff of breath brushed across Teo's cheeks before the jaguar leaned in even closer and sniffed him. Teo probably smelled like dinner. He was also probably about to die, so he made the decision to open his eyes. The jaguar blinked back at him.

Perhaps he wasn't going to die. The jaguar had just killed. He might already be appeased. Teo might live.

And go back to what? he asked himself. The empty apartment, and no job, and no money, and fear. He had never felt fear like this until tonight.

He locked eyes with the jaguar, whose gaze had never left him. The jaguar remained steady, like the hands holding Teo up. He hadn't eaten Teo yet. He hadn't growled. He had told Teo to wake up, and called to him. "You know my name?" Teo made it a question this time.

The jaguar went as still as a statue. Then he scowled. "You're bleeding."

"You're covered in blood." Teo had no idea why he was arguing.

The jaguar pushed at him, and it made Teo's pounding head hurt more. A cry of pain slipped out, and the jaguar spread his hand wide over Teo's ribs. He was very warm, and very soft, suddenly. Teo wanted to cry at how soft he was. "What are you doing here, little muxe?"

The word, which only his grandmother and a few of the other older ladies from the south used, brought Teo's head up despite the pain. "You know me?"

"You know me," the jaguar countered in that unfamiliar voice, rough and animal. Teo could do nothing but shiver and listen. "You know what I am. What are you doing here?"

The question sank through Teo's muddled thoughts, until he slowly turned his head to glance around them. He was in the entryway of the oldest house in the narrow collection of old houses that took up an entire small block. The houses were the place that jaguars of this family had been given, or had taken, generations ago. They were given many things in exchange for their protection, although not even the sacred cats had protected the neighborhood from encroaching whites, who took the land along the cliffs and the sea, and the valleys, and the hills, and left the

Mexicans only the edge of the city, with the strange fairies in their own neighborhood on one side, and the trees on the other.

A newspaper stand was on the first floor of the old house where cigarettes and liquor and some magazines were sold. The stuff was put out, and people left money for it on the counter, hidden or in plain view, it didn't matter. No one would steal from the jaguar, not even the cops.

The jaguar could find where you lived, and bullets couldn't kill it. It attacked with the unspoken blessing of the community, and it repaid every gift it was given. That was why what belonged to it was respected.

That, and a blood-deep ancestral memory of their kind that had been passed down in stories and legend.

For that reason it was best to appease it with offerings. Extra pennies with your tobacco. Milk and chickens. Tortillas. Jars of broth. Fresh fish and tongue. Baskets or blankets, sometimes, but usually food or money. Even during the war when many things had been scarce, people had left beans from their gardens, and ration cards, perhaps because they'd known the younger jaguar was still protecting their sons across the ocean. Now that there was plenty, many of those who had returned had taken up as their elders had taught them, although they left stranger things, like bottles of soda pop and cans of spiced meat.

If not left on the counter, offerings were placed outside the doorway of the newsstand.

Which was where Francisco and the others had left Teo, tied up and helpless. Exactly as they had threatened to do.

Teo remembered Francisco's furious words. *If you want him so much, we'll give you to him.*

He squeezed his eyes shut and made himself say the words. "I'm your sacrifice."

Then he tensed, waiting. For what, he didn't know. The touch of teeth, a snarl, mocking laughter. But there was nothing. Not even more sniffing.

After a long enough pause to make him feel foolish, he reopened his eyes to stare at the unmoving jaguar. "Are you going to kill me and eat me?" he demanded, feeling like a petulant child. But he couldn't stop his complaints now. "Then do it. My head hurts, and I'm tired." He was scared too, shivering despite the body curled over him.

Again, the jaguar considered him in silence. Teo bit his lip when he felt measured and judged by those yellow eyes. He didn't want to know how the jaguar saw him, so he dropped his gaze to one muscled shoulder.

"Are you rejecting me?" he asked in a breaking voice. Maybe there *was* something wrong with Teo, the way Francisco and the others told him. He should have been relieved to know he would be unharmed, but instead he couldn't feel anything but pain and an awareness of the amount of naked skin so close to him. "I'm not even good enough to kill?"

He was very cold, but the reasons for it slipped through his fingers. He licked his lips and continued to speak. "This isn't what I thought I'd say to you, if we met again," he murmured, letting his eyelids drift down and then back up. He shifted to put himself closer to the cat. If he was about to die, then he was as free to talk as he was around the older women, instead of tripping over his tongue the way he sometimes did around the men his age. "I don't know what Francisco and the others want from you, or what they've done that they think they have to appease you, but they've offered me up, and they aren't going to be pleased to see me alive."

A short, raw sound from the jaguar brought Teo's gaze up to his face. Words were easy now. "The grandmothers won't like what they did to me, but they won't blame you." But thinking of the old women reminded him of his grandmother, and he pushed out a shaky breath that felt like a sob. At least she wouldn't be here for Teo's death. He smiled for that. "If you don't kill me, Francisco, his friends, might, but I will have the satisfaction of knowing that you will then punish them. If not for killing me, then for insulting you by trying to offer me as a sacrifice. You *will* seek them out, won't you?"

The jaguar drew his eyebrows together, becoming a wrathful king. Teo almost felt sorry for Francisco, but couldn't manage it in his sinful heart. He nodded instead, assuming a deal had been struck, then leaned his head back into the wall to study the jaguar. The jaguar was so very handsome, and he had chosen not to kill Teo.

"Is it because I didn't offer myself?" Teo wondered, with an ache in his chest. "Would that be better? I could. All I would ask in return is that you don't let them take my grandmother's things." He struggled to sit up, confused when the jaguar helped him and growled along with his words. "My grandmother made you stew and soup. I know she did. You should help me honor her. I'll offer myself if you will protect her memory."

Again, he thought he would feel the slash of claws before the life slipped from him, or the sting of teeth. But without a sound, the jaguar moved, and then Teo was hauled up so suddenly that it shocked him into crying out.

He threw up, his eyes leaking tears and his face burning. He threw up until his stomach cramped, but he was no longer shaking. Then he was turned again while he was weak, and lifted from the ground. Strength curled around him and held him against a chest with a pounding heart, and if this was death, it was nothing to be afraid of. He only felt tired and worn and safe enough to let his eyes fall closed and stay that way.

The last thing he remembered before the black of sleep was the sight of a flat jaguar in bright colors, snarling at him from the wall. Then nothing.

ONCE AGAIN, he woke to pain in his head and an aching body. But this time he was warm and comfortable, curled onto his side on a soft mattress under a pile of blankets. His shoulders and both of his wrists burned, although not enough to make him want to move. The sun beamed through a shuttered window. It demanded he open his eyes.

He already knew he was not in his bed at home, but the painted figure on the wall was still a surprise. The wall itself was white, and someone had painted a giant creature there, almost like a kind of fairy. The creature was dancing, or simply in motion, and appeared to be human although it was wearing a fantastic shawl, or cloak, of bright colors, perhaps even feathers. The headdress had feathers too, but also gold and jewels.

Teo was not in his little room in his grandmother's small apartment, obviously. A dresser stood against the far wall, but none of his jewelry repairing supplies were there, or the secret stash of comic books he could never bring himself to throw away. None of his needles or thread were in sight either, and his pretty scarves and shawls were nowhere to be seen.

He stared at the painting again. He had seen artists try to paint like that on city projects run by the WPA, imitating ancient styles. But this was different. The artist had taken the basic image from history books and public fountains and made it real. The play of muscles in each arm and leg made it seem like a living man, a study of a particular person instead of a fanciful god.

The creature had skin the same shade of brown as Teo, and the same dark brown hair, worn long like a woman's, in a plait on one side, although this was an image of a man, bare-chested, in a long skirt. Perhaps that was what some of the ancients wore. Teo didn't know. He tried to imagine himself wearing that much finery and almost smiled. He liked the colors, especially the jewelry. He thought maybe he could incorporate that style in the future, when he might have enough money to buy precious metals and make himself some proper bracelets, instead of repairing broken necklace clasps for a small fee at the market.

A hushed breath announced he wasn't alone, and he swung his gaze to the doorway, where the jaguar waited.

Teo had to blink away the image of the jaguar like someone in those sorts of paintings, decorated in paint and feathers, wearing only a small cloth, or perhaps the skin and claws of a big cat.

The jaguar's large, solid body was not on display today, except for his bare arms. He wasn't as tall as some would think, but he was taller than Teo, and seemed even taller with the proud, royal way he stood. He had slightly lighter skin than Teo, but darker hair that he'd worn short even before the war. It was only a little longer than the military cut now, and beginning to show signs of curving waves. He was wearing black pants and a thin white cotton shirt with torn-away sleeves. Teo thought of him naked the night before, what he'd been able to see, and his heart began to beat faster.

The jaguar spoke in the same rough voice. "Whenever our people get in trouble, the newspapers and the police will say 'they used to sacrifice humans; that is why they are brutal. Why they are savages and deserve how they are treated.'"

Teo raised a hand to wipe the sleep from his face, then inched himself up a bit more. He thought about those words, then nodded. "The Romans crucified people. It's in the Bible. They were brutal too, but no one mentions that, do they?" Teo lowered his voice uncertainly. "If that's what you're trying to say."

If he was not a sacrifice, he should get up. He stared at his hands for a moment, studying the neat bandages at his wrists, where rope must have been tied too tightly, then pushed himself up. It was only once he was leaning against the headboard of the bed that he realized he wore no clothes. He opened his mouth, then shut it. He'd been bleeding. His clothes would have been ruined, and the jaguar wouldn't have wanted stained bedding.

Nonetheless, Teo felt heated when he glanced over. "Is that why you didn't kill me? No sacrifices anymore?" He picked at the sheets, which smelled like they had been stored away until recently, and found he couldn't lift his head as he waited for the answer.

He stared at his own chest. Teo was nothing worth looking at for so long. He was pretty, but so were many. His lines were soft, not hard and strong like the jaguar's, who was like a man, like some of the well-dressed pachucos that Francisco envied and tried to copy. Although unlike those young men, there was no flash around the jaguar. The jaguar didn't need to remind anyone of his strength. It was always on display, whatever form he took.

Once again, Teo had the memory of the jaguar crawling over him, naked and bloodied, and felt hot all over. He wished for one of his shawls to throw around his head and hide his face.

The jaguar hadn't answered, so Teo skipped on to a new thought. "You brought me into your house," Teo told him, with wonder in his voice.

He took the noise the jaguar made as one of confusion, or maybe surprise. Teo shot him a brief, embarrassed look. "You took me into your house. I'm thinking about what Francisco and the others are going to say. Lots of boasting about what men they are, probably, to cover their fear." He didn't wait for the jaguar to express confusion this time; he just went on. "They think of themselves as tough, but they've never been in any real trouble. They like to drink too much and harass the girls… and me." Teo pulled at his hair and began to comb it with his fingers, wincing when it pulled at his scalp. He reached up and found a painful, hot lump, as well as some dried blood, partly matted as though someone had tried to wash it out. He glanced over again. "They don't really have anything to do, but they live to be in everybody's business—in mine especially." He stopped toying with his hair and flicked a thoughtful look to the watchful jaguar, who remained as handsome as he had always been, even when he'd been a boy.

Francisco wouldn't like that. "This is almost worth it, whatever happens," Teo continued. "But eventually, you'll throw me out, and

Francisco will have even more to say then. He had plenty to say before he—" Teo put a hand to his head and thought of being dragged from the apartment, Francisco's voice loud with imagined betrayal.

"Why did they do it?" The jaguar asked the one question Teo didn't want to answer. He didn't even want to think about it.

Teo glanced to the opposite wall, the wall with the window, where a jaguar-man made in paint stood guard. He swallowed and considered his words. "There's no one to protect me anymore, not that my grandmother could do much. She did what she could. But Francisco's father owns that building, and he raised her rent all the time, whenever I told Francisco no, I think. I don't know how she managed to pay it. There was only so much sewing work the two of us could pick up, and her eyesight near the end…."

He trailed off, and thought there was a small motion from the doorway, but when he turned there was nothing. His lingering fear from last night was making him imagine the jaguar was upset, perhaps on behalf of Teo's grandmother. If anyone deserved to be avenged, it was her.

"An old lady. He chose to punish me through her." Teo worked his jaw. "Francisco thinks of himself as the future master of a bunch of farmhands, when he doesn't own a hacienda and these haven't been farmlands for almost a century. He also hates me enough to spend much of his time observing me and seeking me out." Teo gave a disdainful sniff before the jaguar's silence reminded him of how much he'd been talking, and he shut up.

He pulled at the sheets and blankets around him to look beneath them. The jaguar had removed all his clothes. Teo supposed it was too late to be shy, even if he felt hot and embarrassed for no reason he could name. He sucked in a breath, then flung the blankets from him. The jaguar wouldn't want to see him anyway; Teo had the body of a man, despite how he dressed. His only curve was behind him. His cock slid against his thigh as he got to his feet to turn away from the far-too-revealing sunshine.

Teo was soft. He had long lashes and a plump mouth that he had never been allowed to paint with makeup because his grandmother hadn't believed in it, for men or for women, as she hadn't approved of the way modern women dressed. Since he could not wear stockings and sleek skirts like the women in magazines, Teo chose colorful blouses that he embroidered himself with red and purple flowers to make his eyes flash.

With his earrings brushing his neck, he was pretty enough to make Francisco gaze hotly at him, even at his most cruel and bullying.

Francisco and the others didn't understand what he was. Teo didn't have an interest in masculine things. He found it easy to talk with women and enjoyed what they had to say. He liked delicate and colorful things and always had. According to Grandmother, where she had been a girl, sometimes those like him were called something else, a muxe. They were a blessing, she'd said. She had known where Teo's interests lay before he had, and had explained that some muxe liked men and some of them didn't.

Teo did. Although, as his grandmother also would have said, he had yet to find a suitor.

He straightened up, very aware of his nudity and unbound hair, and forced himself to look into the doorway.

The moment Teo saw the jaguar's gaze on him, he realized there might be a different reason for the jaguar to take Teo into his home, and his shiver traveled all the way down his spine and made his toes curl into the floor.

But the idea was ridiculous. It had to be.

Teo began to comb his hair again as he tried to think of a different reason. The jaguar had mentioned sacrifices. "Do you not kill humans?" He raised his head too fast and had to take a moment as he got dizzy. "Because I know you do. Everyone knows. You, your family, you wanted people to know sometimes. Like… the gang of kids that beat up the shop owners and shook them down for money, after they killed old Mr. Gomez." An accident, some claimed, as if Mr. Gomez hadn't been beaten in his own shop for trying to protect his livelihood. "The police did nothing, but the gang leader was found the next day…." Teo slashed a hand across his throat to indicate the death wound. It had not been done by a knife. The police had done nothing about that either. To them it was all internal struggles among the spics, like the girls who had been pulled off the streets and attacked in the dark. Shortly afterward, several men had gone missing. Parts of them had turned up later.

When the powerful tenement owners who had left their buildings to rot and mold and burn had died in their mansions, *that* had attracted some attention from the police. With no slashes in those bodies, however, they'd had no proof of anything, and they wouldn't come into this neighborhood to take dramatic action except in force.

All of that wasn't mentioning the crimes the jaguar had prevented with a growl in the dark to remind everyone of his presence. Teo went still. "Oh," he realized. "I haven't done anything wrong, and you serve strictly as a protector? Is that it?" He put both hands over his heart and stared. "You think so? That I've done nothing wrong? Grandmother says—used to say—there are men, and there are women, and there are others, like me. But what I want is a sin at the church."

"There are things older than churches," the jaguar reminded Teo quietly, as if the paintings on the walls weren't testaments to that.

That was a good thought, even if part of Teo suspected it was blasphemous. It was only a small part of him. The rest of him peeked up through his lashes, pleased deep in his soul to know the jaguar didn't think of him as a joke or an abomination. "Some of the churchgoers *do* consider you to be the work of the devil," Teo offered in return, letting a grin slip out to show that he was teasing.

The jaguar startled him by responding seriously. "The jaguar are older than him too."

Teo didn't know what to make of that and glanced down. When he raised his eyes again, the jaguar was gone. He hadn't made a sound.

Teo sighed and began to look around for his clothes, but there was no sign of them. With nothing to tie his hair, and it still sticky with his blood, he had no choice except to leave it loose. He had no intention of staying naked, and pulled the sheets from the bed to wrap around himself. Before he did, he noticed an indentation in the other side of the bed, as though someone had sat beside him during the night. He looked at the dresser, then at the paintings on the wall, and couldn't stop shaking as he realized this was probably the jaguar's bedroom and he had slept in his bed.

He left the room before he could dwell on the thought and burn all the skin of his face with his blushes. With no idea of what direction to take, he wandered down a hallway, stopping every few feet to peer into rooms or study the artwork along the walls. The area seemed to be greater than the space of one house, and he wondered if the jaguar family had connected all the houses on the block over time, until the house itself was its own kind of manor house.

A large room was in the middle of the house as he came down the stairs, like a grand entranceway from the movies, with a very high ceiling and windows to bring in all the light they could. Like almost everywhere else Teo had seen, someone had sketched or drawn on the walls along the stairs. At the top was a vivid daytime scene, like any other landscape painting, but this one of the market on a busy day. Other walls had more of the ancient style art on them, or simple sketches. Beneath them, the paint was peeling and cracked.

But Teo didn't give himself much time to look. He continued downstairs into what he thought was the main house, the oldest house, until he found the jaguar in the kitchen.

He was in front of a huge icebox, drinking soup from a jar.

Teo hurried forward to grab it. "Now I see why you brought me here!" He clucked and set the jar on a wooden countertop while he pulled the sheet tighter around his body and searched through the cabinets. He found a spoon and then pulled a pot down from where someone had hung it long ago.

The jaguar seemed frozen as he watched. Teo waved at him as he considered the stove, large and marked from years of use. "I'll cook." Teo got the stove lit, then went to the sink, which had running water, although not much pressure. "Have you been eating your offerings cold this whole time?" He shook his head for that and for the dust on everything in the kitchen he could see. Then he poured the soup into the pot to let it heat.

He peered in the icebox, which was probably from the last decade but still nicer than any Teo had seen. It held bottles of milk and little else. "You should go to the market instead of solely relying on…." He realized he sounded like a scold and stopped himself there. He studied the floor, which also had a fine layer of dust, except for a trail to and from the icebox. "If you brought me here to cook and clean, you could have just said so."

"You offered yourself." There was almost a question in the jaguar's voice, but Teo found himself flustered by his choice of words.

"Yes," he admitted, and tried not to think of lying in bed with the jaguar next to him. "But… I had nowhere else to go. If you didn't hear, my grandmother died a few weeks ago." He got quiet for a moment and made the cross at her memory, and then he coughed and carried on. "As I said before, they often raised her rent. I don't know where she found the extra money for that, much less how she fed us both—and you, when she…. What I mean is, I won't be able to pay rent. So I thought…." He had offered to let the jaguar kill him. In pain and disoriented, he had offered exactly that. His grandmother would have been ashamed of him.

But the jaguar stood there, letting Teo move around him in his own kitchen and watching him with a cat's careful interest. Then he lifted his chin. "Why did they sacrifice you? They have never sacrificed a human to me or anyone in my family. Not in my memory. Then they did. And they chose you." He leaned in. "Why?"

Teo couldn't be near the strength of him as he answered that, so he moved away to find a bowl. He poured the warm, if not hot, soup into it and handed it over. He surprised himself by smiling when the jaguar slurped noisily from the bowl, then seemed to catch himself and sipped politely at the soup instead. Teo had to remember the jaguar had lived alone since the war. And he was a man. Manners would have to be taught. That is what the ladies had always told him, with a laugh.

Before he had finished it off, the jaguar pushed the bowl back in Teo's direction. It was mostly broth, but Teo accepted it blankly, then had to consider his roiling stomach. The jaguar wished to share, so Teo wouldn't reject the offer. He took several careful sips, recognizing Mrs. Navarro's touch in the kitchen before he pushed it back to the jaguar.

"Thank you." Now that he'd eaten a little something, Teo could admit he wasn't well, and quickly sat down at the broad table adjoining the kitchen proper. Paint supplies lay all over it, which meant the jaguar left the house after all, if only to buy paint. Somehow Teo had missed him, even with all the time he'd spent looking.

He thought of the night before and lowered his head.

He finally answered the question. "Why did they choose to sacrifice a person? Or what they thought you would do to me, I can't really say. But"—he kept his hands at his face—"Francisco thinks I would make him a good mistress. But he doesn't want to be the sort of weak man who would want someone like me, so he torments me instead. That is the simple answer." Teo took a breath. The jaguar came closer. Teo glanced up at him despite himself. "The longer answer is that you, and your family, have fascinated me ever since I was little and my mother sent me to live with my grandmother so I could take care of her, but really because Grandmother understood me better." He couldn't meet those eyes and kept his gaze on one bare shoulder. "I think he was jealous. And I was angry and embarrassed that I had been so obvious. We had words when he caught me on my balcony keeping watch for you, and to save face, he and his friends hit me and tied me up and left me here, thinking, no doubt, that you would kill me, or that you'd ignore me, and I would be humiliated."

"But I brought you into my home." The jaguar repeated Teo's earlier words as if now he understood them. "Francisco. He was not…?" The jaguar straightened up and fell silent. He frowned at the paint supplies on the table next to Teo and raised his head. "You may stay here." He huffed, like a housecat who had sniffed a pepper. "But you may leave, if that's what you want."

Teo hadn't thought himself a prisoner, but he supposed he wasn't thinking clearly today. "I stay, and in return I'll cook and clean and wash the blood from your clothes?" Teo said it aloud in order to consider the sound of it, while ignoring the twitchy frown on the jaguar's face. Then he tried a shrug. "I don't want to go home. The apartment still smells like her… the memory of her. Have you ever felt that?"

He turned to the jaguar with the question and saw the sadness and understanding flicker across his expression. Then it was gone, and the stoic, somewhat confused warrior remained. He must have felt the same when he'd returned to find his grandfather had died.

Teo considered his situation. "But I want my things, her things, if Francisco and the others haven't taken them." He shook his head when the jaguar snarled angrily. "Wait, that coward won't go near the apartment. He has to see if I'm dead or not first… and I've no inclination to go outside yet. My head still hurts." He paused, and the jaguar quieted, as if awaiting his answer. Teo slowly brought his gaze to the jaguar's face and studied it until he couldn't contain his blushes. "I'll stay."

The jaguar moved, stalking across the room to Teo without a single sound reaching Teo's ears. Teo caught his breath and raised his chin as far as his pounding head allowed. The jaguar stared at him, almost too handsome to bear, dressed while Teo was in a sheet with his hair unbound, and after a moment, Teo let his gaze fall. It was that or do something foolish.

But whatever the jaguar had wanted went unspoken. Without another word, the jaguar turned and grabbed some of the supplies from the table before padding noiselessly from the room, leaving Teo to wander his house without direction.

TEO *HAD* slept in the jaguar's bedroom. He discovered that on a more thorough search of the first house. He didn't venture into the others. This house was where the jaguar spent his time. This one Teo had to learn.

He had gone back upstairs after poking around in the kitchen and exploring parts of the first floor, and found the jaguar naked and stretched out on top of the covers in that room, his face in the pillow. He'd had paint on his fingers where there'd been blood the night before.

Teo had stared at his back, and his ass, and the smooth muscle of him, the faint lines of scars over his skin, until his eyes had stung, then hurried down the hall the way he'd just come. He sat on the stairs and considered the entranceway, and the room beyond it that could have been a parlor. It was strange to imagine a family of jaguars welcoming visitors, but the sisters must have had suitors if they'd married and left. Teo had been young and oblivious to things like that at the time. He should have paid attention.

After resting and composing himself, he'd moved on, returning to the second floor. He skipped past the jaguar's bedroom and found another bedroom that didn't appear completely abandoned. This one was smaller, with lace on the dresser and light wallpaper instead of paintings. It was possibly one of the sisters' rooms when she'd been unmarried. Most of the drawers were empty, but Teo found bedding in one and a slip in another. Teo had never worn a skirt before outside the apartment, and wasn't sure how he felt about only thin white cotton covering him. But more digging got him a simple dress to go over the slip.

The dress was several years out of style and sewn for curves, but Teo had never worn anything so modern, since his grandmother had favored the skirts of her childhood village. It made him want to seek out stockings, either nylon or the silk kind some women wore again now that the war was over. He decided to look for pants tomorrow and keep the dress on. Or he could go naked. The jaguar seemed to. Perhaps wearing clothes got to be a bother when you spent much of your life as a cat.

Teo was not a cat. So he would need pants. Or more skirts.

Dressed, he rested again, long enough to feel real hunger. So he went back down the hall, observing the mural of the neighborhood for a second time, the shops, the theater that had closed now that the bigger theater in town had removed its sign of *Se Sirve Solamente a Raza Blanca*. This time he looked for familiar stalls and people in the market, and noted with surprise that the jaguar had depicted the roof of the apartment building where Teo and his grandmother lived, and the curve of the balcony outside Teo's window. Both were visible in the background, although there was no sign of Teo himself.

Teo had spent countless hours on that roof or on his balcony, trying to catch a glimpse of the jaguar. Others had noticed, although not the jaguar himself, fortunately for Teo, even if he had admitted it to him today.

The jaguar hadn't taken it as an insult. Teo should be happy with that, he decided, and gave up looking for himself in the painting in order to go down to the kitchen. With his pounding head, he didn't get much cleaning done, but he stopped to rest and drink some milk before he returned to his new duties.

Caring for the home was for women, but the jaguar seemed to already know about those who were both girls and boys, and the work made Teo happy. It gave him something to think about that wasn't his grandmother, or being left for dead, or the shivery warmth at knowing he'd slept in the jaguar's bed.

But they needed more food, so eventually he went through the kitchen to the pantry, which was stocked with dusty jars and cans of meat like those the jaguar must have eaten when in the Army. Another door was at the end of the pantry, and when Teo opened that, he was in a small storage space that led out into the newsstand.

The doors to the newsstand had been left open all night. The jaguar might have brought Teo inside this way. Curious, and a little sick, Teo went outside to see for himself where he'd been left like a dressed chicken. A spot of his blood was on the wall. Someone had placed a candle beneath it, which was a surprise. He wondered who had bothered, and whether people thought he was dead or that the blood was from another victim.

He blew out the candle, then went inside to the counter. He was unamused to find it covered in dust as well, but wiped it off with his hands since he had no towels. The stack of papers the newsboy had dropped off in the early hours had been cut open, which was why there was some change on the counter. Teo tried to put it in the register, but since there was no money in there, he figured he would take it inside for the jaguar. It was the jaguar's money. Teo did not want him to think Teo would take it or anything else.

He was still at the counter, bent over a newspaper, when someone unexpectedly walked in. Teo sprang up, then stood there, uncertain of what to say to Mr. Sanchez, who seemed equally startled. Teo realized he was bloodied and bandaged and wearing an ill-fitting dress. He also might have been presumed dead until that moment.

After a long silence, he waved his hand to indicate Mr. Sanchez should go ahead with his business, and Mr. Sanchez silently put out the money for his evening supply of nickel cigars, with a few pennies extra. He didn't take the cigars himself, so, with a small jump, Teo handed them over. Then Mr. Sanchez left, eyeing Teo warily until he was out of sight.

He could have been wondering how Teo was still alive, or how he'd ended up in his current state. Possibly he suspected Teo now belonged to their jaguar in a way that a man like Mr. Sanchez wasn't going to speak of.

Suddenly exhausted, Teo left the paper and took the money into the house. He placed it on the table in the kitchen, then made his way upstairs. He cleaned up in the washroom, pulled off the dress so he could sleep in the slip alone, then curled up on the narrow bed in the girl's bedroom.

IN THE evening he went out to the newsstand again, hoping for more soup. What he found was a counter so full of offerings it looked like an altar. He blinked in surprise, but dutifully collected them all, from the cookies wrapped in wax paper, to the dried chilies, to the rosary, which was perhaps not meant for the jaguar. He wrapped it around his wrist like a bracelet, fitting it over his bandages, then gathered up the pot of beans—still warm—and the delicious-smelling tortillas someone had also left.

He was making sure the simple meal was ready when the jaguar appeared in the kitchen. He had put on pants and didn't seem to notice how Teo swept a look over him and swallowed hungrily. If anything, the jaguar seemed focused on the dress.

But he didn't remark on it. He accepted a plate with a puzzled expression and sat at the table, where he waited to eat until Teo finally came over too. Once Teo sat, however, the jaguar leapt on his food without any further attempt at politeness.

“You’re quieter now.” He spoke only after several minutes spent cleaning his plate. Teo got up to get him more, and some of the cookies as well.

“I’m a little confused,” Teo confessed. “You were left a lot today. Money and some food. Even some cheese and wine. Is it a festival? A day in one of the old religions?”

The jaguar paused long enough to narrow his eyes at Teo, as if Teo were being slow. “No,” he said at last. He noticed the cross at Teo’s wrist and wrinkled his nose before he resumed eating. “I believe they were meant for you. Perhaps it’s an apology.”

Teo gave a start, then slowly took his place at the table again. “Couldn’t be,” he insisted, and gestured at the pile of coins. “Here is the money from the newsstand today. But you should know that Mr. Sanchez…. Do you know him?” He might. The jaguar had known Teo’s name, after all. “He saw me. Like this. In your house. This morning.” Teo drew in a careful breath. “I thought you should know. If you wanted to change your mind.”

Again the jaguar stopped. But this time he pushed his plate away and regarded Teo until Teo nearly squirmed. When the jaguar raised his chin, Teo knew he was about to make one of his pronouncements. “If he saw you, then he’s already told others, and the offerings are for you. Because you are here, and they want you to be happy.” The jaguar studied him with a slight frown.

“No, I’m not—” Teo didn’t get to finish.

“Why shouldn’t they offer to you?” The jaguar was quiet, but his softness demanded an answer. For someone who adopted the poses of a king on high, the jaguar had a low, gentle way of speaking. Even the roughness in his voice seemed to be smoothing out the more he spoke.

“They want me to keep you happy, maybe,” Teo insisted stubbornly. He shrugged. “Some of the older women were fond of me,” he admitted. “They might want to make sure you don’t eat me.”

That earned him a snort. “They should have brought you your own clothes,” the jaguar pointed out. “They suit you better than my sister’s dress. You can wear my clothes, in the meantime.”

Teo tried not to preen to think of the jaguar noticing him in his usual clothes, or to imagine how it would feel to slip into the jaguar’s clothing. “Ah,” he murmured, flustered for the third time in one day. “Thank you.

But I prefer mine. No insult to you, cat, but dressing as a man would not make me *me*. Maybe I'll fetch my things tomorrow."

He hadn't eaten, but he'd already learned his stomach couldn't hold much today. He took their dishes to deal with them and couldn't help but notice the jaguar didn't leave, although he had no reason to stay. The silence was, mostly, comfortable between them, but Teo had another question to ask. He debated bringing up the subject, but then saw no point in denying a fact of life in this house.

"In the newspapers today, there was a piece about a missing man from the bluffs. The one who had the string of girls that he kept hopped up, including some girls from the neighborhood." Teo clucked his tongue. "He vanished last night." And the jaguar had returned home only partially in his human body, covered in blood. "Do you think your increased offerings today were for that?"

In a voice more husky than rough, the jaguar answered. "That isn't why they make them." His voice had been rough because he'd had no one to talk to, Teo realized. He probably only spoke when he bought his paints. He gave Teo a significant look. "Some bring them to honor the old ways. Some mean it to ask for something, or they are grateful for someone I have avenged. But most of them are afraid. They should be. We are not like them. We can save or we can hurt. To protect, we often kill. I have killed, Teo, if that is what you're asking."

Teo studied him without fully turning around. "I know."

The jaguar's tone was soft. "If you're afraid, you may go."

Teo left the dishes to air-dry, because the towels were none too clean, but he wished for something to do with his hands. The jaguar's steady regard seemed to scatter his thoughts. "During the war, the Army sent men off to kill too. Regular men." Teo paused. People assumed because he wore feminine clothing, he was silly or stupid. He wasn't. Nor was any woman he called friend. He glanced over again. "I could have gone. I was old enough, almost, by the end, but they would never have taken me."

The snarl was loud and startling. Teo twisted around to face the jaguar, who rose to his feet. He snarled again, quieter now that Teo was looking at him. "They had me stalking the Japanese. People I didn't know, whose crimes I couldn't guess, and our soldiers were too many, and none of them wanted me there until I saved them. There was no protection in those places. You didn't belong there, Teo. Not you."

The jaguar knew him. Teo hadn't forgotten that, though Teo still had no answer on how or why, or how he could say Teo's name like it meant something. Teo bit his lip but couldn't help wondering. "You know my name, but I don't know yours. Do you have a name? They call you different things."

The jaguar lifted his chin, but no pronouncement came out. Instead he frowned as if Teo had insulted him, and sat back down at the table. He pushed out a breath and then answered slowly, almost reluctantly. "My draft papers say Carmelo Guerrero."

"Carmelo?" It was the last name Teo had expected. It was thoroughly Spanish, and the jaguar was a New World creature. But Teo repeated it, taking his time with the secret name and drawing it out with pleasure. "Car-me-lo."

The jaguar put both of his hands on the table and splayed his fingers wide. Teo said it again, as sweet as the cookies he brought over in apology for however he had offended the jaguar, and watched Carmelo flex his hands on the tabletop like a pleased, stretching cat. It must have been a long time since anyone had said his name. Teo offered him another cookie. "It's an honor to meet you… again."

Carmelo turned to him with wide eyes, and for the smallest moment, before he spoke, Teo felt like the most powerful person in the world. Then Carmelo licked his mouth and greeted him in return. "*Mateo*," he said. "You—" And then abruptly he pushed back his chair with such force that it almost fell over.

He straightened while Teo gaped at him, and snapped his head up so fast Teo was surprised to not see a lashing tail. He dropped the cookie to the floor as if he'd forgotten Teo had given it to him.

Carmelo nodded, very serious, as though he hadn't done any of those strange things, and announced, "Dinner was very good. Thank you. I will punish the ones who hurt you," before hurrying from the room.

He began to strip off his pants as he went. Teo was too startled to pretend to look away. A few moments later, he heard water running upstairs. So it was not true about cats and water, with this cat at least.

Teo tiptoed into the newsstand to grab something to read and then dashed upstairs as fast as he could so he wouldn't see, or startle, Carmelo as he came out of the bath. Once in his newly claimed room, he sat on the bed without bothering with the borrowed comic book and listened to the patter of feline paws on the roof. He didn't think many people in this world had scared the jaguar and lived to tell the tale. He wondered how he'd done it.

HE WAS awake before he knew he was or what had made him stir. The moon sent lines of weak light through the darkness, even through the closed shutters at the window. Teo froze as he remembered where he was, and why, and then turned toward the door as he realized why he must have woken up.

There was no indication the jaguar was near. Of course there was not. So far the jaguar had been kind enough to let Teo know when he approached, but that had been courtesy. It was a funny thing to realize, not at all frightening, although now Teo knew those nights he had climbed onto the roof and sat in the dark, the jaguar could have been next to him, close enough to touch, and he would never have known.

He turned, pushing his hair from his face, and realized he'd fallen asleep on top of the blankets and the air was chilly.

Tonight there was no glimpse of Carmelo's moonlit shoulders, and he was too far away for Teo to feel any heat from his body. But Teo stared blankly toward the doorway and the black depths of the hall and licked his dry lips. "What is it?" He'd left the door open when he'd gone to bed, not really thinking about it. Perhaps he should have closed it. He cleared his throat, but sleep made his voice soft. "What's wrong? Should I have chosen a different room?"

There was no answer. Teo was not certain that he wasn't dreaming all of this. But he tried again, any excuse to say the name that only he knew. "Carmelo?"

But if Carmelo was there, if he had ever been there, he didn't answer.

IN THE clearer light of morning, Teo washed his hair and left it loose to dry as he made his bed and shook the wrinkles from his dress. He removed the bandages to study the bruises and marks the rope had left on his wrists. Though it was damp, he plaited his hair so it would rest over one shoulder, then went downstairs to begin his day's work, only to stop in the entrance to the kitchen.

The painting supplies from the table had been moved. He didn't see to where, but he wouldn't have looked anyway, since his grandmother's things had replaced them. Except for a chair, *her* chair, the one his grandfather had carved for her, most of his grandmother's belongings were sitting on the kitchen table. Her bed wasn't there, neither were her pots and pans, but he saw her jewelry, her shawls, her combs and hand mirror, her Bible, her photograph of his grandfather. The things she would have wanted Teo to keep.

Next to her things, in some crates that had probably once held magazines or tobacco, were Teo's clothes. More than that, there was his rolled-up kit for repairing jewelry and his box of embroidery supplies. Even a few of his comic books were tucked into one of the crates. It wasn't everything, but it felt as though it was.

Teo spent several minutes touching everything as tears pricked at his eyes. Then he slid one of his grandmother's prettier combs behind his ear, took some of his clothes, and went back upstairs to get dressed, correctly this time. He chose a short-sleeved red blouse and pants he'd sewn himself that he could wear with no shoes. He added a few of his necklaces as well, and wished for red lipstick. In his sleek, modern trousers, which curved to the shape of his ass, he felt like a movie star.

He puckered his lips at his reflection in his grandmother's hand mirror and then quickly put it down before he could do anything like he had done at sixteen. He thought he might try lipstick, now that he was free to. Then, in a daydream, as he walked into the newsstand to put out the morning editions and throw out the old, he thought about what Carmelo might think of his mouth painted red.

Several people were already in the newsstand, none of them anywhere near the counter. Teo paused, observing them, letting them observe him, then worried at his bottom lip. Before he could decide if he should speak, the people gathered—still mostly older men, but a few women as well—began to trickle over to the counter to buy cigarettes or movie magazines.

Teo helped them, and by the time the last of them had taken their leave, he'd also wiped down the counter and added to the pile of out-of-date papers he wanted to throw away. He went through the racks of comic books, noting sadly that most of them were over a year old. Carmelo had probably never ordered more.

But eventually, as the sky got brighter, he tore himself away. He collected fresh eggs and sweet rolls from the offerings, then went inside to clean up and see if Carmelo wanted breakfast. He really should go to the market. But he didn't keep the money, even for that, because it was not his to take. He left it on the table, next to his grandmother's belongings, and was at the stove when Carmelo came in.

He heard nothing, but his heart began to beat faster, and when he turned, Carmelo was there. Teo resisted the urge to pull at his hair and wrap the braid around his fingers, but it was difficult with how Carmelo looked at him, as though Teo was the morning sun. Teo struggled in the silence to remember how to speak. "Good morning," he said at last and, too late, thought that he should have asked about last night. "Would you like breakfast?"

That got him a nod, so he busied himself with eggs for a while, then served them with most of the pastries. If meeting Carmelo's burning gaze had been difficult for him before, it was impossible when they were so close to all of his grandmother's things. Teo dipped his head. "Thank you. This is more than anyone has ever done for me who wasn't family."

Teo went to pour himself some of the tea he'd made from the herbs in the back of the pantry. He took several sweet rolls and picked at them while he scrubbed at whatever stains he came across. When he glanced over, Carmelo was turned in his direction, as though Teo moving around in his kitchen was worth all his attention.

"More people were in the newsstand today," Teo continued, breathless at the jaguar's stare. "They were there to gawk, I think. There was no sign of Francisco or any of his friends."

Carmelo had had a busy night. Teo didn't think he'd had time to exact whatever vengeance he had in mind for them. Nonetheless, he kept an eye on Carmelo as he waited on a response.

Carmelo leaned forward as Teo mentioned Francisco, then sat back and made a small interested sound Teo couldn't interpret. A moment after that he grinned playfully.

Teo's everything stopped. He hadn't known Carmelo could smile like that.

His hands fluttered uselessly in the air. "Did you do something to them?"

The crooked, pleased smile vanished from Carmelo's face, replaced by a scowl. "You doubt me?" He raised his head. "My people were once gods."

Teo's mouth dropped open. Then he raised his head too. "That may be true," he allowed, "but *you* can't even feed yourself without old women cooking for you."

The silence made his ears ring.

His hands were useless in the air, half-raised in apology, and then Carmelo's gruff words made him curl them into fists and hurry forward. "Your boyfriend and the others hid themselves last night. They now know you are alive and in my house." Carmelo narrowed his eyes as Teo came closer, then grinned again. The show of teeth was much less playful this time. "I imagine the idea torments him."

Teo shook his head but stopped in front of Carmelo when he realized he had no idea what to do once he reached him. "Boyfriend? Francisco?" He nearly spat on the floor before he angled his chin up even higher than a jaguar who had once been a god. "Francisco isn't man enough for me."

"He doesn't think so. He never has." Carmelo made a growly sort of huff, a displeased sound, much like a cat whose paw had gotten stuck in the rug. But then he flinched and looked away.

Teo stared at Carmelo's profile in astonishment. He toyed with the tip of his braid and put a hand up to make certain the comb was in place and displayed to its best advantage. He crept closer, then stopped when Carmelo tensed.

"Carmelo," Teo whispered, watching the shiver work through that body before he looked back to Carmelo's face. "How did you know my name? Out of everyone in the neighborhood, you—oh." For a second, Teo was flattered, hopeful; then he remembered the mural of the market. "The scene of the street that you painted," he remembered out loud and stepped away when Carmelo tilted his head in question. Teo's heart was pounding despite his silly, crushed feelings, so he kept his face turned down until he controlled himself.

"Is that what you do?" he wondered when he was at a safe distance. He was genuinely interested, even if it created another ache in his chest. "You stay in here and watch the town? That's.... I've been lonely too. You'd know, you must have seen me." Embarrassment made his face sting. "You aren't like us, but you shouldn't be alone.

Not you. You're too…." He bowed his head to needlessly adjust the comb, which was easier than saying aloud how beautiful Carmelo was. Carmelo said nothing, so Teo went on, babbling like a child. "The mural is remarkable. I want to look at it more whenever I stop there. I want to see what I've missed. It's so strange to think that you paint. I would never have guessed."

"My grandfather." Carmelo's voice was rough again, but only briefly. "My grandfather didn't mind. And the walls needed a new coat of paint."

"It's more than that," Teo scoffed, thinking of the paintings in the jaguar's bedroom, figures from the past but entirely in a style of their own. He didn't know what to make of Carmelo's silence. Then Carmelo darted a glance at him, and Teo again thought of the lonely life Carmelo led. No one else had ever seen his artwork.

"Are you bothered I mentioned it?" Teo couldn't understand why, unless Carmelo was embarrassed. "I'm sure talent and skill comes naturally to you and your kind."

Carmelo tossed his head, but his frown was short, as though he was already dismissing his own work. "It's not hunting. Only hunting comes naturally. Even the Army knew it." He glanced at Teo again and opened his hands on the table. "They sent me first with a bunch of wolves." He snorted. "They learned that cats do not follow a pack."

"No, I suppose not," Teo agreed awkwardly. If Carmelo didn't want to talk about his painting, then Teo wouldn't, but it seemed wrong when he clearly enjoyed it. Teo tucked the subject away for later and approached the table once more. The new topic was also of interest to him. "You were young then. I remember how you looked when you left," he admitted, with less shyness than he would have yesterday. Teo had often wished for Carmelo to come home on leave in his uniform, but he never had. Draft or no draft, Teo hadn't thought the jaguar would go. But his grandmother had pointed out a jaguar wouldn't do well in jail, and many of the other young men in town had gone, so Carmelo had to try to protect them as best he could. The old man had still been here to watch over everyone else. Perhaps Carmelo's parents had been somewhere close as well.

Teo had often wondered what had happened to his parents, why they'd left, and why Carmelo had stayed. He thought, with how Carmelo waited for him to speak, that he was being invited to ask.

"Do your kind not usually live with others? Am I bothering you?" Teo still wasn't sure if last night had happened or been a dream.

Carmelo slowly turned toward him and drew in a long breath before he answered. "We are particular about who shares our space. But we have family. We form bonds. But the neighborhood grows smaller, there was less for them to fight for, so my parents traveled south to meet with more of our kind and see if there was another place that would welcome us."

"They went where they were needed?" Teo imagined the heroes in his comic books and stared at Carmelo with wide eyes.

Carmelo parted his lips as if he had something to say to that. He breathed hard for a few moments, then shook his head. "I don't understand you," he offered at last. "The others know to keep their distance from us."

"Your grandfather went into the newsstand all the time." Teo hadn't raised his voice, but he felt like he was arguing. "I remember you in there too, when I'd go in." As he'd gotten older, Teo had gone in there far too often. Once, at sixteen, Teo had gone to the newsstand with a flower in his hair because his grandmother hadn't let him borrow her hair combs, and he'd glanced shyly around. Carmelo's mother hadn't seemed bothered. She'd made a noise, like a human version of a growl, and then Carmelo, although Teo hadn't known his name, had emerged from the shadows to wish Teo a gruff good morning. It was the only time they had spoken, and Carmelo probably didn't remember, although Teo had sighed over it until Carmelo left for the war shortly after. "Your mother was behind the counter many times when I was younger. She smiled at me, a knowing kind of smile with teeth, but not a mean one. I liked her."

"She might return to visit soon." Carmelo said it as if he was trying to comfort Teo, but his voice was as gruff as it had been that day when Teo had been sixteen. He couldn't possibly be upset that Teo had liked his mother. "She and my father write often."

Teo slid his hands to his hips. "So in the meantime, you live alone and paint your view of the streets because everyone is afraid of you?"

Carmelo clenched his jaw and got even surlier. "They don't want to know me. They only want the cat. And that they want at a distance."

Teo was so startled at how Carmelo referred to the jaguar part of himself that he forgot to blink. "You don't think of yourself as like us, do you? But you still eat, you sleep." He gestured desperately, for what he didn't know. "Your sisters got married, so you must love. You could have come down! I—" Teo didn't finish. He didn't think he had to.

He scrubbed at his cheeks and hurried back to the sink. When he glanced over again, Carmelo had risen to his feet. "The cat is for the hunt. Not for market days. No one would welcome that. Not even you, Teo."

Teo shook for the pronouncement, which was possibly, very painfully, true.

Anyway, he thought stubbornly, not every day was market day. But of course when he thought of it, Carmelo was long gone. It wasn't fair. Teo had been watching Carmelo since he was old enough to touch himself. He'd been watching him more since Carmelo had returned. He thought, if it came to it, he would not have minded the jaguar alongside him at market days, even if it meant no customers.

But he didn't think it would. Teo hadn't remembered wrong. Carmelo's family had, in their way, spoken to others and belonged here. Something had convinced Carmelo otherwise, and Teo wasn't stupid. The war was the obvious cause. Carmelo had killed for reasons other than what he'd been raised to, reasons the cat might not have liked.

He shouldn't let them hold him back. He should take his place in the neighborhood and marry someone to make him happy. Teo would restrain himself from finding whoever that was and clawing their eyes out. Carmelo should have someone, to feed him properly if nothing else.

Of course, Teo wasn't quite brave enough to seek him out and tell him that, and wasn't foolish enough to risk his place in Carmelo's house by bringing up unwanted memories. So he cleaned and went through his things, bringing some of it upstairs. Then he used what food he had on hand to make a strange stew. He didn't know if Carmelo expected them to take all their meals together, so that night when the stew was done, he waited for a long time before he finally gave in and ate. The food was good and he was hungry. He ate a lot but still left enough for several men, and put a bowl and spoon out for Carmelo.

There was no sign of him in the house and no whispering footfalls on the roof as Teo went to bed. He lay awake for a while anyway, wrapped in his grandmother's blanket and wondering what she would think of this.

He thought she'd approve. She'd always revered the jaguar. It was a good thought to fall asleep to, after offering her a prayer.

HE DIDN'T wake up in the night. But in the morning, Teo found his light had been turned off, and the door mostly closed, where he'd once again left it open.

TEO SPENT another morning getting the kitchen into better shape and taking stock of their supplies. He'd been pleased to see his stew had been eaten, every last drop. Carmelo seemed to eat breakfast and dinner, but not a lunch, which was strange, but then he was often sleeping by that time of day. But with two of them in the house, he couldn't expect to live off offerings alone, no matter how generous. Teo was going to have to go to the store soon.

Determined, albeit with a nervous stomach, Teo drank some tea and then went into the newsstand to get any money there so he could attempt a very public trip to the market. He made it as far as the counter before his grandmother's closest friends, three old women, swept in as one and surrounded him.

They smelled like cooking oil and salt and rose perfume, and Teo had to close his eyes at how sweetly they clucked over him and worried over the cut behind his ear. The wound was small, the lump slowly disappearing, but they muttered to each other in the mix of Spanish and their native dialects that Teo had always had trouble following. He'd missed them and hadn't known it until this moment.

He wanted to ask them what they were doing here, if they had been the ones to light a candle for him and who had brought so much food, but they didn't give him a chance. They peered around the newsstand instead and pinched his face so he'd have more color in his cheeks, then exchanged a look when he assured them he didn't need color in his cheeks.

Mrs. Zurar told him if he wanted color and stars in his eyes and plump lips to tempt a man, he should eat a hot pepper before he went inside. Teo gave her a shocked stare, but the others shushed her before he could speak, and then Mrs. Marín handed him a bundle of white cloth.

In his loose grip, the bundle came undone to reveal a simple shawl made of thread so fine it could have been used to make lace. It nearly was lace, woven with a pattern as intricate as a spider's web. The shawl had been created to be pretty, not to keep anyone warm. Teo grinned at them and pulled it over his hair, only to immediately wish he had a mantilla so he could look like Dolores del Rio in the movies he'd watched as a child.

He repositioned his comb to pretend he was wearing one and struck a pose, then froze as his doorway was darkened by a policeman. The old women went still as well, then one by one nodded at Teo and slipped from the newsstand, each one now only speaking the language of her childhood and not the Spanish it was just possible the white cop might speak.

Teo took a breath and faced the cop with his hands folded on the counter in front of him. The cop's gaze went from Teo's hair and the shawl and then to the small pile of flowers and bread someone had left on the counter as an offering. This cop wasn't the one who usually walked the neighborhood, but he must know who owned this shop. He didn't come inside.

Teo tried to force his mind to think in English so he could speak in it too, but the cop didn't seem to expect anything from him. He looked Teo over, raised his eyebrows, and gestured outside. "There's blood on this wall." He had a significant glance for that, as if even he knew it was Teo's blood, and he wasn't sure what the hell Teo was doing in this house. But he wasn't about to interfere. He stared at Teo for another moment, then snorted in disgust and moved on.

When he was long gone, Teo spent half an hour going back and forth from the kitchen with pots full of water to rinse the dried stain away as best he could. He had more tea while he thought about what the people in the neighborhood might think, what Francisco must think, and then gave up on the problem for now and went on to something he could fix.

He grabbed his sewing from upstairs and brought it down to search for a spot with good light and a comfortable seat. Across from the entryway and the parlor no one used was a small room that got the afternoon light. He couldn't tell what it had been used for before, but claimed it for his sewing room for now, and went to work on the sewing he had been hired to do before all of this.

He had barely begun when he noticed he wasn't alone in the house. Carmelo hadn't gone out the way Teo had imagined; he was down in a corner of the entrance, bent in concentration, with a small paintbrush in his hand. Judging from the amount of paint smeared up his arms, and dotting his shirt and pants, he'd been painting for some time.

The morning light might have been with him, but it was leaving now, which possibly didn't matter to his eyes. He acted as though his painting wasn't important to him, but he seemed another creature altogether as he flicked the brush through a bit of paint and then carefully swept it across the wall.

Teo couldn't see what he was working on, but couldn't have taken his eyes from him if he'd been painting Teo himself. Teo wanted to tell him about the old women, about the cop, about what was for dinner, but he held his tongue and stared at every graceful, contained motion, the serious expression on Carmelo's face.

Perhaps the older religions wouldn't care for a god who created and felt as Carmelo did, but Teo found it wonderful. It certainly didn't make Carmelo any less powerful. His muscles surged and flexed as he moved, the light hit his eyes and turned them gold, and his intensity should have melted the wall. In all his fascination with the jaguar, Teo had never imagined this. He had never truly thought he would be allowed to be this close to him, although he had hoped someday for a husband gentle enough to accept him as he was. Carmelo would not be that husband, but Teo studied his hands and thought of how they would feel on him until his breathing quickened and he could no longer sit still.

Carmelo turned to him, instantly, as if attuned to everything in the house despite his focus on his painting. He held himself without seeming to breathe, although at the distance, Teo could not be sure. For a heartbeat, he appeared ready to frown and turn away, and then his gaze caught Teo's.

When he faced the light, and Teo, he made a sound, as if something had hit him, and Teo tore his eyes from him moments too late to do any good. He didn't know what the fever in Carmelo's expression meant, or the stunned fire in his eyes, but he dropped his head to busy himself with his sewing until his new shawl of almost lace fell over his face like a veil, and even then he didn't look up.

SOME OF the tension inside Teo had eased by the time Carmelo came into the kitchen for dinner, but it returned when he noticed Carmelo had washed up before he had come in. They had not spoken a word to each other all day, and yet, aside from Teo's embarrassment at being caught in his daydreams, it had not been uncomfortable. After a while, Carmelo had returned to his painting, allowing Teo to observe him all he wanted.

Teo had continued to sew until his head had begun to hurt from so much concentration, for the extra money and to enjoy the quiet between them for a little longer. But finally he'd gotten up to prepare dinner, pausing in confused delight when Carmelo had stopped to watch him go, and frowned, as if he had enjoyed having Teo nearby and hadn't wanted him to leave.

Comments and questions were trapped in Teo's throat, much like they had been when he'd been younger and even speaking two words in Carmelo's presence had felt impossible. The comfortable silence of the afternoon was gone, so he sat at the other end of the table and darted looks over. His face was hot, and he didn't notice a single detail of what he ate, though he had prepared it. Whenever he glanced up, he met Carmelo's eyes, and he was compelled to stare down at his plate and struggle for something to say.

"I cleaned up outside," he finally volunteered, regretting it the moment he said it.

Carmelo narrowed his eyes at the reminder of Teo as his sacrifice. "I left your blood there to shame them."

"Oh," Teo said weakly. He hadn't expected Carmelo to have noticed the stain or to personally want to clean it. "I didn't think…. He might be shamed. But I think he's waiting." A jolt went through him at the thought, a stab of real fear, like he had only ever felt when Francisco had pulled him from his balcony.

He closed his eyes at the guttural, angry sound Carmelo made, as though Carmelo knew he was afraid. The sound was meant to instill terror, but not in Teo. Teo opened his eyes and looked over at the tense, furious creature staring back at him. When he drew in a breath and tried to smile, Carmelo let out a short snarl, an unfinished huff, and spoke with obvious effort. "He deserves shame, and as much fear as his heart can take. He should experience how it feels to not know if he is going to die, as you did."

Teo's mouth was dry. "I've never had anyone want to"—he tried to think of a less heroic word and couldn't—"avenge me. Never anyone who actually could, and would."

"They hurt you." Carmelo had bent the fork in his hand, making Teo consider for the first time that the jaguar might be more than a man who could be a cat—or a cat who could be a man. The jaguar might be closer to a god than Teo had realized. He thought of the scars he'd glimpsed on Carmelo's back and wondered if they'd hurt, and how long they'd taken to heal. His protection of the neighborhood had a cost Teo had never noticed. Even with great strength, with silence and speed and claws and teeth, Carmelo had been wounded. And still, he acted when it was asked of him.

Teo shook his head. "Yes, but—"

He was interrupted. "They left you there. To humiliate you, you said, but they didn't know I wouldn't kill you."

It was worse to hear Carmelo say it. Teo breathed out harshly. "No."

"You were bleeding, Teo," Carmelo murmured, almost pleading, but it was the use of his name that made Teo bow his head.

"I don't want you to bleed either." Teo had no other objection. "I don't care if Francisco suffers. Let him suffer. But you're different." He cut himself off this time, and bit his lip when Carmelo's voice grew even gentler.

"I will do the same to them, whether or not they choose to show their faces. I'll do more, if they try again."

Tears had stung at Teo's eyes when the old women had brought him his gift, but this time Teo didn't fight the few that rolled down his cheeks. He took a deep, shuddery breath and got up from the table so he could hide his face. He put his plate on the counter and stopped with his back to Carmelo. He pulled at his shawl and let it fall around his shoulders. "You don't have to. But"—the jaguar didn't take orders, he listened to offers, Teo had to remember that—"if you want to, you may."

The exhale came from so close behind him that he jumped. He felt the heat of Carmelo's breath on the back of his neck and then the awareness of the rest of his body directly behind him. Teo's hands went slack on his plate, and he pushed them against the counter to keep himself on his feet. Carmelo could not know what he was doing to him. Being in this house with him was worse, and better, than Teo's every young dream.

Carmelo's rough voice sent another shock through him. "You should have asked me for protection in the beginning. If I had known you were scared of him, I would have protected you." He seemed closer, and his strength and intense stare had Teo breathless, although Teo didn't turn around. Carmelo pressed his cheek to Teo's ear. "Mateo."

When he said *Mateo* like that, Teo wanted to throw himself against him and demand that he be taken. Carmelo had called Teo that from the beginning, as though he knew the name well. As though he had thought it before and said it to himself in the quiet of his room.

Teo shuddered as he reminded himself that couldn't be true. "I had nothing to offer."

Carmelo put his hands on the counter on either side of him. He edged closer when he already had Teo bracketed and safe in his arms. "I wouldn't have asked you for an offering. Not you, Teo." His words stroked along Teo's skin. His growl made Teo shiver.

Teo couldn't wait any longer. He tilted his head to the side and pulled his braid away, baring his neck even further. Behind him, Carmelo stopped breathing. A moment later he moved in, his arms and legs keeping Teo up, his mouth there against Teo's ear.

"Teo?" It felt as though Carmelo was asking him for something, but Teo couldn't think of what. He bent his head and heard himself make a soft exhalation when Carmelo's lips brushed the back of his neck.

This morning he'd been caught staring. Then he'd thought, impossibly, that Carmelo had been staring in return. Now it did not seem so impossible, if only he knew what to do. "I've never had a suitor," Teo told him, and curled his hands into the counter.

He looked down at Carmelo's arms, the spots becoming visible, and felt his blood pound through his body for the hoarse growl of Carmelo's answer. "You had a suitor."

Teo couldn't think of anything except pushing against Carmelo until Carmelo pushed back. He shook his head when words failed him and tried to question what he was doing, but nothing could have stopped him from angling his head to bring Carmelo's mouth against his skin. Carmelo ripped one hand from the counter to grab hold of Teo's hip. He growled, short and quiet, and then slid his hand up to Teo's chest. He would be able to feel Teo's heart under his palm, like a drum, but all the strength in him was quivering, tense and tight, when Teo breathed out and then moved to feel Carmelo's mouth on him again.

Carmelo pressed parted lips beneath Teo's ear and pulled Teo against him, which was exactly what Teo wanted. He huffed another small, furious breath, and then Teo was tight between his body and the counter. Teo was shocked, but he sighed for it all the same and wriggled until the jaguar pinned him down. The jaguar continued to growl. "You should be afraid. Everyone is afraid of me." He warned Teo from him and then moved to place another kiss at the other side of Teo's neck. He rubbed his cheek into Teo's skin and inhaled before repeating Teo's name. "Teo."

Teo told him, "Yes," because there was nothing else to say, and Carmelo put his mouth under Teo's ear, and then behind it, where it hurt. Teo tensed, and Carmelo stopped and drew in a long, shuddering breath before pulling his hands away.

Teo turned on shaky legs, and Carmelo immediately returned his hands to him, catching him as though Teo was about to fall. Then he glanced to the side of Teo's head and raised a hand to brush behind Teo's ear, where his mouth had just been, where Teo was still tender from Francisco's blow. "I shouldn't have touched you."

Teo stared at him in aroused shame until he remembered Carmelo had been the one to pull him closer in the first place. Teo's mouth had never ached before, hungry for a kiss that hadn't come. His blood had never pounded like this. He remembered pushing his body into Carmelo's and curled his hands at his sides.

He glared up, only to be shocked into silence when he was tugged forward. Carmelo ran his cheek across his forehead and smoothed his palms over his face. A rumble came from deep in his chest as he butted his head against Teo's jaw and exhaled with deep pleasure.

Teo was so very confused. He gave himself a moment to run his palms over Carmelo's shoulders, and then he shook his head and put his trembling hands behind his back. Carmelo lifted his head to stare at him. If he was measuring Teo again, Teo didn't care. He was tired of men desiring him who were unwilling to do anything about it.

He tamped down the nerves in his stomach and lifted his chin. "I am going to bed," he announced, with a pause at the end that said everything he couldn't. He waited, a stupid, foolish second, and when there was nothing following that, not a word, or a growl, or the laughter Teo still couldn't help but expect, he slipped away and hurried from the kitchen.

IN THE dark of his room, it wasn't as easy to run away. For a long time, Teo lay in the dark and turned around again and again until he was caught in the slip he'd chosen to wear to bed. Even hours later his skin burned at the memory of Carmelo's mouth and how Carmelo had pulled him close. He was certain the rumble he'd felt had been a purr, and twisted around again at the thought, until the slip trapped him on his side, with his legs sticking out of the blanket and his face toward the door.

Now that he was alone, all he could think of were Carmelo's hands pulling Teo flush against his body and Carmelo's growl when he'd insisted Teo had a suitor. When Teo put his hands on himself like that, he could hardly breathe at the care he had to take for it to feel the same. He wasn't as strong as the jaguar, and he still had to take care to not bruise his own skin. He had felt the force Carmelo had been denying. He found that amazing, and touched himself again, at his neck where he'd been kissed, and then down at the edge of his slip, where he had not.

He had thought of Carmelo killing, but not of his strength and what it took to control it, and imagined Carmelo worrying over it. He again felt Carmelo's mouth at his ear, so close to where Teo had been struck, and didn't know whether to feel pleased that Carmelo had remembered and been concerned, or irritated that he thought Teo was so weak that a little pain would break him.

Teo wanted him so much. He should not have stopped. Or he should have finished what he'd begun and followed Teo to his bedroom.

Teo's heart began to beat faster. He lifted his eyes to stare out the doorway. He kept his hand where it was because he was a sinful creature. In that, he was not alone.

"What did you mean?" Teo asked the darkness and stretched out his other hand. "You said I had a suitor." Carmelo had been angry enough when he'd said it to let Teo see the jaguar. "Who did you mean when you said that?"

The cat emerged from the shadows without even a whisper of a sound, big and sleek and deadly. Even in slivers of moonlight, Teo could see the power in every step, yet the massive paws seemed to float above the ground for all the noise they made. Teo could not hear the cat breathe, but he could feel the heat of breath against his hand when it stopped beside the bed. The glowing eyes fixed on him until Teo understood why more people didn't, *couldn't*, run when the jaguar appeared to them.

He realized he was shaking and couldn't allow that, not again, so he pushed his hand out until his palm was pressed to a wet nose and muzzle, and then teeth when the jaguar opened its mouth. He felt every inch of those teeth, and then the jaguar pulled its head up and locked eyes with Teo again.

Then it began to change.

Teo gasped at the lengthening of bone, the creak and pull of shifting muscle and skin that Carmelo must have been used to. He snatched his hand back as the cat changed and grew, as it groaned quietly in discomfort, and then Carmelo was in front of him, naked and as beautiful as the painted man on the wall in his bedroom. Teo caught his breath as the colors of the jaguar faded from Carmelo's arms and stomach and thighs, and then Carmelo stiffened his shoulders and raised his head.

He met Teo's gaze, then turned his face away with a soft snarl.

Teo sat up, fumbling in the tangle of the slip. Carmelo flicked another glance in his direction, angry or annoyed, Teo couldn't tell in the dark, but he settled into the same pose a second after, his body on display.

Teo looked. It was okay if Carmelo wanted him to, which he must. Teo crawled onto his knees and leaned forward to stare at the impression of feet and toes and knees, and then the meat of his thighs and the cock between them. He'd seen the rest before, but he studied it all again, and then finally brought his gaze up to Carmelo's averted face.

"You could have said something," Teo pointed out at last, which brought Carmelo's eyes back to him. Had Carmelo been a suitor? Teo felt he would have noticed that, and he hadn't seen anything. Yet Carmelo stood here to make it clear that he was, so Teo reached out, daring to touch the jaguar because the jaguar had offered himself.

He had offered himself to Teo.

Teo ran his fingertips almost all the way down to Carmelo's knee and felt the muscles go tense under the touch. He sighed and lifted his head. "You could have come to me at night, if you were worried about daylight and people's fear. You saw me watching for you. You had to know I would have let you in."

Carmelo made a scornful noise. "In your grandmother's house?" he demanded, correct in thinking Teo would never have dared. But then he lowered his head so Teo could not look away from him. "And you had the other boy."

Teo tossed his head at the reference to Francisco and hissed, "I didn't want *him*," and then he sat back to face that glittery stare. He raised his chin but whispered his blasphemy. "Would that have stopped a god?"

"*No.*" The denial was almost inhuman. Carmelo made a noise and then swept forward. He ran his hands over Teo's cheeks, slid them down to his jaw, so Teo turned his face up to him and closed his eyes.

The kiss was soft, yet Teo gasped. He curved his hands over Carmelo's shoulders and pushed his palms over the short length of his hair and wrapped his arms around him so the kiss couldn't end. Carmelo kissed Teo's lips and his throat and then into his mouth without a breath in between. He kissed deeply, with Teo's head thrown back, and ran his hands down Teo's spine, and panted heavily when Teo allowed each kiss and purred, "Carmelo," into his ear.

"I had a suitor," Teo told him, trying to lie on the bed and growing frustrated when Carmelo wouldn't let him. He had a suitor. He found this news astonishing. But Carmelo stopped with a growl and dropped both of his hands to Teo's thighs.

Teo felt the warmth through the cotton of the slip, but before he could do more than rock forward, he was lifted and hauled against Carmelo's chest. He curled into the familiar heat of him and peered up as Carmelo settled his arms under his knees and at his back. He'd carried Teo like this before.

Teo kissed his collarbone and then his throat and felt Carmelo stumble. Carmelo should not have been surprised; Teo had wanted this for a very long time. So had Carmelo, Teo was beginning to realize, and sighed in understanding when Carmelo carried him into his bedroom and set him carefully on the bed.

But then Carmelo pulled himself away again, leaving Teo to shiver all alone. "Your grandmother," Carmelo began, bringing Teo's attention from the moonlight on his shoulders. "You and your grandmother needed money. I thought you would take it from that boy, or that he would claim you as his and he'd protect you." He kept going, although Teo shook his head. "But you didn't. I couldn't have you in the streets, Teo, so I left it." He inhaled deeply. "I left it, for her to find, for you, when the rent was due. She was proud, so I only left what she needed, not everything. But I would have."

Teo froze, trying to imagine the jaguar leaving an offering at his grandmother's door. Had his grandmother known it was from him? Was that why she'd never said a word about Teo climbing onto the roof at night?

Carmelo had insisted so furiously that Teo had a suitor. Teo hesitated only a second before he wrapped his arms around Carmelo's waist. "I didn't know," Teo told him and cleared his throat to make it louder. "If I had, I would have left myself at your door." He put his mouth to Carmelo's skin and smiled foolishly at the rumbling sound of pleasure that answered him. "I had a suitor," Teo whispered and let Carmelo peel him away so he could be kissed all over again and then urged onto his back on the bed.

The slip was stuck beneath him. He regretted wearing it until he felt Carmelo's hands pushing it over his stomach. He lifted himself to help and brought his arms up, and then, when it was gone, he trembled. But Carmelo didn't appear to find anything wanting with his offering. His hungry gaze devoured Teo, and then Carmelo crawled over him and exhaled over Teo's hard cock. "You're not afraid of me," he said roughly, and took Teo's cock in his mouth.

Teo grabbed at his hair in surprise and then fell back to moan at the ceiling. Carmelo's hands were firm at his thighs. He could feel the tremble of Carmelo's control, and the heat of his breath, and the wet sin of his tongue. Carmelo pulled away to lick at his own spit and gave Teo's hip a kiss when this made Teo shake and bend his knees. Carmelo ran his hands up to Teo's stomach and down to his thighs, and then between them. Then he used his mouth again, and rumbled for Teo's fingertips pressing into his shoulder blades and the nape of his neck. Teo tried to pet him, to slide his touches through his short hair, but the curve of Carmelo's shoulders drew his hands.

He held on to him until he was gasping and his stomach was tense and hot, and he arched up to spill his seed into Carmelo's mouth. Carmelo licked at it until Teo let out a small cry, and then he rose up to cover Teo with his body. His grin was that of a pleased cat, and his cock was stiff against Teo's hip.

Teo stared at him, wanting to be welcoming but uncertain of what to do. He stretched up to press their mouths together and lick at the curious flavor of himself, and he was rewarded with a headier, deeper purr as Carmelo draped himself over him. Teo opened his legs and then released a shuddery, awed breath as Carmelo started to move. The drag of Carmelo's cock against Teo's skin sent sparks through him. He stretched for it and brought Carmelo's mouth to his.

If Carmelo was scared of hurting him, Teo was content to leave it for now. For now he had this, power aroused at the thought of touching him, strength whispering his name before it kissed him, a killer who let Teo stroke caresses down his back and who purred when Teo grabbed at him to pull him closer.

He didn't last long, not with Teo touching him and finally wetting his palm to coax his seed from him. Carmelo groaned when Teo squeezed his cock but then bent his head to watch, his muscles straining to keep himself up as he painted Teo with thick stripes of come.

Teo had to admit the sight of Carmelo's cock sliding through his fingers had made him hungry for more, although he'd have to wait. He huffed in his best imitation of an irritated Carmelo, then collapsed onto the sheets when Carmelo raised his head to study him.

Carmelo changed position, kneeling up suddenly and resting on his elbows with their faces close together. Teo thought of the cat, and judgment, but then realized it wasn't that. This was Carmelo unable to take his eyes off Teo. He slid his hands up the length of Teo's arms, pushing them above Teo's head at the same time. Then he nudged Teo's face with his own, making Teo snort in surprise and then laugh.

Carmelo released him, his chin already going up in offense, so Teo scratched his fingernails through his hair until he came down to him again and offered him another kiss. These kisses were slow. Teo had a chance to learn them better, and gave a few in return.

After a while, Carmelo rolled onto his side and found the slip Teo had abandoned, which he used to wipe up Teo's stomach, although Teo hadn't complained. The slip meant more laundry, but he wasn't upset about that either. He was very willing to mess up the sheets in this bed.

He scooted backward after considering that, cautiously fitting himself against Carmelo and relaxing when Carmelo put a hand on his hip to keep him there. He'd never slept next to anyone who wasn't family, if he did not count his first night in this house.

He should never have left this room, he realized, and stared up once again at the dancing figure with his eyes and hair. Opposite it, where Teo couldn't see unless he rolled over, was a warrior in the colors of a jaguar, keeping watch over the pretty dancer.

Teo rolled over. "What if they hadn't done it?" he asked in the quietest voice he had. The words still cracked as he spoke. "How long would you have let me watch you from the roof?"

Carmelo pulled away enough for Teo to see his frown. "I thought you knew I had helped and had chosen not to respond. When they left you at my doorstep—" A silent snarl transformed his face, and then it was gone. "—I thought they were mocking me. Until you… until you were surprised I knew your name." He came back to speak roughly into Teo's neck. "I know your name, Teo." His reproachful tone left Teo feeling sorry and foolish, even though he couldn't have known. "I have always known you. Even when I never knew what to say to you."

Teo's breathing caught noisily. He clutched at Carmelo's ribs. "But you left and I was alone. You returned and I was still alone." He hadn't even hoped for this.

Carmelo did not look up, and his rumblings were quiet. "I thought you were afraid. And after, you should have been."

Teo understood his meaning. He'd been barely more than a boy when Carmelo had left, and the ways of war were not the ways of the neighborhood. He pressed his cheek against the top of Carmelo's head, and Carmelo reared back to regard him with surprise.

Teo left his hands on Carmelo's body and brought himself closer. He studied him, with no distance between them, and then nodded.

"You should have come to me," he pronounced, very seriously, because he had worn a flower in his hair, and only an idiot would have failed to see why.

Carmelo blinked. "You brought me no offerings, Teo," he returned, just as seriously. So Teo leaned in to offer his mouth, and his hands, and his skin, and his heart.

TEO WOKE first, sometime before dawn, too warm and itching with the need to clean himself. He lingered in bed despite that, considering the sleeping man next to him. When he did finally move, he was pleasingly sore, although Carmelo hadn't taken him. Last night in the kitchen he'd thought that had been going to happen. Perhaps it would have, if Carmelo hadn't stopped to worry that he was hurting him.

Teo liked delicate things, but he wasn't delicate. As he washed and went to his former room to dress, he considered that his suitor ought to learn that. He plaited his hair over his shoulder and slid a pretty comb into place and once again wished for red lipstick, determining he would venture out today to buy some, and perhaps a short skirt or the fabric for one. Then he settled his shawl over his shoulders and went down to prepare breakfast.

He didn't know what to think when he saw Carmelo was no longer in bed, but wasn't entirely surprised to find him in the kitchen. What made Teo pause was Carmelo in a chair by the table, drinking milk and frowning at one of Teo's old comic books. He'd put on pants, probably still worried about shocking Teo.

But he raised his head when Teo entered and made Teo's legs go weak with how he stared. Teo turned his head for both his blushes and to show the hair comb to its best advantage, and felt his blood grow hot when Carmelo wished him a rough "Good morning."

"Breakfast?" Teo wondered with his chest squeezed tight and his heart pounding. He was very hungry. Carmelo probably was as well. But Teo didn't move toward the stove. His feet took him to Carmelo, who gave the book another quick scowl before he tossed it to the table.

"The art is bad," he commented critically. "The printed color doesn't stay in the lines. All the people look the same."

"But the story!" Teo scolded him. "The hero! In that one the detective solves the crime… which is an old one, but no older than the books in your newsstand. You've neglected your business."

His protest earned him a steady look, and then Carmelo glanced away. "I'm not a hero, Teo."

"You saved me." Teo shrugged, since this was obvious, and shivered all over when Carmelo huffed and reached out to pull him closer. He drew Teo into his lap and very carefully brushed the edges of his shawl with his fingertips. When Teo settled over him to face him, he did it again before lifting the cloud of fabric and arranging it over Teo's head. He wouldn't look away.

Teo studied him, equally pleased with what he saw. The sunlight beginning to enter the kitchen flattered Carmelo. Anything would flatter him. Teo chewed his lip, then admitted the truth. “Have people left you offerings for their daughters? To capture your attention?” Even with their fear, Carmelo would have been someone others would have wanted. Matchmaking widows and grandmothers had no doubt left their granddaughters’ cooking on his counter, sent young beauties in to buy their newspapers and cigars for them. Teo knew he looked smug. “But you left gifts for me.”

Judging from his disgruntled sniff, Carmelo didn’t enjoy that being thrown in his face, but Teo smiled and leaned in closer. Carmelo brushed his cheeks with his thumbs, then drew his hands over Teo’s hair, pushing the shawl slowly down to Teo’s shoulders. Teo kissed him, forgetting all about breakfast until long after the sun came up.

HE DIDN’T make it to the drugstore to buy lipstick, but he did finally slip into the newsstand after breakfast, with marks from Carmelo’s mouth beneath his blouse and the taste of Carmelo’s seed still thick on his tongue. No newspapers were left from the previous day, but he wiped down the counter at least, noting which cigars were running low and putting the change in the cash register.

Carmelo hadn’t asked him to do those things, but someone had to until he would. Teo clucked his tongue for that and for the basket of tamarinds someone had thoughtfully left. He debated taking them into the house to make himself tamarind water, and of course, Carmelo would be there. Carmelo would either be sleeping or painting. Or sometimes, Teo had learned, he repaired things, if he knew how. That might be worth watching.

But he lingered behind the counter, staring at the simple offering in consternation. He ought to do something in thanks for it, although he had no idea who had left it or how to repay them. He supposed it was more general. Carmelo protected them as best he could; they fed him as best as they could in return. That didn’t leave much for Teo to do anything. He wasn’t sure of his place in that.

With a small measure of guilt, he stayed to clean the shelves behind the counter, then smiled while a few customers began to trickle in. Some of them even greeted him. He spent a while chatting with them and accepting their money and handing them cigarettes, and even more time learning how to make tamarinds into the best sweets, according to Mrs. Navarro.

He was politely agreeing with her when Mr. Navarro, at his wife's side, turned to the door before going still. Teo followed his gaze, and his blood rushed so loudly in his ears he was deaf to whatever the Navarros said as they stepped away.

Francisco and his crowd of four friends stood in the doorway, their hands in their pockets, their backs slouched as they tried to appear unconcerned about where they were.

Teo's throat tightened. They were merely boys posing, too frightened to cross the threshold of the jaguar's home, and yet Carmelo was right. They had tried to kill him. Or, if not kill him, they hadn't cared if he'd died.

They were Teo's age. They had known him for most of his life. For all that he'd disliked them, he had never feared them until that night. All because they—because Francisco—had caught him watching for the jaguar. Because he'd known what it had meant and been jealous, even though he had never thought to woo Teo himself. He hadn't thought Teo was worth the sign of public respect.

Carmelo had been jealous of Francisco, wrongly, stupidly, but he'd never tried to hurt Teo for it, and he had killed many times in his life. He was an admitted killer, and Teo had slept safely in his bed.

Teo put a hand to his chest, as if that would slow his heart, but then lifted his chin. "Come in," he dared them loudly. "Come on, if you're as brave as I am."

They had to prove themselves at that. Others were watching.

Francisco led them, standing up straight the moment he passed through the doorway. His gaze went to Teo, and though he was smiling, his eyes were dark. He studied Teo's hair and his face for long enough that anyone with sight would notice. Teo wondered what he saw, why his smile briefly fell away before he turned to gather strength from his friends.

"So he didn't eat you." Francisco spoke at last. He came closer. Teo was very proud of himself for not flinching. Francisco's voice was soft until he again faced his friends. "He wasn't even fit for that!" he jested loudly, making Teo swallow.

Teo glanced toward the house, but Carmelo was far away. He took another breath and remembered Francisco was nothing but an annoying fly to him. He sniffed.

"It's strange that you aren't more frightened, if you really think that." Teo could see the confusion on Francisco's face and couldn't believe anyone so stupid had thought Teo would be grateful for his attentions. He petted his pretty shawl for strength and raised his voice. He could make pronouncements too. "You offered the jaguar something you felt wasn't worthy of him. You intended insult. He noticed."

Francisco glanced around at his friends behind him and then at the few others in the newsstand, as if only now realizing his mistake and needing support. No one was going to support him, even if they sympathized. The cat could single them all out if he wanted to, one by one. Even the religious, the ones who denounced the old gods in church, or the doubters, the ones who talked to the fairies and recognized that the beings were only people and not gods, wouldn't confront the best protection the neighborhood had. Their jaguar, their warrior, their guardian was there for them, though he wasn't one of them. If Francisco had crossed him, no one, not even Francisco's father, could save him. They might not even try.

"But he didn't kill you," Francisco argued. His tone was belligerent for a moment, then quieted into something different, something that burned him. "He took you in."

It would torment him, Carmelo had said. The jaguar saw a lot.

Teo smiled. "He took me into his home," he repeated, as slowly and softly as he murmured Carmelo's name when Carmelo was scraping blunt teeth beneath his ear and kissing the damp skin. He blushed at his hot, sweet tone but didn't hide his satisfied grin. Carmelo had growled for Teo's first attempt at using his mouth on him but put a hand on the table so he could use the other to slowly feed his cock into Teo's mouth. Afterward he had kissed Teo in that chair, until Teo had been squirming and aware of nothing but the knowledge that he wanted Carmelo back inside him but not in his mouth.

He'd been thinking about how to get that when his stomach had protested, and Carmelo had insisted he stop to eat. He had paused, however, to first settle Teo's shawl around his shoulders once again.

And he thought Teo had been afraid of him. Teo didn't have anything to fear from him.

Teo met Francisco's stare and grinned wider. "He was not pleased that you hurt an innocent and mocked his offerings."

"I…," Francisco blustered and fell silent, then gestured at Teo. "You aren't innocent. Look at you, what you are."

"My kind have existed for as long as humans, for as long as the jaguar. I see no reason to hide myself. A muxe is a blessing," Teo informed him coldly, snapping his head up. He'd cared for his grandmother. He'd care for the jaguar too. Carmelo appreciated his care and treated him with reverence. He had art devoted to Teo and gave him the run of his house, his newsstand. "He's given me everything," Teo realized out loud, then focused on Francisco once more. "Are you saying that I'm not worth his choice?"

"What?" Outrage and hurt made Francisco's voice very loud. He stepped forward with his hands clenched. "You and the cat?"

"*Francisco.*" Teo wasn't the only one who instinctively recognized the low sound of a predator in the dark. He turned toward the entrance to the house and watched Carmelo emerge from the shadowed storeroom. He didn't think Carmelo had been in the newsstand in the daytime for at least a year. Teo couldn't imagine what had made him come out at this moment, unless he had heard everything from inside the house.

Teo was very foolish sometimes. He had focused on the look of that cat, and not what made it a hunter. Of course Carmelo had heard everything with his cat's ears.

Carmelo spared a glance for Teo behind the counter, then narrowed his attention to Francisco. "This is the one who left Mateo bleeding at my door." He wasn't asking. Carmelo spoke as though he did not normally speak Spanish, as if only bestial sounds or ancient languages crossed his tongue. It was how he always spoke, because he didn't often speak to people. But Teo had already forgotten how different it made him. He was ancient and animal like this. He was someone apart. So was his gaze, which Teo had already experienced when tied up and helpless at his doorstep.

Francisco took a step back. So did many of the others gathered around.

In a way it was amusing. Carmelo wore one of his torn T-shirts and a plain pair of pants. He was barefoot. But how he moved, slinking from the darkness into the partial light near the counter, made Teo's breathing quicken. Carmelo was human, but his eyes were intent on Francisco and only Francisco, as if he were being studied and memorized so the cat could find him anywhere, at any time he chose.

Teo made a sound, a happy sigh, and a name he barely kept himself from saying out loud. *Carmelo* was a name for him. For the crowd he was jaguar. Perhaps *tehuantl*, if they remembered.

"This is Francisco," Teo introduced them, unnecessarily, but pointedly.

Carmelo leaned against the farthest edge of the counter with easy grace, as though he was not watching a mouse tremble before him. "Is he here to beg your forgiveness?"

He made it seem like a simple question. Things were very simple to the jaguar. It was the human aspect that created confusion, Teo realized with sudden clarity. It was no wonder, then, that when Carmelo had returned home, unhappy and haunted, he had avoided the newsstand and anything that demanded he be a man.

Teo turned to Francisco, who was visibly struggling to stay where he was. He managed it, Teo would give him that. He hadn't run yet. "My father…," Francisco began to say, but his voice shook, and he elected to stop talking.

The others stayed quiet. They had lived here a long time and had spoken with the jaguars before. But not this one. Teo thought they wanted to see what he would do. Teo was pleased at how Carmelo held their attention, how they held back with respect. Even the ones who didn't like Teo weren't going to approve of his murder. They might not know what to feel about his feminine interests, or what he was doing in the jaguar's house, but they didn't like the bullying son of a rich man either.

Francisco attempted to state his case again. He wasn't arguing anymore, and Teo wondered if he knew it. Francisco's tone had become pleading. "But Teo is…. You weren't supposed to…." He looked at Teo, as if expecting Teo to save him.

Teo had been on his own, mourning his grandmother and watching the night sky. He hadn't asked to be dragged from his home and beaten. He recalled the fury in Francisco's voice and lowered his eyes. He raised them a moment later so Francisco could see his pleasure at the thought of what Carmelo had done to him in his bed. He even smiled. Ever a sinful creature, Teo enjoyed what he was about to say. "Your sacrifice was accepted, despite your intentions."

Confusion gave Francisco an ugly scowl, and then slowly, surely, he understood what Teo was telling him. Teo had never wanted Francisco, but if Francisco had presented himself like a man, Teo might have accepted him anyway. Instead, in his jealousy, he'd thrown Teo at the man Teo had truly desired, the man who had desired Teo in return. It was quite an offering to make. Francisco simply hadn't realized it until now.

Teo deliberately took his eyes from Francisco. He scooped up the coins of today's earnings and stepped to the edge of the counter before holding them out to Carmelo. "Here," he insisted in a whisper, although Carmelo had yet to touch the money Teo had already taken inside the house for him.

Carmelo gave a short, rough growl as he stared at the offered money, a sound that sent a few out of the newsstand. Francisco released a noisy breath, but Teo didn't bother to turn toward him. Carmelo frowned down at him, as though he was trying to figure out Teo's purpose in handing him his offerings so publicly when he could have taken them whenever he wanted. But he reached for them after a few moments and then startled Teo into a small jump when he took hold of Teo's hand and poured about half of the coins back into his palm, as gently as a groom sharing his wealth with a new bride.

"Mateo." He said the name that made Teo's heart stop, and spoke only for him. "I come to you now."

Teo's mouth dropped open. He very, very slowly pulled the money to his chest and stared, unblinking, as Carmelo smiled at Francisco, because Carmelo was a cat, and cats toyed with their food. When Francisco uttered a small noise, like a whimper, and his friends echoed it, Carmelo turned at last. He ducked his head away from Teo's amazed, worshipful stare and disappeared back into the storeroom, where he seemed to vanish.

But of course he didn't. He was there, listening to everything, probably as tense as he had been last night when he'd stood naked in front of Teo and waited to see what Teo would do.

Teo twisted to consider the remaining crowd, the Navarros, an old widower who liked to roll his own cigarettes, Francisco's friends, Francisco. Teo studied them all, then tugged on his braid and grinned.

Francisco stumbled for a step on his no doubt quaking legs, but recovered himself with surprising dignity. He reached into his pocket to pull out a few dimes, which he slapped down onto the counter. But he couldn't raise his head and didn't meet Teo's eyes. He left without another word.

With him gone and his friends quickly following him, Teo pulled his lacy shawl up over his hair. Then, clutching at his gift, he ignored the lingering crowd and followed Carmelo into their house.

As Teo had anticipated, Carmelo hadn't gone far. Teo found him in the kitchen, standing between the table and the doorway to the rest of the house, turned so Teo could not see his face.

The power to scare the cat was a heady thing, but it was nothing to how it felt to touch him. Teo dropped the money onto the table, where it sat with the rest of the offerings he had brought these past few days, and then slipped his arms around Carmelo's back. Carmelo released a breath for that, and for how Teo immediately pushed his hands under his thin shirt to feel his skin.

"Husband," Teo tried out, slowly, sweetly, and shuddered in delight at Carmelo's short, satisfied snarl. After so public a statement from his reclusive Carmelo, Teo had to say something equally as bold. "Carmelo." Teo was more certain with every rough exhale from the brave jaguar in his arms. "It's been a busy morning. I'm very happy you came out to see me, but I have had enough of the full light of day and the rest of the world for now. I would like to go back to bed."

There was a loud growl, and then Teo was lifted from his feet before he'd realized that Carmelo had turned. This time he was awake as he was carried upstairs, but he closed his eyes and leaned his head against Carmelo's familiar warmth. He was in the jaguar's arms, and in a few moments he would be in the jaguar's bed. This was where he was meant to be.

Hyacinth on the Air

1961

HYACINTH PULLED his candy cigarette out of his mouth long enough to take a trial sip of his cup of joe. Since he could still taste the coffee, he used the cigarette to stir as he poured in a few more tablespoons of sugar. The coffee was thick enough to chew by the time he was done, but at least it finally tasted right. He took another swallow and then tossed the soggy bubblegum cigarette aside.

He drew a new one out of the pack and licked the sweet dusting from one end before he let the cigarette rest between his lips. Then he leaned into the mic and lowered his head to track the motion outside his booth.

He'd chosen a song about longing, and he echoed the lyrics as it ended. Walter turned toward him at the sound of his voice and then looked away when he noticed Hyacinth watching him.

The song itself bordered on silly, but Hyacinth felt ridiculous and juvenile as Walter's bluebell gaze slipped away from him. The candy cigarette hung from one side of his mouth as he spoke intimately into the microphone. "For those of you just tuning in, that was Lee Dorsey waiting on a girl in 'Ya Ya.'"

Hyacinth sucked on his cigarette and stared at Walter's pretty pink-and-gray shine. All humans had their own light, but some glowed and shined more than others, and Walter was one of them. An aura of gentleness and charm surrounded him that Hyacinth thought was stronger than any magical allure he'd ever seen.

Walter glanced over and raised his eyebrows to find Hyacinth's gaze on him. Hyacinth could not imagine why Walter would be surprised, but licked at his cigarette again when those blue eyes, magnified by thick, dark-rimmed glasses, landed on him. The glasses were the same rich shade of black as Walter's hair, which was currently slicked back into symmetrical order. His tie was the same color. It should have made Walter look dull as dishwater, especially against his crisp shirt of plain white. Instead Hyacinth shifted in his chair and heard himself start to breathe heavier. Walter could wear whatever stark colors he wished, but there was no hiding his true beauty, not to fairy eyes.

"There's a lot to be said for pining." Hyacinth exhaled into the microphone and let Los Cerros hear his yearning. "Especially as Lee Dorsey does it. Will 'Ya Ya' make it to 1961's Top Hundred Chart? I hope so." He hummed over the silence and reached for another record, only to stop and reconsider. "In fact, let's hear it again. Fuck it."

There was a thump from the other room as Walter almost fell out of his seat. Once again Hyacinth remembered too late that "fuck" was one of those things he wasn't supposed to say on the air. It didn't matter that he had the highest ratings in the city, in fact the highest ratings that this station had ever seen, and a devoted group of listeners. Among the human population some people were offended when he said things like that.

In his seventy years among the humans, Hyacinth had yet to figure out why such a small bit of talk was such a problem. He had enlisted for their war, even if he hadn't fought. Love, along with words like "fuck," was harmless compared to bullets. He knew what the humans said, what they had said when they justified the horrific things they had done, that words spread ideas and that meant they were to be feared. But he had seen what came of limited speech and refused to believe that anything he said or did on the air could be anything but beautiful. He was speaking with love. That should surely count for something.

Nonetheless, he was not supposed to speak of such things for vague, puzzling, *human* reasons. Sometimes it was the small things that humans found the most threatening.

"Shit," he said distinctly, over the playing song, because Walter had a thin line of distress between his eyes now, as if they were both in trouble. Hyacinth thought about using his mouth to make that wrinkle go away and then forgot whatever else he'd been going to say as he imagined Walter's shirt and tie askew, his pants gone, his hair a mess and his flowery blue eyes wide and dark.

Hyacinth had often thought about taking Walter's glasses away while sucking him, leaving Walter blind and helpless. Maybe Hyacinth would even wear Walter's glasses while he sucked his cock.

It was a strange urge but worth exploring. Walter tended to be quiet. He might make noises when aroused, hopefully even loud noises, noises loud enough for the entire city to hear. He might be so confused by Hyacinth's stealing his glasses and wearing them while raptly laving his cock with his tongue that he'd tremble and stare and gasp for more.

Hyacinth's sister always told him that he was confrontational, that he was too public even for a fairy and he was going to get them in trouble with the humans. That was probably true. Hyacinth loved for his voice to be heard, but in this case he wanted the volume and noise for Walter. Everything, every loud, desperate cry Hyacinth longed to hear would be for Walter.

He supposed that made little sense to others, most especially to Walter, who shied away from attention. But the world *should* see and hear Walter like that. If Walter were Hyacinth's steady, as the human teenagers said, Hyacinth would ensure the whole world knew how special Walter was. If Walter allowed it, Hyacinth would sing his praises to the world even more than he already did.

It was not likely to happen. The painful reality was that Walter wasn't his to keep and didn't seem to want to be.

A knock on the glass window separating Hyacinth's booth from the small outer room with the phones startled him, and he realized the song had stopped playing and there was dead air.

If he'd had a producer to regularly sit in that room, that wouldn't have happened. But no producer wanted to work with "that crazy, flit fairy," no matter what Hyacinth's ratings were. Instead of a producer, or even an assistant, he had Walter, the station's lawyer and Hyacinth's personal watchdog.

"I've done it now," Hyacinth confessed absently to his audience, though he kept his eyes on the delectable human in the other room. "Once again I've forgotten that I'm not supposed to say things like fuck." He said the word on purpose this time, and Walter seemed to know it. His eyes narrowed. It was delightful. Hyacinth had to restrain a giggle. Giggles, as he had been told more than once, were not a sound an American human male adult should make. Even a ridiculous being should know better, it seemed. Hyacinth thought that was a load of bullshit. He was convinced most of his audience did as well. "Are you offended, listeners? Walter is here, and the way he's pursing his lovely mouth tells me you might be, or that you should pretend to be."

Walter put a hand to his mouth and looked startled, though it wasn't the first time Hyacinth had remarked on his full mouth, or even the most detailed thing he'd ever said about it. He recalled once waxing rhapsodic about the cherry blossom pink of Walter's lower lip and how he longed to nibble it. That was, incidentally, something else an American human male was not supposed to do—express tender feelings of any kind, and especially not toward another human male. Hyacinth had more trouble remembering that rule; mostly he chose not to, as Walter could attest.

Walter's blushes were the same shade of pink as his lips, brighter than the soft glow of his shine. His pained frown, however, had been less delightful. Hyacinth had spent a wretched week apologizing for embarrassing him, and then Walter had gone out and gotten himself a *girlfriend* and insisted stiffly Hyacinth had nothing to apologize for.

Hyacinth made a disgruntled noise to himself at the memory and extended a hand over the pile of records he'd pulled from his collection. His record library took up most of the room. They were all his, except for some of the current Top Forty hits, a condition for working here that the station had been happy to give him. In fact, most of the others at the station tended to give Hyacinth what he wanted as long as they could stay away from him. It was either his reputation for trouble or his habit of working without a shirt that had earned him the distance. It seemed Hyacinth was too much for some square, uptight humans to handle.

For Walter he'd wear a shirt, or at least consider it, but Walter had never asked him to cover up his bare skin. Hyacinth wasn't sure if that should upset him or give him hope. He'd ask his listeners, but discussing Walter with his listeners made Walter frown at him more.

Hyacinth sighed and picked a record. His magic, as always, helped him find what he wanted, a song to suit his mood and to end the night.

"It's almost midnight. Time for Happy Hyacinth to fly away home. But before I go, and before those phone lines start lighting up, one last song to say good night. Something uniquely human, though possibly touched with magic. For all of you out there getting hot and heavy in those cars parked on the bluff, and for whoever else might be up, I give you Patsy Cline."

He put the needle on the record, turned off his mic, and flicked his candy cigarette to the side. If ever there was a time to believe in the powers of human magic, it was when singers like Patsy Cline or Etta James came to exist. Whenever he heard them, or any music that gave him chills, he knew it to be true. Surely something incredible must have come to pass to allow the birth of the early blues singers, as well as the outspoken rebels of the music world whose music had been stolen to create rock 'n' roll. Those voices that told of infinite sadness and unreachable desires could slow even fairies and elves down. There was lots of other music like that, but Hyacinth wasn't allowed to play anything "too wild," which meant anything by any magical beings, and never any Negro music that wasn't on the Top Forty.

Hyacinth rose from his backless, cushioned chair to stretch. He hoped Matt, the jockey who followed him, was somewhere close and ready for his midnight to six shift, but then the thought was gone, and Hyacinth was flying out the door and into the next room to talk to Walter.

"Tired of babysitting me?" The music coming over the station's speaker system made his words sound sadder than he meant them. Hyacinth stopped directly in front of Walter and landed as Walter straightened.

The producer's room had dim lighting. Hyacinth had never understood why, but then the glitter haze around him tended to make anything that didn't have a natural shine of its own seem lackluster.

Walter looked up at him. He was beautiful, gleaming with a blush and glowing with his innate charisma. It was a quiet pull that Hyacinth found hard to resist, although Walter's fellow humans seemed to not be nearly as affected as he was.

"I'm not doing a very good job of watching you." Walter grimaced. Hyacinth was standing far too close to Walter by human standards, but Walter hadn't objected or stepped back. Hyacinth felt so warm he was dizzy. It only got worse when Walter held out a bottle of Coca-Cola for him. He'd taken the cap off and put a straw in it. His gaze went to the straw as Hyacinth took a sip and then skipped away to the table and the telephone.

Hyacinth had seen the lines light up but not Walter taking a call. "Are you in trouble?" he asked. He let the wet tip of the straw drag along his bottom lip.

"*You're* in trouble." Walter exhaled noisily, sounding not a little frustrated. "I know it's nothing to you, but you shouldn't have said that."

"Which part?" Hyacinth usually preferred sweet candies, but sometimes, times when the music and Walter had his insides twisted, he wanted sour cherries or hard black licorice sticks. He downed his Coke instead, swallowing every sticky drop because Walter had gotten it for him. It did nothing to quench his thirst. In all his years, Hyacinth had never felt this… this awful, awful, terrible yearning.

"You know which part." Walter pushed his glasses up by the bridge and met Hyacinth's gaze for far too long. "I can talk them out of the fine for the language if I stress, again, that you aren't human. But the other thing… the other thing…." Walter trailed off and looked away to clear his throat. "My *mouth*?"

Hyacinth instantly looked at Walter's mouth and licked his own. "Remind me to start my shift tomorrow with 'Lollipop' by the Chordettes." The song was a few years old, but Hyacinth never got tired of it. Humans wrote popular music to be as harmless as possible, and yet their censors never noticed things like how sneaky some of the lyrics could be. They would worry about teenagers having sex, yet allow them to listen to a song where a girl praises the lovemaking skills of her boyfriend by comparing his kisses to candy. Hyacinth had discussed this in a broadcast just last week.

"Aren't you even a little concerned about what you're saying on the air?" Walter demanded quietly and then threw his hands up when Hyacinth had trouble focusing enough to answer. "You might think it's funny to tease me and say those things, but trust me, they don't upstairs. You might as well be a Communist for the things they say about you."

"If they don't like it, they can fire me." Hyacinth did his best to stop mentally unwrapping Walter and putting him in his mouth. Then he blinked and shook away the image of licking Walter like a stick of candy and the "pop" sound he imagined Walter's cock would make sliding free of his lips. "Communist?" he repeated blankly. It had only taken one talented human seer to discredit that ridiculous McCarthy fellow a while back. Although, of course, then humans had added "dangerous criminal magical elements" to their list of things to be afraid of. Hyacinth had a feeling he was going to end up a modern-day, bewinged Socrates, but he dismissed that fear for now. Walter appeared to be grossly mistaken about something. "*Tease* you?"

"You wouldn't care if you got fired?" Walter's fingers curled over Hyacinth's for a moment as he took the empty bottle from Hyacinth to throw in the trash. If Hyacinth had allowed it, Walter would have been in the booth right now, straightening up after him. Hyacinth couldn't be blamed for loving a human like that, though honestly anyone who really, truly looked into Walter's eyes would fall in love with him too.

Speaking of which…. Hyacinth reached out to wipe an imaginary speck off Walter's pressed dress shirt.

"No, well, yes I like being employed, and I love what I do. But no, I wouldn't mind too much if they fired me. I've done many things in my life, and this is only one of them." Hyacinth had no idea why, but whenever he spoke of his past Walter got a troubled expression on his pretty face. Hyacinth never spoke of his past for very long anymore. He was more interested in the future anyway. "Speaking of love, Walter…." He switched to a new topic and Walter jumped.

"Were we?" Walter was so confused by the turn the conversation had taken that Hyacinth was led to wonder, not for the first time, if Walter had ever experienced great passion. He didn't think so, and even if he had not been so madly in love with Walter, he would have wanted to push Walter against the table and knock the phone off the hook with the force of their lovemaking. He would have done it simply to allow Walter to experience the passion he deserved yet would not reach for.

Because he also suspected Walter was actively resisting that passion, and because he respected Walter so dearly, Hyacinth did not push. He restrained himself, as always. Damn humans and their illogical hang-ups.

"*Yes*." Hyacinth practically hissed it. "We are *always* speaking of love." Walter shouldn't act so puzzled by those words. Just because he didn't love Hyacinth in return didn't mean that Hyacinth didn't sparkle with love for him. "Your shirt seems so well starched as to be untouched, and I was thinking that these late nights with me must be cutting into your time with… what's her name?"

Edith. Her name was Edith, and she was polite and sweet, and Hyacinth wanted to pay a werewolf to rip her to shreds… or cheer her on if she made Walter truly happy—a confusing muddle of impulses. He pretended not to know her because there was a special sort of hurt in hearing Walter say her name.

Walter seemed pained as well. "I…. Edith. And no, we… that is, *she* ended it. Last week."

"Oh, Walter." Hyacinth wanted to clap and shout and couldn't have been happier when Matt hurriedly slipped in behind them and began his shift with the fast, smooth voice of Ricky Nelson singing "Hello, Mary Lou." "Good-bye heart," Hyacinth murmured and dared to put a sympathetic hand on Walter's shoulder. Walter looked at him, his eyes so dark that he could have been aroused.

Walter might have wanted to call Hyacinth out as a liar for feigning sympathy while Hyacinth was also clearly ready to jump with joy, but if that was the case, he didn't. Walter stayed quiet.

Hyacinth's pulse thundered in his ears. "If you're free, you can always come out with me," he offered as levelly as he could with the galloping rhythm of his heart and Walter's serious gaze making his wings flutter enough to lift him up. "Robin's Egg and I are going into the fairy village to watch this artist who apparently paints with his toes while reciting Sartre from memory—"

He stopped at Walter's stare. Walter had never once taken him up on an offer to go to a show in the fairy village, as it was called. The village, near the edge of town, was becoming more and more frequented by beatniks and bohemian humans, usually artists, and had a reputation as a hangout for, as the station owner put it, "beings and other degenerates and perverts," although mostly beings called it home.

In their years out of the shadows, most magical beings had not dared to venture outside of certain city enclaves. It was little wonder they were so misunderstood, or that many were, like Hyacinth, continuing to try to figure out the humans around them.

"Do you ever just go to a movie?" Walter gave a small, jerky, awkward wave that Hyacinth didn't really understand, though he tried.

"This late?" Hyacinth shuddered to think of the surfing or monster movies that might be playing at a drive-in this late at night. It was hard to watch monster films without cringing at the thought of what a demon or werewolf might say, and surf films were so boring. "Nothing good will be playing." He bobbed thoughtfully in the air and pulled a handful of sour cherry candies from his pants pocket. “Though there might be something somewhere. I admit, toe painting with Sartre is more something I need to see simply to see it more than something I want to see. It *is* late. Maybe I should go home.” It was only when Walter shut his mouth and stepped back that Hyacinth realized he should have asked Walter to a movie and not cared what was playing.

Walter had a briefcase full of papers that he always intended to do during Hyacinth’s broadcast and that almost never actually got done. He picked it up and headed for the door.

“Going home seems dull,” Walter remarked as he passed, with a strange little smile. “For you, that is. Not up to your usual standards.”

Hyacinth tried to think of his usual standards and remembered that the night before last he’d met a Russian firebird at this little hidden door club—a real firebird! In person and not merely a voice on a record!—and had spent the next day describing him to a scowling Walter. But he couldn’t help it; he’d never met a firebird before. His wings had been exquisite, as had his songs of lost love. Hyacinth had lost people before—human lives were short and fragile even without a war, but those songs in the firebird’s clear, echoing voice had kept him shadowing Walter afterward, this strange pang deep in his chest.

He’d felt as if something would happen to Walter if Hyacinth took his eyes from him for even a moment. Walter, however, had not seemed interested in Hyacinth’s accounts of the firebird’s beauty. Point of fact, he had not seemed pleased to know Hyacinth was so impressed with the performance. Perhaps Walter considered Hyacinth’s nights too wild.

Last week Hyacinth had learned to play the bongo drums and had nearly gotten arrested with the other musicians when their party had been raided in a search for marijuana. It would take more reefer than any human could ever hold to get a fairy hopped up, so Hyacinth hadn’t been smoking any, which—combined with human belief that fairies were too simple to know better—was the reason he’d been released. Not that any of the other smiling, laughing people around him had seemed especially criminal.

Criminals or not, Walter had been quite upset to learn Hyacinth had almost been arrested, and Hyacinth wanted to make Walter happy more than anything.

“I would love to watch a movie,” Hyacinth blurted, but Walter was already at the door. Hyacinth must have been imagining that

Walter wanted to sit at a drive-in with him. Walter had gotten himself a girlfriend once, after all, and humans did seem to prefer one gender to another, at least publicly.

Walter sighed at him and clutched his briefcase. "Really?" he wondered, with his head down. But he didn't wait for an answer. "Have fun, Hyacinth, but not too much fun. And please don't…." There Walter paused, his voice cracking. The pink color settled over his cheeks and drifted down his neck. "Don't talk like that again tomorrow. Please?"

"Why not?" Hyacinth called at his back, but then Walter was gone. Hyacinth slowly sank to the floor and stilled his wings. A moment later he put the entire handful of sour cherries in his mouth. They didn't seem nearly sour enough.

WALTER SLIPPED into the other room in the middle of the next night's broadcast. He looked harried, with a few hairs out of place and signs of wrinkling on his tie. The hour was late and Walter had worked all day, but here he was.

If it wasn't a Friday night, the night Walter loved to watch his *Twilight Zone* show with all its brilliant, strange, almost impish logic, he should have been out with some willing human girl, maybe parked on the bluff with the teenagers who tuned in to hear Hyacinth and used his voice and his music to fog up their windows. But instead Walter was here with Hyacinth, and it didn't matter if he was forced to be, Hyacinth felt himself glow poppy-bright when he saw him.

"Walter is here, kids." He addressed his audience while eating up how Walter paused and glanced at him. Walter's gaze traveled over what he could see of Hyacinth from where he was, which was his body from the waist up, bare, golden chest and lavender wings, green eyes and brown hair with odd strands of purple, the ever-present rain of his glitter.

"It's a nice night. I imagine the bluff is packed with cars and closely entwined bodies." Hyacinth drew out the words, envisioning Walter beneath him in the backseat of Walter's car, the window cracked to let in a breeze. Some human traditions appealed more than others, and the idea of accepting Walter's virginity—at least with males, being or human—in the roomy backseat of a car made Hyacinth grow hard. He would give Walter so many orgasms. He would wrap Walter's climaxes in a bow if he could.

He switched out the music as he talked, abandoning the Top Forty in the middle of a song for something older. Walter liked older songs more than a human in his midtwenties usually did. Songs Hyacinth had heard when men had been marching off to Europe and the Pacific made Walter smile. Music from when Walter must have been a child, perhaps. Or maybe songs he didn't associate with the sound of Hyacinth's voice.

In this case, however, Hyacinth chose something from the previous decade, something else lightly yearning.

"How about it, Walter?" Hyacinth pressed dreamily, not at all surprised when the faint scratch of the needle brought Walter into the booth with him. "The windows down… this song barely audible over the sound of heavy breathing…."

"I don't have—" Walter swallowed and didn't finish. "Now the police are going to race up there to chase the teenagers away," he said instead of whatever he'd been going to say.

"How awkward for the police, having to enforce stupid laws." Hyacinth talked over the song and hardly cared. "Any cop who listens to my show would have to think they are stupid laws." Any cop listening to Hyacinth play his odd choice in music and swear and talk about sex and detail his love for Walter could not hold any respect for laws that stifled the expression of true, deep, pure feeling.

"However." Hyacinth exhaled sadly in the next moment. "Walter is right, listeners. Be warned, the fuzz are on their way." He didn't understand why the humans made exemptions for the "unusually uninhibited" nature of magical beings in these matters but not for their own kind. They arrested their own kind. They locked them up or gave them treatments that turned them into strangers. Hyacinth felt himself droop. "Take care, kids."

After a few moments, he raised his head. He was surprised to find Walter looking directly at him.

"Wouldn't that be"—Walter waved his hand in that same confused gesture from yesterday—"tame, for you? Square? Parking on the bluff outside of town? It's what teenagers do."

"With the right person? Not even a little bit tame." Hyacinth tried to follow; Walter seemed even more serious than usual, so whatever he was getting at must truly bother him. "In fact, with you it would be—" Walter tensed, and Hyacinth stopped abruptly and searched for a new topic. "Are we in trouble for yesterday?"

Hyacinth had remembered to tone it down today. Walter should have been happy. But honestly, trying not to say what he was feeling was exhausting. Hyacinth poured more sugar into his coffee and gulped most of it down.

Talking like that was a problem. Walter kept trying to stress this fact. Things were different for humans, he'd say, but he never said *why* in a way that made any sense, which was probably the reason Hyacinth couldn't seem to stop. When Hyacinth had first started work at this station, he'd seen Walter less than he did now, but it turned out that talking about things you'd like to do to your station's handsome, charming, gentle, male lawyer got humans so outraged that they'd sent that same handsome, charming, gentle, male lawyer down here to keep an eye on him.

It displayed an astonishing lack of logic to his way of thinking. A reward like that was only going to make Hyacinth talk more to keep Walter with him forever, and judging from his ratings and his fan mail, the people liked it. Those ratings were the only reason Hyacinth hadn't been fired yet.

Not that it mattered—the records around him were his, and would go with him when it finally happened, and in the meantime, there was still the music, and Walter, his little bitty pretty one.

"How did you not get thrown out of the Army?" Walter leaned against the shelves, far away from Hyacinth but still close enough to make Hyacinth burn.

Hyacinth leaned into the mic. "Walter is asking about my past, listeners. Walter never asks about my past." Somewhere Hyacinth's sister was shaking her head at his crazy ways. Walter gave a start, as if he hadn't realized he'd been on the air. His eyebrows came together. Hyacinth straightened up and let his wings carry on without him. "You see, Walter, fairies are quite good at staying up all night and manning radios without getting tired. We are also, one might say, good for morale, if you follow my meaning, which I believe you do." Walter's blushes were so very lovely. "So, rules were stretched on our behalf." A lot like the rules allowing werewolves in the service to be on leave during the three days of the moon's peak, when they were less in control of themselves.

That the weres had frightened their fellow soldiers on those days went without saying, Hyacinth supposed. Not to mention the number of matings that must have occurred when feelings would have been impossible to deny. The armed forces did seem to find it awkward when it turned out their soldiers often loved one another.

"Silly, isn't it?" he went on, caught up in how Walter was waiting on his answer. "Disgracing good, honorable men out of some fear that they will nellie up the Army if they express their love for me, but if I express my love for them, the generals pretend not to hear."

"Hyacinth!" Walter bit out and then shut his eyes.

Hyacinth watched the buttons on the phone in front of him light up and then on the phone at his side as well. "It's the way things are, Walter. I'm just saying it." He held up his hands to prove his innocence. "Truth is the business of fairies."

Walter surprised him again. "You… you loved them?" he asked quietly, squeezing the words out like his chest hurt before opening his eyes wide. "Ignore that. Change the subject. You are supposed to be playing music, or promoting your upcoming appearances."

"Yes. Yes, I am." Hyacinth had to agree, even while he frowned at Walter and worried that he was ill. Humans got ill so often. It was another hazard of loving them. Hyacinth angled his head back toward the microphone as he thought about that. "Be sure to listen to my show every weeknight six to midnight, and to come out to the show at Lincoln High this Saturday night. There'll be live bands and dancing, and I'll be there to keep it interesting and say hello to all you kids. Remember, all proceeds at the door go to the renovations of the… I don't know. Some old building."

"The campanile in the old town square," Walter filled in, and gave him a look that wasn't happy.

"A bell tower!" Hyacinth wrinkled his nose back at him. "I thought we were going to donate to the NAACP? Did they nix that upstairs? Well, hot damn, everyone, let's give to them anyway, whatever it says on the posters. It'll be fun. Come out and see me, and I promise I will keep my shirt on this time. Maybe." He hated wearing clothes, especially in crowded, sweaty rooms. Pants were one thing, but a shirt…. He sighed loudly and looked up at the clock as Walter cleared his throat. Walter was smiling, faintly, and Hyacinth wondered what he'd done right to earn that smile, not that he'd ask and risk it disappearing.

"Now it's time for requests. That's right, you heard me. Requests will be taken for the next… let's say five minutes."

He put on a Dion record and switched off the mic before turning back to Walter, who pushed up his glasses. He didn't say a word about Hyacinth changing plans for the station's event, although it was undoubtedly going to give him headaches that he'd never mention to Hyacinth unless forced to. He exhaled and skipped a look over Hyacinth's chest.

"Hyacinth." Walter's hesitation was not new. His request was. "Wear a shirt to the event."

"*Walter*." Hyacinth needed an icy cold soda pop. Or more coffee and sugar. The way his voice was rasping was going to make Walter nervous. "Why?" He hadn't expected *that* after all this time.

"You'll…. You'll attract attention. Trouble. Stares." Walter's voice was growing quieter but increasingly compelling. It almost hummed with a desperate energy of its own. "I have enough to deal with already. *Please*. Do this for me."

"Walter." Hyacinth wanted to press himself to him. "Walter, you beg so sweetly." He didn't mean to say it; it slipped out.

Walter put a hand to his stomach, then drew it up to smooth down his tie. "Do I?" he asked faintly, not calling Hyacinth a flit or a sissy or expressing disgust the way some human men did when confronted with an interested male fairy—not many human men, it was true, though most denied the fact later. One more reason Walter was special. Walter had never once tried to insult Hyacinth or hurt him or deny his attractiveness. He simply hadn't responded to it.

Nonetheless Hyacinth hadn't thought Walter would understand that remark. No offense to the departed Edith, but Walter did not seem the type to plead softly or playfully in bed with a lover. Walter didn't seem comfortable even having a lover, or maybe that was a *female* lover, or…. Hyacinth was thinking wishfully again.

"You do," he said anyway, just as sweetly. "It makes me want to give you whatever you desire when you beg like that."

Walter made a noise deep in his throat and tore his gaze away. "Is the microphone on?"

Hyacinth shook his head. "It's off now. I'm sorry for before." He almost really was.

"You don't understand why it upsets me, I know." Walter nodded and then pointed at the phone. "You have a request."

Hyacinth lowered the music volume and turned the mic back on to take the call. "Happy Hyacinth here. You're on the air, kid."

Giggling was his answer at first. Human teenaged girls, Hyacinth thought, somewhat irritably. He loved them, but some of them could try even a human saint's patience. "We ain't got all night," he barked, in the finest impression of a black-and-white movie gangster he could manage. It earned him more giggling and then, at last, a question.

"Is *Walter* going to be at the Lincoln High concert?"

Hyacinth could tell from the way they said *Walter* that these girls were regular listeners. Walter probably could too; he pulled away from the shelves with an alarmed expression on his face.

"Of course." Hyacinth was terrible, even for a fairy. He took shameless advantage of his audience to get what he wanted, which was Walter at that dance with him. Walter narrowed his eyes, so Hyacinth shrugged. "What? You don't have any demands with your girlfriend gone. And someone is going to have to make sure I stay out of trouble. Walter, be my chaperone! I will wear a shirt for you!"

The girls began giggling again. Their parents might not know what to do with Hyacinth and his kind, but the next generation would be more used to beings and their ways if it killed him. Hyacinth smiled so brightly at Walter that Walter flushed down to his starched collar.

"But—" Walter tried to protest, then fell momentarily silent, a disgrace to watchdogs everywhere. It was enough to make Hyacinth wonder if Walter was like this when practicing law or if he only caved to him. How he hoped this was only for him. "But those events you host are notorious." Walter pulled at his collar. He pursed his lush, pink mouth. "And I can't dance," he added.

"That's almost a yes, ladies." Hyacinth addressed his audience to keep from falling to his knees. For all his teasing tone, Walter had only to look at his wings to tell that Hyacinth meant it. His wings stirred up so much wind that papers and candy cigarette wrappers flew to the floor. Hyacinth cleared his throat, but his voice stayed husky. "I can teach you to dance, Walter," he promised heatedly. "*Every* kind of dancing." He was not being subtle; perhaps that was why Walter recovered enough to look troubled.

"I'm supposed to watch you," Walter insisted, in a tone that said he had burdens to carry up mountains.

"You want to watch?" For a long moment Hyacinth was honestly confused. Walter didn't seem the type at all, but Hyacinth would take it if that's what he could get. "All right, Walter. It's less fun, but okay. You can watch."

The innocent girls on the phone went silent, no doubt lost at the remark, so Hyacinth opened his mouth to explain it to them. He caught himself in time when Walter's delicate, rosy blush turned brick red and Walter couldn't seem to look Hyacinth in the eye any longer.

"That isn't…. Dear God, Hyacinth. You can't be serious. You wouldn't…." Walter let out a strangled cough and made a hand gesture that Hyacinth almost understood.

Hyacinth made a sound. "Walter, *tsk*, we have young, sensitive listeners."

"Don't mind us." His audience was smarter than people thought, Hyacinth decided, even if he was secretly grateful it hadn't been one of those anti-being hate groups calling in. He didn't like seeing Walter's face during those calls.

"You horny bitches," Hyacinth chided the girls, and heard Walter quietly dying. "Now tell me a song to play or I'm hanging up on you and you will never get to find out if I ravish Walter or not."

They picked "The Werewolf Twist," and Hyacinth promptly hung up on them, though he did get up to grab the record and put it on. He made sure to conspicuously turn the mic off.

Walter took a deep, deep breath as if he'd forgotten what air was like.

"Will you come to the dance with me, Walter?" Hyacinth didn't want to get yelled at for calling young ladies bitches. He wanted an answer. Walter gave him a vague stare and seemed to truly be at a loss. "It's a dance, Walter. A concert. It will not be even close to an orgy, trust me."

That perked Walter up. His eyebrows came together and he pushed his glasses though they hadn't slid down his nose yet. "No, I suppose you'd know the difference, wouldn't you?" He put a hand to his stomach again. "The station will probably make me go."

Hyacinth clucked his tongue. "Walter, if you don't want to, then don't. *I* would never make you." Humans were so vexing. "Of course I wouldn't."

“How do people say fairies are immoral? You only want everyone to be happy,” Walter wondered out loud, then scrubbed at one cheek and lifted his head. “You’re already certain I’m going to go, aren’t you?”

“That isn’t how fairy magic works,” Hyacinth informed him primly over the rush of his fluttering wings and pounding heart. “But I *am* famished and could use some dinner. Would you…?” Hyacinth paused to remind himself that he was a beautiful, attractive, glamorous fairy. He was *born* to tempt humans. Any other human he would have already had by now. For Walter he was compelled to *wait* by love magicks unknown to him. “Would you like to get some dinner with me?”

At the words he was abruptly aware that he’d never asked Walter to dinner. He’d been so caught up in dreaming of seducing Walter into his bed forever that he’d never thought of the simple, if indirect, human idea of *dating* him. If Walter said yes, this would be a date. Surely even Walter had to know that. Hyacinth had not been shy about his feelings.

Walter considered him. He was still pink from being caught on the air before—at least Hyacinth assumed that’s why he was blushing—but Walter didn’t seem angry. He even gave Hyacinth a small smile. “You’re always famished.”

“Is that a yes?” Hyacinth had to stand up or his wings were going to lift him *and* the chair. He clapped his hands together. “I’m thinking Chinese food for you. I prefer sweets myself, obviously, but when with humans, I try to do as they do.”

Walter’s face at those last words was precious—befuddled and startled and absolutely starving.

“Walter?” Hyacinth got no reaction, and flicked on the mic since that always seemed to get a rise out of his recalcitrant watchdog. He addressed his patient audience as “The Werewolf Twist” howled to a close. “Everyone, should I take Walter out to get chop suey—I bet he’s never eaten Chinese—or should we go out and get pie and coffee?”

Walter moved at last, though it was only to gape at him. “Hyacinth, you… made it sound like a date. You can’t do that.”

Hyacinth’s feet hit the floor hard. “Why not?” He felt like he was *always* asking that around Walter. “I swear I will never understand humans,” he moaned into the microphone.

“Of course you don’t.” Walter was almost bitter. “You’re special.”

How quickly Walter could have him flying again. Hyacinth floated closer, just a touch helplessly. It was almost shameful in a fairy in his middle years… if fairies could feel shame. Someday he was going to have to get Walter to explain that particular emotion. He imagined it as something ugly and unpleasant and controlling.

"Special?" Hyacinth repeated, warm all over.

Walter began to stutter. It was indecently charming and only got worse when Hyacinth touched down in front of him. "I mean, you're a being. You… you don't have rules, or fear. You can't get hurt." Walter was not bitter; Hyacinth had been wrong. If anything Walter's words were tinged with something sad.

Hyacinth frowned as delicately as he could with the ache in his chest. He wanted Walter to feel it too, to know it existed, so he grabbed the hand Walter had left at his stomach and put it over his heart. Walter looked up into his eyes, and his were such a deep, dark blue that Hyacinth was drowning.

"I can get hurt, Walter. It doesn't feel good, having you humans regard us as freaks, those of you who do. But some of you like us, more than can admit it. I suppose that's why I don't understand what frightens you. Most of us mean no harm. Most just want to live our lives with love and freedom." His honest frustration had him growling like a were and then dropping Walter's hand to turn away.

"Hyacinth." Walter exhaled his name in the strangest, most beautifully hopeful voice, before he groaned. "You left the mic on. Again. Because you"—he couldn't seem to get the words out evenly—"you seem to enjoy putting me on display." He shifted as if he couldn't be still.

"Sorry." Hyacinth tried to be, if only because Walter was trembling. "Is that a problem?"

"You don't understand." Three words were all Walter could seem to push out. He shut his eyes, then opened them when Hyacinth swept back over to his chair and flounced down. He was struggling not to pout and to recall that for creatures who lived such short lives, humans liked to take their sweet time.

"Of course I don't." Hyacinth chewed his lip because he was out of candy and he really was starving. He was in no condition to try to explain to Walter, again, how much he longed to show him off. He tried to sum it up. "Anyone as lovely as you should have the world hanging on his every word. No one should find anything wrong with that."

However, he would admit that the number of calls they were getting at that moment was slightly more than usual. He might have gone too far. Again.

"Dear God." Walter made a move for the phone, but Hyacinth beat him to it.

"Do you think he's calling in to complain too?" he asked and enjoyed the shocked but amused smile that Walter couldn't quite hide. High off his moment of victory, Hyacinth took another slug of heavily sugared coffee and answered the phone.

"Chinese, then?" he asked, before the caller could manage a word.

HE ENDED up taking Walter out to a diner for coffee and pie, only to find the diner out of pie and full of teenagers who had probably staked out every all-night diner in town to watch for them. Stale donuts and coffee were not the same thing as a shared slice of pie, though even the plain cake had been delicious with Walter sitting across from him in their little booth, looking around at the others in the diner and practically squirming in his seat.

Walter had not remarked on it being a date again, which Hyacinth had realized some time before dawn as he'd been puttering around his kitchen while trying to make a real pie. He'd discovered he had no talent for piecrust, while also coming to the crushing conclusion that he might have scared Walter away forever by taking him somewhere public, even though Hyacinth had kept his hands and his feet and his mouth and every inch of his skin to himself.

He'd left his somewhat burned pie at Walter's desk in the office Walter almost never used, then gone out grocery shopping, which was the only reason he had bits of a hard, spicy licorice to snack on now while he stared morosely at the door.

His parents had told Hyacinth he would get more settled in his middle years, which were fast approaching, but he hadn't expected this *slowing*. Then again, perhaps this was love, in which case it was everything the humans sang about and more, uplifting and terrifying and painful. It was unpleasant, and fairies did not care for things that were unpleasant. Yet when Hyacinth thought of flying away, or of giving up, or of simply seducing Walter to at least have his body, he felt so heavy he could barely move, much less fly.

He ate more licorice and put on another song without speaking into the microphone. No doubt some people were curious about his night, whether Walter had gone with him, and if so what had happened, but he was in no mood to answer.

With that in mind, he turned the mic back on and silently apologized to Ray Charles for talking over the agonizingly lovely melancholy in his voice.

"He ate only one donut, listeners, but he *smiled.* He smiled even without pie, with a cup of terrible black coffee in front of him. He told me of his parents. He began to speak of law school and of what he had hoped to accomplish by going into law and how he'd ended up working for this station instead, and for a moment, when I reached out for the sugar, his hand touched mine."

Hyacinth wanted to relive that moment for eternity, because Walter had not pulled away, even with so many others there, all of them knowing who he was, who Walter was. But the next part hurt, so Hyacinth put his head down and wished he had paid more attention to the ways of humans when they courted one another.

"Then another group of people entered the diner—where they really should make more pie if they're going to run out of even apple by 1:00 a.m.—and Walter bolted." Hyacinth sighed. "He ran out of there like he was in some kind of stomach pain or distress, and oh, you humans don't like to share details of your bowel movements with strangers, do you? Walter is not going to be pleased with me. If he ever appears."

Hyacinth looked over at the glass and the empty, Walter-less room beyond it. An hour into his shift and no watchdog lawyer, it wasn't a good sign.

"He was with *me*. Surely nothing would have happened, if that was what worried him." The thought of human violence made Hyacinth shudder, because he would likely heal, but Walter might not. But after all this time, nearly fifty years since the beings had fully reemerged into the human world and fallen indiscriminately in love, the humans must have learned to tolerate if not accept.

Not seeking to understand one another was what had led the humans into decades of war. Hyacinth did not want to see decades more. He found it stupid and wasteful and ugly.

He pulled the mic to his mouth. "I tell you what, kids, you young, young humans looking for glimpses of the future and sparks of magic. I'll give you magic. I'll give you the future as long as you keep tuning in, but I warn you, change hurts, even when it's for the better. But oh, if you could feel what I'm feeling…." He stopped on a loud inhalation as the outer door opened and Walter entered the other room.

"At last," Hyacinth breathed and reached for the Etta James LP at the top of the pile, exactly where his magic had wanted it to be. Walter stopped too, standing in the doorway and meeting Hyacinth's stare for the first, stirring notes of Hyacinth's new favorite song. Then Walter dropped his head, and Hyacinth felt something inside of him grow cold, almost as if he were getting sick how the humans described it.

He turned off the mic and went to the door. "What happened?" He knew that expression; Walter had heard from upstairs, and it hadn't been good.

Walter stayed where he was, though he let the outer door close behind him.

"The station owner heard about our… he heard about last night. Of course, even if Bobby Allen from KSNC hadn't come into that diner last night and seen us and told everyone, he would have found out anyway because you're famous." Walter kept his eyes on the floor and lowered his voice. "You're famous in this town. So it was in the gossip this morning in the paper. I'm—" Walter couldn't seem to breathe. "—I'm newspaper gossip."

He lifted his head to stare at Hyacinth in amazement and then marched over to his usual seat and dropped into the chair. A second later and his head was on the desk.

Hyacinth tried not to notice how this made Walter's back muscles stretch and how thin the starched white of Walter's shirt was, or how Walter flexed his hands over the surface of the desk. He focused on his human's pain. Walter was groaning softly.

"Why can't I be normal?" Walter whispered, and even though Hyacinth wasn't sure Walter wasn't talking to himself, he answered.

"Is normal good? You seem to find me unusual, but I'm normal for a fairy. Normal enough, anyway." Hyacinth wasn't exactly normal. If fairies ever were to call another fairy lacking in sense and inhibition, they would say that about Hyacinth for his determination to bring the humans into the sunlight with them. Other fairies simply didn't care where they were when they were seeking their happiness; Hyacinth deliberately sought his happiness in public. Luckily, fairies differed from humans and most other beings in not judging others, much, for their sexual and personal tastes.

Walter barely glanced at him. "I'm not a fairy," he mumbled into the silence. Silence, because the song was over.

"Hold on, Walter, I'm listening." Hyacinth flew into the booth, flipped the record to play the B-side and his new second favorite song, and then flew out to wait on Walter's words. When he returned, Walter was sitting up. He seemed to respond to Hyacinth's attentiveness and how Hyacinth clearly wanted to hear what he had to say.

"People were…." Walter swallowed as if his throat were bone-dry, and shifted in his seat. An odd blush painted his cheeks. "People were looking at me." His very shine seemed to shiver.

"Why shouldn't they?" It all made sense to Hyacinth. "You're pleasant to look at, Walter." He ran a hand over his chest to touch his nipple, to demonstrate. Then he nodded. "Very."

Walter's gaze deepened and darkened. His lips parted. Then he turned away. His blush deepened as well, making him glow prettily.

"That's why." Walter closed his hands on the table, then stretched them out. "*You.* Everyone *knows*." Walter put an emphasis on the word that was puzzling.

"Knows what?" Hyacinth blinked a few times. "Not to be difficult, I simply don't understand."

"That you… that I… I mean…. *You.* With you, I…." Walter did a good impression of a man in agony. He shut his mouth and shook his head.

"Oh." Hyacinth felt somewhat calmer now. He skipped back into the booth to pick a new record, because Walter might not be ready for that B-side yet. He flipped on the mic to introduce the song, then commented, "You mean that I want you. Of course they know. I've told them all," before turning the microphone off again so as not to upset Walter.

"I *know.*" Walter spoke up from the doorway, and Hyacinth looked to see that Walter had followed him. His blush was still there, but Walter seemed to have recovered enough to frown. His tone was almost eerily calm, like the winds around a mermaid's lair were supposed to be.

"I know I've tried to explain this, but human men don't… well, they *do*… but they aren't supposed to…." Walter took a long, deep breath. "The things you feel, that you make me feel…." He coughed and left that heart-pounding, potentially wonderful thought unexplored.

Hyacinth wanted to explore it. He thought exploring it would make him very happy indeed. He hoped it might make Walter happy too.

"I do? Do I make you feel?" Hyacinth almost twirled, but he was too old for that. "Tell me what I make you feel, Walter," he demanded, knowing he had Walter's attention, knowing now that he might have always had it. "I've never been sure, and I did not want to press with you so shy. Tell me."

"I'm not shy," Walter blurted unexpectedly, fierce for one small moment before he looked horrified and dropped his stare. His inhale was shaky, but he glanced back up. "You *have* been trying not to press, haven't you?" He had noticed Hyacinth's progress in the field of human wooing, but Hyacinth couldn't tell if Walter approved of his restraint or not. Walter breathed in again. "But that wasn't what I meant." He went on after breathing out, shaking his head once. "No. I can't do this with you right now."

"Because I'm on the air?" The denial after coming so close to more made Hyacinth leap clumsily up and forward. "Walter, I have a confession. I'm not normal for a fairy. Or, since we wouldn't say normal or abnormal, I'm *different.* I'm different too, Walter, more than you can know. I don't only have no care for time and place the way most fairies have no care. I *want* to have you for all to know."

"*Hyacinth.*" Walter swung his gaze up. He seemed frozen, his back to the shelves, his hands out at his sides.

"Before the human authorities stopped us, Walter, I would do so many things with you. I would wring orgasms from you until you burned. I adore your mouth, but I'd need you to have mine first, and I'd need to hear your sounds. I would keep you naked and walk with you in the park, leading you forward to the places of the softest grass so I could stop and kiss you. How long could we get away with that, do you think?" Hyacinth asked dreamily, imagining it. "I bet you are a very clever lawyer, Walter. I bet with you to fight for me I could kiss you again and again and again until they forgot about all the supposed indecency and saw only my need for you and your beauty."

Walter was making sounds, very nearly the sounds that Hyacinth had always wanted to hear from him, harsh, dry sounds of air that would not come and secret little moans that Walter was trying to bite back.

Hyacinth looked at him, at the shimmer of sweat at Walter's forehead, and the pink of his flush, and the aroused blue of his eyes.

"Why, Walter," he said, suddenly feeling very stupid and unable to say why.

Walter gave one body-long tremor and then forced out more words. "That isn't something people advertise, Hyacinth. People aren't supposed to. They aren't supposed to want—"

"Other men?" Hyacinth interrupted him impatiently and got a hurt scowl for his trouble. That scowl said he was missing the point, and he *wasn't*. "Again, I know I say this to you a lot, but why not?"

If he didn't love Walter so much, his stubborn silence at that would have greatly annoyed him. As it was, Hyacinth did the one thing he knew was guaranteed to make Walter respond; he flipped on the microphone to let the city hear them.

"Should I ask the audience?" he inquired as nicely as he could with spicy, hard licorice candies melting on his tongue and his cock pounding and hard at the images of Walter that he'd conjured up. Walter shut his eyes. A shiver and a groan were his only answer.

WHENEVER HE was in a crowd of humans, it was difficult for Hyacinth not to think of most of them as children. Even during the war, he had thought that about many of them, although they had looked the same age he had. He thought it had something to do with their innocence, or perhaps just how far they still had to go in the world and how destructive they might be if not properly guided.

That was his audience out on the dance floor and huddled close to the stage around him, but they seemed so young. They not only had no answers for him, they looked to him to explain the unfair and arbitrary rules of their society. As if Hyacinth could tell them why some human skin colors were considered more or less beautiful, or why some love was supposed to hide itself, and how even the love that was allowed had to follow such limited rules.

The rules were stupid and they were ugly, and Hyacinth would not allow ugliness in the room with him. His bosses and the hate groups of frightened humans might claim he was obscene or inciting indecency, but these children loved him for how he loved them. Everything was so simple.

Or it was simple to him. Perhaps not to others. To Walter.

Walter had gotten a call from upstairs before Hyacinth had a chance to question him further on why he could not admit what was between them, and since then Walter had been careful to sit in his little room and leave the glass between them. But he had stared, how Walter had stared at him. He had stared without hiding his gaze, and Hyacinth had found he could not look into Walter's sad eyes without that *wrong* feeling inside of him, as if he had pushed too far when he knew from Walter's shine that he had not.

That shine spoke of Walter's greatness, of his quiet strength. He was more than Hyacinth's equal; Walter was remarkable and capable of so much more than sitting in a booth and making sure Hyacinth did not swear too much. It could not be that Hyacinth had asked for what Walter could not give. It had to be that Walter did not want to entrust Hyacinth with himself, and Hyacinth could not figure out why.

He had no one to give him an answer except Walter himself.

Hyacinth looked away from the humans and scattered beings dancing to the music he had put on and glanced around the stage until he found his lovely watchdog.

Walter was tucked away at the side of the stage, almost behind a curtain, and he looked away when he saw Hyacinth watching him. He shivered as though the room wasn't hot with so many dancing bodies and he hadn't rolled up the sleeves of his white shirt.

He'd worn a tie to the event, as well as a jacket that he'd left somewhere. He'd chosen an outfit that he might have worn to work. Hyacinth had asked Walter to this dance. With humans, Hyacinth had thought that meant something. Walter could have dressed differently, but had not.

Hyacinth had worn a shirt after all, as requested, slicing holes in the back for his wings and then awkwardly sliding the thing on. He'd drawn the line at a tie, but it hadn't mattered, because Walter had not remarked on the shirt except to suck in a breath and go even more impossibly tense.

Hyacinth's fans seemed to like the shirt. They crowded around the stage, calling up comments and questions, inviting his opinion on the subtle changes in their clothing. Town teenagers trying to be as wild as the beings in the village; Hyacinth adored all of them in their borrowed lipstick and misappropriated skirts.

He wondered if Walter had noticed the blurring of the rigid human gender and racial lines, and looked back at him. If he had, Walter wasn't commenting, just as he was remaining silent on the subject of how close many of the humans had started to dance to each other during the slow songs, or what was no doubt in all the pocket flasks he had glimpsed.

Two fairies were in the crowd, and Hyacinth could feel the glimmering attraction they were giving off in waves, how it drew human boys and girls to them. Walter should have been alarmed, he should have said something. He had not.

Hyacinth couldn't stand seeing him so lonely in the shadows. He fidgeted desperately until it was time for a local group of girls to perform a few songs in the style of their favorite singers, and then he flew to the side of the stage the moment he was free.

"Walter, please, now I truly am sorry for how they stare at you. I never meant to make you feel ashamed. Please come out to stand with me." It tumbled from him, shockingly quiet. He did not want this to be public, he realized, not if Walter was this distressed.

Walter stared at him, the line between his eyes appearing and then disappearing. Hyacinth waved behind him toward the part of the stage and the dance floor that they could still see. "It's not an orgy, you see?" Even the children trying to sparkle like fairies in their jewelry and makeup were, mostly, behaving themselves.

"I don't." Walter looked out at the crowd too, out at the two fairies, neither of whom was wearing a shirt. Despite the fact that this meant one pair of visible breasts, Walter had not asked either of those fairies to put on more clothes. Hyacinth plucked at his shirt and hated how it pulled at his shoulders and the itchiness on his skin that was somehow different than the fabric of Walter's clothes. He didn't understand why Walter would ask that only Hyacinth cover up.

"Don't what?" Hyacinth delicately came to rest on the ground before Walter.

"I don't feel ashamed." Walter looked at Hyacinth and then away again. "Maybe I should, but I don't. That's what makes it so terrible."

Hyacinth went still. He realized his blood was singing. He leaned down without thinking and let his hands skate over Walter's chest. "Terrible?"

He watched Walter's throat move as he swallowed. "To tell you no."

The slow, hoarse words brought a burst of glitter out of Hyacinth, startling some people on the edge of his vision, not that he cared.

"Then why do you?" He pushed his palms against Walter's chest and felt Walter's heart beating so fiercely he thought Walter was frightened. Walter's face held no sign of fear, only sadness as Walter frowned and looked away.

"Why me, Hyacinth?" Walter exhaled softly. "I've thought about it for too many nights to count and I still do not understand why you'd bother this much. I keep thinking you'll tire and give up, but you don't. Then I think… I think maybe I should let you do the things you talk about."

Hyacinth let out a greedy, eager sound that made Walter swallow again before going on.

"But I never can reason it out. You have already said you've loved other humans." Walter looked up at him. "It would be a mistake to ask you about them, if… if it was like this."

"What?" Hyacinth tried to think of other humans, to recall their names. At the moment it was difficult to recall his own. He thought of his youth, the scandals he and his friends had left behind them in speakeasies and USOs. He smiled as it came back to him. "Of course I loved them. Those who are still alive, I count among my friends to this very day, Walter."

Walter had that look of pain and worry again. Hyacinth at last thought he understood and shook his head. "But that was different. Your colors, your shine, called to me from the first moment, and though you have steadfastly held me at a distance, I couldn't help but know you further. I thought we were at least friends."

"Yes, of course we are," Walter answered immediately. He was a thing of rare beauty.

Hyacinth bowed his head to let his mouth rest close to Walter's ear. "Is it such a surprise that I'd desire you?" His entire being was drawn to Walter. He would keep him forever if Walter allowed it.

Walter started to turn toward him but stopped himself, his mouth close and far away. "Was it… was it like this with the others?" It was the second time Walter had asked that question. This time Hyacinth was unsure what he meant by it. He had a feeling Walter was asking him something else.

He let his lips graze the shell of Walter's ear. "You must know there is only you, Walter." He put his hand up behind Walter and grabbed a handful of the thick, rough curtain.

"That can't be true," Walter gasped for him and lifted his head in what he had to know was a silent plea for Hyacinth's mouth on his skin. He shivered at the touch of Hyacinth's glitter all over him, that scarce whisper of sensation that humans often compared to a tickle.

"Why not?" Hyacinth felt himself drifting as if under a spell. Walter's warm skin was at his lips, the humanness of him salty and new.

Walter was trembling. "People will see," he groaned in a strange, raw voice and grasped at the shirt he had insisted Hyacinth wear. His breathing was loud and fast.

He was afraid, Hyacinth thought, and again remembered those humans who had gone off to die, and how dancing and love should never evoke the same fear as wars and murder. His human was fragile too, just as those boys had been, and Hyacinth would protect him. For Walter, Hyacinth would pull back. If that was what Walter wanted, if Walter needed to wait, Hyacinth would do that, no matter the pain.

"Please not yet," Walter begged him, his hands in Hyacinth's shirt to prevent him from stepping away. "Don't go. Just, please, give me something, something…."

"Normal?" Hyacinth finished for him sadly and was surprised by Walter's answer.

"Simple." Walter dropped his chin. He was pressing forward, by small, unbelievable inches. "Stop finishing what I'm trying to say. It's not that. I want…." He still could not say what he wanted, except that he needed something simple before he could dare to try anything else.

Human music filled the room, slow and exquisite, simple enough for its meaning to be clear. Hyacinth listened to Walter breathe and did not press Walter in return except to say, "A dance is simple, Walter."

Once again Walter surprised him. "I can't dance, enough girls have said so." He said it confidently, easily, not rejecting Hyacinth, but offering a reason why he thought this was impossible. Perhaps it had been simple Hyacinth needed with Walter all along.

"One thing at a time," Hyacinth marveled, because humans, Walter, were so *different*. "I'm not a girl, Walter." He put a hand on Walter's waist.

"I know." Walter moaned it with that same hint of anger and sarcasm Hyacinth had heard from him before. Walter must have wanted to say that, probably for a long time. For all his advanced age, Hyacinth felt like a youngling again. Humans required trust, and he had not earned it first as he should have.

"I…." Now *Hyacinth* was stuttering. "I meant that perhaps you weren't meant to dance with girls." He thought of human melodies, uniquely human words for what it meant to love one gender more than another. "Perhaps you were meant to dance with men." He swayed, just a little, just a small step, and felt that burst of glitter and love escape him again when Walter shivered into him and followed. "Perhaps you were meant to dance with me. And perhaps…." The new thought might be frightening, but Walter listened and stayed with him. "Perhaps you were not meant to lead when you dance with me, Walter."

Walter's shudder this time was stronger, and his breathing came harder, but he did not speak or stop moving.

Hyacinth moved gratefully with him and spoke against his ear. "Understand me, Walter; there is nothing about that which I do not find beautiful. Nothing about it I don't respect and admire." Walter's tremors against him were like the fluttering of wings, almost like happiness. Hyacinth closed his eyes and felt no urge stronger than to stay as he was with Walter right now until the end of his days.

But the music stopped. More eyes turned toward them.

Walter raised his head. "Your audience is waiting." He spoke quietly, his body tense as he finally pulled away. His face was dark with more than a flush of embarrassment. Hyacinth put a hand to Walter's blushing cheek and floated, feeling the sparkling haze around him deepen.

"Let them wait," he decreed, ready to swoop in and take Walter in his arms. Walter's entirely too reasonable eye roll stopped him.

"Oh, *fine*!" Hyacinth realized he was smiling, that he was glowing, so brilliantly and obviously that anyone who knew fairies would know why. He was also drawing all eyes, and they would see Walter. They would know. Yet Walter stared back at him as if their dance had not ended, waiting in his gaze, *longing*.

"But I can't be blamed for anything now, Walter," Hyacinth sang out gleefully and flew to the center of the stage to let the human's magic speak for him and say what anyone with eyes could already see.

APPARENTLY HUMANS *could* blame him for how the evening had ended. Hyacinth, twitching and flying from one side of the courthouse to another, had tried to argue otherwise, to explain the spells cast when humans sang the truth and how he had merely played the songs that his heart had wanted to hear, but the human judge had disagreed. According to the judge, it was somehow Hyacinth who had incited the riot.

The police coming in to break up the party and harass people had started the riot. Hyacinth had at most inspired more freedom in the behaviors on the dance floor. Now he was stuck in the back of a courtroom and trying not to storm forward and demand that everyone be released, which didn't work and seemed to anger the judge.

There hadn't been anything resembling a fight, much less a riot, until the police had burst in. The youth had wanted to have a good time. There was no crime in that. He hadn't forced them to drink more or dance or to imitate the fairy by removing articles of their clothing to reveal their skin and then to allow the other youth to touch that exposed skin.

Hyacinth had given them the truth, that was all, that they were beautiful and there was no shame in what they felt for each other. He had praised Walter and let himself sparkle with unmistakable love for him until the audience had cheered and whistled and grown more boisterous. Lovely, simple things like happiness should not instill fear in those in charge.

He touched his cheek, though his bruises had already healed. The human children spread out around the courtroom were not so lucky. He noted every single injury and listened to their statements of mingled defiance and fear while he searched for Walter. Every time he saw the damage on their innocent faces he could hear the echo of Walter telling him that it was different for humans. Their pain made him shake as it had during the war. They should not suffer so, not for being themselves, not for loving each other, and not for daring to openly admit to loving creatures like Hyacinth.

And yet they did. The humans around them punished them for such minor differences it made Hyacinth shudder with anger and fear. He felt a deeper stab of terror at the thought of Walter taken from him, never to be seen again.

Walter and the station owners had disappeared with the judge into the judge's chambers some time ago, something Walter had asked for in a calm, authoritative tone Hyacinth had never heard from him.

He heard it again now and raised his head to watch Walter and the station owner and the judge come back into the courtroom. Other lawyers were around too, though Hyacinth did not know who had called them, as the young humans hadn't been allowed to move from their seats in hours. Walter looked out over them as he strode over in Hyacinth's direction.

Hyacinth stood up and sparkled as defiantly as he could. "Walter."

Walter was marked from the scuffle as well, a cut on his forehead that had only recently stopped bleeding. His shirt was mussed and ripped in places. But his bluebell eyes were narrowed, and Hyacinth realized that Walter was upset. Walter was *angry*.

"You and the other fairies are free to go. The exemptions for fairies stand." Walter almost spit out the words, and Hyacinth understood his fury. The very idea of the exemptions left a bitter taste in the mouth, although of course he couldn't speak for the other two fairies, both of whom had been forced to put on borrowed human clothing as they waited.

"Us beings who don't know any better?" Hyacinth shot a brief glare at the judge, although of course the exemption might only apply to fairies. Fairies got treatment that even the most beautiful were wouldn't have gotten. A troll in a fight like that would have been beaten into submission and locked up by now. A human might suffer the same fate, and Hyacinth sometimes heard stories about what humans said, and did, to their own kind for loving a being. "What about you? What about them?" He deliberately raised his voice so the children would know they weren't alone. Some of them turned toward him. A few of them looked to Walter. He could tell from the expressions on their human faces the shame they were feeling. He knew Walter saw it too from how Walter went still.

"Walter." He put a hand to Walter's sleeve. "Walter, it won't always end like this." Not that Hyacinth was any kind of a seer, but he had lived a long time already, longer than many humans, though they seemed to live longer and longer as time went on. He still had hope. Walter could too. "In a small way I started this by sharing what I felt, yes, but I am not ashamed of that."

"You aren't capable of shame," Walter pointed out with quiet logic, and Hyacinth shrugged.

"Maybe it's like your human appendix and serves no purpose, so as a culture we dispensed with acknowledging it." Hyacinth studied the humans, his audience, the future. "I told them that I adore you. That hardly requires the police."

"Adore me?" Walter made a strange squeaking noise, as if this was news to him. Maybe his head injury was making his thinking slow.

"Isn't that the word? Love? Want? Need to see you regularly to keep my glitter falling?" Hyacinth raised his voice again and heard a tiny, muffled laugh from one of the watching lawyers. He smiled. Oh good, someone else who saw reason. "Desire to hold and fuck and kiss?" he went on, even louder, because the judge was feverishly banging his gavel now. Hyacinth kept his eyes on Walter's panicked blush. Walter looked startled and thoughtful all at once.

"I want all the pinks and grays of you, Walter. Every shining inch. I'd marry you if the humans would let me." Human-being marriages were legal in ten states. Marriage between two men, between two women, between two pixies and others like them, was sure to follow eventually, since it was already legal among same-sex beings, the ones who bothered getting married.

"They *were* on their way over to release you," Walter relayed distantly, then blinked at him. "Marry?" He seemed utterly confused. "Isn't that too normal?"

"Blissfully." It would give Hyacinth the legal right to show Walter off to anyone who would listen.

Whatever response he'd thought he'd get for that, a kiss maybe, or Walter coming nearer, he didn't get it. Walter stayed where he was and frowned. "It's not that easy," he commented, so low it must have been to himself. "Or it is that simple… and that terrifying." His frown deepened, but before Hyacinth could step in to ask what Walter meant, Walter stiffened his shoulders.

"I don't know how seriously the public defenders are going to take this case." Walter met Hyacinth's concerned stare. "As you know, there's a stigma in working for beings, even when civil liberties are involved. That's why beings are dependent on the few being lawyers for good representation. Humans who deal with the beings… most of these lawyers will barely defend them."

At that, he abruptly turned around and walked back to the judge before Hyacinth could think to grab him or ask what he was doing.

"If anyone else here needs a lawyer, I'll represent them," Walter called out as he passed the furious station owner.

"Walter." Hyacinth exhaled his name in shock and delight. Walter's shine had never been so obvious. The way would part in front of him. Seas and law books would open up. No human could deny Walter's strength now, however much it might surprise them. The children around Walter started to pipe up, obviously seeing it for the first time.

Hyacinth buzzed with all the magic in the air. It felt like music to him, and he didn't think he was the only one. For a moment, he would swear the humans were dancing too. Even the fear he felt, fear for Walter, for what it might cost him, couldn't take his joy from him. This was Walter as he was meant to be.

"And you ask me why, Walter?" Hyacinth spoke to himself. "You dared to ask me why."

As if he'd heard, Walter glanced back at him, eyes wide and very blue, and then he turned to begin his arguments.

HYACINTH WAS thrown out of the courthouse shortly afterward for some reason involving obstructing the completion of duties, which apparently meant making too much noise as he'd watched Walter accept client after client as if Walter had any possible way of defending them all. Only one other lawyer had taken any of the cases with something besides reluctance.

Hyacinth had done his best to stay, and when that hadn't worked, he'd gone home to clean up and then on to Walter's home, but Walter still hadn't been there. By then returning to the courthouse had gotten Hyacinth barred from City Hall for life. That left Monday at the station to see his watchdog again.

But Walter wasn't there. Close to six, Hyacinth walked in to find the station silent except for the sound of the music of the evening shift ending and Betty at the front desk informing him that he was wanted upstairs.

Hyacinth thought his reaction was very well behaved after finding out Walter had been fired and that he was being kept on with a new producer—at least how the humans would see it. They had tried to ignore fairies for fifty years. They were willfully ignorant of what dimmed, darkened glitter meant, or that fairy magic had its less benevolent purposes, rare though they were to see in use.

Hyacinth had nodded without speaking or agreeing to anything, then come downstairs and walked into his booth for his shift with barely a glance at the unhappy-looking human on the other side of the glass.

Merely entering the booth made him think of Walter. Then Hyacinth saw the microphone and knew he should leave now and find Walter, stake out Walter's home until Walter returned, and determine their future together, off the air.

Unfortunately for the station, it was not Hyacinth's way to go quietly.

He skimmed through his records, considering songs, and then promptly at six slid over to the chair and flipped on the microphone.

"Hello, kids, I suppose you've heard a lot by now. Some of you might even be surprised to hear my voice, but Hyacinth is here, and I'm not going anywhere." He looked over at his new producer. Then he smiled. "That's right. I'm not going anywhere until Walter is returned to me."

Hyacinth wasn't ancient or especially powerful, but he could send out his magic in the most basic way he knew. Fairy magic was about fortune. When used well, it was for finding things, or illuminating good people, or easing difficult situations. Used for malice, it made simple things difficult, got people lost, hid objects in plain sight, broke down mechanisms that should have worked.

He focused and thought about the locks in the doors to the station's electrical room and to the roof with the radio tower, and how it might be if they were no longer functional. Then he did the same to the door to his booth. When that was done, he took the mic again.

"I love Walter, and I believe Walter loves me, and for that they fired him and are attempting to silence me with some"—he glanced casually over—"frantic and frightened sort of human."

One thing he had left working were the phones, because how else would they get Walter and bring him here if the phones didn't work?

"Did you hear that, listeners?" He repeated himself for the joy of saying it. "Walter loves me! As I'm sure those of you at the dance heard. But he is down there right now seeing that each and every one of you who stood with me gets protected from some stupid old laws." He sighed. "Isn't he marvelous? Doesn't he shine?"

Hyacinth spent a few moments imagining what he might do when he saw Walter again and then coughed. He was going to have to do this without sugar. He hoped this wouldn't take too long.

"So you see, it wouldn't be right to do this show without him. He has made it what it was. He inspired me, and in tribute to him, until he is standing in front of me, I'm going to honor him with dead air."

And although Hyacinth had speeches and monologues left to say about Walter, at those final words he shut his mouth and pushed the mic away from his face.

He wrinkled his nose at his producer, who was on the phone and looked a little like Walter when he was being yelled at, except less handsome, and who, a moment later, dropped the phone and tried to push open the booth door.

Hyacinth waited until the man had given up and left to run down the hall and probably upstairs, before he let out a deep breath. Silence was a lot harder than it looked. He considered the microphone again, tapped out some Elvis on the tabletop, and then flung himself out of the chair to pore through his stacks of records.

"This one is—" He stopped himself from saying *one of Walter's favorites*, and sighed again. This was going to be a problem. They'd better hurry, because try as he might, fairies were not known for taking long stands. They always meant to, but sometimes other things were so distracting.

Like thoughts of Walter and how Walter danced beautifully no matter what he thought, and how his listeners might like to hear about that.

Hyacinth came to terms with how in love with the sound of his own voice he might have been during the first hour, while the station handyman was trying to unscrew the booth door despite his constantly breaking tools. He seemed surprised to find the tools so shoddily made. Hyacinth could only think that if humans spent more time with beings, they'd know when fairy magic was afoot.

After the attempt to break in had failed, the station owner himself had come down to try to talk to Hyacinth through the door. He seemed to think talking equaled yelling. Hyacinth had responded by stripping off his ridiculous blue jeans and sitting back down in his chair while the man had panicked at his nudity and fled.

Personally, Hyacinth liked his body, especially his cock. He was hoping Walter would too, which was what he was occupying himself by thinking about when the outer door opened again to reveal Walter at last.

Walter looked exhausted. He might have changed his shirt in the past days, but Hyacinth didn't think so, judging from its sad, nonstarched state. Faint stubble was on his jawline, so he must have shaved at least once, but his glasses were smudged, and his hair was a mess.

As he hadn't done the mussing, Hyacinth decided he preferred it in its usual symmetry. He jumped to his feet just the same, as if it were any other day except this day, when Walter very probably loved him back.

"Walter!" he called out and wondered briefly if he still had an audience at all, if anyone could possibly be as frozen and fragile as he felt in that moment that Walter stared at him through the glass. Walter could break him, he realized. Fairy healing or not, his little Walter could break him without even trying. He only had to leave. Hyacinth had to hope, trust that he would not.

Walter's gaze dropped. He looked wrung out and already weak, but paused at the sight of Hyacinth's naked body. He took a small, terrifying step back. Then he blinked and raised his head again. He closed the outer door behind him.

Hyacinth remembered the inner door. He didn't have enough magic for much more, but he imagined the lock working again, enough for the door to pull open when Walter touched the doorknob.

Hyacinth inhaled. "Walter is here." It was all he could say. The silence had taken his strength, or his magic was all run down for a while, but either way it seemed to work. Walter stepped into the room.

"Is this a protest? As your lawyer, the station's—" Walter paused, visibly saddened. "—as *your* lawyer, you should have told me you were planning a protest."

Hyacinth grabbed a record, without caring about what it was, not even that it was from the current Top Forty. He put it on without looking, scratching the record itself with an awful sound that barely made him flinch, though Walter blinked again.

The song wasn't terrible. Hyacinth's magic wasn't completely gone. The song was, in fact, his favorite song in the entire universe. Walter was here for him, at last.

"To hell with the station," Hyacinth sang with relish. "Where have you been?"

"At the courthouse and with some of the kids. Some of them no longer have homes, so I had to find organizations and individuals to care for them before I work out anything else." He took off his glasses to wipe at his eyes, then put them back on. His gaze went over Hyacinth's body again before he looked away. Hyacinth almost preened for him. "The cat's out of the bag," Walter remarked a second later, as if that made any sense. But Walter seemed so distressed. Which cat and what bag was what Hyacinth wanted to know. He very carefully did not skip over to throw himself on Walter and pet away the line between his eyes.

"Does it matter?" Hyacinth asked as gently as he could. "There are advantages to people knowing. I can demand to see you, for one."

"You can," Walter agreed mildly, perhaps tired. "And you did."

"That doesn't sound good. Did you mind? I needed them to see." Hyacinth waved a hand. Surely he'd explained this enough that Walter understood.

Walter made a weird face, not angry but unhappy. He huffed a little, then shook his head. "I didn't even do anything. All this trouble, and I didn't even get to do anything."

That was a surprising, and amazing, and *incredibly* pleasing statement. Hyacinth mulled it over and then almost fell into his chair his legs were so unsteady. He touched his cock because he couldn't help himself. Walter's blush was perfect.

"I can fix that." Hyacinth's voice took a moment to return to him, so he patted his knee to make his meaning more clear. "Come here, little bitty pretty one."

Walter stayed by the shelves for a few seconds longer, and then he straightened and walked over. He didn't sit on his own, but he didn't do more than make a shocked sound when Hyacinth took hold of his wrist and tugged him down.

Walter put his feet on the floor and sat stiffly for a long moment, so motionless that Hyacinth wasn't sure he was breathing. Then Walter sighed, a sigh of impatience or relief or arousal, or perhaps all three, so Hyacinth leaned in and slid a hand around Walter's waist. He almost gasped when Walter immediately shuddered back against him.

"Walter." It slipped out softly as Hyacinth turned Walter's head and pressed a kiss to the side of his pink, fruit-blossom lips. His hands felt heavy and glued to Walter's body, and his mouth could not stop seeking out Walter's mouth, especially when Walter parted his full lips and exhaled his name.

"Hyacinth. Hyacinth, you know I love you. Please." Walter pleaded with sweet innocence. Hyacinth kissed Walter's cheek and dragged his hands over Walter's chest and down to his stomach. The muscles were tense beneath Walter's rumpled shirt, but Walter did not stop Hyacinth from pulling the cloth away to touch him. He shivered, once, but Hyacinth thought it was for the glitter landing and disappearing on his skin.

"I'm sorry if I ever hurt you, Walter. But you should know you are beautiful like this." Hyacinth spoke the truth with kisses along Walter's neck, with his hands under Walter's shirt and then in Walter's lap. Walter arched up into his touch in a sudden, almost pained motion. His breathing hitched into a faster rhythm.

"That's… that's you," Walter panted quietly for him, sliding his legs open when Hyacinth touched them. "You're the beautiful one. But, Hyacinth, Hyacinth, this feels…." Walter didn't finish, but he didn't have to, not with his cock hard and his mouth open and hungry. Hyacinth kissed him again, the corner of his lips, the curve of his ear, even the frame of his glasses.

"How does it feel?" he asked gently. "Tell me, please." He wished he could see those bluebell eyes right now, wide and dark with lust, but this was good too. Walter wanted him and had said so. Walter was shocked and writhing in his lap. Walter's cock was full and hot, and he continued to whisper Hyacinth's name. His voice was hoarse, as though he'd been saying it for a long time already. "You love me."

Hyacinth abruptly recalled the rest of what Walter had said and bent his head to kiss the bared skin of Walter's neck.

Walter put a hand out on the table. Hyacinth watched his fingers curl along the edge and kissed him again for the wet, choking sound he made when Hyacinth peeled his pants away to better caress his cock. At last. At fucking last. Walter hard and begging for him. Walter pleading for Hyacinth to love him as he should be loved.

"Hyacinth," Walter exhaled unsteadily and rocked into his touch. "Hyacinth," Walter tried again, swallowing audibly. Hyacinth ran his other hand up to Walter's nipple.

Walter spread his fingers out on the surface of the table. For a moment he looked like he was trying to point. And then he was holding desperately to the tabletop. "God, Hyacinth, the microphone."

Hyacinth turned to look at the mic too, at the little glowing light on it and the On the Air sign above the door that was lit up.

Walter shifted against him. Hyacinth shut his eyes at the sensation of Walter wriggling in his lap and heard the increase in Walter's breathing. He frowned, not entirely sure he wasn't imagining it, but it was true, Walter *was* squirming against him in what could have been embarrassment, except that his cock was perfect in Hyacinth's hand, and Walter's movements were steady and regular as he ground his ass against Hyacinth's hard prick.

Things with his Walter suddenly made so much more sense.

"You like this. You *like* when they can hear," Hyacinth realized aloud so everyone listening over the airwaves could understand too. Walter put his head back and moaned, in shame or pleasure or guilt, Hyacinth could not say.

His skin was hot. Hyacinth opened his mouth to let Walter feel his pleasure, if he couldn't already feel it against his tight backside. He sucked kisses into Walter's throat, and there behind his ear, and trailed glittery touches wherever Walter allowed, which was everywhere. He pulled Walter's shirt away and urged his head to the side by the length of his tie. He stroked his dick and soothed a brief touch down his hip, over the curve of his sweet little ass, and though Walter tensed for that one moment, a groan escaped him too. Walter was not shy at all. The revelation was enough to make Hyacinth hold Walter tighter against him, right against his cock so Walter could not mistake his delight.

This was what Walter had meant all those times he agonized over being heard on the radio. He was so shiny that Hyacinth fell in love with him a little bit more.

"Shall I leave the mic on?" he whispered into Walter's ear and then buried his face in the back of Walter's neck at Walter's shocked gasp, and the nod that followed. They might be arrested again, they might be disgraced, they would be fired, no question. Hyacinth didn't care. And neither did Walter.

"Please." Walter barely seemed to get the one word out, but Hyacinth thought it was just what he should say.

"Yes, Walter," he agreed, "why not?" and told Walter to stand up, asked him to lean down, hands flat on the table. Then Hyacinth stripped the last of Walter's clothes from his trembling body and turned him back around to kiss him once more before he shared the rest with the world.

He'd thought Walter might be afraid, and perhaps he was, but his marvelous eyes were fixed on Hyacinth's, his glasses were askew, his mouth swollen. Any moment, anyone could come through that door to try to stop them. But at this moment no one, not a single person, offended or aroused, was calling in.

They were listening, as hushed as Hyacinth in the face of Walter's beauty. Then Walter frowned, unhappy or worried at the delay, and Hyacinth ran his hands down Walter's ribs. "Oh, listeners," he began, not looking away from this different, wonderful human that he loved. "If you could see him, you would understand everything I have been trying to tell you." Walter's blushes were like cake icing. Hyacinth licked at him, his collarbones and his stomach, his hip, then dropped down before Walter could tremble with longing for one more second.

Walter turned his head as he moaned, finding the microphone with little effort. Hyacinth took Walter's cock in his mouth, and the entire town heard Walter's hungry cry. The sound was better than music, with a magic all its own. Hyacinth thought the town agreed. Walter did it again, and again, wet and choking as he came and Hyacinth swallowed. Then Hyacinth stood up to turn him back around so he could drive more of those sounds from him while thrusting between his thighs. All of that, every slap of flesh and flutter of wings and agonized groan from Walter as he slowly grew hard again, and still they didn't get a single caller until it was over.

Hyacinth came across Walter's ass, his hands tight on his burning hot skin, and kissed Walter's sweat-dotted skin and whispered how much he loved him. Walter murmured, "Oh," as if still surprised, but ran his hands over where Hyacinth had used his body as if each part was new to him. "Oh," he said again, all shocked pleasure, and then turned around to place his hands on Hyacinth. His eyes were stunned and lovely, and he made a soft plea to be kissed again while Hyacinth was breathlessly reconciling his shy Walter with this come-splashed, pink-cheeked lover.

"Oh, listeners," Hyacinth repeated, in complete awe at what he had been given. "I love him so very much." And then, as though this declaration and Walter's pained, yet pleased, groan of "Hyacinth" for an answer was the last straw, the phones finally began to ring.

Hyacinth imagined a thousand voyeurs and hypocrites on the other end of those calls, and, very likely, a thousand grateful humans and fairies as well, people all hungry for the same love and joy he felt. He wanted to answer them. At any other moment he would have.

But for now he leaned down to kiss Walter, then reached over to turn off the microphone.

A Giant Among Men

1982

FOG SETTLED over Los Cerros almost nightly in the fall and winter. It rose around sunset to engulf the bluffs, then crept in along the creeks to blanket the rest of the city. By nightfall, unless a storm was blowing in, everything but the growing suburbs around town and the thick forest to the south was hidden by cold gray clouds. The fog rolled over the fancy houses on the coast, the yuppie apartments springing up near City Hall, and the historic buildings of the barrio, settling between buildings and trickling out along the highways to cause accidents during the commute.

Human development had destroyed or decimated many of the creeks that led from the trees to the sea, but a few remained, some even free of the garbage that careless humans had tossed into them. Oro Creek, a tiny trickle barely worthy of the name in the summer, was flush with water now from recent rains, and cold enough to send the fog from its banks out into the alleys and streets of the old quarter.

Tank liked the city best in the fog. Of course, trolls were supposed to hate cities and like scary, unpleasant things that made humans piss themselves, but not all trolls did, just as some humans got a kick out of softly glowing lamps along misty streets. But these days, the humans seemed especially and easily frightened. They were afraid even of the air itself, as though this was that cheesy movie about the fog that came in and brought vengeance and death with it.

Entertaining film, even if Tank had never heard of any curse working like that. But he reconsidered the swirling, chilly air and pulled his leather jacket tighter around him. His fingers glanced over the *Viet Nam MIAs/POWs Never Forget* and *Love Is A Many-Gendered Thing* pins on his lapel as he straightened his collar.

Streetlights and neon signs shone through the fog, but it was the red, blue, and white flashes that caught his attention. He began to walk faster, skirting around an elderly human woman trying to push a cart of books over a crack in the sidewalk. Tank lifted the cart for her without stopping, finding it cute that a lady her age had a flower behind her ear. But he had no desire to stick around for her expression of horror when she raised her head and saw what had helped her.

Maybe she thought Tank was a large human, because she called out her thanks in husky Spanish, the language of most of the older humans in the neighborhood. Those coming toward Tank on the narrow sidewalk knew better and got out of his way without saying a word.

Tank kept his gaze on the lights as the shape of a police car emerged from the fog, parked sideways in front of Mami Wata's.

The area in front of the bar was well lit. Mami's wasn't that kind of bar, despite what humans thought a bar that catered largely to beings would be like. Plenty of other bars around the village were the kind of places for anonymous anything, where people saw a big scary troll and got hard with fear. But Mami's was something to look forward to at the end of the long, lonely week. Seeing the cruiser out front made Tank's heart thunder in his ears. He crossed against the light and scowled at angry cab drivers to silence them.

Even early on a Friday, the place should have been loud with music and conversation, but though elves and fairies were outside, huddled against the chill as they smoked, they weren't talking much. That could have been due to the cop perched on the hood of the car as he filled out paperwork, or it could have been due to the reason the cop was there.

Tank came to a halt. Mami's entrance was on a small side street that continued for a few hundred yards before ending at a line of trees and a fat swollen portion of the creek. The part of the building that faced the main drag through the neighborhood was a wall the color of the daytime sky, with a few tinted windows, impossible to see through.

The windows had been broken. And over the lovely, calming blue, someone had spray-painted the words Let Them Die Too.

Fog was damp at the back of his neck. Tank stared at the red, dripping letters until his eyes burned, then turned his attention to the entrance to Mami's.

Mami herself owned the whole building, located at the corner of a block that had been cut short a few years ago by an unexpected deviation in the path of the creek. A shift that had coincidentally occurred around the time Mami had bought the place. A more recent change was the banner at the door that read Research Not Hysteria, which explained that Mami's would now have a door charge of a dollar, with all proceeds going to the group that had begun protesting at City Hall and to the hospitals for the care of the humans already struck down.

A Silence Equals Death poster had been hung up outside one of the leather bars closer to the fairy village, but someone had taken it down. Bad for business, Tank supposed, and in a small defense, he could admit so far not a single fairy had come down with the mysterious, fast-moving human illness, what they were calling the gay cancer. No being had, that Tank knew of. It didn't keep them from being blamed, along with the users and the homosexuals—the outcasts, as the other humans called them. Businesses at the other end of the neighborhood, in what had been known as the Village before it had begun to blend with the older barrio next to it, had been vandalized too.

Despite what some humans thought of the area, crime used to be fairly low here. The area wasn't wealthy, but it wasn't a skid row either. The old quarter was a neighborhood largely occupied by the elderly and a growing population of beings. There were urban legends to explain the crime rate—something about a beast that stalked criminals, but Tank thought it was more that people couldn't report crime, since the police hadn't used to venture too far into being territory. Some of them still wouldn't go into parts of the old barrio.

He didn't think it was a coincidence that many cities' gay districts had formed alongside, and in some places, in the center of areas thought of as disreputable because of who lived there. Down here in the old quarter too. What surprised him was that whoever had painted this wound onto the side of Mami's had felt safe enough to do it. Tank was also shocked the cops had responded to the call.

The officer at the car raised his head and jerked when he saw Tank, hand going to his gun before he moved it back to his paperwork. He gave a stiff nod. "Krieger."

The guy hadn't been on the force when Tank had, but Tank's reputation had carried on. Tank grinned to show teeth capable of grinding bones to make his bread, or at least of cracking bone to get to the marrow. He came closer to tower over the little man, rudely pleased when the human got to his feet and only reached his chin.

The fairies and elves were watching with interest, so Tank leaned down and sniffed the air, although he couldn't actually smell a human's blood, despite what was said of his kind. Giants, trolls, ogres, it was all the same—big, stupid monsters from stories and legends. Unlike the giant in the human favorite about the boy thief and his beanstalk, all Tank could smell was lingering cigarette smoke and the cop's coffee breath. He narrowed his eyes, hoping a stray bit of light caught them and reflected back. Trolls lived in dark spaces; it helped to see in the dark. He couldn't help it if the shine in their gaze frightened smaller creatures. "They catch who did this?"

He knew the answer. No one was going to waste time chasing down someone who had spray-painted a building owned by a being.

Nonetheless, the cop swallowed and shook his head despite his obvious fear. "Wouldn't tell you if I had, Tank—Krieger." He looked young, even for a human. He must have done something naughty to get assigned to working the old quarter, especially now, with disease and fear around every corner.

Tank made a fist and squeezed it to crack his knuckles. He showed his teeth again, although his stomach turned sourly. "If I can't trust the force to take care of these things…." He trailed off there, almost merry about what he wasn't saying. Tank had been hired onto the police force after protests about the lack of beings in the department. He, and most of the others hired with him, hadn't lasted long. On the books, violence wasn't the official reason he'd been kicked out—it was something about the budget. Los Cerros PD weren't known for shrinking away from fights, but there was a difference in their minds between a human cop beating in some heads to ensure his authority and a being who took note of where the justice system had failed his kind and acted to prevent it happening again.

With a gruff snort, Tank turned from the quivering cop.

Rawlins was working the door; he was big, for a human, as though some wolf stock was in his family line. He put out a hand before Tank could drop a buck in the donation bin. Tank waited because he appreciated the guy's balls in thinking he could stop him. Then he kept waiting, even with his heart going a mile a minute, because he'd never seen Rawlins show so much tension.

"No one was hurt?" From where he was, Tank couldn't see around the corner behind Rawlins that led to the small dance floor, so he couldn't see all the way to the bar either.

Rawlins shook his head but didn't relax his pose—shoulders back and arms crossed so he could reach for a weapon if he had to. He kept a highly illegal pair of knuckles in his jacket pocket and a whole mess of charms hidden in his belt. In addition to that, he was a decent brawler and loyal to Mami unto death.

"This thing." Rawlins didn't say what the thing was, and Tank didn't ask, because everyone knew. It was all they were talking about when they weren't discussing that TV show with the talking car. "The doctors gave it a name, but it's scaring people worse now. No frat boys tonight. The clean-cut straight boys and girls haven't been slumming in a few days." Rawlins made it a point to bar those types from getting in, no matter how loud they got. This was a place for beings to feel comfortable, not an adventure for curious college kids who couldn't mind their manners. Respectful humans were allowed inside, but they had to impress Rawlins first.

"In fact, if you ask me, they're the ones who did this. Them or some group like 'em." Rawlins grunted and stared down the street. It sounded right. Beings weren't getting sick, but an ignorant, drunk human wasn't going to think about that, or the effect his words would have on the dying humans who saw it. Hellfire, the president of the country wouldn't even admit there was a problem. It was only the community leaders, like Mami or the lone gay human city councilman, who were doing anything about it.

Like the door fund, which sent many of the sick humans to a town up north run by werewolves who weren't afraid of illness and who took care of them as the disease progressed. Tank had never thought of weres as especially nurturing, but, in fairness, most of the ones he'd known had been soldiers at the time. The town had been mentioned in *Time Magazine* for its activities, although the article had been about the downturn in skiing tourism. It made no mention of the wolves' hard work, or the work of people like Cassandra, who slowed the disease when they could.

It was all she could do, she said. Something about her strength and the strength of nature's devices. Tank hadn't really understood it, since a witch of her power could supposedly shift a human into a toad, although he'd never seen that happen with his own eyes, so perhaps that was a myth.

At least she was trying to do something, which was more than anyone in Washington had done. These people deserved something better from their leaders than the treatment they'd gotten so far.

Tank glanced inside the bar once again, though he still couldn't see much of anything. He grunted at Rawlins. "Mami okay?"

He didn't mean physically, although if she had left the bar, an attack on her would have been possible, even in the part of town that belonged to them. Tank hoped it had been a group of outsiders who had painted that bullshit; if it was locals turning on them, it would hurt that much worse. Mami would pretend not to care, but she'd had decades upon decades to build up a thick skin.

Tank was more concerned for everyone else. He scowled when Rawlins opened a hand and shrugged, as if he couldn't say how anyone was taking this. But then Rawlins heaved a breath. "The mood is tense in there, but no one's hurt. It's mostly the little ones, the fairies and elves."

A tense bar wasn't a good place for a were, if you could find one in the city. But the little ones lived around here and didn't like to be alone. This was where they would go, even terrified. Tank nodded, grasping what Rawlins wasn't saying. "If you need me…." He left it unfinished and dropped his donation in the bucket before continuing inside.

In dim lighting in a regular, mixed bar, no one would know Tank was a troll, except for his size and the reflective glint in his eyes. In full light it was inescapable; he was the color of mossy dirt, shifting browns and greens, with thick earth-brown curls that he shaved off to keep his familiar, comfortable buzz cut. His ears were large and had a vague point, though nowhere near as pointed as an elf or a fairy's. And of course he was big. He ducked through doorways and didn't bother trying to fit inside most cars.

Elves, always busy with something, didn't seem to mind that he was much larger than them. Fairies, on the other hand, couldn't seem to decide if they liked the idea or were worried he might accidentally crush them. Tonight, though, in the multicolored, soft club lighting, the regulars saw him and gave small sighs of relief, as if Tank were there to protect them.

Considering his reputation at the leather bars, Tank should have found that amusing. But he went directly to the bar and sat on his usual stool after it was quickly vacated by an apologetic elf.

Down at the other end of the bar, Simon was listening to a fairy earnestly explain something that would never be heard over the music and the agitated fluttering of the fairy's wings. Simon had stopped with a dishcloth in his hand, which normally put him in a bad mood—he hated being interrupted with a task unfinished—but there was no sign of the little man's temper on his face.

Tank exhaled and politely said he'd wait for Simon when Dahlia approached to ask about his order. Simon bobbed his head at whatever the fairy was saying, then drew in a long breath and began to answer. Tank couldn't hear that either, but he knew it was good because it always was when Simon offered direction.

That's what Simon called advice—"direction." He also didn't call what he did magic, though it had to be, even if no one knew what kind of magic. It wasn't like the human gift of the sight, and it wasn't psychoanalysis, but something between the two. Simon's magic was probably unique to whatever Simon was.

Elf was the term most used to describe Simon, kind of a catchall term for the slim sprite-like beings who had no name or whose names had been lost, but he wasn't like the other elves, even the other black or mixed ones. He had the same slight build, the same sweetly tipped ears and tendency to always be doing something, but he was taller, and his hair wasn't any unusual colors. It was naturally black, and darker than his skin, but only just. He dyed it anyway, purple at the moment, and had shaped it in a mohawk before shaving the sides. He'd left his hair tightly curled instead of forming it into stiff, straight spikes.

The punk-fairy look was at odds with his clothes. Today he wore a pink cardigan with a fur collar that only accentuated his long lovely neck. He probably had on a kilt or something too, or lace like those New Romantics had worn. Tank didn't understand the fashion these days and didn't pretend to. He was a leather and jeans kind of guy.

Tank studied Simon's high cheekbones and lush mouth while Simon offered life advice to the worried fairy, but looked away when Simon glanced toward him. In the corner behind the bar was the staircase that led to Mami's office and probable living space. There was no sign of Mami herself. Tank wondered who'd called the police as he turned back around.

Simon glowered in front of him, arms crossed over his chest, wispy tendrils of fur, or maybe it was feathers, brushing his throat.

Tank straightened. "You ever get tired of that? People asking you for the same thing all the time?"

"Do you?" Simon didn't bother to tilt up his head to keep eye contact. He didn't have to. Tank slouched back down.

He didn't feel like commenting on what Simon was implying. "My usual," Tank grunted but then noticed Simon was still holding the dish towel. He had no wish to be on Simon's bad side. "Please."

He slapped his money on the bar when Simon gave him an unimpressed look but turned to grab the bottle of Everclear and set it in front of him. It was illegal for anyone human to buy the stuff in the state, but beings with high metabolisms did not have that restriction. It tasted like shit, but Tank liked to have something to hold on to while he sat there.

Simon took the money and slid the change to him without assuming it was a tip the way most bartenders did—and how Tank always wished he would. Then Simon picked up a glass from the space by the sink and began to dry it. He wouldn't have time for that later, but for now it was slow enough he would work uninterrupted to his heart's content.

Interrupting elves in their work and watching the tiny explosions had been one of Tank's favorite pastimes as a child. Trolls had terrible senses of humor.

Tank cracked open his bottle and poured out a little into the glass Simon pushed toward him. Simon stared as he downed the first shot, then rubbed his wide nose as if nervous and went back to his glasses.

Tank watched his long fingers as he went steadily through all the wet dishes, then finally let out a shaky breath. "You're okay." It wasn't a question. Or, Tank hadn't meant it as one, or to allow a tremor to slip into his voice. He quickly glanced away.

"It'll take more than that," Simon answered defiantly, but nearly dropped the last glass. He caught it in time and set it carefully down. "You're okay?" he returned before Tank could think long about what might make Simon's hands stop trembling.

Tank snorted. "Me? Tank the Troll?" Tank wasn't fond of his name in the clubs, although he knew he'd never be rid of it. He was more than just a troll. He was a veteran. He'd served the community, for a while anyway. He liked crosswords, though he wasn't much good at them. He was proud to be a troll, but troll meant something different to him than it did to others. Nonetheless, he made himself smile. "Everyone knows you can't hurt a troll."

Simon's strange old-world magic, or new-world knowledge of people, was reflected in his expression when he raised his head to study Tank. He stared at Tank with fathomless eyes, as if he knew exactly how much Tank disliked his street name and was waiting for Tank to say it.

Not for the first time, Tank wanted to ask about Simon's magic and what Simon thought he was. There was probably a nice way to ask. Tank had no fucking clue what it was. He looked away and poured himself another shot. "I didn't ask you for direction," he complained before he downed it, then lifted his gaze in time to catch Simon covering his mouth with one hand. Simon didn't meet his gaze.

"I know." Simon put down the towel and then reached into his apron to pull out and count his tips so far. Tank considered the money Simon had handed back to him and contemplated demanding to know why his money was never good enough. Maybe one night he would, one night when he couldn't take it anymore. But not tonight.

"So no one tried to confront the assholes who did it?" Tank didn't think Simon would have, but Tank also wasn't much good at reading people who weren't begging him to hurt them.

"What would you do if I told you they had and had gotten hurt in the process?" Simon managed to be heard above the music and sound calm at the same time.

"Did you get hurt?" Tank raised himself off the barstool, and this time Simon's head went back. His mouth dropped open for a second before he gave himself a shake, and then he pointed at the stool and didn't move until Tank sat down and controlled himself.

Too late, Tank realized that his action had set a few fairies and elves scurrying to the opposite side of the bar. He cleared his throat. "Sorry," he apologized gruffly, but at a volume only Simon would hear.

Simon stepped closer to the bar and slid the bottle out of the way. "Everyone is fine, Tank." His voice could be what clouds looked like, when he wanted. Other times it was like the wind in the trees when a storm was rolling in.

He was right. There wasn't a scratch on him or a button in the wrong buttonhole.

Tank forced himself to speak again. "And Mami?"

Simon's wide-open, understanding gaze shuttered. "She's tough, you know that," he said shortly, then left for the opposite end of the bar.

Tank watched him go, then spread his hands out on the scarred wood of the bar. Simon made a slow bartender when a complicated drink was asked for, but that was elf thoroughness. Each drink, no matter how fruity, was made correctly, though fairies didn't bother ordering alcohol most of the time. Tank briefly considered the pale green concoction the elf secretary down the bar ordered and the tropical pineapple-laden drink that was for an unfamiliar fairy, and then he glared at his clear booze.

Simon didn't look over. The fairy didn't leave once she got her drink, lingering to smile at Simon and pet his hand when handing over her money. Simon didn't bring her any change.

Tank took a pull from his bottle, then sighed and poured out more to sip in the manner of a polite human. It stripped his tongue, but he hid his grimace and occupied himself keeping an eye on the place.

Lots of quiet chatter inside, much different from the nervous silence outside. Not many were dancing, but it was early yet, even if it was a Friday. Tank didn't dance, but he didn't mind watching. Fairies were so delicate and graceful. They loved it. Elves had to be convinced to dance, as far as he could tell, though they devoted their entire beings to it once they were on the dance floor.

He looked back to Simon, who had sent the fairy on her way and was once again listening to someone's story. Maybe they weren't asking for direction. Maybe they were asking for his number. Whichever it was, it wasn't Tank's business.

He returned to glaring at his bottle anyway.

"Lots of people come to this bar to meet other people." Simon's voice, like a hint of a footstep in the dark, made Tank go still. After a pause he risked a look up. Simon tilted his head toward the person he had been listening to. "Not only other beings like them, to talk and know them, but also to search for love."

Tank forgot to swallow. Sometimes he thought Simon saw everything.

Simon blew out a noisy breath. "That's what they usually ask me about. If you were curious."

Obviously Tank was fucking curious. He sat here every goddamn weekend wondering about it.

"You're giving relationship advice?" Tank hoped that was what Simon meant, although he hadn't known Simon to date anyone.

"I don't give advice," Simon corrected him, his expression indicating he thought Tank had had too much to drink, when Tank hadn't had anything really. Again, Simon stopped, as though he was waiting for Tank to say something.

Tank had a lot of things to say. "Direction," he amended himself instead of saying anything else. "I bet a lot of people want direction right now."

Tank gave a lot of direction too, but his was more about fucking, growly threats for his bitches to spread their legs and keep quiet until he told them to speak. Tact and sympathy were not his strong suits. He figured Simon knew that too. The old quarter wasn't that big of an area, and word got around.

"People always do, but I don't know how much they listen. Their loss." Simon lifted a shoulder in a half shrug. "Anyway I could be wrong." He screwed up his face as he thought about it. "I'm not, though. I'm always right, about them at least. Don't ask me how."

"Stopping to deal with their questions doesn't bother you? Pretty soon people will think that's all you are. They'll only want you for that, and what they think you can give them." Tank was a dumb troll, but he realized what he was really saying about two seconds after he'd said it. "Shit on a shingle," he swore. "That's not magic. You're just listening."

Simon cut him a significant look. "It's magic enough. *Some* people never hear a goddamn thing they're supposed to."

"I've got my ears open, and I've got some big fucking ears." Tank frowned. "But I've never heard you offer me any direction, if that's what you're getting at." Not once had Simon even hinted that he would, something Tank usually tried not to think about, like he tried not to think about the tips Simon wouldn't accept from him, and what Simon did on weeknights. He took a breath to calm himself, but it did nothing for his racing heart. "Not unless you're talking about all the times you told me to go to hell," he finished, and grinned to show teeth.

Simon scowled at him, then froze with his arm extended as though he had been about to tell Tank to go to hell one more time. He blinked. "You're fucking with me," he announced, once again unimpressed and cool as he lowered his arm. "You're too good at acting dumb. Now there's direction you should take—stop acting stupid. Especially with the people who know you better than that."

Tank's heart hadn't slowed, but he kept his grin. "Who would believe it? Stupid, scary ogre is what the people want."

"You aren't nearly ugly enough to be called ogre," Simon observed flatly. "And I doubt a scary, stupid ogre would be as popular in the clubs as Tank the Troll."

Tank didn't drop his gaze to his bottle and glass, but it was a close thing. There were, in fact, trolls who were considered beautiful, usually the blue and white giants who seemed to be made of ice and frost. Ogre was generally used as an insult for the less attractive ones. If you didn't think trolls had feelings, you did things like that, you called them ogre or delighted in stories about children killing giants for their money.

"Who says I'm popular?" Contrary to what Simon thought, Tank had plenty of less-than-bright moments.

Simon put his hands on the bar and leaned forward. He raked a look over Tank's chest and then his face. When he was done, he reached for the dish towel and wiped down the edge of the sink with jerky motions. "They tell me it's really something, an encounter with you. If you're into that." There was nothing in Simon's voice that said he might be. Tank was glad. No one should hurt Simon, ever, for any reason. He made a noise, and Simon flicked a glance at him. "Yet you spend your weekend nights here at the bar, alone. You don't talk to anyone. Do you not want anyone to know you're capable of more than inflicting pain?"

"I talk with you," Tank defended himself, then quickly emptied his glass and poured himself another as a snarl slipped out of him. "I didn't ask for your direction." His throat felt scorched and made the words strained. Simon had gone tense, and Tank didn't want him to leave yet, although he could still hear Simon's words replaying in his mind. "I'm not disrespecting your gift. But the boards over the windows don't make me feel any less exposed. Even…." Tank made a face, but mostly to himself, and clenched his hands into fists. "Even a big, scary troll. I don't want to fight with you."

"Mami's is where you come to relax," Simon murmured after a few moments, and let his shoulders fall. "The place where you can think about being more than Tank the Troll. Of course you don't want me telling you what you need." Despite the forgiving tone to his words, Simon seemed unhappy. He stared at Tank for a long time, then glanced down the bar. "Don't go, all right, Tank?" He flashed a smile, all white teeth and nerves, then went to take someone's drink order.

Tank swallowed the burn of more Everclear and wished for water. Everyone was on edge, Simon too. Tank should have remembered that, instead of acting like a jackass. He tried a smile when Simon returned, the soft kind he had almost forgotten, and blurted out the first thing that came to mind.

"It's not that I'm afraid or anything." Tank was such a fucking dumbass.

Simon made a noise of rude amusement, like a laugh or a sob caught in his throat. When he was really laughing, he threw his head back. Tank had made him do it once or twice, but this wasn't a night for much laughter. Strangely, he didn't think Simon was crying either. The graffiti must have made him more nervous than he was trying to show.

"Okay," Simon agreed at last, although Tank hadn't made any offers that he knew of. Simon studied him with glittering eyes. "You want direction from me, Tank, you are going to have to ask." Simon wasn't being fair. He gave advice to people all the time. Why should Tank have to ask?

Tank made himself let go of the bottle before he broke it. "If your magic doesn't work on me, you could say so." He stuck his tongue in his cheek, which made the statement only slightly less belligerent.

Simon narrowed his eyes and leaned over the bar. He inhaled sharply when Tank didn't move away, but he didn't retreat. "Here's some direction for you," he started, glaring upward with the heat of a thousand suns, and Tank fully expected to be told to go to hell, or maybe to sit on his bottle. Instead, Simon met his stare with a darkly unhappy twitch of his eyebrows, and a heaving sigh. "Stop sitting there night after night dreaming about what you want and actually ask for it."

Then Simon closed his eyes and pulled back. He turned to toss a lopsided smile behind Tank. "Hey, Mami," he greeted his boss unevenly, then gave Tank one last glance Tank didn't think he was meant to see before he went to the other end of the bar.

Mami held herself gracefully at the foot of the stairs. Anyone else would have been posing, but Mami moved with that kind of grace and decision all the time. The sway of her hips from side to side as she moved was music of its own. The outstretch of her dark, dimpled arm was far more welcoming than a simple wave. Her face lacked a definite age, much like Cassandra's, but unlike Los Cerros's most powerful witch in residence, Mami rarely smiled. At least, not with her entire face. Smaller, mysterious smiles often came and went on her lovely countenance.

She glided forward in Tank's direction with an enigmatic twist to her full lips, pausing only to order a drink from Dahlia and to pat the yellow-and-red wrap holding her hair atop her head. She wore the wrap like a crown, and the gold necklace pressed against her Adam's apple enhanced the unearthly glow of her skin. Despite having the appearance of a queen, she was wearing a crop top and jeans.

Tank cracked a smile and felt his face heat as she approached him. Only her watchful eyes, like a serpent's, reminded him not to be lulled by her beautiful face.

Treat Mami and her causes with respect and you would be fine, possibly even rewarded with her friendship. Disrespect her and hers and her gaze promised death by drowning.

Tank inclined his head so she wouldn't have to stretch to look at him. "Hello, Mami. If you find who did that, let me know. I'll handle it." The offer was easy to make.

From the far end of the bar, even over the music, he heard Simon snort.

Mami's smile got slightly less enigmatic. "Tank. I was worried."

"For me?" Tank was flattered, until he realized she probably meant that she was worried he'd already done something and gotten himself arrested. He held his hands up in false innocence. "I can take care of myself."

"I am certain of that," Mami agreed throatily, with a wink that made Tank grin.

They were interrupted by Simon handing Mami her Old-Fashioned. He stepped back without a word to either of them and then twisted to face the displays of bottles, which he began restocking in short, furious gestures.

Mami took a sip, sighing a little, probably because Simon took his time but made the best drinks. Or so Tank had heard. Tank had never dared to request anything but his usual bottle.

Tank studied the line of Simon's back, noting that Simon was wearing high-waisted black plaid pants. The ends of the tie for his apron trailed down over his ass like a tail. Tank wanted to wrap them around his fingers and tug. Simon would complain, a lot, if he did that, so Tank sighed and turned to Mami.

She was enjoying her drink, and possibly the sight of Tank ogling her employee. "I was worried, but not for myself, or for you. I was worried for my Simon. You'll see to him, won't you, Tank darling?"

Simon had turned to face them before Mami could finish gesturing at him. "Mami!" Simon protested, hands to his cheeks and then in fists at his sides. He took a breath. "Mami, really. This is no time for that."

"There is no better time. We will carry on." Mami was not asking, or suggesting. Tank's CO in Nam had been less intimidating for all his barking. Mami gentled her voice. "Simon, you have to go forward, even when it hurts. Although…." Mami spent a moment considering Tank, until Tank realized he was frowning at her for the way she'd spoken to Simon. "Although I do not think this will hurt. Not much, anyway. Will it, Tank?"

Tank nodded immediately without knowing what she was talking about. Simon looked at him with wide, startled eyes, then shook his head and focused on Mami again. "Mami, please, he doesn't want to do this."

"Hey, you don't speak for me," Tank objected, fascinated with the whispery thread of embarrassment in Simon's voice. Protecting Simon would be an honor. "What would you like me to do?"

"The situation in the quarter is serious. The humans are scared, and though we like to think we are sheltered here, they surround us. If they do not find some way to slow or stop this soon, you know things will only get worse, for us and for the humans who share our tastes." Mami placed her drink on the bar. "Simon won't listen to me despite that. That is why I need you, Tank."

Simon scowled. "It's not going to do any good." Very few people would have been that openly angry with Mami. She liked him a lot to tolerate it.

"Nonsense. It will keep you safe. *He* will keep you safe." Mami patted Tank's arm. "Darling Tank will escort you home, since you insist upon walking."

"*Walking*?" Tank heaved a beastly breath of disbelief, liking it when Simon gaped at him as if Tank taking Mami's side had never occurred to him as a possibility. Or maybe he thought Tank wouldn't care about him walking through the quarter after two in the morning in a time like this. "So you don't know everything, little man." Tank was unable to resist the urge to poke at him, even as relief flooded through him at the thought of being able to protect Simon.

"You see?" Mami was smug and elegant as she patted Tank again. She took her leave with another small smile, leaving only her drink and the scent of Dior behind her.

Simon swallowed. "You don't have to." He went to wipe the bar, then seemed to realize his towel was missing. "You can go do whatever it is you do after your nights here." Tank wondered what Simon thought he did, since he'd already noticed that Tank didn't take anyone home. "This is your place to unwind. It doesn't have to be more than that."

A thinking man would have pondered that before speaking. Tank narrowed his eyes. "My nights here are the best part of my week. Walking you home isn't going to change that."

"But—" Simon cut himself off, then squinted up at Tank for what felt like a long time but was probably a few seconds. Then he dropped his head to study the top of the bar. "I'll tell Mami you said that," he informed Tank, an emphasis in the words Tank didn't understand. He would have asked, but then a series of androgynously dressed pixies lined up at the bar, and Simon hurried away.

TANK DIDN'T usually stay to close the place, but a promise to Mami was a promise kept. He would have done it anyway, had he known Simon had been walking home alone. A part of him thought that might be why Simon had never mentioned it, but then he remembered Simon's surprise at how easily Tank had agreed, and he realized Simon hadn't thought Tank would care.

The hot pool of anger in his stomach made his vigil easier, that and the sandwich Mami had brought him from the kitchen for dinner, and the careful looks Simon kept giving him even while he avoided Tank's part of the bar.

That was new. He and Simon usually talked more on these nights, when Simon wasn't working. The bar wasn't that busy. The cop outside must have left hours ago, but many beings were steering clear. Mami came and went too, using the phone by the bathrooms a few times. By last call, not many were around, and those still there were easily convinced to leave when Dahlia called them a cab.

Having finished his bottle some time ago, Tank helped them clean up and watched Rawlins walk Dahlia to her car. Then he pulled his jacket close around him and stepped outside to wait.

No patrons lingered for a final cigarette tonight. Tank considered the wall, once a pure sky-blue but now painted over with a patch of white. The spray paint was still faintly visible through it.

He started when Simon stepped out from around the back entrance. Simon seemed equally startled. He froze at the sight of Tank, then reached into the interior pockets of his big faux-fur coat and withdrew a pack of cigarettes and a lighter. He stared at the wall as he lit one and took his first drag. The flame from the lighter flickered, revealing something new in the paint, a symbol drawn in the same white color. A blessing maybe, though human magic wasn't Tank's area.

"You mind if I smoke?" Simon blew a ring of smoke to the side, where it blended with the fog.

Tank couldn't see more than a few yards ahead with all the fog, yet Simon had been going to walk home alone in this. Tank stifled a grunt and shook his head. Smoke wouldn't hurt him, and he doubted it would hurt Simon, even if he was a different kind of elf.

The wet air made everything feel colder, even to Tank. But Simon didn't have gloves. He buttoned up his coat and avoided Tank's eyes. "You really don't have to do this, no matter what Mami thinks."

"Shut up." Tank huffed, which at least got Simon to look at him. "I know that. What do you think, I'm going to laugh at where you live or something?" Tank could see him trembling, and while Simon might be a regular smoker, he didn't smell of tobacco most of the time. He was probably nervous. Tank hoped he was nervous, and not scared of him. He went on when Simon jumped, lowering his voice. "I won't hurt you, Simon."

"I'm not afraid of you, Tank," Simon snapped at him, then dropped the cigarette and crushed it under the heel of his boot. He wrapped his arms around himself and shivered. "Come on." He headed into the fog with barely a pause, leaving Tank to follow.

If anyone else was wandering through the mist, Tank couldn't hear them. He stayed close to Simon, then took a giant step to put himself at Simon's side. Simon glanced up at him, as wide-eyed as he'd been when Mami had asked Tank to do this.

"You didn't think I'd want to see you home," Tank remarked.

"I thought you'd have other things to do," Simon corrected, then stopped short when Tank snarled, "Well, I don't."

Simon made a motion as though he wanted to reach for another cigarette but changed his mind. "I know you won't laugh at my apartment," he admitted, soft and quiet. "You're more decent than you like people to know."

"*You* know." Tank didn't know why he kept pointing out how Simon was special. Sooner or later, Simon was going to notice, if he hadn't already. "You cold?" he pressed before Simon could say anything.

"I should buy gloves," Simon admitted, but flapped a hand to dismiss that before shoving both hands in his pockets. He started walking again. "I don't expect you to fight for me if there's trouble. But…." He paused to sigh. "Thank you, Tank."

"Fighting is what I'm good at." Tank let an animal noise carry through the still streets. "Crunching bone and painting walls with blood. It would be my pleasure to hurt anyone who hurts you. My great pleasure."

"You sound like a human." Simon stopped at a corner, as if he were really going to wait for the crosswalk light even though there wasn't any traffic. Tank steered him forward by his elbow, then took his hands away.

"I sound like a troll." Tank hunched his shoulders against the chill. "If you think beings don't kill, or feel fear, you're wrong. Even fairies can strike out in a frantic moment and cause pain. Of course…." Tank paused thoughtfully. "It wasn't beings who thought up Agent Orange. The effects of that will last longer than any curse."

Simon exhaled loudly. "Do you ever wonder what the older ones were thinking to come out of hiding as they did?" Everyone, even the beings who hadn't come from Europe, even the beings who had never been in hiding in their various homelands, knew the story of the fairies and elves who had fled the war in France and Belgium and, in doing so, proved their existence to the world. The West, being what it was, thought of them as new, as foreign interlopers, and had spread the idea to the countries that had previously accepted their magical residents.

"They were afraid. Who doesn't do dumb shit when they're afraid?" The pool of anger in Tank's chest was growing as he realized how many blocks Simon walked, alone, every night. "*Some people* do dumber shit to prove they aren't afraid."

He'd made his point. Simon leaned closer and raised his head to be sure Tank could see him roll his eyes. "*Some people* are saving money instead of spending it on cab fare. Answer the question, Tank, seriously."

Tank stared ahead, although the fog told him nothing. Finally he gave in. "I imagine they were thinking they were facing the dangers of the human world anyway, why should they stay hidden? They were at risk whether or not the humans knew they were fucking there. They chose to have a voice, to fight, in their way. Fighting for survival is…." Tank didn't know the words to finish the thought and snorted heavily in frustration.

Simon gave him a careful look. "I suppose some people react to fear differently than others."

Tank shook his head. "The original fairies were brave to run as they did. They could have stayed hidden and wound up dead. Running toward the fight is pointless bravery most of the time. And in my case, it means less. Takes more to kill me, that's all."

"I meant with compassion." Simon surprised him by curling a hand around his arm. "Like you doing this. Like what Mami does."

Tank felt himself smiling despite the topic of discussion. "C'mon. Mami doesn't always react with compassion and you know it."

Simon laughed, then put a hand over his mouth as if Mami might hear it this far away. "True," he admitted. "But when she attacks others, it's those who deserve it. Not innocent, sick humans. Not us."

Tank nodded and followed as Simon turned a corner to head farther into what had been the barrio. He thought about the groups of humans now fighting back, and the human scientists and doctors claiming they were trying to help. Of course, then he thought about the president, that useless piece of shit.

"How about you?" Simon asked, making Tank glance down. Simon stared ahead. "What do you do when afraid?"

He shivered, and Tank didn't think it was from the cold, or that Simon was asking an idle question.

"Thought you knew," he answered, embarrassed for no reason and grunting to cover it. "You keep going."

"Keep going." Simon sounded thoughtful, and young. Tank had no idea how old he actually was. Old enough to work in a bar at least. "You sound like her. 'Keep going.' I'm furious and scared, and she tells me to go forward anyway."

"Yeah." Surprisingly, Tank had no anger for that. "What else can you do?"

The noise Simon made was so beast-like a were could have made it. Tank approved. Simon seemed to know that and looked up at him. "Fuck those assholes who are doing this to the neighborhood, though, right?"

"Oh yeah." Tank was close to growling himself. "Fuck those guys. Sic demons on them, and fairies too." There was nothing like a pissed-off fairy or a pixy for vengeance. The slow kind that showed no marks on the outside but drove people to their limits and then broke them.

Tank noted Guerrero's Books and Comics through the fog. "You live this far away from the bar and you walk home every night?" He didn't sound happy about it because he *wasn't* happy about it.

"It's a good neighborhood. Most of my neighbors are old, and any troublemakers are usually passing through on their way somewhere else." Simon sounded proud, but then he tossed his head. "My place is small, but it's affordable, and… I needed some distance from the fairy village."

"I like fairies." Some people didn't, Tank knew that. Some people thought they were too flighty, too sexy, too unstable. But he hadn't thought Simon was one of them.

"I do too." Simon didn't disappoint him. But he did sigh. "But sometimes I feel like I get all the crap from being what I am, what we are, but none of the good stuff that they get. They are seen as beautiful. They're in *Shakespeare*. Even stuffy humans will make allowances for pretty fairies. Me? I can't fly. I don't heal that much faster than a human. I don't sparkle. Frankly, I'm not even sure how much of what I am has been diluted by human blood over the years. But when the fairies and the humans who love them are blamed for this, I'm blamed too."

Tank opened his mouth, but no sound came out. Simon slowed, then stopped. He raised his head to stare at Tank. "I'm being unfair. After all, fairies are still the first to get blamed, despite all that. Maybe it's because they were the first to emerge from hiding. But… but wouldn't it be nice to fly?"

A smile cracked Tank's face. "You want to fly?"

Simon hid his face behind one hand. "It just seems like fun."

"Say the word and I will give you all the airplane rides you want," Tank told him, serious despite the smile he couldn't shake. He flexed his arms when Simon looked at him in disbelief, although with his jacket on, there was no muscle to see.

"I'm never going to hear the end of this, am I?" Simon wondered, although he didn't seem angry.

Tank grinned at him for a moment longer, then straightened as he had an idea. "Hey, you tired?"

"Of course I'm tired." *There* was the familiar irritation from his spiky little man. Simon heaved a sigh. "I worked a full shift, and no one is sleeping well these days with how the cops aren't doing shit and—" He stopped when Tank shushed him.

"Want to hear something? It might not happen, but it's not far out of the way." Tank hooked a thumb toward a different street. "Ever been around Cassandra's shop late at night?"

Simon raised his eyebrows and shook his head but said nothing when Tank took his elbow for the second time and led him down a new path. He took his hand away when they reached the end of the street with Cassandra's magic shop on it. Then he sighed happily at the first echoing note.

Simon bumped into him but didn't move away. He only tilted his head toward the sound.

Tank didn't know what language the song was in, Italian maybe, though it had seemed like German or something before. He didn't know what it meant, but he guessed it was opera. He wouldn't have thought he'd be a fan of opera, but that voice carrying through the fog sent shivers along his skin and pricked at his eyes. He closed them and inhaled slowly as the voice soared high and clear and exquisite and then dropped away.

It didn't start again. Tank had come too late to hear the full song.

"What?" Simon wiped at his cheeks furiously and then scowled at Tank as if embarrassed to be caught crying. Tank brushed Simon's damp cheek with his big fist, then realized what he'd done and stepped away. "Tank." Simon couldn't seem to catch his breath. "Tank, what, who was that?"

"I have no idea who he is. But I hear him sometimes as I walk home on the weekends. He must visit someone around here." If the song was over, Tank ought to get Simon home. "Come on. When he stops, he's done. He won't go on. Sometimes I don't hear anything for weeks. You were lucky."

"Things like that still exist," Simon said softly, like someone talking to himself. When he didn't move, Tank relaxed his hand and turned him around to go back the way they'd come. "I forget, you know? People like us get to hear things like that. We get to make things like that, even now. Thank you."

"You're welcome." Tank didn't duck his head like a dumb kid, but it was a near thing.

Simon glanced around them, then twitched. "Don't you live near here? Really, Tank…." His tone was irritated, but he was still wiping at his eyes, as if the lonely singing had stayed with him.

"I'm walking you home." Tank was firm but kept his tone as light as he knew how to. "I don't need the sleep, and anyway I've got nowhere else to be."

Simon's frown was obvious even at night and in concealing fog. "Why is that, when half the village enjoys begging for your cock?"

"That doesn't mean crap." Tank huffed. Simon had said he wouldn't give direction, but he kept pushing. Tank waved over his body. "Big, dumb goon like me? Who would think of me as the settle-down type?"

"The fairies like you." Simon grew quieter. "They don't look at appearances, not like that. They can be gentle."

How Simon knew what Tank wanted was not something Tank was going to ask about. Not tonight. He tossed his head. "Fairies aren't what I'm interested in. I like strength."

"Ah," Simon remarked. Only the one word, but Tank felt as though it was the end of something. Maybe the strange late-night opera had affected him too. They didn't talk for a while.

He stopped when Simon stopped and turned to him. They were in front of a small, three-story building. A single bulb was burning over the entrance. Simon pulled a key from a chain around his neck.

"Good night, Tank," he said and then raised his head. He tilted his chin that much, enough to make Tank aware they were standing close, and Simon was shivering with the cold, and it would be very easy to pick him up and warm him. Tank stared into his dark eyes as the mist swirled around them, and then Simon gave him a small smile, like one of Mami's, and stepped back. "I told her," he whispered sadly, then nodded. "Thank you again. You don't have to wait."

"Huh?" Tank answered stupidly, then wanted to kick himself. He shoved his hands into his pockets. "I'll wait," he insisted anyway, not understanding Simon's smile, and not certain he wanted to. But he took up position and waited as Simon went inside. He stayed until the third-floor lights went on, and then he turned and headed home.

THIS TIME when Tank saw police lights through the gathering fog, he headed directly into Mami's. A bunch of volunteers worked out of the building down the street, a lot of them protestors, but some lawyers and doctors from the gay community out to combat the mysterious cancer, or syndrome, or whatever. Tank would find out what had happened there later.

He rushed past Rawlins and went straight to the bar. "Are you okay?" The question spilled out the moment Simon turned toward him with his eyes wide and hurt. Tank reached out without thinking and placed a hand over the one Simon had left on the bar.

"Tank." Simon let out a breath. "It's nothing. More broken glass. Bullshit terror tactics. Only… only they were in there at the time. Someone could have been hurt."

"And the cops showed up?" Tank frowned in surprise. Two cruisers were out there. He stared down at Simon, handsome in his dress shirt and bow tie, intriguing with his single, long earring, and he made up his mind. "I'm walking you home again."

"What?" Simon pulled his hand out from Tank's to gesture in frustration. "I'm not going to show them I'm afraid—" he started in, but stopped short and stared around Tank. Tank turned and took in the sight of a cop, a human cop. No, not just any human cop, but Detective Calvin fucking Parker walking past Rawlins with his badge out.

"Krieger!" Parker called over the music. He wore a trench coat and a wrinkled suit like a movie detective, but underneath his chin was a long, electric-blue scarf he could not have picked out for himself. Calvin Parker was a black suit, dark tie, scotch neat kind of man—on the surface. Under the surface was something else. Tank wasn't sure what, exactly, but he knew the fairies saw it. They might shudder away from most cops, but Calvin Parker had them practically humming.

"Parker," Tank greeted him cautiously. "You're investigating across the street?"

Parker reached him and lowered his voice. "Ugly business. The kind of thing I expect to see in old newspapers, not in front of me." He put his hands in his pockets and stood at ease, as if unaware of the mix of interested and suspicious stares focused on him.

Tank gave him a suspicious look of his own but then shrugged and decided to play along for a bit. "Find anything?"

"Can't say. Ongoing investigation." Parker smiled as he said it. He had a strange face, almost handsome when he smiled or laughed, but then dour and serious the rest of the time. "But," Parker added, lowering his voice even more, "bricks through windows is hardly the work of masterminds. So far whoever it is has been lucky in the lack of witnesses. Very lucky."

"The fog helps." Tank wondered if Parker was implying magic had been used, but didn't think so. For one thing, Cassandra would have been all over that. For another, Tank didn't want to think that someone from their community had done this.

"So do witnesses who won't talk to the police." Parker's smile disappeared. "Before you snarl, I know why they don't. But I can't do much without them."

Tank thought of what some human cops had done to the humans those beings loved, but made himself swallow his growl. "They know about you," he admitted after a while. "If they do talk to a human cop, it'll be you. But you let them down and it's over." Parker should never forget that, even if he had once been the department's golden boy. "What are you doing down here?"

"My new precinct." Again, Parker smiled. Tank couldn't read if he was pissed or pleased. He doubted he was sorry. Parker didn't only have a mind that made the rest of the city's detectives look lazy, he had committed the unforgivable mistake of falling in love with a fairy—and lived openly with her. They'd probably be married if fairies were into that kind of thing. It was legal in this state, after all, at least if the pair was hetero.

"So they sent you down here." As punishment, but Tank didn't say that part. He did allow himself a grin. "Congratulations."

"I'm in good company." Parker gave him an answering grin, then sobered up. "First things first. I need to show I'm serious, and I am very serious about this, Krieger." He never had called Tank by his nickname. Tank had never appreciated it as much as he did at this moment.

Tank nodded. "So am I. Never expected the PD to give a shit, though."

Parker didn't waste time arguing that. "Bosses sent me here, they can deal with the new order." So he planned on actually doing his job here and making the other cops do theirs as well. Tank didn't know whether he believed it, but the idea was certainly intriguing.

Parker glanced around again, his gaze lingering behind Tank for a moment. Then he focused on Tank. "It's strange. This neighborhood used to take care of itself. In the old days, this kind of crime wouldn't have been tolerated. There were stories." How Parker had heard about the avenging beast, Tank had no idea. He blinked, and Parker met his gaze and held it. "Which is a shame. If there aren't going to be their own kind on this force any time soon to serve and protect them, then someone acting on their behalf might be helpful, for the beings and for the humans who live with them."

Tank felt his mouth drop open and snapped it closed.

"I'm so glad I saw you coming in here," Parker went on, much too smoothly. "You were always a good man. I'd hoped you'd be the first being to make detective. Well, whoever finally does is going to be someone special. For now, we have to work with what we have, right, Krieger? I know you wouldn't get carried away the way they used to say you did. You have the best interests of the community at heart, after all, as I do."

Tank stared back at him, trying to examine what he'd been told without giving away too much. He hadn't managed a word by the time

Parker nodded at him in farewell, then nodded toward someone in the corner, possibly Mami. He turned and left at that, not apologizing for busting into the privacy of the bar, but leaving a handful of bills in the donation box as he went.

"You know Detective Parker?" Simon questioned from behind him. "Are you… friends?"

"Not exactly." Tank couldn't think of how to explain what he thought Parker had suggested he do, so he didn't. But he turned to Simon, who was regarding him in amazement, like most of the other bar patrons. "If anyone hears anything about who is doing this, they can tell me, if they don't want to tell him."

Simon narrowed his eyes. Tank felt like he was being read, but then Simon shook his head. "I don't trust him, even if he does have a fairy lover."

"And a child," Tank added absently.

"What?" Simon's voice broke.

"A little thing, I hear, with tiny, tiny wings that formed early. No glitter yet." Babies were probably adorable. Tank always felt like he might crush one, and avoided them. "I'm still walking you home."

Simon didn't even object. He stared hard at Tank, then glanced away. "I didn't know you were so powerful."

"Powerful?" Tank snorted and started paying more attention. "Because I know Parker? I thought you knew everything."

"I *listen*." Simon crossed his arms. "It's not my fault you never say what you really want."

"Are you mad at me? Because of Parker?" Tank plopped down into his seat, making the barstool creak. "Look, I'm the same as any other troll, all right? Most of the time I don't need humans around. Humans are assholes. I also think beings can be assholes. But I've worked with him, Parker, and… he's okay. He doesn't get an award for following his heart and choosing his fairy. Any decent person should do that. But it did take guts. I'll give him that. And he's clearly got shine, because the fairies can't take their eyes off him."

"They look at you that way too." Simon picked up a towel and slapped it over his shoulder. It made his earring swing back and forth. "That isn't quite how I see things. And other elves… not at all. I wish I knew if that was normal, for whatever I am… am supposed to be."

"I think you're fine, however you are." Tank's confession would have been better on a dark and foggy street so he could hide his face, not that Simon was looking.

Simon lowered his gaze. "That's because you don't see like humans do. You're too pigheaded."

"Which is why I'll be waiting for you outside tonight," Tank agreed, and got confused when Simon regarded him scornfully. He reached for a bottle of Everclear before Tank could say a word, then set it in front of him with a challenging air.

Tank sighed. Simon waited.

"If I ordered something else, would you accept the tip I'd give you?" Tank demanded, softer than he'd ever been in his whole life.

Simon pursed his lips and only looked delicious for it. But he glanced away first. "Try it and find out," he dared, equally quiet.

Tank could have asked how Simon knew he wanted to ask for something else, and if Simon knew what he wanted. If Simon thought Tank was powerful, he wouldn't after that. "People like the hard-drinking troll," Tank answered at last, and slid his cash onto the bar. He didn't mean for their hands to touch, but when they did, he recalled how he'd put his hand over Simon's before, and Simon had let him. He was such a fucking idiot.

He opened his mouth to say so, but Simon stepped neatly away. He went to the register, then came back with Tank's change, which he left in a water ring from someone's glass before disappearing to the opposite end of the bar. And there he stayed.

PERHAPS IN defiance of recent events, Mami's was as busy as usual on a Saturday, maybe more. Tank grew restless with that many elves and fairies buzzing for his attention and went for a walk a few times, grabbed a slice of pizza, but he was back by closing. He waited outside this time, amid the lingering smokers and all their fluttering wings.

He wasn't often in this position, and he thought it showed in his fidgety movements—movements that stopped the second Simon came around from behind the building. He was once again in his thick coat, and once again had forgotten gloves. He went still for a heartbeat when he saw Tank, then offered him a small, puzzling smile and came forward.

"You're here." Simon's earring was metal, and probably cold against his skin. Tank struggled to take his eyes off it.

"Every night, if you want," he promised, then heard a laugh. He twisted around with a scowl on his face that sent their audience back a few steps.

Simon touched his arm, and Tank remembered their audience didn't need more things to be afraid of and nodded. He rolled his shoulders and adjusted his jacket, then followed Simon into the fog. More people were out tonight. He could hear them and occasionally glimpse them, but no one came near.

Simon walked without pausing to light a cigarette. He must have been tired, because he didn't move fast. Tank stayed at his side, glancing discreetly at him every so often.

Or not so discreetly. "Are we friends, Tank?" Simon wondered, in a whisper like moonlight.

"Yeah. I mean, I hope so." Tank wanted to put his mouth where the chilled metal of Simon's earring touched his skin, and thought that Simon tied up in his bed and glowering at him before his eyes went glassy with desire was something he'd kill to see, but friends sounded good too. "If you want."

"Are you friends with the men at those clubs?" Simon evidently changed his mind about the cigarette. He held one close as he lit it and made a face after he blew a perfect ring.

Tank shrugged. "Some I like more than others. But no, not friends. They don't want to be friends. It'd make me too real to them, I think. They don't like it when I stick around after, even when I just want to take care of them." He didn't know what to make of how Simon stared at him. "I like that we're friends. That you don't mind… me."

"But you enjoy what you do there, with them." Simon listened even to the stuff Tank hadn't said. He picked a bit of paper or tobacco from his tongue, then gave Tank the small, confusing smile again. "I don't even know what that is. Sorry."

"Don't be sorry." Tank felt more gruff and huge than usual and didn't know why. "I don't like everything, but I don't mind making people happy. As for the rest, you don't have to know about it if you aren't into that, and anyway… anyway, I don't like the idea of anyone else hurting you."

Simon raised his eyebrows, although Tank didn't notice anything that should have gotten that reaction. "How do you hurt them?"

"Gonna get you flustered if we keep talking about this," Tank pointed out, but he was the one with the voice rough and his body hot. Simon would not be deterred, he knew that. So he nodded. "If they want rough stuff, I give them that. Tie 'em up some, or cuffs, whatever. Paddles, if they like that. Floggers. Some want bruises. Some got respectable work to think about. It's not about pain like that, though. I mean, it's there, but it's not like a fight because I don't want to crush them. I want them to give in, and they always do. It makes them real happy, and I like that. It's like what I do, but it relaxes them and gets them hard and if they're scared of me, then it's because fear might get them off too. But mostly it's because they feel so much, I make them feel so much, they can't think. That's what they really want. Then I get to make them come, or tell them to, which is the same thing, and they're mine, for a while."

"That's all?" Simon appeared amazed, even if his tone was warm. "But I… maybe it's because it's you. It doesn't seem scary when you say it all like that."

"You interested in submitting to someone, Simon?" Tank would challenge anyone who dared to try. Simon's pretty neck wasn't meant to bend for just anyone.

Simon focused on his cigarette. "I wouldn't know anything about that," he said at last, which wasn't an answer. He nodded too, after a moment, then kept walking. He offered up his cigarette, so Tank accepted it and took a drag. Bitter smoke made him wrinkle his nose, but he blew it out and handed it back. Simon glanced at it before putting the end in his mouth.

"You know, this thing could spread that easily. Human colds do." Simon looked in the direction of a passing stranger, tracking his footsteps in the dark. His voice was like the creek after a rain. "I could catch this disease. I have no idea what I am, or how much of me is human. I could."

Tank flinched. He forgot, sometimes, that his protection did not extend to everyone in the being world. He thought again that acting fearless was easy when you were never in much danger. Hellfire, he could catch it too, for all he knew, if not now then someday. These things evolved, and they barely knew anything about it.

He waited at the crosswalk this time, because he could hear revving engines and squealing tires somewhere close.

"Is that why you don't take anyone up on their flirting?" he asked when they continued on their way again. He almost led them in the direction of Cassandra's shop but then remembered the tears in Simon's eyes and decided against it.

"Customers." Simon shook his head, then snuffed his cigarette out under his boot. "I can serve their drink exactly how they like it, and I can listen if I have nothing else to do, and offer direction they never heed. But in the area of who I date, I am quite particular, and I'm not interested in any substitutions."

Tank thought of the elves he'd known and their focus on work to be done. "One thing at a time?" As a joke he could have done better, but Simon laughed.

The laugh had an edge to it. "He's not a *thing*. But yes, you could say that."

"So you're waiting?" Tank stifled a snarl. "He must be something, the lucky bastard." Simon missed a step and came down hard, then said nothing when Tank took hold of his arm and kept it. "Don't know if I think much of him, if he's leaving you hanging. That must hurt."

He meant emotionally, but Simon wouldn't stop staring at him. He allowed Tank to lead him on toward his apartment and kept staring, eyes dark and deep. "Tank, you… you hurt people all the time. Why am I different?"

"I'm a troll. I like a fight." Tank tried to dismiss it before he embarrassed himself more, but Simon was Simon, his fierce little elf-man.

"It's not a fight if they ask you to, and they like it," Simon insisted.

"No, but it helps scratch that itch. And it's how they like me." Tank scowled, but of course Simon wasn't afraid. "I make them bleed, leave bruises, tell them what to do, fuck them. It's almost enough."

"But you want more." Simon had read him all right. "A fight is good. The leather is good."

"The fucking is good," Tank interrupted.

"The fucking is good," Simon said as if Tank hadn't spoken. "But you want more. You want to have what *you* want, not what they ask for. Maybe it's leather still, but it's not how you are with them. It's being friends and taking care of them…." Simon trailed off. "What do I know about it anyway?"

He shook off Tank's arm and walked faster.

Tank had a hard time catching up to him, despite his longer legs. His breath came in bursts. "No, go on. What were you going to say?"

Simon turned a corner. "You want something else, Tank. You want your fights and crunching bones, but you also want easy nights of conversation. You want someone who doesn't think of you as Tank the Troll. You want to hold someone who is a challenge, someone strong and controlled, and you want to unravel them until they are only for you. You want them to want you to stay afterward. And you want a sweet drink made of fruit and sugar, but you won't ask for one, will you? That isn't what Tank the Troll does. So you sit and you imagine and worship from afar."

Simon stopped dead and released a weighted breath. "You want someone beautiful who you don't think you can have," he announced unhappily, making Tank's chest seize up. "You want Mami."

Tank tripped over nothing and slapped a hand against the iron grate over a shop window to keep on his feet. "What the fuck? You think I want Mami?" He raised his voice without meaning to. "You see everything and you think that?" Every harsh exhale left him like puffing steam and then rose up to disappear.

"I don't see everything," Simon reminded him, but lowered his arms and wobbled for a moment, as if he wanted to fall back or lean forward.

"Did you see me sitting on that stool night after night?" Tank demanded, and felt slow and stupid, humiliated at what he was admitting. Simon gaped, as if Tank had completely thrown him. Tank pointed at him. "I should spank some sense into you."

Simon raised his chin and got his mouth closed but didn't otherwise respond to that. In the silence, Tank could hear squealing tires from some idiot driving too fast, but he kept his gaze on Simon. He'd gone that far, he might as well bare his chest. "It's you who talks to me. You I watch. You I can't have. Doesn't matter if I drink something pink or not."

Tank panted into quiet, still air, then turned sharply at another screech of tires and the tinkling crash of breaking glass.

Simon sucked in a breath. "Tank…."

Tank pointed at him again. "Find a phone, call the cops. Ask for Parker if you can." He squeezed his fists, cracking the knuckles, then ran toward the sounds of violence. Simon shouted after him, his voice ringing with fear or fury, but Tank didn't slow until he was back at the corner and the noise was louder.

Lights had come on in some of the second and third-story windows around him, but they didn't illuminate much. The headlights of the old sedan parked half on the curb were the best available light. Tank wondered if the area's elderly residents were as disinclined to phone the police as its being residents, then shook off the worry when he counted three human outlines in the light from the car.

Three. Tank grinned as the burning pool of anger he'd been sitting on rushed hot through his veins. Only three puny humans, armed with bricks they were tossing through windows. They hadn't thought to wear masks, but he didn't recognize them. They were calling out encouragement to each other. One held a can, probably beer. Tank couldn't tell why they were doing this from their ordinary sweaters and jeans, but he had no plans to ask them.

He picked up speed as he crossed the street, grabbed one by the back of his head before the asshole could turn around, and shoved him into the front of the building he and his friends had been vandalizing—Prieto's Pasteleria, Tank noted blankly. The owners had recently hired two elves.

The human hit the wall with a satisfyingly heavy sound. He'd been too drunk or surprised to get his hands up, and when he spun around in shock, there was already blood streaming from his nose. His friends turned to look at him, then at Tank. Their heads went all the way back as Tank straightened.

"We aren't all delicate and tiny." Tank let his voice rumble and shake and took one stomping step forward. "If you little humans want to try to scare me, you are welcome to try."

A sound seemed to echo his words, like a snarl, and one of the human's eyes snapped to somewhere else in the shadowed street. His mouth fell open. Tank went for him first. He grabbed him by his hair and swung him into the car. He dropped like a stone and Tank rounded on the next one, as yet unbloodied. "Fee Fi Fo Fum," Tank recited in his face when the fool wouldn't move, and the man tightened his grip on the brick in his hand.

Tank laughed as the man swung, then caught the human's fist and squeezed his fingers against the brick until something cracked and the man howled. He fell to his knees before Tank let go. Bloody Nose was nowhere to be seen. He must have run. Tank turned to find him, then blinked to see him curled up on the ground, his hands at his stomach and chest. Blood was trickling from between his fingers.

Tank craned his neck to track the flash of movement above him, but there was nothing on the roof of the sweets and pastry shop that he could see. He returned his attention to the two remaining humans. The one he'd tossed against the car was back on his feet, although he seemed torn between defending himself and running away. Tank came forward and threw him to the sidewalk by a handful of his shirt. "Stay down." Tank snorted dismissively at him and the one clutching at his broken hand.

"Not much of a fight," he announced a moment later, and swept an assessing look over the storefront. Broken glass and probably some damage inside. The air smelled like spilled beer and a little like blood. No paint, so he stalked over to the car and punched the window to reach into the backseat, where of course there were cans of red spray paint and more beer. He grabbed a can of paint, shook it, and came around to the hood of the car.

He was dotting the *i* in "hysteria" when he heard a siren. The humans both stirred, glancing up in alarm.

"Consider yourselves lucky. If you'd hurt anyone, I wouldn't be leaving you to the cops." Tank tossed the can of paint in a trash can, then turned toward the noise of fast-approaching footsteps.

"Tank!" Simon ran up, breathless and unsteady. "Tank, you're… fine." Simon skidded to a stop and took in the scene—the three groaning men, the graffiti on the car, the damaged store front. He glanced up to Tank's face, then at all the lit windows and their silent audience. "We should go."

"The neighbors aren't going to tell." Tank was somehow as sure of that as he was that someone else out here had wanted him to take care of these assholes. But there was nothing in the dark, not even for his eyes to see. "And these sons of bitches are drunk."

"*Tank.*" Simon tugged at his sleeve, then gasped loudly and grabbed Tank's hand.

Punching through the window hadn't been the best idea.

Tank was bleeding, but all he could seem to feel were Simon's chilled little hands. Simon should have remembered to buy gloves.

"Pretty sure I told you to stay put," he remarked, flexing his fingers to check for breaks.

"Fuck off, you idiot," Simon hissed at him. "Now come on before the cops get here."

"You're confusing," Tank informed him, and noticed the throaty growl in his words. He coughed, but it didn't do much good. It hadn't been enough of a battle to get rid of his anger, although he was satisfied these humans would hesitate before returning to the quarter. "If they arrest me, go to the volunteers and get that human with the glasses for my lawyer."

Blue, red, and white flashes were closer. He hadn't expected such a fast reaction. The cops must have started car patrols in the old quarter. That had to be Calvin Parker's doing. More of the residents were coming to their windows, no longer so afraid to openly look at the disturbance. Tank stared at Simon, who remained concerned for him and kept trying to pull him away.

"They need to know they don't have to be so afraid," Tank murmured and put his hand between the cold metal of Simon's earring and his neck. Simon froze, not even breathing. Tank wondered how tight Simon's bow tie was and how constraining it felt. He wondered about the chain with the key Simon wore around his neck and how it would feel to have that chain in his hand. He wondered what Simon would do if Tank asked for—demanded—what he really wanted. Then Simon met his gaze, and Tank stopped thinking altogether for a while.

A police cruiser pulled up, followed by a plain car. Two uniforms came out of the cruiser and went over to the vandals. A tired-looking Parker emerged from the plain car, ignoring his crackling radio as he walked past the three on the ground. Tank finally pulled his hand away from Simon's warm skin. Simon made a small noise of complaint.

Parker considered the building, then the car, with no expression. "We need a bus?" he asked one of the officers, who mumbled something but then went to the car, presumably to call for an ambulance. "Are those *claw marks*?" Parker then wondered, without seeming to expect an answer. "All I need now is to deal with a werewolf. Christ, I need a smoke."

But he didn't light up. He came around to peer inside the car, then up at all the windows and the lights that were quickly turned off, before he approached Tank.

Simon leaned closer. Tank put his clean hand on his shoulder to reassure him.

Parker most likely noticed that too. "Looks like our vandals ran into some trouble," he remarked, making Simon tense.

Tank huffed a laugh. "Could have been worse."

"Yes, it could have." Parker had probably noted Tank's bleeding hand and any flecks of paint on his clothes. "But it wasn't. When they sober up, they might have something to say about their car, but I can't imagine anyone listening. It's their spray paint, after all."

"Oh yeah?" Tank wasn't surprised exactly, but he'd imagined at least one night behind bars before he made bail. Maybe a fine or a short sentence after that. Not this.

"Can't speak for everyone of course," Parker mused, "but as I said, I serve the community's interests."

"You did say that," Tank agreed, almost blankly.

"So we understand each other. You and your friend and me." Parker didn't look at Simon as he said that. Tank kept himself from glancing toward the rooftops, but only just. "Come on down to the station tomorrow, Krieger, in case anything else needs an explanation." Calvin Parker leveled a brief, serious look at him, then directed all of his remarkable attention to Simon. "You'll keep an eye on him, won't you, Mr. Mounier?"

He crooked a brief smile, then returned to his suspects while Simon frowned after him.

"He knows my name." Simon turned to Tank, who raised his hands.

"It wasn't me. The man somehow knows things." Tank protested his innocence, but Simon had already caught sight of Tank's injured knuckles, and took hold of his hand again.

Tank remembered everything he'd said to him in the moments before he'd rushed here and let out a small breath as he realized how very fucked he was. He had no clue what to say to make it better either. "You okay?" he settled on at last. "This wasn't so bad. I mean, I've done worse."

Simon tightened his mouth and took a long, deep breath. "You were yearning. I could hear your yearning, and it was for *me*." Stunned didn't begin to describe his tone. "You yearned, but you didn't ask because you are a big, scary, stupid, *stupid* troll."

“Huh?” Tank was familiar with Simon’s thin-ice voice of irritation, but not the way Simon was studying him. “You don’t need to read me. I already told you everything.”

“This isn’t reading.” Simon managed to sound furious while fussing over his wound. Tank decided he liked it. Then what Simon had said sank in, and he made an unintelligible sound.

Simon took another deep breath. “I’m tired. And you haven’t finished walking me home.”

“You want me to?” Tank’s voice jumped so high one of the cops turned to look.

Dark, fathomless eyes met his. “Have you already forgotten the way?”

Tank shook his head. For once he was smart enough to not say anything.

“Then come on.” Simon turned and began walking, Tank’s injured hand still in his.

TANK FOLLOWED Simon up three narrow flights of stairs and ducked through his doorway without a word. He could stand straight once inside, although he could touch the ceiling with no strain. The apartment wasn’t much. It opened into a kitchen from which Tank could see the living space, which was also Simon’s bedroom. Several bookshelves, crammed full of books and knickknacks, but neat, were scattered around the room. A small brown couch, draped in several brightly knitted afghans, was against one wall. The curtains looked hand-sewn but thick enough to keep out the cold, although Simon immediately released Tank’s hand to go to his radiator and check the temperature. He removed his coat despite the chill.

Tank studied the hanging baskets in the kitchen, the spotless countertops, and the loudly running refrigerator. Simon’s apartment had the same amount of color and patterns as a fairy’s space, but every project had been completed and put away when done.

Simon returned to the kitchen, scooting around Tank to turn on the oven. “It heats the place faster,” he explained as if embarrassed, but then stopped. “I could make something, if you’re hungry. Or, no, I should clean you up first.”

Like that decided him, Simon seemed to relax. He took hold of Tank's hand and led him to the sink, where he wet a towel and began to dab at the cuts.

Give an elf a task and they were happy. Tank stared as Simon picked out a few shards of glass he hadn't noticed and then fought the urge to swear when Simon put his hand under the tap. The cold water stung.

"You cook?" Without the glass in them, Tank's minor wounds would heal in no time. They weren't even that painful, but he thought Simon could use a distraction. And he was curious. Tank was always curious about Simon.

Simon grumbled at him without looking up. "Bartending isn't my life's dream or anything, Tank." He grabbed a new towel to dry Tank's knuckles, then held the towel there for a moment. "I've always cooked, but I've been trying to learn more. On weeknights I've been using the bar's kitchen to offer a few things. It's slow going with how I am, but so far it's been popular. And… I grew up thinking I was a not-quite elf. Most black beings in this country have no connection to their history, or each other. For years most of them didn't even know what they were, and they did their best to hide their differences in order to stay alive. Anyway." Simon seemed embarrassed by his show of emotion. "So, I've been trying to learn West African cooking too. I'm probably nothing like my ancestors, but it's been interesting, learning it all. Mami has helped. Sometimes I think she's ancient." He glanced up in sudden alarm. "Don't tell her I said that."

Tank smiled in genuine amusement and not as a threat. "Your secret is safe with me," he promised without looking away. Simon blinked at him a few times, then swallowed and lowered his attention to the towel and Tank's hand. He removed the towel and made a pleased sound to see the wounds had mostly stopped bleeding. Nonetheless, he held the towel against them again.

"I eat TV dinners." Tank felt like his breathing was too noticeable in the silence. Simon lifted his head, his pretty mouth open in confusion. Tank cleared his throat. "I meant, if you ever needed a guinea pig. For your cooking." Simon only stared at him, soft and wondering. Tank tugged his hand free. "Unless you wanted someone else. I know I'm just a grunt."

Simon had cleaned away most of the blood, and the bruises and scratches would disappear soon as well.

Simon wasn't done worrying. He snatched Tank's hand to study it one last time, holding it in both of his hands. He was larger than most elves, but he still made Tank hold his breath and remind himself to take care.

"I'd be happy to cook for you," Simon told him, quite formally. "If you were to ever come by the bar during the week, I could make you something."

"You need an escort home those nights too?" Tank asked hopefully, and wondered how he'd never noticed the way Simon stared at him when they were this close. Of course, he hadn't been this close for this long before. "What?"

"Your expression." Simon wrinkled his forehead, as though Tank was a mystery and not a hulking, obvious troll.

Tank had already told him everything. Yet speaking now made his stomach tense and sent shivers along his skin. "I like looking at you. I like that you're touching me. Pretty, regal Simon is touching me. Even when he knows how I feel about him."

Simon opened his eyes wide, then gave a toss of his head that sent his earring swinging. "Tank Krieger, you walked me home and possibly saved my life tonight. Or if not my life, the life of some person who might have been nearby the next time those humans went to trash a business. You—" Simon stopped there and swept a look over Tank's chest and shoulders. "Tank, you sit at my bar and you never ask me for anything."

He sounded like he wanted Tank to ask. Tank licked his lower lip and kind of thought his pounding heart and trembling limbs were laughable. But Simon regarded him steadily, so he made himself say something. "I really don't scare you?"

"Scare me?" Simon made an expression of disdain. "Those humans scared me. The college boys who come in looking for the being experience scare me. The way the humans are falling ill so fast scares me. You… you casually talk to the cops, Tank. And you speak to Mami like you're almost her equal when she's as strong as a dragon. People literally beg you to do what you want to them." He was breathing heavily. "You don't scare me, but maybe you should. You're powerful."

"I'm a garbage man." Tank knew Simon read people right most of the time, but Simon had to be confused now.

Simon reached out with one clean, slender hand and poked him hard in the shoulder. "You're a giant among beings, Tank, and I…

I…." Without finishing his sentence he leaned forward and threw himself at Tank with a desperate jump. He held tight to Tank's chest as he pressed their mouths together. His lips were parted, his breath damp. He slid to the ground before Tank could exhale. "I'm sorry," Simon exclaimed immediately. "But I—"

Tank placed two fingers over Simon's mouth, shutting him up in the gentlest of ways. Gentle felt strange after years of trying to forget it, but Tank liked the bottomless hunger in Simon's eyes for it. He hadn't realized that's what that endless dark was until Simon had kissed him. Tank was only a dumb troll after all. Some things took him a while.

With his fierce elf silent and hot with embarrassment, Tank felt free to slide his fingertips over his mouth and then over his cheek. Simon shivered but stood still while Tank explored the line of his jaw and then the side of his neck. The collar of Simon's shirt stood in Tank's way, but Tank didn't feel the need to remove it, not with the bow tie to tempt him. He tugged it experimentally, his finger thick between the bow and Simon's shirt. Simon made a startled, pleased noise.

He'd hidden this well, under all those buttons. Tank snarled to think of it but then wanted to kiss him as softly as a troll could when Simon frowned. Simon's fears were Tank's to vanquish now.

"Will you hurt me?" The question was like being buffeted by the winds at the bluffs along the coast, Simon's voice as thin as the ocean air.

"If you want." Tank couldn't take his eyes off him. In the bar Simon was deliberate and knowing, a wise queen bitch. Now he was stunned and quiet, barely holding himself still as Tank petted him.

"What about what you want?" Simon managed to maintain eye contact, but when Tank offered a smile, a shudder tore through him. He was breathing hard already.

"You asking?" Tank inched closer, studying the proud angle of Simon's chin and the vivid shock of his purple hair. "I want you." That was the short answer. Tank hadn't let himself think much about the rest. Now he did. Simon might be pierced in other places besides his ears. Tank could pull him forward by his suspenders and slide his hands behind his back. He could hold them there until Simon was aching to move, and all the while Tank could be fucking him slowly. That's it. Nothing against pain for pleasure, but watching Simon come undone would be the best thing he could imagine. "Lift your head," he growled finally, when Simon only shivered and waited.

"Like this?" Simon was uncertain and wonderful. Tank pressed a kiss to his forehead and burned for it. Stupid troll, trying to be a tender lover. But Simon let his eyes flutter closed as if he liked it.

Tank curled his fingers around the chain still hanging over Simon's collar from when Simon had let them into the apartment. He twisted the thin rope of silver links, pulling it taut, and nearly roared in satisfaction when Simon came in with it. "Yeah." The pool of heat inside Tank didn't feel like anger or lust. He raised his scraped hand and cupped Simon's head to tilt it back. "That's it, little man. Part your lips for me so I can kiss you."

The moment Simon did, with the faintest tremor of anticipation, Tank's heart stopped. Simon grabbed his jacket, clutching the leather in a way that was almost as adorable as the noises he made while Tank kissed him, again and again, a little bit harder each time. He wanted those lips swollen. He wanted those eyes wide open and dazed. He wanted Simon, all of him.

"If you had told me, I would have given you this." He spoke against Simon's mouth, then his temple and his neck. He released the chain, undid the buttons of Simon's shirt, and left it hanging from his shoulders, with the bow tie and suspenders in place despite how he'd removed the rest. His hands were too big, the actions felt rough, but Simon only breathed harder and pulled Tank closer. He sounded surprised, then hungry, when Tank's fingertips skated over his smooth skin, and when Tank found a nipple, unpierced, and scraped it with a fingernail, Simon fell against him. He was trembling and his eyes were wide.

"Tonight?" Simon murmured, with enough need to send Tank's hands down to his ass to haul him up. Simon released a shocked, worried sound as he glanced down to the floor below, but then he curled his arms around Tank's shoulders and allowed himself to be placed onto his countertop. He leaned into Tank. His weight was precious. It felt like trust. Tank was not going to let him down.

"No," Tank told him, as if his hands weren't itching to hold that chain again. "Not like that. You don't know yet about it all. And I want…." He had to force himself to pause and think of something other than his cock sliding into Simon's ass. "I want to take my time with you. See if I can get you to forget all about reading anything. No direction except the ones I give you."

Simon let out a startled gasp and held tighter to the collar of Tank's jacket. He nodded and exhaled noisily.

That was it. That was what Simon wanted from him. Tank could give it to him.

"Open your legs." Tank's body was wide. Simon grunted when Tank pushed between his thighs, but then groaned and scratched his fingernails through Tank's hair when Tank urged him back and kissed him. He was so good, openmouthed and pliant and moaning against Tank's lips. "Simon." Simon was Tank's only thought. "Simon."

"Tell me what to do." Simon was bossy and Tank bit him for it, gently tugging at his bottom lip even as he was palming Simon's dick through his pants. Simon was hard for him, for this. Simon had wanted this all along. Tank shouldn't be so lucky.

"Not tonight," Tank growled at him. Enough had happened tonight already. But he captured Simon's wrists easily and pulled them down to the counter. "Keep them there. Close your eyes while I touch you." Simon's bare skin was temptation. He shivered, but he closed his eyes. Tank was going to make him come and said as much. "I'm going to touch you and you're going to come, but not until I say so. Will that do?"

He didn't think he was leaving any bruises, but the heat inside him was brighter, hotter than anything from a fight or any club fucking. He opened Simon's pants and pulled out his cock.

Simon sounded like he was choking. "Tank. I've waited… I've wanted…." His hips were already leaving the counter. He still tried to argue for more. "You can't just tell me to—"

Tank snapped his teeth in his face. "I can and you will, won't you?"

Simon opened and closed his mouth. For a moment he looked at Tank, though Tank felt no desire to punish him. His eyes were shiny. His lips ready for another kiss. All he had to do was say yes.

"It's not safe. With me it might not be safe. You have to be careful." Of all the things Tank had thought Simon might say, this was the most unexpected, and maybe the only thing that could have made Tank lean forward to kiss that mouth anyway. It was his place now, his right, to fight for Simon and protect him. He nodded so Simon could shut his pretty eyes again and focus only on what he was feeling.

"No reading," Tank bit out against Simon's throat, then again under his bow tie. "You feel this?" He knew Simon did from how he shook. He began to slowly jack Simon's cock while their faces were still close together. He got to taste Simon's first shocked inhale.

"Say yes." Tank meant it for an order, but it was low and careful. "Say you'll come when I tell you. Tell me you're mine, and I'll take care of you. Simon." Tank breathed the name and felt foolish. "Simon." He put his other hand to Simon's thigh, then moved it up to his chest, to the chain and then that bow tie. He licked at Simon's mouth and denied him a kiss, once and then again, until Simon whined in the most incredible way. But he kept his eyes closed.

He pushed up his hips again, and Tank held him down, leaving him to writhe.

Simon frowned blindly but then leaned forward to bury his head against Tank's shoulder. His hands were still at the counter. His breath was fast. "The others…." He held out, stubborn and fierce as ever. "Am I as good as them? Please, I've waited…."

Tank had never been so hard or so hot. "No others. Me for you. Say it." He felt huge and delighted in it, towering over Simon in Simon's kitchen, panting above Simon's head while he squeezed Simon's cock and drove him crazy.

"I don't know what to do." Simon was a thousand breathless fears. Tank was going to crush them all.

He snarled. "Keep going." He ran his lips along the shaved part of Simon's hair. "Keep going," he ordered quietly, as if Simon weren't whimpering and clinging to him. "Say yes."

Simon exhaled into his shoulder. "Yes," he said, furious and desperate before he whispered the rest. "Yes. Me for you."

Tank reached down to his painfully tight jeans and freed his cock. He spat onto his hand and then gripped them both firmly. Simon jerked at the sensation and then melted against him. He was breathing Tank's name, urgent and soft.

"As good as them…." Tank chided him as gently as he could. "You think any of them comes apart like you?"

Simon's hands finally left the counter. He grabbed desperately at Tank's leather jacket and gulped air.

"Not until I tell you," Tank stressed, despite being pleased as all get-out, and Simon nodded, although his hold on Tank was almost frantic.

Simon's throat with his buttoned collar and bow tie was beautiful. He rocked forward with increasing strength, but the only sounds that left him now were pleadings. He grasped at Tank's shoulders like a hungry kitten but put his head back when Tank reached for the chain with his key on it. A stupid, scary troll didn't deserve anything so amazing. Tank wanted to make him wait until he was on the edge of pain. He wanted him to come now. He pulled on the chain as lightly as he could and released his own cock to cup and squeeze Simon's balls. He stroked him, rough and then gently, again and again, and though Simon bit his lip, when he leaned back and opened his eyes, his gaze was wide and dark.

"No seeing. No reading. No thinking. Only what I tell you when we're like this." Tank let go of the chain to pull Simon flush against him. He worked the head of Simon's cock with his thumb until Simon was shaking. "That's what you want." Tank wasn't asking, but Simon answered him with a weak, perfect cry. Tank trembled too as he bent his head. "Then let me watch you come," he demanded with his lips over Simon's ear and then heard himself minutes later, still whispering encouragement as Simon caught his breath. Simon was good. Simon took direction because he was so good. The honor was Tank's.

He finished himself off while Simon was quiet and still in his arms. He came into his hand and then wiped it on an already stained dish towel. Simon protested then, a small sound, and opened his eyes. The exhausted pleasure in them made Tank stand tall. Then Simon shivered, apparently cold with Tank no longer so close to him, and Tank hunched down around him again.

The corner of Simon's mouth twitched upward, then downward. "I liked it. Was that… was I—"

Tank kissed him to keep that misty voice and all its sadness and worry and shame away. Simon put both hands in his hair and murmured against his mouth anyway. But when Tank eased off, all he said was "Tank," and then "I'm tired."

Tank had him in his arms and across the apartment in seconds. He was such a dumbass. Too excited to get what he wanted to take the care he should. However, once he sat Simon on top of his bed, Simon lay down on his back and pulled at his bow tie. It slid open with a sound that nearly got Tank hard again.

He blinked and went to the couch to grab an afghan. "If you're cold," he explained, as though Simon didn't have his pants and boots on. They both did. "You want something to eat?"

"No." Simon took a while to speak. "But, the oven."

Tank nodded and dipped into the kitchen to turn off the oven. Then he returned to stand like a lump at the foot of the bed. Simon, rumpled and half-dressed, stared back at him. "Was kind of worried about your cock," Simon remarked out of nowhere, slurring his words. "But I think I can handle that."

Tank glanced down at his cock, soft now but still a reasonable size for a troll of his stature. He supposed, if he was an elf, even a taller than usual elf, he would have worried about it too.

"You want that?" He was stupid, but words said in passion weren't always real. "You want me again?"

Simon snorted and then reached up to take hold of the thin chain at his neck like Tank had done. He sighed and nodded.

Tank slid onto the mattress to touch him and ignored the creak as the small bed took his weight.

"Better than the radiator," Simon all but purred when Tank stroked his cheek, then shut his eyes. He trusted Tank to wipe up the spunk on his stomach and pull away his shirt, the bow tie too. Tank removed his shoes, then tugged the afghan up over him. He was as delicate as any fucking fairy out there.

"I should probably…." Tank fought to say the words. "I should probably go."

Simon's face twisted. Tank noticed his earring pressing into his cheek where he'd snuggled into his pillow, so he moved the earring to the side. He gave a start when Simon grabbed his wrist. "Ask." Simon kept his eyes shut tight. "Ask, Tank."

"Simon…." Tank was so slow sometimes. "Am I your one thing?"

"You're not a thing," Simon returned immediately, then opened eyes bright with tears.

Tank settled over him on his hands and knees. "Fuck," he said, with feeling, and put his hand to Simon's cheek. He thumbed at the trails of salt. "Shit. No one should cry over me. Especially not you. My Simon."

Simple, silly words, but they made Simon smile. "My Tank," he answered, and even while crying, he managed to make Tank feel like the slowest goddamn creature alive. Fuck, even Calvin Parker had seen how Simon felt about him.

Tank didn't feel any sting at his eyes, but his cheeks were burning, like all the heat in his body was coming out through his skin. Trolls didn't glow, but he felt like he was, and grinned for it.

"This kind of thing still happens," he murmured in awe. "This kind of thing happens to us, even with everything." For one strange, heady moment, Tank wanted to sing, and he'd never sung in his life. He lowered himself carefully down to lie next to Simon and was still caught off guard by Simon slowly curling up against his chest.

THE FOG raced in early on Sunday night, bringing freezing air with it that signaled winter had finally arrived in Los Cerros. Tank didn't mind, although he turned his collar up against the cold. He'd walked from the precinct down to the village that afternoon, stopping only for coffee to warm him up as he'd prowled the stores.

He got catcalls from more than one fairy, but most of them only winked at him. The village and its spillover into the old barrio were not large areas, and word traveled fast. The clubs might not have heard yet, but they'd been built to keep out the rest of the world. Tank passed them with barely a glance anyway. The posters were hard to miss, but the mood of the neighborhood remained lighter with the recent vandals in jail.

He liked that. Nothing was over. They still had shit to deal with and way too many humans who needed care, but today at least, everyone's hearts were a little lighter.

Parker had shrugged, his closed-off expression going even more blank than usual. Tank was certain it was an act. No one who made fairies buzz and who continued to pretend that Tank hadn't beaten the crap out of those humans last night could be that unaffected.

The guy was kind of a hero, even if he'd never call himself that. Which was fucking stupid, considering he was going to be out there every night until there was nobody left who needed protection.

Tank clenched a fist at the thought, and glanced around misty streets as he headed toward Mami's. He had no idea what he'd expected to see there on a Sunday night, but it wasn't the crowd lined up by the door. The white splotch of paint hadn't been redone to match the rest of the wall yet, but everyone had returned anyway.

He hadn't thought a few drunk idiots getting hauled in by the human cops would make that much of a difference, but Parker had been right about that too, he guessed. He hoped he kept it up. Tank would hate to have to stand against him.

No, that was a lie. Tank would love it. That sounded like a good fight.

He bypassed the line and approached Rawlins, who stopped in the middle of accepting a candy cane from a proudly pregnant fairy to stare at him in astonishment.

"Yeah, yeah, I'm never here on Sundays." Tank dropped some money in the donation bin. "He here? What's the mood?"

Rawlins lifted both eyebrows, then stuck the candy cane in his mouth. "Don't tell me you're scared," he mumbled around the stick of peppermint, then waved him and the fairy in.

"I'm checking on things," Tank growled at him and the listening fairy, then stomped past both of them. Dancing wouldn't really begin until later, but so many people had returned to Mami's that a lot of them were standing and talking on the dance floor. Tank huffed when they didn't get out of his way fast enough, and he refused to acknowledge the way they then turned to look at him.

"You'd think I wasn't Tank the Troll or something," he grumbled as he sank into his seat, which had been mysteriously left empty despite the limited space. Dahlia smirked at him without bothering to try to take his order. Tank scowled at her then turned toward the other end of the bar.

Simon was glowering at someone who had tried to touch him to get his attention when he was in the middle of replacing a bottle of whiskey on the back shelf. He'd chosen a long dress shirt, with rolled-up sleeves and another bow tie tight at his neck. Outside of that, he'd left his silver chain with its single key to dangle loosely over his chest.

Tank let out a rough sound at that, and Simon raised his head. The regal tilt of his chin gave no hint that his cheeks were probably hot with embarrassment right now. Tank had felt that against his palm last night and again that morning before Simon had made him breakfast.

He was the luckiest fucking troll in the world.

"Tank, darling!" Mami took up the space next to him as though no one else was sitting there. In fact, the pixy on that seat moved with barely a raised eyebrow. Mami held up her hand to signal to one of her bartenders and smiled at Tank. "You grace us with your presence on a Sunday? So the rumors are true."

Simon had said Mami was never going to let him hear the end of it. Tank had found it hard to believe that Mami had been matchmaking in the middle of all this, but he was beginning to realize that nothing was going to keep Mami from anything.

He swallowed as he met her eyes, which were almost exactly like a dragon's now that he thought about it. He should have trusted Simon's description of her more.

"Mami," he greeted her in return, then jerked his head toward Simon. "I thought I might walk him home."

"You work in the morning." Simon arrived with a protest and Mami's drink. He handed it to her with grace and exchanged a look with her that ended with Simon fidgeting with his dish towel. Then he turned to Tank. "That would be nice."

"I really don't need the sleep." Tank truly didn't, any more than the fairies did, but that wasn't going to be enough to make Simon happy. "And I want to," he added, and appreciated how Mami sighed and patted his arm.

"Wonderful," she approved, and Tank got the impression that Simon's face was definitely hot to the touch. "At last, my darlings," she cooed at both of them, then sipped her drink and addressed Simon. "You can leave at midnight if you want. We should be slower by then, and the mood is good." She turned back to Tank. "Thank you for this, Tank. You're our hero."

Tank froze, because hellfire, what was he supposed to say to that? He liked a fight, that was all.

But as he opened his mouth, he caught sight of Simon's small, pleased nod, and wisely shut himself up. Mami patted him again, like this was also a good thing Tank had done, then left with her drink.

Simon met his stare, then glared at a call from down the bar and disappeared in that direction. He put his hands to his face as another elf placed his order, as though Simon *was* burning up. Tank didn't blame him. He was warm too, blazing hot in fact.

Simon poured out a beer and a soda for the elf, rang him up, and pocketed the change before making his way to Tank. "You're staring," he pointed out, cool as anything even though Tank was getting him flushed.

Tank grinned like a loon. "I like looking at you."

Simon yanked a dish towel from his shoulder and slapped it down on the bar. Tank wasn't fooled; Simon's eyes were fixed on him and hungry for every detail. "If you had said something like that before, we wouldn't have spent months on opposite sides of this bar."

They still were on opposite sides of the bar. But Simon was working, so Tank resisted the urge to point that out. He had to ease Simon into awful troll humor.

Tank placed his hands on the bar, his blood singing at the challenge between them. "You didn't say anything either."

Simon had been afraid. So had Tank, shameful as it was to admit it.

Simon looked him over, his gaze lingering on Tank's mouth before he darted it away. "That isn't what I do, Tank," he reminded Tank in a voice like falling leaves, then sighed heavily when someone at the end of the bar called for the bartender.

Tank watched him go, watched him listen for a long time, then close his eyes and explain something. He took care as he did it, wrinkling his brow as if his advice wasn't nice but it was all he had. And when he was done, he turned away from the bar and grabbed several bottles.

He measured and added ice and shook the whole thing, then added a slice of pineapple and a cherry with the stem attached to the edge of a tall, frosty glass. He handed it over, accepted the generous tip that he deserved, then appeared before Tank again.

"You ready to order?" His eyes were so pretty Tank stared at his shirt to avoid doing something foolish. Of course, that allowed him to gaze longingly at the silver chain at Simon's neck.

He glanced at Simon's face. "You've still never given me direction."

"You still haven't asked for any." The argument was different when Tank had to hide a smile and Simon gave a delicately aroused shiver.

Tank wanted to touch him. "I was here every Friday and Saturday night. Obviously I was looking for something."

Simon gave him a narrow-eyed look and then turned to grab some more bottles. He began mixing a drink without remarking on what

Tank had said. He took a step to grab more of the pineapple but stopped when Tank reached out and gave his apron strings a tug. Tank didn't put enough force in it to keep Simon where he was; nonetheless Simon held still and then twisted to stare at him.

He exhaled, an interested sound that made Tank's heart beat faster, and then continued on his way. He grabbed a slice of pineapple and a glass, and returned to the spot in front of Tank as he worked.

"I should have slapped your hand," Simon said, quite primly for someone with a mohawk, and Tank choked out a gruff sound that was more encouraging than anything else. Simon brought his gaze up; his eyes were dark and deep.

Tank's mouth unexpectedly went dry. He leaned forward. "When we figure out how to be safest, I am going to make you beg. I'll give you all the direction you need. Where to touch and when to use your mouth and when to wait, until you're making those tiny, pleading whimpers I already like so much." Simon flattened his hand on the bar and flicked a look up at him. Tank let his voice get rough. "But I'm not going to give you my cock until you can barely think, and even then I'll only give you the tip. You'll have been waiting so long that your eyes will roll back and you'll whisper my name because it's the only thing you can think about, stretched open but unable to get off, unable to do anything but beg me. And then—"

"Tank!" Simon interrupted him, scandalized but breathing heavily.

"You're going to beg until your voice is raw, and then I'll fuck you till you come," Tank finished, breathing harder himself despite his grin. "That's what I fucking want."

Simon licked the edge of his mouth and then his soft lower lip. "Okay," he agreed, and slid his hand down the length of the chain at his neck before letting it go. He frowned curiously upward. "Do you think that singer will be out tonight when you walk me home?"

"I hope so." Tank had the feeling there was a dumb, punch-drunk expression on his face. He didn't care. The streets would be dark and cold, but he was going to be with Simon, and if they were lucky, they would hear something beautiful before he took Simon home.

Simon finished the drink, then focused on Tank with all his not-elf magic. "Is me begging for you *all* you really want, Tank?"

He tapped the glass.

The bottle of Everclear was at the ready. Tank stared at it, then at Simon, and then at the garnish on that big, pink drink. He sighed and ducked his head. "I'd also like something with cherries in it," he admitted, and Simon placed the drink neatly in front of him.

"Good boy," Simon praised him, with perhaps more of a trollish sense of humor than Tank had given him credit for.

Tank looked at him, then pulled the glass closer while Simon put the other bottle away. He set his money on the counter, and sighed again when Simon didn't keep the change. "But—"

"You are a giant among men, but you are the one person I won't accept money from." Simon didn't turn around to answer. "You are not any other customer, Tank."

Tank grumbled at him in something between annoyance and pleasure and then took a sugary, fruity sip. "Clarence," he mumbled, and gnashed the cherry between his teeth. Simon made him feel like he could have anything, and it was a new, and uncomfortable, feeling.

"What?" Simon angled his head as though he hadn't heard Tank right.

Tank lowered his gaze. "My name. Is Clarence." He drained the entire glass in one go and winced at the cold of it. Other than that he liked it. This drink wouldn't get him drunk, but it was pretty good. He wondered about the green, minty-smelling ones while Simon studied him. Then he acted like the tough, scary goddamn troll he was and looked up again.

Simon was pleased despite his smug sniff. "About time," he allowed, then came closer. He smiled in perfect understanding. "You told me your name. Because you want me to know, and… and so that when I beg you, I will call you Clarence. I will be the only one to call you that." He was some kind of mind reader. He was incredible, and he was going to moan the name until he lost his voice. His quirked eyebrow said he knew that too. But his quick puffs of breath said he was interested in the idea. "Stay, okay?" Simon requested in the next moment, then went off to take some drink orders.

Simon didn't mind knowing Tank's real name. Simon wouldn't even mind saying it. Tank was truly the luckiest troll in the whole goddamn world.

Tank settled in to watch him and keep an eye on the crowd. He patted his pocket, and the fairy-knitted gloves he'd bought for Simon, then ordered another pink thing from Dahlia, who barely stared at the sight of the huge troll with the fruity drink in his hands.

He grinned at her and anyone else who gave his drink the stink eye. Tank the Troll was in love, and he could face anything, be it cops or humans or fear itself, or a complicated, frosty drink that tasted like cherries. Tank was in love and Simon was in love with him, and that kind of thing happened, even to those like them, even with everything else.

Of course, if anyone or anything tried to take that from him or anyone else here, he'd grind their bones to make his bread. It would be his very great pleasure.

The Imp and Mr. Sunshine

2005

RENNET SAUNTERED into City Hall with the smell of dynamite lingering in his hair and an excited twitch in his tail. Los Cerros City Hall wasn't as much one building as it was a complex of buildings close to the center of town, with the library and post office across the street, the courthouse at the corner, the police station next to that, and a collection of government offices in the middle. The clock above the courthouse was striking three, which meant it was coffee break time. In the'80s and '90s that hadn't meant much, but now it meant that many City Hall employees wandered outside to a nearby coffee shop or to the small cart by the police station.

Daryl, the security guard at the desk by the entrance, was watching a basketball game on one of his monitors and holding a steaming cup of tea. Because coffee break time put Rennet in such a good mood, he considered warning Daryl to keep his cup of tea level. But then Rennet figured Daryl should have been guarding the place, not watching the game, so he said nothing. He grinned a little when he heard a splash and a string of profanity as the cup finally tipped, and turned in time to see Daryl jump out of his seat to grab some paper towels. Daryl spared Rennet a dirty look, as though Rennet was responsible for his mishap, and though Rennet knew himself to be innocent—well, semi-innocent—he grinned wider at him, showing the nubby, ineffectual fangs that added to his diabolic appearance.

Daryl almost tripped backward in his haste to distance himself from Rennet, which was insulting, but at least he didn't cross himself as he did it. Most of the humans in town didn't bother with that gesture in Rennet's presence anymore, or with the one they thought would ward off the evil eye—which wouldn't have worked even if imps had been the cause of it.

Most humans, at least the ones in this town full of beings, seemed to have finally accepted on some level that imps were more closely related to fairies than to demons, but just because the humans didn't think Rennet was after their souls didn't mean they were comfortable with him hanging around. These days Los Cerros prided itself on being a liberal town, tolerant of its beings, but the truth was, if you weren't a fairy, the humans didn't know what to do with you. Dragons were revered from a distance, elves were useful if strange, demons good for dirty work, werewolves feared but lusted after, and imps, well, imps were imps. Untrustworthy, malicious, and most of all, ugly.

Rennet dusted some traces of dirt from his shoulders and shook out his wings behind him, leaving more dirt as well as some wood chips to fall to the floor. His wings would be too wide to fit in the hallway when unfolded to their full span, so he tucked them against his back as he headed toward the office of the deputy mayor. The skin of his wings was sensitive, and he could feel grit rubbing at the delicate membrane. He was suddenly aware that he probably should have showered before coming here, but it was too late to turn around now.

Margery looked up from her desk at his approach, and her heavily made-up eyes widened behind her glasses. Margery was maybe twenty-five, young for her job, but more than capable, despite what most thought when meeting her. She was not only young, but had a love of spangled, low-cut tops and big earrings. The intern who had never left, she worked as secretary to the big boss man—not the mayor. Everyone knew the mayor wasn't the one running the town. She looked Rennet over slowly, then wrinkled her nose the tiniest bit before shaking her head in disapproval.

She glanced at the watch on her wrist in the next second before sighing. She pointed to the bank of chairs against the opposite wall, where a nervous white man in a suit was already sitting. Rennet hopped up into the seat next to the stranger and perched there, looking, he imagined, like a grinning gargoyle come to life.

It wasn't far from the truth. Imps had the build of fairies but on a slightly smaller, yet more intimidating scale, which meant they were lean with large wings on their backs. But the similarities ended there. Imps were capable of sustained flight and so had thicker muscle to support their heavier wing structure. Imps also, for whatever reason, did not possess the variety of colors that fairies did. Fairies were only slightly more sparkly than one of those human boy bands that were currently so popular.

Rennet's hair was one color—brown, a couple of shades darker than his skin. Mud brown, some said, though mud didn't have hints of red in it, like he'd been formed from rich river clay. Neither was he delicate. His wings resembled a bat's more than a butterfly's, and his tail was something unique to imps, long and flexible and ending in a point. The tail had a wicked mind of its own most of the time, but for now it was curled around his side as he considered the stranger next to him. The man was probably someone asking for something—a new stop sign, a crosswalk, a talk with the licensing board. People always came to this office to ask for things. Los Cerros's deputy mayor was very in demand, probably because he had a way of making things happen that was almost magic.

It was a shame that the humans who didn't think magic was outright evil tended to think of magic as something easy, and not something that required work and sacrifice and cleverness. Any human magic worker could have told them that practicing magic was like practicing medicine, or rocket science, or any other specialized field, but instead they chose to believe the movies.

Rennet made a disappointed noise at the thought. The man next to him flinched as if startled, then cautiously peered at Rennet. Rennet looked back, giving the man plenty of time to notice his lack of a shirt and the layer of dirt that coated him. That was in his first glance. In his second, he probably noted Rennet's smeared eyeliner and the tousled mess of his hair, the collection of spiked bracelets at his wrists and his tight, ripped jeans. Of course, he would not have missed what Rennet was. That went without saying.

The man swallowed.

Rennet reached out and pointed to the man's very respectable necktie. "Got a little something here," he observed, then flicked the man's nose when he looked down. Margery made a noise, the kind mothers made when their kids were being unruly. Rennet ignored it, at least until the guy gave him a nervous smile and tried to scoot unobtrusively to the other side of his chair.

"Aw, I was being friendly," Rennet exclaimed in dismay, not really too upset, since he'd expected those results. Margery pushed out her red, red lips at him. Rennet stared back at her with his red, red eyes and was secretly delighted when she remained unimpressed. "I'm kidding." Rennet turned back to the stranger with a small bounce. He glanced at the closed door and suppressed a sigh before moving on. "No, you look good. Not nervous at all. Whatever anyone says, you totally have a chin."

"Rennet." Margery had a wonderful mouth, a beautiful figure, and absolutely zero tolerance for Rennet's shenanigans. Under different circumstances, he would have worshipped her. As it was, with his heart quite safe, he made a rude gesture at his favorite toothsome wench. It was a gesture a British airman had taught him decades ago. Margery snapped her fingers at him and pointed to another chair.

Rennet slid his ass over the arm of his chair into the new one, leaving his feet and his tail hanging in the air. He jerked a thumb at the stranger. The guy was skinny and sweaty and flushing with color. He appeared harmless, but Rennet had a bad feeling. "Who is this guy, Margery?"

At the question, the guy unexpectedly lifted what passed for his chin. "Who are you?" It probably took all the balls he had to ask. Rennet would have respected that, if he'd cared to.

"I'm Rennet the Imp." Rennet angled his head to stare at the room upside down for a moment. He didn't want to see the confusion on the man's face. Humans never knew what to make of his name. After a moment or two, he looked back up with a smile on his face, his tongue at his little teeth out of habit more than in an attempt to intimidate. It wasn't like the fangs could do much; they weren't even sharp.

The man didn't seem as confused as he had a second ago, though he was still pulled as far away from Rennet as he could possibly get.

"I know that name," the man remarked with a frown. "You work with the police sometimes, don't you?"

Rennet dusted some more dirt off his shoulder. "Yeah, well. I'm good at blowing shit up, and sometimes they like me to help out with training." He didn't say with what; he assumed it wasn't necessary. The imps who survived childhood lived a long time and tended to find or make conflict; that meant most of them had served as soldiers at one time or another. If you wanted to increase someone's chances of survival, you had him or her spar with something bigger or stronger, or, in the case of an imp, stranger and not above using dirty tricks. Los Cerros had a fairly low crime rate for a town its size, but its police department liked to be prepared. Maybe it was because so many beings had congregated here in the last few decades.

He considered how long it had been since he'd gotten to kick a little ass, then licked at his teeth again. "Mostly I do odds and ends for people around town." People rarely asked Rennet to fix anything, but he was very good at pest control, demolition, finding the source of the drain blockage that no one else could find, that sort of thing. Occasionally people approached him wanting revenge on someone, a hex or two, as if that was how it worked, as if Rennet was for sale or some kind of human worker of magic.

But at his words, the man suddenly leaned forward for the first time. He reached in his pocket and pulled out a little tape recorder, although he didn't turn it on. "So what's your business with The Incredible Unflappable?"

He didn't finish the nickname. He didn't have to. Everyone in town called the deputy mayor "The Incredible Unflappable Mr. Sunshine" behind his back. The man had certainly earned the nickname. Anything, no matter what the level of crisis or importance, was taken with the same sangfroid and listened to with the same careful attention. Once or twice The Incredible Unflappable had even been known to smile during a moment when anyone else would have been tearing out their hair. It both fascinated and unnerved people, being and nonbeing alike.

Rennet considered the nosy newcomer and the emphasis in the question, but forgot about it the moment the door to the inner office opened. He jumped to his feet, and the other guy followed suit, only to flail and fall forward onto his hands and knees. His tape recorder hit the ground too, and broke into several pieces.

It looked like his shoelaces had knotted together. Rennet had no idea how that had happened, not that he ever really did. Sometimes these things just happened, and those times tended to be when Rennet was around. He couldn't help that.

All the same, however, he curled his tail around his leg and kept it there as he raised his head.

John stared back at him, hardly taking notice of the man on the floor between them gathering up the pieces of his recorder, though of course he had. John noticed everything, even if it didn't seem like he did at the time. For all that he seemed bland and calm and harmless,

John was pretty fond of springing traps on unsuspecting idiots. Every time he did it, Rennet wanted to come on his face as a reward.

"Rennet." John managed to sound surprised without appearing surprised. His phone sex skills would have been amazing if he'd ever gone into that field. Unfortunately for Rennet, John Summers had gone into the respectable, if cutthroat, field of local government, so Rennet would probably never get to experience being brought to orgasm by his dry, faintly curious voice alone. "It's been a while. I didn't expect to see you today."

John turned up one corner of his mouth in a smile that made Rennet smile back without thinking. John had curved lips and even white teeth. He had skin that tanned in the summertime but remained pale the rest of the year. His glasses were thick, black, and practical, the eyes behind them hazel and unremarkable. He was tall and his shoulders were broad, but his brown hair was thinning on top. Overall he was extraordinarily plain for a human, but that did not stop humans and beings alike from wanting him.

Rennet had to take a moment to remember his own name and then to make himself respond in American English. "Well, I was in the neighborhood. Just finished a job. Thought I'd stop by." He was aware that he sounded like an idiot spewing out disconnected sentence fragments.

Thankfully John only inclined his head slightly in his direction. "I heard the explosion. I thought it might be your doing."

"Tree stump." Rennet shrugged. He could have *not* used dynamite to blast out the stump, but what was the fun of that? "You heard that? I thought you were at Seelie Court today?" Not that Rennet was stalking the deputy mayor, of *course* not. There had been a snippet on the news about a street festival for the fairies, as though every day weren't a festival with fairies, and the news reporter had said the city council would be attending.

"Just got back. It was… eventful." John looked Rennet over, then reached out to wipe something from Rennet's jaw without explaining what he meant by *eventful*. "I have an appointment in a few minutes, and a budget meeting before my dinner tonight, but I thought I might take a break for some coffee. Would you like some?"

He was unfailingly polite about it; he always was. Rennet tried not to nod his head too obviously or to glower when John finally acknowledged the man on the floor, helped him to his feet, and offered him coffee as well. A shameless coffee addict, John kept a pricey espresso machine behind and to the side of Margery's desk, though Margery never touched it. As far as Rennet knew, only John was allowed to. He set about preparing several tiny cups, including one for his loyal secretary, who accepted it as her due.

"Eventful?" Rennet cleared his throat to ask. There were no traces of fairy glitter on John's suit and tie, but there wouldn't be, and Rennet was crazy to have looked for it. Knowing that didn't keep him from peering closer. The suit was rumpled, but when wasn't it? John lived in a suit. The cloth wasn't too expensive, but he had them tailored to fit. Rennet swept his gaze down John's back and over his ass, then raised his eyes in time to meet John's inquisitive stare. "I don't care," Rennet said in response to the silent question of how he wanted his fancy Italian coffee today. Then John came over to hand him his cup and, probably, to ensure that Rennet didn't spill it on the stranger without a name.

"*Very* eventful," John answered blandly, though with another long look at Rennet that was more confusing than anything else. John turned to Margery. She got an espresso with a hint of nondairy creamer that left it almost the exact color of her skin. Rennet got his black and earthy and unsweetened. He drank it boiling hot, and stared down at the interloper over the edge of his oh so breakable tiny cup.

"How's my evening look?" John finally got his own espresso, black as well, and blew on it while discussing his schedule with Margery. Rennet perked up but was stopped from saying anything when the stranger continued to watch him. Margery, oddly enough, was watching him too.

"You'll be late, but you'll make it," she replied. She looked stern, as if Rennet was up to something when he wasn't.

"Late for what?" the other guy asked.

Rennet put down his empty cup and waved at him. "Who *is* this guy, Margery?"

"Reginald Campbell, reporter for *The Star*," Margery informed him in a tone that said Rennet should have known that.

Rennet held up his hands. "Never trust a Campbell," he remarked and grinned. "As someone once told me."

“Someone once told me that you were the enforcer of Mr. Summers’s political will, Mr. Rennet. You should consider the source of your information,” Campbell the reporter snapped back, sweating but getting braver. Rennet stared at him, then directed a look over at John. John was calm, even smiling faintly, which could have meant anything. But he wasn’t intervening to shut Rennet up, so after a long minute, Rennet arched his eyebrows.

“Just Rennet,” he corrected the reporter, in case this was on the record. “Rennet the *Imp*. What kind of idiot would hire an imp for matters of a delicate nature? I’m an embodiment of chaos, asshole. I don’t do good or evil. Didn’t you learn this in school?”

“Asshole seems harsh, Rennet,” John commented, taking his empty cup and setting it next to the espresso machine. Rennet would need at least two shots to feel any effects from the caffeine. John removed his jacket and rolled up his sleeves before preparing a second cup, just for Rennet.

“See?” Rennet continued with his mouth dry, trying not to stare at John’s forearms. “Sorry about the asshole thing, but you honestly think I take orders from this guy?”

Margery coughed around her sip of espresso.

“Then why are you here?” Campbell demanded nosily and took his first swallow of his drink. Rennet widened his eyes in innocence a second before Campbell swore and spat out his hot espresso. Campbell looked pained; he must have burned his tongue. Life was a bitch like that.

Rennet couldn’t help a small look toward John. John had his eye on him and a little furrow in his brow. Rennet tried to pat the reporter sympathetically on the shoulder, but John’s forehead wrinkle remained.

“Are you two friends?” Campbell lisped a moment later, swatting Rennet’s hand away from him. He looked horrified that Rennet had touched him at all, and turned toward John.

John offered him a faint smile and drank his coffee.

John shouldn’t do things like that, shouldn’t stand aloof and patient and unreadable with Rennet anxious in front of him. There was no telling what Rennet might do when he felt like this, even when he was trying to behave. A part of Rennet suddenly wondered if he *was* the enforcer of John’s political will, or if the only reason he wasn’t was because of John’s tactful silences around him. Perhaps John had a reason for often remaining silent in his presence, and that reason was to protect his political opponents. Rennet had no control over himself in some regards, and unlike most humans, John knew that. One off the cuff remark from John might set certain events in motion.

Rennet wasn't sure whether to be grateful for John's silence or annoyed, but the thought of himself as John's enforcer, of John using him, made him breathe a little harder.

Then he remembered how threatened some humans could be about beings and humans working together, even when it was only as friends. Times were different now, they claimed, but Rennet had a good memory. He wasn't about to risk anything.

"I do work around Mr. Summers's house. He's my boss." Rennet glanced around the room. John let out a disappointed sigh, and Rennet turned to him in confusion. His face felt unusually warm when John handed him his second cup and their fingers touched.

"Oh." Campbell made a disgruntled face, as if the truth was boring and not one of the most destructive forces on Earth. "You have an imp for a handyman? That doesn't seem like a good idea, no offense."

Rennet thought about saying "None taken." He narrowed his eyes instead, letting the threat hang in the air.

"*Ordo ab chao*," John interrupted Rennet's badass moment. "Out of chaos comes order. Compared to a budget meeting, Rennet is"—John glanced down, and Rennet didn't get the chance to duck away from that careful look—"invigorating."

Rennet swallowed dryly, scarcely remembering to blink for the time that John held his gaze.

"They say you seem to thrive in a crisis," Campbell interrupted. When the sound of his voice made John look away, Rennet turned on Campbell. Campbell seemed startled to be on the receiving end of a glare but didn't stop talking. "Imps are related to fairies, aren't they?"

"Oh for fuck's sake!" Rennet let out a small explosion, which was only fair since he'd contained the last one. His espresso, and the tiny cup with it, flew in all directions, staining shirts, soaking papers on Margery's desk. Humans yelped in surprise and mild pain over the sound of his rant. "Fairies! It's all anyone cares about, with their pretty little wings and their sparkle and their grabby hands!"

The truth was, Rennet had been glued to every second of that brief news segment, had seen naked and half-naked fairies throwing themselves at John, all of them, no doubt, curious, and dying to be the one to get a reaction from The Incredible Unflappable. John hadn't welcomed any of their attentions, but he'd hardly seemed to mind them either. Other people might not have seen the pink tint to his cheeks, but other people didn't watch John like Rennet did. Other people didn't know fairies like Rennet did.

"Rennet." John didn't raise his voice, but Rennet grabbed John's tie of pale rose-colored silk and started to dab at the spreading coffee stains on John's collared shirt. The shirt was white with tiny pink pinstripes, and it would have to be washed immediately if John didn't want it to be ruined. Rennet released a sound of frustration and gave John his tie back. John quietly requested Margery stop by the dry cleaners for him after work. He didn't even have the grace to act surprised that he was now covered in Rennet's espresso.

"I didn't mean to do that," Rennet exclaimed anyway. "Fuck." His palms were still tingling with warmth from John's chest.

"Of course you didn't." John let him off the hook even if Margery and Campbell seemed less forgiving. John was being polite; everyone knew it was the imp's fault. "But now I am definitely going to be late. I'll have to go home and change."

"Fairies are rarely on time anyway." Margery handed him some tissues in the middle of mopping up her desk. She gave Rennet a hard look, and he blinked back at her. For once he had not caused the confusion.

"Fairies?" Rennet demanded faintly. "What?" He flashed back to seeing John on the news, John with his rose-colored tie and hints of pink under his dark suit, John in a sea of bright wings and naked flesh. John had an appointment for dinner that didn't sound professional. Rennet raised his head. "You have a date with a fairy? You have a date, in public, with a fairy?"

He didn't recognize his own voice, it was so rough, not that it mattered to Campbell, who seized on the question like it was a dragon's scale. "You date a lot of beings, Councilman Summers?" he pressed eagerly, definitely on the record now. It wasn't a scandal, exactly, a councilman in *this* town dating a being. Even dating a male being might not destroy John's career in Los Cerros, as it would have in many other places—provided the being was friendly and attractive and endlessly fascinating to humans.

A fairy would be all of those things.

Of course John would want one. Of course someone like John would be brave enough to date one despite his job. Rennet should have known this was coming, but for once he hadn't felt any kind of warning that trouble was on its way.

He didn't know if the tremor in his chest was fear or jealousy. No one was going to hurt John for this, at least not physically. Knowing John, he might even get the city to love him more for it. The Incredible Unflappable with some beautiful, smiling, gentle fairy by his side.

Rennet took a deep breath and avoided John's eyes by brushing more dust from his stomach. He hadn't seen John in a few days, so he'd invented a stupid reason to see him. It should have been an easy, harmless visit. Yet even accounting for the presence of an imp, this encounter had turned disastrous quickly. He couldn't look up. "I should go. I just wanted to say hey, and I've done that… and quite a bit more, now… so…."

John talked over him when his words stuttered to a stop. "Mr. Campbell, you asked that question as if there is something surprising, or even shameful, about wanting to date a being." John's voice was warm, pleasant, but Rennet shivered. Mr. Sunshine meant business when he used that voice. "Beings are citizens of Los Cerros, some of our best citizens. Your attitude strikes me as old-fashioned, bordering on bigoted." John was putting a bold face on it, but Rennet knew the truth. Dating a being was still a deal-breaker to certain voters. John was refusing to be cowed. Rennet would have admired him more for it if John hadn't said it because of his date. His date with a *fairy*.

"Come on, you're a public figure, one of the most popular public figures in town, and you're single. People will want to know your type." There did not seem to be a way to shame Campbell.

"Fairies are everyone's type," Rennet commented, trying to sneak toward the door. He had to take a moment to forcibly remove his tail from John's leg. Damn thing could have a mind of its own. "Who wouldn't date a fairy?" Rennet addressed the ceiling. "They're pretty and the kind of wild that is perfection between the sheets—if you could get a fairy to bother with sheets." Fairies possessed chaos too, but the light kind, the right kind. The kind that broke your heart but blew your mind. The kind humans wanted, the kind they might accept their deputy mayor and favorite councilman dating.

It hadn't always been that way. Humans hadn't always cared for same-sex couplings, although many were more willing to accept those than they were human and being pairings. Then the past decades had brought the humans new diseases, new fears to make them act cruelly to each other, and to the beings around them. Fairies in particular seemed to stir up strong feelings, although the disease that had destroyed so many young, handsome humans never touched them. To this day there were some who thought of fairies as shameful, out of control, irresponsible twits, little more than bimbos with wings, or seductive manipulators who used glamour and magic to ensnare humans. But to most, they were sexy, and they were fun, and they were beautiful. They would always be beautiful.

"Something bothering you, Rennet? Have something to add?" John turned that sunshine-warm voice on him. Rennet didn't know what John's purpose was in asking him that, but quickly shook his head. He still couldn't look at John.

"A councilman should be able to date whoever he wants." Rennet's throat was so dry. The words came out hoarse, deeper than he'd intended them to. His bracelets jangled when he ran a hand through his hair and swept a thumb over the pointed tip of his ear. He looked at the splashes of espresso everywhere, how they were spreading out over the stains he'd left in the carpet on a previous occasion, then looked at Campbell's shoelaces, which were still tied together. His gaze skipped up to the espresso on John's shirt. Fairy sparkles didn't stain; they left no traces. He was such a fool. "Whoever he wants, right? Even a fucking fairy. Thanks for the coffee. See you around."

He skipped out the door and back down the hall before the word "thanks" was even out of his mouth.

"JUST SO you know," Rennet slurred into his little flip phone, "it doesn't count as stalking if it was an accident."

"Accidentally seeing the guy you like on a date with someone else is not stalking," Daphne agreed coolly, halfway across town and probably in bed. "However, lingering on a rooftop to stare at the restaurant he is in, is, in fact, still stalking."

"Only to humans!" Rennet defended himself quietly from his position on top of the Madison building, staring down at the cobblestone boulevard in the nicer part of town, which was filled with expensive restaurants and pricey boutiques. He wasn't allowed inside of any of them. Well, he was, but he felt such pressure not to move or touch anything that it was hardly worth it. He'd only go if he had the money to replace everything he accidentally or not-accidentally broke or ruined, or if the staff were especially annoying and he felt they deserved the trouble.

The chef in the particular restaurant Rennet was studying had once exclaimed that with Rennet in the building, soufflés would not rise. John had called that slander, since it was only about 50 percent of the soufflés that wouldn't rise, and Rennet had grinned and offered to flatten the other 50 percent. It was Rennet's best memory of the place.

The rest of that evening had been awkward. Rennet had been stuck at a table surrounded by fancy humans in fancy clothes with his chest bare and his tail restless, only too aware that he was attracting attention. Staring over deliciously breakable dishes and enticingly lit candles at his calm, collected, and all too human boss had not made him feel any better. John could not have known the stares he would receive for being seen in public in that kind of place with an imp, or how the way he had ignored the negative attention had only made it harder for Rennet to control himself. Rennet had been itching with the need to move after the first glass of wine and had torn out of there not long after that, leaving shattered china in his wake.

Now, on the occasions when he ran into John in public, they mostly ate at food carts or in fast-food places where no one minded a mess. It was accidental, when he ran into John, most of the time.

"No, I'm pretty sure it's stalking to everyone." Daphne was both sleepy and reasonable. Rennet didn't know how a human who was only in her thirties got to be so reasonable. She was so *young*. The young were supposed to be devil-may-care, subject to whims and fantasies. Instead, she was in bed with the TV on mute, and he was on a roof, staring miserably at the doors of a restaurant he couldn't go into.

And drinking. He was also drinking. The liquor was brown, and it was almost as old as he was, and Rennet thought it was perfect, because it was a spectacularly bad idea, even if he couldn't exactly remember why it was a bad idea at the moment.

"But's a fairy," he whispered, sliding his cheeks on top of the little stone gremlin next to him. "A *fairy*." It was one thing to know John went on dates. It was another for it to be with one of Rennet's rainbow-colored alleged kinfolk. He'd even seen the fairy, a male as expected, as John preferred males. A fairy who had put on a shirt despite the discomfort. A fairy with red and yellow hair, orange wings, and the sort of magic that made soufflés *always* rise.

"I could get a soufflé to rise if I really wanted," Rennet mumbled, making Daphne snort.

"I am so not bailing you out," she asserted. She was as calm as John. Well, almost. No one but John was that calm in the face of Rennet's improbable nature, but Daphne did come very close. Rennet wondered what that said about him that he chose such people for friends. His mother, had she been alive, might have said he must be maturing at long last. Daphne did not seem to agree. "No way. I have work in the morning."

It was a testament to the liquor that Rennet didn't feel the need to protest that he would not end the night in jail. "I have no intention of doing anything to get arrested," he argued instead. There had been a brief moment where he'd considered calling in a bomb threat to the restaurant, but thankfully he'd called Daphne instead. He had friends in the PD, but not *that* many friends.

"I need to go to sleep now." Daphne made rustling sounds, like she was sliding under covers. "You should sleep now too, but I know you won't."

"'M fine." Rennet rubbed his face against the cold stone of his compatriot. "I can sleep when the date's over."

"Really? Because you know how that is going to end." Daphne was cruel and mean. If only that wasn't why Rennet liked her. "I am surprised the fairy even bothered with dinner, instead of just going back to John's place. Which as we both know is where they are going to bow chika wow wow."

"Shut up." Rennet squeezed his eyes closed, then whipped upright at the sound of stone cracking. One of the gremlin's wings fell off. Rennet picked it up and numbly tried to reattach it. He was going to have to come back with some glue. "Sorry, little fella. 'S the price of being wi' me."

"Okay. You need to stop drinking before things get any more out of control," Daphne huffed at him. "If you come over here right now, you can sleep it off on my couch and not on a bench in jail."

"Do you think he likes fairies? You think fairies are really his type?" Rennet put down the broken wing and focused back on the street. He couldn't see *inside* the restaurant; that shouldn't count as stalking at all.

Daphne's sigh was long and exhausted.

"Okay. I will shut up and come down from the roof." Rennet gave in, mostly because he was tired. "But there is no accounting for what will happen when my feet touch the ground."

"Don't threaten me, Rennet Imp. I work with two-year-olds. I know how to handle pandemonium."

"Go to bed, you," Rennet snarled tiredly at her and was not surprised when she hung up on him. He supposed he *was* having a bit of a pity party. But a *fairy*. John had to pick a fairy and then *tell* Rennet about it. Why would he be so cruel, saying such things to see Rennet's reaction?

Rennet would never understand the human heart. He didn't even understand his own, true, but the human heart was a puzzle. He remembered the love of his adoptive mother. He could think of Daphne. He had personally witnessed a great, tragic love once, as well as the aftermath. He could vividly recall soldiers protecting one another. But when it came to romantic love, the human heart was careless in its assigned tasks, even by his standards.

He put his head on the broken gremlin and sighed while imagining passing out on Daphne's couch. He dropped his arm and his phone slipped from his hand. Rennet fumbled to catch it before it fell into the street, nearly releasing it again and touching several buttons before he got a better hold on it. He heard beeps, and when he saw a name lit up in green immediately hit "end" to end the call he'd inadvertently made.

He was a victim of his own chaos. He shoved the phone into his back pocket, grabbed the bottle, and jumped off the roof, swooping with slightly too much speed to the street below. He hit a city trash can and skidded into a car, which was parked illegally anyway, as there was no parking on the boulevard. Rennet tried to tell the car that when its alarm started blaring, but the alarm blared on, so he skittered off, spinning away from a startled couple and belatedly folding his wings behind him.

He took another pull from the bottle, noting sadly how empty it was, then winced at the sound of his phone buzzing in his pocket.

"Rennet," John greeted him the moment Rennet answered. Rennet dashed away from the car to hear him, and then he could detect restaurant noises in the background as John spoke. "You called me."

"'Cident," Rennet told him seriously, then shook his head. "Accident," he clarified. "Gremlin did it." He turned his head up to the sky. "Sorry, buddy."

"A gremlin did it," John repeated dryly, like he was standing in front of Rennet and not on a date in a ritzy place with a prettier, sparklier, less drunk version of Rennet. "Is that a car alarm? Did the gremlin do that too?" John's tone abruptly changed. "Have you been drinking?"

"Why does everyone sound so worried when they say that?" Rennet inquired of the world in general before focusing back on John. "If you like chaos as much as you said you do, then what's a little drink or two?"

"Or a little bottle or two?" There was something hidden in John's voice, something sneaky.

"Why, Sunshine," Rennet purred at him, "are you laughing at me?" It seemed like a good guess, though it hadn't had the sound of laughter. The subtle note in John's voice had been tighter, like anticipation. That was something Rennet recognized when he heard it, although usually around him it was anticipation of something horrible. He draped himself against the trunk of a tree strung with white lights and fell backward when his tail slipped free without holding him up. The sound he made when he hit another damn trash can was loud enough to rattle his bones.

It was suspiciously silent on John's end of the conversation. "Aren't you on a date?" Rennet demanded over the embarrassment that imps could still feel. "Why are you talking to me? On your date. On your red-and-gold fairy date—" He stopped at John's sharp inhalation, then quickly kept on talking before John could start to notice things. "Sunshine, John, I *think* someone might be knocking over trash cans downtown. You should come here and take care of it."

"Or you should call the police," John remarked, with only the smallest of pauses this time before he spoke again. When he did his voice was so friendly it was dangerous. "Since, as you pointed out, I am on a date, and that is hardly reason enough to cut it short." The next thing Rennet heard after that was silence.

Rennet had a feeling the call had been a bad idea, even if he hadn't meant to make it. He tipped the bottle back and swallowed until all of it was gone. Then he tossed the bottle in the trash.

Well, he meant to toss it in the trash. He missed. That happened in life. Unfortunately, as Rennet was immediately reminded, Los Cerros was a town that took littering very seriously, especially when the littering was done by a shitfaced imp who had a habit of getting drunk and knocking over trash cans.

RENNET SAT up so fast his head spun, but he stayed up, which meant he was getting sober already. There was an uncomfortable thumping in his chest and a sticky feeling in his mouth, but even that would fade soon. Imps never stayed intoxicated for long, and they always got sober in the worst moments.

"John," he blurted foolishly, blinking to make sure he was awake. "I told them to call Daphne."

John stood outside the bars by the door. He was wearing a dark suit with a dark tie, and he looked decidedly unrumpled by fairy hands. He also had a small smile on his face, which Rennet shivered to see. John looked him over, not that Rennet thought he was much the worse for wear except for some possibly smeared eyeliner and disordered hair. That was his look most of the time, to be honest.

"They always call me first, Rennet," John said, slow and smooth, although Rennet didn't think it was out of consideration for Rennet's mild, fleeting hangover.

Rennet didn't know which part of John's statement to focus on first—the fact that the PD apparently had standing orders to contact the deputy mayor when Rennet fucked up, or the fact that John had said *always*.

It wasn't like Rennet got arrested every other week. It was once a month, tops, and that was usually over teeny misunderstandings like this one. He'd been aiming for that trash can, anyone with eyes could see that. Things had just escalated, as they always did, and not for the better, unless he counted the incident with Bobbi. Bobbi was the deputy keeping an eye on him tonight. She had stumbled while avoiding his tail, and landed on the floor, where she had promptly found her missing wedding ring. The ring must have rolled under a cabinet. She would never have found it if not for Rennet's presence.

She was grateful, despite the bruises that would form on her probably rosy and dimpled knees. Rennet would have given her another smile, but his eyes were on John. He tried to gauge how irritated John was, if he was irritated at all, but John was even more difficult to read than usual.

"Well, I didn't tell them to, so don't go thinking I did this on purpose." Rennet slid back down onto the bench, shoving aside Ralph's feet. Ralph, his cellmate, had also imbibed a bit too much. He smacked his lips at the manhandling and rolled onto his side.

"I know you didn't," John said evenly, bringing Rennet's gaze back to him.

Rennet froze for a moment, uncertain which statement that was a response to. "You have better things to do than put out more fires in your off hours," he continued after a second, moving his wrist. He missed his bracelets. He didn't know why the police insisted on taking them when they threw him in here, or his shoelaces for that matter. He wasn't going to hurt himself, and if he wanted to hurt someone else, he wouldn't need a physical weapon to do it. Decades of fighting experience aside, the threat Rennet posed was simply not containable. A human could spend a lifetime trying.

"But I am very good at putting out fires, Rennet." John's reply sent pinpricks through Rennet's skin. John's tone was close to slippery, not quite satisfied.

Rennet licked his dry lips. "*Yeah,*" he agreed dumbly, and watched John's gaze finally move from him to take in the rest of the scene; Ralph passed out and wearing clothes spotted with his own vomit, and then Rennet sprawled out next to him, smelling faintly of scotch. Rennet couldn't imagine it was a pretty sight, but John looked him over again and quirked his mouth.

Rennet couldn't feel annoyed at being a joke. He liked the way John's lower lip pushed out when he did that, like he was restraining himself from saying something he really wanted to say.

Rennet grinned sloppily for him, though he wasn't very drunk anymore. "How do I look? Like a monster on a bender?"

John's mouth stopped doing sexy things, as though Rennet hadn't amused him, but he seemed to take the question seriously. He made a low "hmm" sound and tapped the bars. "You look like rock stars try to look when they want to seem debauched."

Rennet slapped a hand over his twitching tail as unobtrusively as was possible in his current state. "Don't try to flatter me, human," he rasped after a moment. "I am a fearsome bogeyman."

"Yes. Fearsome bogeymen are often picked up for littering and public mischief. Mischief," John went on, deadpan and perfect, "so fearsome."

"Public mischief!" Rennet lurched to his feet in outrage and stalked over to the bars to peer around the corner at Bobbi. "Public mischief?" he demanded in a howl. "What does that even mean?"

Bobbi waved him off, which was even more humiliating. Rennet crossed his arms and glowered for a good minute, right until he realized he had brought the little half smile back to John's face. He angled his head up and sniffed. "Apparently assaulting a police officer rates as mischief in this town."

"Is that what happened? Because I heard when Rourke slapped the cuffs on you after you argued with him and ripped up your citation for littering, you purred at him and leaned back to give him some kind of standing lap dance, only to knock him on his ass."

"No." Rennet shook his head, but John's stare was unwavering, and, just possibly, slightly pissed-off. "Okay yes! But it wasn't how it sounds! Rourke was being a prick because I've kicked his ass a few times at the gym. Naturally, I had to point out that maybe he'd be less of an asshole if he got some once in a while. Then he blushed. John, you *know* I can't help myself around a blushing maiden. So I pressed the issue." By pressing his ass against Rourke's crotch.

John got even more impassive. Rennet chose not to delve into that moment anymore and moved on. "And the original charge of littering still stands. I got the ticket."

"It's been handled. You are going to spend a weekend cleaning up Oro Creek."

"The fuck I am." Rennet pushed out a breath and took a few seconds to resettle his wings and his nerves. He sank a nubby fang into his lower lip before looking back up. "Fine. Yes, sir, Mr. Deputy

Mayor Sunshine." It wasn't even sarcastic, that was the worst part. Rennet couldn't shut up. John had handled it. John had handled it for him, like he always did. "What did I do to deserve that?" he asked quietly, unsure if he was being punished or rewarded, and felt his pulse race when John inclined his head toward him and lowered his voice to answer.

"You purred at Officer Rourke for putting you in handcuffs, and then you leaned back to grind your ass against his dick." Mr. Sunshine didn't manage a smile this time.

"It wasn't how my evening was supposed to go," Rennet defended himself weakly, the words tripping from his tongue in blatant disregard of his wishes. It was too distracting, knowing he'd provoked John into coming down here, knowing that John was *provoked*. He had to keep going. "Did I cut your date short?" He didn't say he was sorry. No matter how much Rennet tried to make them, red eyes could not convey innocence, even on the rare occasion when he *was* innocent.

John stepped away from the bars. "As a matter of fact, yes." He momentarily turned in Bobbi's direction and left Rennet staring after him. "Officer. We're ready." John paused, then considered Rennet again. "Though, as you know, fairies are not known for making it to the entrée before going for dessert."

Rennet curled his tail up around his body. "I didn't see you leave the restaurant early," he argued, then caught himself in the admission to stalking. He flung himself down on the bench. "Don't judge my choices! Scotch was a factor."

"As I recall, that's what you said when you started the riot at the strip club, except that time it was vodka." John had this way of lashing him with words, and sadly for Rennet, it was so hot that it made his guts spark. His insides were on a slow fuse, and John knew it.

There wouldn't have been a riot at the strip club if Destiny had kept her ass out of John's face. That detail at least Rennet managed to keep to himself. "Thus ended my one week of working security at The Velvet Peach. Vodka leads me to bad decisions," he sighed instead, and slid toward the door when Bobbi came in to let him out.

"Like giving you C-4 leads you to bad decisions," John commented as he stepped aside to give her room, making Bobbi laugh. Rennet would have scowled, but he was a free imp, so he hurried past them both to go claim his jewelry and shoelaces. He liked those shoelaces; the purple looked good with his work boots.

"As if a little boom boom doesn't turn you on, Sunshine." Rennet scoffed at him as he went, enjoying Bobbi's tiny, shocked laugh, though he doubted it got any reaction from John, and he was not feeling brave enough to see for himself.

Rennet wasn't sure he'd see John again after that. John disappeared while Rennet was claiming his property and using the bathroom, but when Rennet stepped out into the parking lot, John was there, chatting with some detectives. Rennet kept his distance, shoving his hands into his pockets and waiting with hunched shoulders under a streetlight.

He had no reason to be waiting and knew it, but after a few more minutes, John pulled away from the group and nodded toward his car, and Rennet followed him.

"Nice to see you, wolf!" Rennet turned at the last second to yell at one of the detectives, an especially tall, broad one with a nice frown and a crooked nose.

"Fuck you, imp!" the detective called back, in a not entirely unfriendly way, for a were.

"Anytime!" Rennet leered at him, then turned and caught John studying him. That werewolf was now the second being to make detective in this town, which made him more than deserving of some proud ribbing and mild flirting as far as Rennet was concerned. John possibly disagreed, though it could have been a trick of the shadows. "What?" Rennet prodded him artlessly. "I don't not *not* mean it."

"Rennet." John's exhale wasn't weary, not exactly, but there was something in it that slowed Rennet down and made him lift his head to listen to the rest. "You won't be sleeping with any weres."

Rennet thought about telling John that orders and imps did not go hand in hand. He might have done it if he were not also absolutely convinced John was speaking the truth. The Incredible Unflappable had issued a decree, and Rennet, for all his power, was still trailing after him. He got into John's car, the one with the butter-soft leather seats and the residual odor of gunpowder from Rennet's last ride in it, and rubbed his cheek along the side of the passenger seat.

He didn't buckle up, but thought it was wise that John always did, since John was not an imp and so not close to indestructible, no matter how magical and omnipotent he seemed to others. John took a second before starting the car. He pulled out of the parking lot and then headed south. He was taking them toward Rennet's part of town.

The first time John had given Rennet a ride, Rennet had warned him about the risks of having an imp in the car. John had responded that driving was a risk anyway, with or without any passengers. If Rennet hadn't already been smitten, that would have won him right there.

He cleared his throat to break the silence, wishing John had turned on the radio, or the early jazz recordings he was so fond of but which reminded Rennet of his childhood and long lost friends. "What do you want? A promise to be good?" He fidgeted, trying to feel more leather against his skin and at the same time not make John's car stink of a holding cell. "An apology? I can't apologize for what I am."

"I like what you are, Rennet." John really shouldn't say things like that so easily.

Rennet sucked in a breath and swallowed it instead of breathing. He coughed, his eyes watering, and tossed his head. Didn't Rennet have it bad enough? At this rate every electrical device in town was going to start malfunctioning. Bread wouldn't bake. People wouldn't be able to blow-dry their hair before going to work. They would have to live with crackers and wet hair. They'd blame him, even when their new curlier hair attracted someone they hadn't had the courage to talk to before and the crackers led them to try recipes that turned out to be delicious. They always blamed the imp. John would blame the imp too, sooner or later, but even if he didn't, it was a mess he didn't deserve.

"You're just pissed because I ruined your date," Rennet said after a while, turning restlessly in his seat the closer they got to his duplex. John didn't respond other than to turn to him at a stoplight and lift an eyebrow, practically daring Rennet to think of John enjoying that fairy's company and what kind of dirty fuck John and that fairy might have had if Rennet hadn't called him away.

"John…." Rennet's chest was tight. He couldn't stop his tail from creeping toward the parking brake. "John…." His throat was so dry, his skin hot. "You don't have to take me home."

John glanced at him again. Rennet couldn't see well enough in the dark to make out his expression, if he even had one. In times of turmoil, John got more impassive than the Mona Lisa. Not that John should be in turmoil over Rennet asking to go to his place—that was Rennet's job. If anything, John was probably trying to think of a way to say no.

This was it, Rennet thought when John didn't answer, the way he thought every time John hesitated like this until finally inviting Rennet back to his place, inviting him *in*; this was the last time they did this. John had finally had enough of Rennet's waggery and pernicious ways and wanted nothing more to do with him. He was going to cast Rennet out and find some nice fairy to date until he settled down with some reasonable and politically appropriate human. Rennet was going to have to leave the country in order to not jinx that wedding.

John broke into Rennet's vengeful thoughts of torrential downpours and bad DJs and wedding guests with food poisoning to ask a question. "Can you give me the alphabet backward and forwards?"

Rennet was barely tipsy now, but it still took him a second to follow. John wanted to know if Rennet was drunk before he took him to bed, so he was giving Rennet a test.

"What language?" Rennet answered smartly and perked up when John made a muffled sound of amusement. He was still heading slowly toward Rennet's neighborhood, which was almost at the edge of the city limits. He'd already driven through most of Old Town, where faded Spanish-style buildings stuck out among converted apartment buildings and funky clubs. Rennet lived out where the woods and part of Oro Creek crept up among the houses, and small specialized shops were easier to find than grocery stores. It had been the barrio, once, and then the district beings and other outcasts had called home, before slowly aging into something midway between elderly and historic. "I'm not drunk," Rennet added to make it clear, though John knew him enough to know the alcohol would already be wearing off.

"I wouldn't want you to regret anything in the morning," John said, which was an indirect sort of answer, not to mention mistaken as shit.

Rennet gave him a long look. "Do I ever?" he breezed, and waved a hand at the window as though his tail weren't wrapped around the parking brake.

"I wouldn't know. I've never seen you in the morning." John was a mystery in the dark of the driver's seat. Rennet tilted back his head and let his eyes fall most of the way shut. It was as close as he could get to being inscrutable as he studied John. Maybe it worked, or maybe that was chaos magic, because they hit a light, and after a few seconds, John straightened his shoulders and turned right to circle the block and go back the way they'd come. He headed north and west, toward the gentle hills that gave the town its name. Respectable people lived in the hills, people like John. Rennet eased back against the plush leather and shut his eyes all the way. He wasn't relaxed, but he could pretend to be now.

If it was any other night, John would have played his vintage recordings and spoken of his day, perhaps offered to pick up dinner, and Rennet would have leaned back in the seat and enjoyed himself even with the sliver of tension keeping him awake and making him restless. Tonight something was different, and it wasn't Rennet's brief stay behind bars. That was hardly unusual.

"That Campbell guy…." Rennet opened his eyes and noted vaguely they were in a nicer part of town already. "Why was he in your office? Since when do you get chummy with the press?"

"The old political reporter for *The Star* retired. I wanted to meet the new guy and get a feel for him…." John trailed off, as if he was considering his words. He didn't often do that when they were alone. Rennet frowned, but John finished his thought at last. "I'm up for reelection this year, so I said yes to a small piece to see how he'd handle it. Then you showed up."

"Yeah," Rennet agreed and frowned harder, "and you let me talk." Not too many people would give Rennet so much freedom around a reporter, especially not someone in the vicious world of local politics. John had basically let Rennet run his mouth, most likely to see what would happen and how the reporter would react. Rennet had a sudden picture of John as a kid, setting off fire alarms and leaving toads in strange places to startle his classmates. "You were a hell-raiser as a boy, weren't you?" he mused, and noticed John did not deny it. John clearly had good memories of childhood. "Troublemaker," Rennet teased and then had another thought.

"So you *were* using me." He wasn't offended. If anything, he was proud and turned on. The list of people who had not only accepted what Rennet was, but fully understood it, was small despite how Rennet had lived for a long time on several continents. He ran his fingers over the leather as they went through streets of upper middle class homes, heading uphill. “Am I your enforcer, John?”

He loved how unapologetic John was. He only gave a nod and kept his eyes on the road. “More than once you have been referred to as my thug,” John admitted. “I don’t know that Campbell has heard that yet, but it’s come up once or twice from some council members. Any time they stub their toe, they whine about it, even the ones who say they don’t take the rumor seriously.” He finally glanced over. “But I wouldn’t call you my enforcer, Rennet. I would say that things can get mired down in that council and sometimes they need shaking up… or an explosion or two. It’s the only way to get things done.”

So he wasn’t using Rennet directly, he was simply taking advantage of the occasional fallout. John was giving him the warm fuzzies here. Rennet wet his mouth. “So you find me in a room talking to a reporter and you decide to let me talk to see what happens. You clever fuck. Did you learn anything, get his angle?”

This time John gave a small sigh. He dropped his shoulders. “Yes, I learned something this afternoon.”

“You don’t seem happy about it,” Rennet observed without thinking, remembering too late all the complex rules about human boundaries and privacy. But he didn’t want John to be upset when for once there was something Rennet could do to make it better. “You could use me.” He resettled against the seat, not quite flexing the muscles that controlled his wings. “You can always use me.”

“I know.” John gave that sigh again, small and sad, but shook his head to close the subject, at least for now. Rennet, however, was not done. He kept poking at it, partly because the image of himself as John’s lackey was a good one. Obviously nothing could ever really control him; he couldn’t control himself sometimes, but John wanting to, now that was something.

“I’m serious.” Rennet slid toward him. His voice was too hoarse to be seductive. “Please use me.”

John pulled into his driveway. He didn’t have a garden, he had grass and trees that he paid someone to look after because he never had the time. His house was too big for one man, but smaller than most of his neighbors’ homes, although it was just as old and full of valuable things for Rennet to break and then repair or replace.

John parked at the bottom of the steps leading to his porch, then turned to look at Rennet with narrowed eyes. When the lights came on, Rennet could clearly see the flush in his cheeks. "I don't want to use you, Rennet." John enunciated each word as if he was fighting to stay calm and then got out of the car.

Rennet was so stunned it took him a moment to follow. He was never a graceful creature outside of a fight, but he tripped over his own feet twice on the walk up the stairs and then found a previously unknown spot where the wood had weakened or rotted, and nearly fell through. He scrambled up before John could turn around to help him, as he had no dignity or sense of pride, and then stood awkwardly by while John unlocked the door and went inside.

John flicked on an overhead light and then turned to face Rennet before Rennet could close the door behind them. Rennet fell against the door and raised his hands, betraying himself and not especially caring. He angled his chin up and John looked him over before stepping in. He curled his hands around Rennet's forearms, then slid them up to Rennet's wrists, pushing the spiked bracelets up, making them dig into Rennet's skin. The move brought John intimately close, but though Rennet tipped his head back and let a short, frustrated breath escape, John didn't kiss him.

"His name was Ianthe," John whispered, almost against Rennet's mouth, making Rennet squirm. "I think he genuinely liked me."

If Rennet were human he would have been pinned, but he wasn't. His wings were pressed against the heavy wood of the door, painfully so, but he could have moved. John couldn't have stopped him. But he shivered weakly at John's words and panted for the hint of anger.

Rennet had anger of his own, and grinned to show his pearly whites. "Sorry," he offered, not sorry at all, but grunted when John pushed him harder against the door. His legs parted immediately when John slid a knee between them.

"Are you?" John wasn't really asking.

Rennet rolled against John's thigh and shook his head. "But I can make it up to you." The throaty rumble coming from Rennet was not a purr, not truly, but John called it that and Rennet had never argued. Arguing was fun, a pleasant way to pass the time, but not with John. With John, Rennet wanted to be the pet that would listen and obey, even if he was more cat than dog. He could, and would, purr for as long as it made John want him.

John considered him. He was breathing heavily and his eyes were bright with lust behind his glasses, but he considered Rennet, what to do with him, what to do to him. Those who thought him dispassionate, unflappable, were so fucking wrong. Rennet closed his eyes and let John hear him beg for it. "Please."

John tightened his grip. "I don't know that you've earned that," he said, egging Rennet on in the worst, best way.

"Sunshine." Rennet's pleading was getting less playful. His purring stopped as he choked on his own words. "Sunshine, please. I'm no fairy, but I can make you smile." He nearly jumped when John leaned in to lick at his mouth, at his teeth, and then pulled back again. Rennet opened his eyes to find John staring at him, already smiling. It was a secret, bitter smile, but his gaze devoured Rennet whole.

"What did you say?" John demanded quietly without letting Rennet look away. "What was that?" Rennet would have glared at him if John hadn't taken one hand from his wrists and slid it down his chest.

"You heard me," Rennet snarled at him. He tried to angle his head to the side, only to stop and shiver at John's breath, warm beneath his ear. "John," he protested, wriggling against the door and all but moaning when John held him still, trapped over his thigh. He would beg to get off; they both knew he would. He would beg for John's hands and mouth, whatever it took. He'd lost his pride some time during the War, and he kept his dignity in John's back pocket.

"I'm not a fairy," he explained, as if John didn't already know that obvious fact. "I'm not pretty or sweet." He put a hand to the back of John's neck and hitched up toward him when John trailed his hand over his hip and then tugged at his jeans. "John, I'm not a fairy. I never will be. But please."

"No, you will not," John agreed fiercely, with his fingers opening Rennet's fly and his lips resting over the tip of Rennet's ear. Rennet tried to shake his head and plead for more. He let words spill out of him in case some of them were the right ones, while John drove him crazy and watched him twist and shudder. Rennet pushed his face into John's shoulder and kept talking. It felt so good, pushing against John's strength and being held back, letting John choose when to make him explode.

"Tighter," he whispered, arching onto his toes at John's breath, dragging his hands under John's suit to pull him closer. His movements, his breathing, were restricted, momentarily contained. Everywhere was hot with too much clothing. Only Rennet's skin was bare, only Rennet was pinned, only Rennet was sinking his teeth into John's collar and dark, dark suit. He'd rip it, tear it, in an effort to hold off coming until John allowed, and John kept going, a strong, firm grip on his cock and soft orders for Rennet not to come at Rennet's throat. Rennet's tail was whipping against the door, a fast, steady beat punctuating the strokes of John's hand.

Inside he was heat and fire, and John had him like lightning in a bottle. "John. Mon humain. Il n'y a personne d'autre," Rennet told him in the language of his childhood, knowing John would not understand the French. He growled it against John's suit and shook with the force of what he was denying. Already the door was creaking, tiny flaws in the wood making themselves known. Rennet could bring the house down. John could *make* him bring the house down, and John knew he could. John knew everything, and Rennet ached with it. He'd never wanted a tragic love. Of course he'd been given one. "John," Rennet begged again, urgently, and lifted his head to moan when John pushed Rennet's hand into the door as if he *wanted* the door to break.

"Rennet," John bit out at last, demanding Rennet come with just the sound of his name, exhaling hard when Rennet came hot on his own chest and all over John's suit. John didn't seem to give a fuck about the stains as he jacked Rennet through the orgasm, until Rennet was wrung dry and whimpering. He stopped when Rennet scratched at his neck, curling his fingers into John's skin in a wordless expression of mingled satisfaction and pain. Then he released Rennet's wrist but didn't move back. He was remarkable, this human. This human more than any other.

Rennet felt the force in John's hold ease and ran his cheek over John's sleeve. When Rennet's presence during sex did not lead to stuck zippers and spilled lube, it led to this, his mind dazed and his body sluggish, content to stay held within John's arms as he regained his strength. "Now let me?" His lips barely moved, but he meant it. He lifted his head a second later. John was looking at him, his mouth open as he caught his breath, too aroused to pretend he wasn't. Rennet wriggled closer to slide their mouths together.

It was not a pretty kiss, but it made John groan, and it let Rennet push him so he could fall to the floor. John's hand cupped the back of his head, his fingers in Rennet's hair as a reminder that he was still in charge. Rennet licked him for that, once he yanked open John's fly and pulled his pants down. He teased John's cock with his tongue, then took it in his mouth, then into his throat. Not for long, just until John's hand splayed out and pressed down as if he wanted to press harder, make him take all of it. He wanted John to want that, loved John inside of him, the lack of fear as John took him.

He grasped at John's thigh, then at his hip, accidentally-not accidentally bruising the skin every time John inched forward into him. His tail curled around John's ankle when he pulled back, but it was only to keep John still as Rennet licked up spit and sucked on his balls, a few more moments to tease before he returned to making John come in his mouth.

If Rennet could not have John naked this time, he would take this and get him naked whenever they did this next. But John's hand curled in his hair, painfully tight, and then he said his name, "*Rennet*," not some fairy's name, so Rennet changed his mind and ducked to let John's seed splatter over his lips and down his chin.

Thus painted, he eased his head back to allow John to look his fill of him. John's fingers slid from Rennet's hair to brush the tip of his ear. Rennet leaned back in, licking come from his lips while John stroked the sensitive spot. He rubbed his cheek against John's thigh, caught John's finger in his mouth for one last greedy suck, then paused to wipe the rest of the mess from his chin. He dragged that over his jeans, then left his hand on the floor.

"You think fairies are explosive," John told him, his voice still uneven, his breathing still rapid. "Rennet, you are pure TNT."

"Pure destruction, you mean," Rennet huffed into John's warm skin, holding on harder for a second when John didn't deny it. How could he? He was Rennet Imp, localized disaster. Rennet made himself let go. "Thanks for bailing me out," he offered without looking up.

"I didn't bail you out." John was cool again, boxing Rennet in with logic, as if logic was the point. "They never booked you."

"Then I don't owe you anything," Rennet snapped, moving away so John's hand wouldn't be on him anymore to make him fizzle and burn. He raised his head, but the flushed, hungry John of the last few minutes was gone. John was collected again, his expression distant and frozen. That mask was worst when Rennet had made it disappear only seconds ago.

Rennet crossed his arms, ignoring the discomfort of drying, sticky come on his chest. John noticed that, of course he would, and for a second the twist at his lips was real and just as bitter as before. "No, you don't," John agreed quietly. "You didn't make me bring you here."

It was a strange thing to say. Rennet edged back and stared up at an angle that should have hurt his neck. "No one made you bring that fairy to that restaurant either." The accusation tumbled out, so true that Rennet knew there was no way he could call it back, no way John could miss it.

He'd finally done it. He'd finally ruined everything. He'd been content to have friendship and sex, he really had been. His heart hadn't needed to do this.

"You have something to say, Rennet?" John pressed in a tone not as even as it could have been, but Rennet pulled himself to his feet and tore his gaze away from John's face. The truth wanted to reveal itself, so he swallowed it down, though he knew there would be consequences for that later. He shook his head.

John let out a long, disappointed breath. "Then I am going to bed."

He made no move toward his bedroom, but Rennet glanced curiously in that direction. He had seen John naked but didn't know what he wore to bed or how he slept, if there was enough room in his bed for an imp, if he'd mind if an imp made room for himself there, wings and all. The thought was ridiculous. Rennet knew better. Almost no one wanted imps around. He wasn't even drunk anymore to be thinking like that.

He raised his head at the same moment that John looked away. "Then good night," Rennet told him and fumbled for the doorknob. Then he ran out of the door and leapt off the porch into the wind.

RENNET SCOOPED up the child climbing over his knees and set him on his shoulders without taking his eyes off the buildings across the street. The daycare for the children of city workers was a small house attached to the library. This meant it was across from City Hall and the courthouse, and on certain days Rennet would find himself there, drawn to the whirlpool of energy, questions, and finger paint. It reminded him of his childhood and all his adopted siblings.

He continued his story while the very determined three-year-old tried to climb him. A few more human children were in the window seat with him, dutifully staring out the window because they'd caught Rennet staring out the window and had wanted to help him find whatever he was looking for. The older ones had been asking questions, necessitating a story time distraction.

"In the old days, humans often thought beings were gods. In fact, they mistook imps for small gods, or servants of gods, which are practically gods, and still very powerful. They thought imps were gods of mischief, gods of tricks, because it was our destiny to cause problems so humans could learn to solve them."

"My dad says imps are liars." Ynez had a sweet, heart-shaped face and a trusting nature. She was curled up at his side, playing with his tail. Rennet tugged her hair.

"Only liars accuse other people of lying all the time," he told her matter-of-factly, sowing the seeds of future discord and only feeling a little bad about it.

As was the way of the world, he got his comeuppance in the next second when Devon piped up from behind him, spreading Rennet's wings out like he was playing an accordion. "Are we spying on Mr. Sunshine?"

"Mr. Summers," Rennet corrected, wondering how a four-year-old had learned about spying in this day and age. "And no. We are… protecting him." Not that Rennet had seen John yet. John hadn't even come out for lunch. He must be having a busy day. Rennet looked at the kids and their curious, innocent faces. "We are protecting him from the bad things that happen when I am around. The slight disaster I think is brewing." He sighed. He sounded like a lunatic.

"Rennet, please stop teaching these kids your bad habits." Daphne came up behind him and started picking up children and setting them on the floor. Rennet turned from the window and gave her his best disgruntled expression.

Daphne set her hands on her hips and spoke to the children. "What stories is Rennet telling you now?" For them, she had a wide, happy smile and an arched, curious eyebrow. They started to fill her in on the tale of The Imp and the King, which he hadn't finished, and when they were done, stopping short of the goodly king rewarding the imp with a golden bower, she finally looked at him. Her eyes were so startlingly blue that Rennet sometimes thought she had being blood in her, but Daphne had always claimed to be fully human. Her frizzy hair seemed to back her up on that score; her chignon could not contain it.

"Now who wants to help me make sugar cookies?" she asked, and hid most of her wince at the resulting excited screams. She was good, offering the kids sugar close to the end of the day so it was their parents' problem.

"Is that a good idea with me here?" Rennet pointed out and got shushed. Devon came back to grab his hand and pull him toward the kitchenette in the other room.

"No cookies will burn on my watch," Daphne promised Rennet seriously, brandishing a kitchen timer and gesturing to the second timer on the oven itself. She had rolled out the dough on a low table while Rennet had distracted the kids with a story, and she sent them over to wash their hands before giving them plastic cookie cutters in different shapes.

"So, god of mischief…," Daphne began quietly while the children were focused on pressing shapes into dough and carefully putting them on cookie sheets. "I don't think I've ever heard that story."

"It's an old family story." Actually, Rennet had read it once, in a book nearly as old as him, a book with yellowed pages, full of stories that made Rennet's chest ache. It was a story within a story, a tale told by a soldier on a dark, stormy night. He also remembered it as a bedtime story from a friend.

Rennet coughed, then accepted the mushed up ball of dough Ynez brought him. "No raw dough for you," he scolded her with a grin and ate it in one gulp. She giggled and ran back to the table. Rennet didn't look at Daphne or give himself time to wonder why he'd found himself thinking of Paris so much lately. "Would you rather I told them how in some human cultures they thought of us as gods of fertility? I will admit that if I fancied ladies more, I'd probably be a father several times over, because my presence plays havoc on prophylactics."

"Rennet!" Daphne hissed at him.

He pretended not to hear. "And probably some human saw our tails and mistook them for our—"

"*Rennet.*" Daphne was not amused. He summoned up a smile for her.

"But I had the sense not to tell the kids that. I'm not so bad, when you think about it." His shoulders fell for a moment. "I'm no politician's wife, but for a regular person, I wouldn't be so bad." He had been telling himself that or something similar since he was a child, when he'd realized that in order to be adopted, one first had to be abandoned. Many imps were abandoned. So were many other being children, but after the war there had been so many orphans, he'd stopped noticing. He'd never seen imp parents, but he couldn't imagine, if some unlucky child ever came under his care, that he would leave them, no matter how much trouble it was.

Then he wondered, quite foolishly, if John would, and decided he wouldn't. It was not one of his proudest moments, considering that John was a human male and Rennet was also a male and therefore they would be making no children. And of course, John wasn't Rennet's and never would be.

Rennet made a very small, very pathetic noise.

Daphne bumped her shoulder into his, then shoved him forward. "Come on. We'll make cookies. You can finish telling your story. And then later if you want, you can tell me the other story that brought you here in the first place."

"The cookies will burn," he protested again, not that Daphne was having any of it. She directed him to the kids' table and handed him bags of powdered sugar and food coloring and kept him there as her frosting slave for the next hour.

By the time he left, right before the parents started to pick up their children, his voice was hoarse, he'd eaten too many cookies, and he'd learned that food coloring did not wash off, it only faded. He'd also learned that bags of powdered sugar were not as sturdy as they looked.

HE SHOWED up at City Hall around three, despite not intending to go in. But he was more known around the building than he'd realized, because after a few people acknowledged him by asking if he was going in to have coffee with John, he realized that for a supposedly unpredictable entity he was getting very predictable.

A meeting was going on, something behind closed doors that ended as he made his way toward John's office. Rennet stopped when he heard John politely disagreeing with someone about cuts. Rennet didn't catch the details; he was busy checking out John while John was distracted. John seemed tired, which was probably Rennet's fault as much as it was the demands of his job.

It was too late to slip away once John noticed him. Rennet knew he had, because John excused himself from the conversation in the middle of the other councilmember's argument and started walking in Rennet's direction. Stuck there, Rennet waited for him and felt like a twitchy youth.

"Should I ask?" John inquired. He didn't lean forward, but Rennet curved his body against the wall anyway and tried to think up a legitimate reason to be in City Hall. He'd never needed one. John had never once asked why Rennet was always wandering through the building. Somehow Rennet had never noticed that before.

"I, um," Rennet said stupidly, because imps were poor at outright deception, and gulped when John took his hand and held it up to inspect the faded spots of food coloring. "Oh. Sugar cookies. I made the frosting. Daphne says I invented a new color."

"This is sugar?" John's thumb swept over Rennet's shoulder, leaving a path through the layer of white powder. He didn't put his thumb in his mouth, which was good, because Rennet might have been forced to kiss him if he had. He'd thought John was angry with him, but John had approached him, and now they were staring at each other in the hallway for anyone to see, and John was touching him. "Were you on your way somewhere?" John went on innocently.

Rennet blinked at him. "To see you," he confessed, and blamed it on the whizz-bang storm of good feelings in his chest when John continued cleaning powdered sugar off him one careful stripe at a time. John met his eyes. This time he did pop his finger in his mouth, for a second.

"Good." He smiled and Rennet was so, so confused—and horny—but mostly confused. He didn't get a chance to demand if John was still angry. John hadn't let go of his hand and gave it a tug. "I need coffee, and I'm starving. I missed breakfast and lunch. Walk with me?"

"You don't… have other things to do?" Rennet wondered in a mumble, staring at their hands as he followed. He pulled his hand free in the lobby when he saw Daryl watching them, then frowned, more puzzled than ever. John kept walking.

"Were you really on your way to see me?" John held the door open for Rennet and a few other people on their way out, then immediately started in the direction of the deli a few blocks down from the courthouse. The place was popular, usually packed with cops and lawyers, though it was a little late for the lunch crowd.

Rennet did not like feeling this lost. "Yes. But I thought—"

"Let's eat first," John interrupted, holding the door *again*, and then urging Rennet ahead of him in line to order before him.

It was a lot like the first time Rennet had ever shared a meal, *tried* to share a meal, with John. Rennet was not a woman, though every one of the few imps Rennet had met had liked to blur the humanity-imposed lines about clothes, and he had been quick to say something about John's habit of holding doors for him. John had responded pleasantly, "I know you aren't a woman, Mr. Rennet," and then held the door for someone else. Rennet had felt uncomfortable and awkward and stupid all at once.

He hadn't felt that off-balance in years, and it had only gotten worse when he'd taken a good look at the restaurant John had chosen. He still didn't understand why anyone would take their handyman to a place like that one—spotless white tablecloths and candlelight. Rennet had been shaking after one glance at a place so immaculate.

With so much effort required to behave himself, it hadn't taken long for him to storm out and hurry away. He'd made it a few blocks down the street, his tail lashing with agitation and his face hot, before John had pulled up alongside him and invited Rennet back to his place to talk about it over coffee.

Rennet had thought there would be less to break in John's home. He'd been inside it before, and had thought it was safe. Then John had handed him a cup and saucer and told him he might as well do his worst and get it out of his system.

The china had been commonplace, easily replaceable. Rennet could still remember the feel of the fragile, thin porcelain in his hand, and how beautifully it had shattered when he'd thrown it against the wall. He'd looked at John then, grinning, and felt something ease in his chest when John let out a short breath and smiled at him. A moment later they'd been kissing, Rennet with his back to the sink and his tail wrapped around John, John pressed against him and sliding his hands into the waistband of Rennet's jeans. Rennet remembered feeling startled at how good it was, how fast, though to this day he didn't know why he'd been so surprised.

Of course John was considered a catch in his circles; Rennet had known that before Campbell had ever mentioned it. John was successful, well-liked, and well put together. Some humans who had harsh standards on physical perfection might have said he was ordinary or commented on his thinning hair, but humans were known to be shortsighted about many things. To an imp like Rennet, to Rennet himself, John was the ultimate temptation.

It had been difficult to leave afterward with John half-naked and bruised as he'd held Rennet up against his countertop. His fingers had been gentle on Rennet's ears, but they'd trailed away when Rennet had moved, and he hadn't said anything when Rennet pulled up his pants and walked out.

Maybe John hadn't felt anything then. Maybe he still didn't. Rennet frowned at him all through ordering his food and listening to John order his, then frowned some more when he sat opposite John at a small table to wait for their sandwiches.

"Something on your mind, Rennet?" John asked him, probably not 100 percent calmly, but Rennet couldn't be sure. John was too good at hiding things. He'd never seemed angry any of the other times they'd fucked and Rennet had left. The only thing that had been different this time was that, if John had been angry about Rennet leaving, he had been less willing to hide it.

Rennet took his eyes off John and focused on the silver tray of condiments in the middle of the table. He was a big imp; he could have this conversation. "I was wondering if you were angry with me." He picked up the saltshaker and opened it, then twisted it closed again, but not all the way. He did the same to the pepper, then the sugar, before raising his head. John had a telling smile in place, though he didn't comment on what Rennet had done.

"Angry isn't the word," John admitted. "Frustrated would be better," he added, then picked up the salt and screwed the lid on properly. He did the same to the pepper, but left the sugar as it was. Rennet wanted to leap over the table and push John to the ground and writhe down his body until he had John's cock in his mouth.

"Sunshine." Rennet wanted to purr, but it came out too rough for that. John lifted both his eyebrows and then stared hard at Rennet for a long time. His smile slowly disappeared.

"Rennet, I am going to ask you something, because I feel like there has been a miscommunication somewhere." John paused, as though he was waiting for Rennet to give him permission to go on. As though that was *exactly* what he was doing, he took a deep breath and continued when Rennet nodded. "When that reporter outside my office asked you if we were friends, why didn't you say yes? I thought you at least considered us to be friends."

He said *at least* like Rennet was making a mistake. Rennet had heard John use that tone in council meetings on people who asked for stupid things.

Rennet took his hands off the mustard bottle before he could get to the lid. He coiled his tail around the leg of his chair. "You're my friend, John Summers," he said quietly, forcing himself to be still. "You're…." Rennet would have been less careful in a minefield. "You are also the deputy mayor. Few humans would claim the friendship of an imp. Some will not even acknowledge a being as a friend to this day, despite years of struggle for acceptance." Rennet paused, and knew when he spoke again that he sounded as old as he was. "They killed beings when I was young, John. They killed the humans with them too. Or we assumed they did, since sometimes they disappeared, vanished into night and fog. Other times they left their bodies out as a message. A few days later we would find them and…. They didn't deserve that." For a moment Rennet couldn't say any more. Then he carefully breathed in and out until his throat wasn't locked. "That was a different time, and a different country, when the humans were killing each other for many reasons, but I haven't forgotten."

"I see." John took his time to answer. He knew some of Rennet's stories, but Rennet had not told him about that particular loss. John was a revolutionary too, like those lost ones, but John was seated in the halls of power. It might save him, but Rennet wasn't going to take the chance. Not with John.

John was probably doing the math for Rennet's age and making reasonable guesses at what Rennet was referring to. Not that John had to search all that far back for evidence that humans didn't think of beings as their equals: there were a handful of beings in the police department, and still only the two detectives. No beings sat in the City Council.

"You were doing me a favor, controlling chaos for once." John spoke again at last. "That was… quite a sacrifice for you to make." Their food arrived, but John didn't dive in to his sandwich right away. "But, Rennet, do I seem like I mind a challenge? That I am bothered by stress?" He sipped at his coffee until Rennet started to get twitchy again. Eating his own food was impossible.

"You seem like you enjoy it," Rennet muttered and put his hands on the table.

John moved forward, setting down his coffee and covering one of Rennet's hands with his own. He let out a short, relieved breath. "Exactly. So do you want to come over tonight?" The faint smile was back. John was pretending, and Rennet didn't know about what. All he did know was that he'd never gotten to be with John two nights in a row.

"*Yes*," Rennet agreed, loudly, startling the server bringing over Rennet's extra pickle, who lost his grip on his tray and sent the tray and the pickle to the floor.

A few people looked over. John continued to smile.

Rennet, tentatively, smiled in return, then reached, one-handed, for the mustard.

RENNET STEPPED over the hole he'd left in the stairs to get to John's porch. John was home already, early, for him, though still working. He was putting up a sign that read Reelect Mr. Sunshine, and it was so unexpected that Rennet had laughed as he got out of his work truck. He was still laughing even when the hole almost killed him.

He reached the porch alive and John came up to meet him, stepping wide of the bad spot. He had his sleeves rolled up and no jacket on. "You have my vote," Rennet told him, a grin on his face. He probably looked stupid.

"Thank you." John responded like a politician and shook his hand. "The printer stared at me like I was crazy, but I'm beginning to like the name."

"People will call you that anyway whether you like it or not, so you might as well embrace it and make it work for you." Rennet wondered how long he could get away with keeping John's hand in his. John hadn't pulled away yet. It was the third time in one day.

"You're kind of a devious asshole sometimes, Rennet." John wiped a bit of sweat from his brow with his other hand. The first time John had said that to him, someone in line ahead of Rennet in the hardware store had spilled a box of nails on the floor and Rennet had stepped up to take his place.

"It's my nature, Mr. Summers," Rennet replied, like he had then, only this time John pulled him forward by the hand until Rennet fell against him.

"I'm well aware." John had a purr of his own, one Rennet didn't think anyone else got to hear. He tilted up his face and let out a small, surprised noise when John kissed him gently. He splayed his hands against John's chest and pushed closer, liking the soft way John was kissing him even as he silently pressed for more. John's hands were at his jaw, holding Rennet where he was while he took his time with Rennet's mouth, but he said nothing when Rennet's tail slithered up between the buttons on his shirt. He tore away to breathe, but only for a moment. Then he slid his mouth back over Rennet's and kissed him until Rennet was half a second from climbing him.

John hit the porch railing, which creaked ominously, but Rennet didn't stop, kissing back and moaning when John slid kisses under his ear and down to his collarbone. Rennet shivered as the evening air hit his damp skin. He didn't know what had come over John, but this was good, even if they were going to break the porch.

He edged John toward the door, not wanting him hurt if the railing did give way, using his hands and his tail to pull John's shirt from him, and nearly choking John with his tie until he got that off too. Rennet threw it in the yard and then pushed John inside the house. Once there he dragged his teeth over the muscle of John's bicep and the tattoo from John's Army days. John tangled his fingers in Rennet's hair the second the door was closed and yanked up his head for a long, filthy, wet kiss that made Rennet stumble on shaky legs when John let go. John was breathing hard. Rennet wasn't exactly steady either.

It wasn't that they never did this. It was more that getting it again so soon after last night was almost enough to make Rennet worry that he'd upset some cosmic balance. He was never this lucky. But John held Rennet by his belt and licked his mouth as he looked him over.

"Bedroom?" He angled his head in that direction. "Not that I didn't like against the door, but I'm not as young as I used to be."

Rennet didn't even verbalize his agreement—he pounced. John staggered back with a startled laugh. It turned into a groan when Rennet got him into the bedroom and shoved his pants down. Rennet took care of his own jeans in the next second and had barely stepped out of them before he tilted up his face for another kiss. John smiled against his mouth, a real one, and Rennet gave his lower lip a resentful bite that John responded to by taking Rennet's arms and pushing him down onto the edge of the bed.

Rennet glared up, not bothering to conceal how aroused he was. "What?" he panted, and ran a hand up his thigh to touch his prick. So John did this to him, made him this eager; there was no shame in it. "Stop looking at me like that," Rennet told him, but couldn't help leaning a little more so John could look all he wanted, something John had no shame in doing either. He stared at Rennet like he couldn't get enough, as if Rennet weren't anything but a fairy. If Rennet's wings and tail were gone he wouldn't even have made a very pretty human. Average, Rennet would have said. Rennet would have been an average-looking human, though his body had always been his main attraction.

John studied him from his tail to his ears, then finally answered. "I'll look at you however I please, Rennet," he informed Rennet with relish, and Rennet closed his eyes and put back his head to swallow.

John was always resolute, but there were cracks in his control to be exploited. Rennet slid farther up on the bed to rest on his elbows, bending one knee. He didn't bother to open his eyes until he heard John step forward. Then he let the spiraling need in his belly show in his expression. "Come on, Sunshine, I've been waiting all day." He barely got the invitation out before John grabbed him by the legs and flipped him over onto his stomach.

Rennet grunted, his face in the comforter, before he got onto his knees. The promise of a good fucking made him flick his wings open enough to make him feel even more splayed out. Then he arched his back and spread his legs. "Je suis le tien." John's hand curled around the base of his tail. Rennet let himself be pulled, lowering himself onto his elbows and sliding his face against the cool bedding. "John. John, please."

He shivered for the sounds of what John was doing. A condom was everything and nothing. It was next to useless, and unnecessary, at least to Rennet, because he was magic and because there was only John, but it was also a sign that John never underestimated Rennet's power and took all reasonable precautions. Rennet was both pleased and impatient, and settled for shaking his ass. John touched him again, a quick little smack that made Rennet snort a laugh, and then John silenced him with a more serious touch. His slick fingers eased Rennet open, slowly, as if Rennet needed gentle when they both knew he didn't. But Rennet didn't say a word, only exhaling as he fought to stay still.

"Rennet, are you trying to behave?" John asked in a tight, shocked voice, and Rennet shook his head to deny it but otherwise didn't move. He wanted to rock back and order John to fuck him, but John was pushing in, getting him ready with human care and attention, and it hurt to deny him. Rennet trembled instead, an uncontainable quivering in his thighs and down his back. He opened his mouth when John finally stopped and put a hand to his hip.

The moan just escaped.

"John." Rennet curled his tail around John's arm to draw him in and hissed as John's cock filled him. John's hold on him was strong, and Rennet stayed motionless for that as long as he could with John over him, inside of him, gasping softly above his lower back, and then he started to move.

He pushed slowly back to take more, and John tugged on his tail, a warning. Rennet smiled where John couldn't see it and leisurely impaled himself again on John's nice, thick cock.

"I don't need to walk tomorrow, human, I can fly." He shook his wings for good measure at the taunt and then dropped down onto his hands as John yanked up his ass to thrust in deeper. It was rough, and Rennet shouted, the comforter slipping from his fingers before he gave up. He got a hand around his cock for one frustrating second before John pushed into him again, and then he had to take his hand away in order to brace himself. The bed rocked, blankets slipping toward the floor, but Rennet couldn't have moved to save them if he'd wanted to.

John took him again, a firm hand at his tail, limiting Rennet's every movement until all Rennet could do was slide against the falling comforter and stretch his wings and be taken. His cock was heavy and untouched, and he howled for it, shaking as John made free use of him exactly as Rennet had dared him to.

"Yes." Rennet burned as pillows disappeared and the bed groaned against the floor.

It shouldn't be legal for a human to fuck like this, to talk like that, whispering, "*Now* look at you," to Rennet in a pleasant, obscene voice until Rennet's legs were jelly and he couldn't keep himself up any longer. John held him, pulled him back, hooked an arm around his hips to continue fucking him. His arm brushed Rennet's cock and Rennet gasped and bit down hard on his lip. The cry emerged anyway, loud, almost as loud as the crack of wood and the ping of screws coming free and hitting the floor.

"Your bed," Rennet choked out a warning, but John pushed a hand against the small of his back and didn't slow, so Rennet shut his eyes and shivered as the bed frame cracked. John started to jack him, an order for Rennet to finish if there ever was one, and Rennet slid a hand down to cover John's and groaned into the sheets and came, clenching hard around John to make him come too. His magic held off on the condom at least—it stayed on and in one piece, keeping John from coming inside him, but the bed wobbled as John finally stopped moving.

Some weakness in the wood, some slightly loose screw, that was all it would take with Rennet in the room and feeling this much. Rennet kept his face down as he caught his breath, and swallowed thickly every time John slid an exhausted hand over his ass and murmured, "Rennet," into the space between his wings. It made the thin, sensitive membranes shiver like a leaf in a breeze. John said it like it was a good thing, as if Rennet hadn't broken his bed. Which Rennet could admit was a first, even in his experience.

After a few minutes, John pulled out and went into the bathroom, and Rennet could collapse onto his stomach. The bed gave a great shudder but thankfully stayed up. He did not know what to say about that. It only became more embarrassing when John stumbled back in, none too steady himself, to clean him up.

"I broke your bed," Rennet wheezed, and John huffed a laugh.

"I think we both did," he joked, like it was nothing. Rennet turned onto his back to look at him, ignoring the discomfort. John wiped seed and lube off Rennet's skin and then met his gaze.

Rennet should have been amused too. He'd been fucked into the mattress and had a shattered bed to prove it. But all he could think was that, thanks to him, John was going to have to sleep on the couch.

He rolled onto his side and then put his feet on the floor. "I should go."

Out of the corner of his eye he saw John freeze, but when he turned, John headed into the bathroom. He wasn't saying anything, not even anything else about his bed. Rennet thought about offering his truck to pick up a new bed frame, then realized John would simply buy a new bed and have it delivered.

He scratched at his chest where it was still damp from the washcloth and waited for John to come out. Then Rennet started talking, the words as fast as the whipping of his tail. "I didn't mean to do that. I can… I can fix it. Don't hold that against me too."

At least it brought up John's chin. "What else am I holding against you?" His tone was more curious than angry, but Rennet could not believe that even The Incredible Unflappable was going to act like Rennet hadn't ruined his bed.

Rennet made a face, then looked away. "I'm not nice. I'm not useful. I'm not even that pretty. I just… I break things. If I were a fairy…." He shut his mouth and gave John a sideways look.

John's silence didn't bode well for Rennet. Gears were turning behind John's sharp eyes and fogged up glasses. "You keep saying that. I'm starting to think it means something very specific to you, Rennet."

Rennet had the sinking feeling that John had found his angle. "Yeah, it does," he grumbled, not at all defensive as he grabbed his jeans and slipped them on. He was going to be feeling this fucking all night, but he ignored that for the moment. "I'm not a fairy and I'm not a human."

"I have noticed." John was a dry fucker, and Rennet was in no mood.

He snarled and narrowly missed a painful accident with his zipper. "I've been around a long time, Sunshine, you can't fool me. If you don't want me to apologize for your bed, then fine, I won't."

John stiffened even more, then startled the shit out of Rennet by making a noise in his throat and throwing his hands in the air.

"Do you do this for the sake of causing trouble, or do you honestly not understand what you're doing to me?" John tore away from him and left the bedroom. Rennet followed after him, dazed at finally provoking John into losing his temper, even if he didn't understand how he'd done it.

"Take your pick," Rennet murmured, blinking when John angrily shook his head. His glance at Rennet after that was pitying. Rennet straightened in annoyance. "In case you hadn't noticed, John, I am an imp! I cause trouble! I break things! It's what I do."

"That's not all you do!" John turned to tell him, and Rennet put his hands out without thinking and came into contact with John's warm skin. It was chaos and it wasn't. It was what Rennet wanted if not what he planned. John looked at him so knowingly that Rennet snatched his hands away.

He wasn't any good at acting, so his voice remained too loud and too frustrated. "It's cool, Sunshine, I'm not about to mess up your life."

"What in the hell does that mean?" John's face and neck were red. A vein was throbbing in his forehead, but he took a deep breath as if he was trying to regain his usual control.

"This." Rennet waved between them and back toward the bed. He should not have had to spell it out. "I'm not going to take this public or anything."

John went utterly still as only John could. After a moment that small, painful smile curved the corner of his mouth. "What?" He was so quiet it made Rennet's stomach tighten. Rennet had been in battle and never felt this nervous around a human. He didn't know whether to back up or charge forward or freeze in place, and thought, briefly, that this was how humans must feel in the presence of an imp bent on destruction.

The words stuttered out of him. "I know I'm your handyman. That you fuck sometimes. We're friends, as humans would describe it. But I can restrain myself, John. Keep it all at bay. So if you wanted to date a human. Or something. You can, I mean, I wouldn't stop you." His weakness made him go on. "But not a fairy. Anything but that." He denied it in the next second. "No, even then I wouldn't stop you. Even if… even if they are beautiful and wanted and everything I'm not. I wouldn't."

John's stare was disturbingly level, although he had to unclench his jaw before speaking. "You wouldn't?" He was so soft, as soft as the sweetest of his kisses and just as treacherous. "You're a real asshole, Rennet," he announced, not quite cold, "and you are completely wrong."

"About what?" Rennet demanded.

John gave a rough snort. "Where should I start?" He turned his back on Rennet and opened a small closet to pull out a blanket. He brushed past Rennet to toss it on the couch in the living room.

"Aren't you going to fix the bed?" Rennet kept inching close to him. "You love handling problems." But John wasn't making a move toward the bedroom. He was watching Rennet and breathing hard.

"Yes, I do." John sighed and dropped his shoulders. "But not right now. Go home, Rennet."

He had never once told Rennet to go home. He had never even told Rennet to leave City Hall when he was working. Rennet frowned at him, and after a second John made a noise and walked away. Rennet heard the bathroom door close, and distantly, the sound of water running. John did not return. So after a while, Rennet left.

RENNET STABBED the buttons on his microwave, hoping the popcorn setting wouldn't let him down, though he'd gotten used to the taste of burned popcorn over the years. It wasn't a real dinner, but it would do until he got something else. He knew he needed to eat; Daphne had been annoyed enough when he'd woken up on her couch that morning, so weak he'd barely been able to move.

Sex and flying would take a lot out of anyone, even someone half his age. Wandering around town before reaching Daphne's apartment at dawn hadn't helped matters. She'd let him in, sent him to her couch, and then woken him up a few hours later by waving orange juice and a handful of granola bars in front of his face before heading out. She'd left Rennet to have an awkward breakfast with her boyfriend, but Rennet felt like he'd deserved it after waking her up so early and shedding strip club glitter over her carpet.

He vaguely recalled trying to explain that he'd gone to the club because he'd wanted to apologize to Destiny, and then Daphne answering that he had better wash off all the body spray and sparkles if he didn't want anyone to know where he'd been. Rennet didn't have anyone who would have cared where he'd been, but when he called a cab to get home, still too tired to attempt flight, he instructed the driver to avoid the downtown area.

After a shower and lunch, he remembered that his truck was still at John's house because, too upset to drive, Rennet had flown from John's porch. So, sadly for Rennet, he'd had to go get it. John hadn't been home, most likely at work, but Rennet had approached his house carefully and then spent some time considering the stairs up to the porch. He couldn't get inside to look at the bed, and even if drunk wouldn't have attempted breaking and entering, but the stairs were out in plain view. Sooner or later John was going to hire someone, if not Rennet, to replace the boards with the weakened wood, probably the ones in the porch railing too.

The wood, like the house, was old. It would have rotted eventually with or without Rennet, but there was no denying that Rennet's presence was costly. So after a while he sighed and set to work ripping away the bad wood and taking measurements for the new.

He'd worked there for most of the afternoon, then left before he thought John might be home. Rennet was not in fighting condition. He was tired and dazed, and there was a knotted, cold feeling in his stomach that was making eating difficult, which sucked, since imps tended to eat as frequently as birds.

He decided to forget the popcorn and go out to get food just as his phone buzzed in his pocket. Daphne had been calling him all day, wondering if he was feeling okay, if he'd gone out anywhere, if he wanted to talk about anything. He appreciated her concern, but it was a little much. His heart was bruised, that was all. If it was broken, then maybe he could understand why she'd call repeatedly to bug him about watching TV or getting out or reading the paper, but it wasn't.

It might be, if John never spoke to him again, but Rennet was not acknowledging that possibility yet. He was going to eat food and then go in the backyard and smash things with a hammer.

He answered the phone without looking at the number or attempting to sound like a professional handyman service. "No, I don't care about local news right now," he snapped irritably, because Daphne could be a plague when she wanted to be.

John answered in a controlled voice, "Rennet."

Rennet stopped what he was doing, aware John could hear him choking. "Yeah?" he acknowledged finally, trying to determine what kind of call this was, if John had gotten home yet. He must have, because Rennet didn't hear any sort of background noise, just the slow in and out of John's breathing.

John didn't bother with pleasantries. He didn't ask or wait for an answer. He said, "Get over here. Now," then hung up, leaving Rennet to stare at his phone and wonder how things had gotten so messed-up between them. Everything was upside-down. Even considering his tendency to pitch screwballs, this seemed excessive.

RENNET SWERVED as he parked his truck, moving too fast when he stopped in the dirt to the side of John's driveway. It didn't help his nerves, and made him even more irritable about his audience.

John was at home, after all, standing on his porch with his arms crossed as though he was waiting for Rennet to pull up. Rennet glanced around before he got out of the truck, but of course there was no clue about John's mindset to be found in his yard. A few of John's neighbors were out on their porches, unabashedly staring at Rennet, so he nodded at some and flipped off some others and then stopped at the base of the steps to squint up at John.

"Right, the stairs," Rennet began, licking at his teeth uncertainly. "I know you didn't ask me to, and I wasn't going to charge you, but they needed to get replaced, and that railing too. So I figured, why not start it today? The weather was nice, and I can replace all of it, including the porch deck, this week. Then you can pick a stain color you want, and I'll stain it. Water seal it as well, of course, why take stupid chances?"

John didn't answer. Rennet scratched at his nose. "You decide on a stain color, and I will take care of it. When you aren't here, naturally. Renovations are stressful for humans, though you… you like stress." Rennet had no idea what he was saying. "You know your neighbors are watching us? What's their problem?"

Unbelievably, that made John's mouth quirk up. He shook his head and let his arms fall to his sides. "Rennet, you dick," he remarked, like he had a host of other things to say and had settled on that one. But he did say it fondly, perhaps knowing Rennet wouldn't be offended. "What did you do with yourself today?"

"This, obviously." Rennet felt like he was missing something.

John nodded. His smile wasn't going anywhere. "What did you do last night? Roam around town?"

"Oh no." Rennet realized that Daphne might have had a reason to ask him if he'd read or seen the news. "Was I a traveling trouble vector?"

"A little bit, yes." John was probably downplaying it by saying *a little bit*. Rennet had been rather upset last night. Rennet wondered how curious he looked that John's smile would get wider. "It wasn't that bad. An elevator got stuck. A baby was born on said stuck elevator, a healthy nine-pound boy. A car crash out by the freeway united long lost siblings. A water pipe burst in The Regent Hotel. The registers froze at a gas station outside of town, charging everyone sixty-nine cents for everything. Then, of course, there are rumors that an especially handsy customer at a certain strip club got salmonella from the buffet and had to be taken to the hospital. And… a few other things happened."

"There is no proof that any of that was me," Rennet pointed out, then discreetly sniffed himself to make sure the scent of Destiny's body spray was gone.

"But this was you." John gestured at the stairs.

Rennet grabbed his tail before it could do something embarrassing, like start wagging. It hadn't happened yet, but anything was possible around John. "Well, I," he started to explain, except that he didn't have an explanation that didn't expose his every desire. "Yes."

John looked out toward his neighbors, then back at Rennet. He exhaled. "I think I've had enough. Rennet, I would like it if…. No." He straightened his shoulders. "Rennet, you are spending the night."

Rennet opened his eyes wide. His heart did crazy pounding things. He took an involuntary step forward before he remembered that he had no idea what was going on in John's head. "I… am?" he asked, clarifying a statement that wasn't confusing. John had said Rennet would be spending the night, and Rennet was already drifting closer.

"Yes." John nodded for good measure, then stood there. Rennet gave a start, then decided *fuck the neighbors*, and hopped up to the porch.

John seemed surprised at Rennet's breathless acquiescence, but only for a moment. He murmured, "That was suspiciously easy," and gave Rennet a searching look, yet despite that his smile stayed in place as he opened the door for him.

Rennet didn't comment on the door being held for him, or on the box of pizza sitting on the coffee table by the couch, or the couch itself, which still had a blanket and pillow on it. But the pizza smelled delicious.

"Have some," John invited. Rennet took him at his word and downed two slices in seconds. He took his time on the third and fourth. John moved around while Rennet was eating, closing curtains and blinds, bringing Rennet a glass of water, before he finally sat on the couch.

"I thought you were mad at me," Rennet got out around a mouthful of a supreme with everything but anchovies. He perched on the other end of the couch and licked his fingers clean, keeping his eye on John while enjoying the food. "You really want me to spend the night?"

"If you want to." John looked like he wished he had a tail to fidget with. He pushed his hands over his knees as though he had sweaty palms, but otherwise he seemed calm. "Do you want to? Regardless of everything else that's happened," he went on, not making any sense that Rennet could see, "you don't have to if you don't want to. *Did* you want to?"

Rennet nodded. John rubbed his hands over his knees again. He was so perplexing.

Rennet slid down a touch and rested his cheek on the back of the couch in order to stare sideways at him. "I didn't know you wanted me to. I thought—"

"You thought we were fuck buddies. Yes. I understand that now, Rennet." John stopped and cleared his throat. "I apologize for giving you that impression, but you always left first, and I didn't want to pressure you. Clearly I should have known you require the delicacy of an H-Bomb." John turned to look directly at him. Then he made a strange, displeased face and shook his head. "I should have asked why you were leaving, but I thought I was being very obvious."

Dinner by candlelight in a nice restaurant was, in fact, very obvious now that Rennet let himself really think about it. He stared at John with dry eyes. "No one ever… I'm an imp." He couldn't find the words. "All those lunches at food carts. You wanted…."

John gave a long sigh as Rennet had the realization that John had taken him out on a date that night, a real one. The kind you went on when you wanted to impress someone. All wrong for someone like Rennet, but beautiful anyway, for the attempt. No one else would have done it.

"I value your friendship, Rennet, and the sacrifices you were trying to make for me, but as far as I am concerned, I've wanted to date you since I met you. You swear in at least three languages. You can fix anything, until you break it again. And you *really* fill out a pair of jeans. You came to my house to take down a tree in the backyard and wound up replacing my gutters, and I couldn't take my eyes off you. You called me 'Sunshine' to my face, and I resolved right then to ask you out, damn everything else." John wouldn't let him look away. "I thought we *were* dating until I realized how you never stay over. And forgive me if I tell you that those stairs out there are sending the message that you wouldn't mind that, dating me. Even in an election year, which, I acknowledge now, might be stressful."

Rennet opened his mouth, then closed it. He slid down onto his ass. He opened his mouth again.

John narrowed his eyes.

"I know you aren't a fairy, or a human," he argued preemptively, and Rennet shut up. "You can stop thinking that I care about that, about any of that. I don't know why you are so afraid of fairies in particular, because you are the sexiest, most interesting man I have ever met. But if that still bothers you, let me make some more things clear before we go on. The fairy, Rennet, was because I thought you didn't care. You hadn't been to see me at work or at home in over a week, and the fairies were around me, and I thought, if you cared, you would say something."

Rennet winced, because he had said something all right, but probably not what John had wanted to hear.

John's expression was hard as flint, but his voice was getting softer. "You're worried about the bed? We can buy a new one, or drag the mattress to the floor and sleep there, it doesn't matter. I can take it, as long as I get to at least know what it's like sharing it with you. I know you can break things, Rennet. I don't care. You make things too, and I want… I want you."

"I thought politicians weren't supposed to be this honest," Rennet whispered when he could finally speak again, then shook his head at his own stupidity and crawled over the middle cushion to climb into John's lap. "It would be safer if you only wanted to fuck me." John's face against the hollow of his throat was wonderful. John's hands clutching hard at Rennet's hips to hold him still were even better. Rennet slid his cheek over the top of John's head and shivered when John stroked under his wings.

"But I don't want to only fuck you," John countered, as pleasantly as he'd ever told someone off in a council meeting. Rennet didn't smile. He couldn't with his heart tripping madly. But he willed himself to be silent and then gave up when his worries made his tail twitch.

"Yeah?" he asked at last, because John acted like that, like dating and all the attached feelings, weren't dangerous too. "Even though I'm an imp?"

"Yeah." John could be gentle even out of bed. "Because you're you." His fingertips strayed lightly over different places around Rennet's back, dipped against his wings as though he'd been curious about them for a while. Rennet had never been still with him long enough for him to touch them. Rennet opened them wider, trying not to shake, and then swallowed when John took the invitation for what it was and caressed them with the same care.

No one had touched Rennet with such thoughtful attention since he'd been a boy. He took it for another minute and then folded his wings protectively around John. "I didn't want you hurt," he admitted in a young, frightened whisper. The very act made him flush hotly in embarrassment.

John murmured his name as if surprised, but that was all except for John's hands sliding over him, John's breath against his skin. After another nervous pause, Rennet nestled his tail against John's side. Then he held still. He didn't so much as twitch. He didn't even want to try. Maybe this was unbelievable enough that his spirit was momentarily satisfied.

It couldn't last. Of course it couldn't, even without Rennet there, but he wanted John to have it. Rennet imagined this was what sleeping next to John might feel like. Then he closed his eyes and willed it to happen. Maybe even an imp might find an ending worthy of a fairy. He could let himself hope for that, and relax at last in John's waiting arms.

RENNET SAW the news—*finally* saw the news, apparently—the next morning, when he was eating a bagel in a diner and a very helpful citizen gave him his old paper so he could do the Jumble. There were a few follow-ups to the stories of the previous day. He read with interest about the baby born in the elevator, skipped over the reunited siblings, and flipped to the fun section, only to freeze at a glimpse of the political page, where there was a big picture of himself outside John's house with the caption "Imp at the heart of City Hall sex scandal." He was pretty sure the picture had been taken the day before. It seemed worse when paired with one of Rennet's mug shots.

"Fuck me," he exclaimed, ignoring the outraged gasp of a woman feeding her toddler a muffin. He gulped his coffee and scanned down for an article to explain that caption, then pulled his phone from his pocket to call Daphne at work as he was reading.

"You couldn't have been a touch more clear?" he thundered at her while reading the words.

The man known as the Incredible Unflappable Mr. Sunshine had no comment despite the strong hints in yesterday's society column that he was sleeping with an employee.

"I don't normally read the society stuff," Daphne yelled over the sound of squealing, tiny humans, "but people kept pointing it out to me all day."

"What did it say?" Rennet's good mood was sinking fast. He had to get out of the diner before he did any real damage. He went outside and started walking.

"The gist? That the previously perfect Mr. Sunshine, who is up for reelection this year, might be having an illicit relationship with an employee. There was a pun or two. He wouldn't like 'being' caught in a relationship, that sort of thing. But…." Rennet had a feeling Daphne was pursing her lips. "But the thing is, everyone, and I mean *everyone*, knew it was you. Or assumes it was. Not that they are wrong, are they?"

"'Regardless of everything else,' John said," Rennet growled into the phone. "That's what he said to *me*. What did he say to *them*?"

"Nothing. Not even today, as far as I know, when the gossip made it to the political page and people were discussing his chances if he had been, er"—she dropped her voice—"*sleeping with* an employee, or if he was, as everyone in town but this reporter, I guess, already knew, seeing you."

Rennet stopped dead. He lashed his tail, knocking over a trash can, which he immediately righted, then kept walking.

"Did *everyone* know about us?" He was more embarrassed at being so surprised by that than anything else. Daphne laughed.

"It wasn't me always driving to the station in the middle of the night to bail you out, Rennet. I have to go. Ynez, sweetie, put that down!" Daphne hung up without saying good-bye. Rennet tucked away his phone and narrowed his eyes as he passed the police station, noting the smirks that accompanied the waves as he walked by today.

He looked up when he realized he was outside City Hall. Coming here had not been his intention, but it rarely ever was. He put his hands in his pockets and slipped in the doors as someone else was leaving. Daryl coughed deliberately, announcing that he'd witnessed that entrance, and when Rennet turned toward him he was almost leering.

Rennet considered. It was bad enough he was in City Hall without knowing for sure that John didn't mind everyone knowing about them. Doing more damage was probably not advisable. John didn't want Rennet as his thug, he'd said. He wanted Rennet as more than a friend, more than a friend with benefits. He didn't need to deal with more of Rennet's fallout.

Then again, he didn't need to deal with Daryl's smirks either. Rennet winked at Daryl, and the wheels of Daryl's chair caught on the edge of a rug as he moved, pitching the security guard forward. He would have hit the floor if he hadn't caught himself on the desk. Rennet sailed on, spreading his wings as he went down the hall.

John hadn't explicitly forbidden him from anything, and perhaps it was time people were reminded that Rennet wasn't some fairy in search of happiness; he was a vengeful, malicious, petty spirit of disharmony with the sensibilities of a rocker. John had said he wanted him. John didn't mind the rest. In fact, John liked it. Even if Rennet had maybe, probably, definitely, damaged his career.

Despite all that, knowing that even, John had told him to stay the night. And Rennet had. Now he was a well-rested imp in love.

He hadn't *begun* to act like a thug.

Margery spotted him and formed a circle with her beautiful red mouth. It only lasted for a second before she pointed to the bank of chairs as though nothing had changed. Rennet immediately folded up his wings and sat down with his knees hooked over the shared arms of two chairs. Margery remained as unimpressed as ever.

"You could have said something," Rennet tossed out, not even a tiny bit angry when she went back to working on her computer.

"And ruin the show?" She arched an eyebrow without looking at him.

Rennet considered the closed door to the inner office. "So he's in there? Who with?"

"If you want me to clear up these appointments so he has a free afternoon, you had better be quiet." Margery was cool as a cucumber. It must be something to watch her and John in action together.

The doorknob turned. Rennet jerked up his head without changing his languid pose. He blinked to see Campbell the reporter smiling as he came out of the office and then blinked again to see John behind him.

They both noticed him immediately, though their reactions were quite different. John had his pleasant yet utterly false sunshine politician face on, but his smile widened when he saw Rennet. Campbell froze in his tracks until John politely nudged him forward.

"Mr. Campbell, I believe you remember Rennet," John prompted, then turned to exchange a few words with his secretary. Rennet turned to Campbell and grinned. He let his tail whip against the floor. If John wanted to be the guy who threw a lit firecracker into the room and then shut the door, then Rennet had no problems being that firecracker.

"I did say never to trust you," Rennet remarked, stretching in a way that most wouldn't while sitting in City Hall. John glanced at him, pushed up his glasses, but didn't say a word. Rennet focused on Campbell with glee. "But that's okay. Intrigue is necessary in the world of gossip reporting. Oh right, you're the political writer. I got confused."

Campbell's eyes went to Rennet's teeth, then away. He scowled. "I'm writing politics now."

"You mean you didn't before?" Rennet sat up. "So you *are* a gossip columnist. Or were, I suppose. Old habits die hard, I understand that. You should see the things I used to get up to before you humans started getting stricter with your laws. I could have a human like you living in absolute *terror*."

"Could you now?" Campbell asked faintly, looking from Rennet to John. He had his chin up in a show of bravery. It wasn't too bad, actually. Rennet rose to his feet, circling Campbell before moving toward John.

"Finally see the news, did you?" John inquired pointedly, stopping Rennet in his tracks with a touch of his hand, a sweep of his thumb at the edge of Rennet's mouth. He pulled back his hand, revealing a speck of cream cheese. Rennet didn't have time to be chagrined that he'd been walking around with that on his face before John sucked it from his thumb.

Rennet thought he might be mistaken about who the firecracker in the room was. He turned toward Campbell with his face hot and his nubby fangs pressing hard into his bottom lip. "You know, you caused quite a lot of trouble," he said conversationally, though his tail was agitated and active. "So before I forget, thanks."

Campbell seemed confused. Rennet patted Campbell's chest in understanding, then flicked his nose when the man looked down. He was probably always going to fall for that.

"Oh, by the way…." Rennet had something else to say before he got even more distracted by John. He glanced in John's direction but then focused on the reporter. "You asked before, about our relationship, my relationship, with Mr. Sunshine. I wasn't entirely honest, but then everyone knows imps are liars." He lied but made it seem like honesty, and felt John's tension, as if John found that highly amusing but couldn't laugh. Rennet took a deep breath and kept his eyes solely on Campbell. "The truth is this human, this human and no other."

That was all he needed to say, really. John went motionless in that shocked way of his that other people never seemed to see, but Rennet could *feel* to his marrow. He could feel it the way fairies saw shine. Campbell stared. Rennet waited, only a little anxious about Campbell's reaction, only a lot anxious about John's, even with everything. John was still John, Rennet was still Rennet and always would be, and the truth had always been the source of the best explosions. The truth could destroy and reshape the world, or just pieces of it.

"I'm glad we could clear things up." John abruptly returned to the conversation, putting a hand on Rennet's hip that made Campbell's eyes go round. Rennet swallowed. John had a threatening, pleased rumble in his voice, the Sunshine version of a purr. "Mr. Campbell, I look forward to reading more of your work. Now if you'll excuse us…."

"I'll hold your calls," Margery interjected, a goddess of secretaries and orderly retreats. John angled Rennet toward the inner office door, and Rennet went. He had a moment to appreciate Campbell tripping due to a knot in his shoelaces, and then John shut the door and pinned him to it.

"I've never been in your inner office before." Rennet got his tongue unstuck from the roof of his mouth in time to say that, and then John kissed him.

"I figured it was time my boyfriend got to see it," John said in reply, long moments later, when Rennet was panting against his jaw and Rennet's hands and tail were yanking John closer by his belt and tie.

"Boyfriend?" Rennet was far too old for the childish term. He grinned to hear it anyway.

John angled his head to whisper above the tip of Rennet's ear. "Someone once told me that a councilman should be able to date whoever he wants. I think I want to date this one." His mouth was obscene. "This one and no other."

Rennet was having a hard time speaking. "Well, that someone sounds reckless as shit," he said at last, and trailed his mouth over John's skin, liking the human roughness, then pulled back to shove John against the door. John went willingly.

"I like reckless," he told Rennet as he started to breathe harder, but reached down to lock the door. Rennet swiped his tongue along John's already wet lips and completely failed to protest when John flipped them to the way they had been and held him in place.

"Like this?" Rennet suggested, offering a wicked grin. Margery would hear. The door might never be the same.

John didn't seem to realize that, or care. He only said, "I don't mind if you don't," then pressed forward.

Rennet shut his eyes and moaned before John even had his pants down.

The Wolf in the Garden

2014

"IS EVERYONE doing well?" Miki asked the plants as he went to the small greenhouse sink to fill the silver watering can with distilled water. The glass-enclosed room wasn't a true greenhouse, but the other employees of Cassandra's magic shop called it the Greenhouse anyway. Despite the humidity, it was the only part of the Dead Man's Garden most of them ventured into.

Unlike the plants in the yard outside, the Greenhouse didn't contain anything useful for magic, but something about the damp windows and iron work and hanging, hungry plants gave the shop atmosphere, or so the customers said. Tourists stopped by sometimes too, humans who didn't practice magic, or curious, shuddering fairies from the village who wanted to glimpse the flesh-eating plants on display.

A harmless little freak show, to most. Miki tutted and rolled up his sleeves. The late afternoon sun broke through the glass around him, leaving him red-faced and sticky with perspiration, not that anyone was around to see. He leaned in, although not too far, over the first—a flytrap. "Hello, beautiful," he greeted it softly. "Let's keep you healthy." He eyed the dirt, then dripped enough water into the soil to keep it damp. It would add to the steamy temperature of the semi-enclosed room.

He paused to make sure his long sleeves stayed in place at his elbows, then moved on to the next flytrap, keeping the soil wet. He ducked out of the way of hanging pitcher plants, noting one of them had trapped something, a small insect lured there by the bright color or the promise of sweet nectar.

The vivid hues of the Old World pitchers were a warning, but most, including the humans who visited the Greenhouse, found the crimson and purple shades fascinating. They giggled nervously at them, recognizing killers even if the plants meant no harm to them.

Miki always kept his face turned from the door as he instructed the pitchers to ignore the giggles. He watered each, in turn, feeling the room incrementally grow more humid and uncomfortable. The pitcher plants on the tables behind the flytraps and different breeds of sundews got the same treatment, though he noted which had fed and which hadn't. He rarely had to supplement their intake of nutrients, but he kept watch just the same.

Some dirt had been spilled along a table, as if someone had tried to touch or take a plant without asking, although nothing was missing. Customers were not supposed to be back here without an employee present.

He tightened his mouth and cleaned up the mess. Then he put away the watering can and swept the floor, since it was almost closing time. That done, he went on to the next room, glancing out over the sales floor. The glass terrariums and mock-antique birdcages filled with tiny plants were another part of the magic store's famed "atmosphere." The practitioners who came in regularly found them charming. A few claimed the tiny worlds Miki had created inside each glass bowl or metal cage induced states of calm, which made their work easier.

Miki scrubbed dirt from his palm and felt warm all over again at the remembered compliment, although he did not remove his outer shirt. By summer the long sleeves would be too warm, even in Los Cerros, with its rolling hills and sea breezes, but he liked the comfort the outer shirt offered.

He almost pulled down his sleeves when he saw the people still milling around inside the store despite it being close to seven. His part of the shop was separate from the main store, where tools from many magical disciplines were sold to the city's more discerning practitioners. Some witches and healers preferred to make all their tools themselves, some only liked to prepare their own ingredients, and others preferred to leave the prep in the hands of specialists.

When he wasn't occupied with the gardens, Miki was supposed to work the floor and offer help if it was needed, but Cassandra, the owner as well as Miki's landlady, had long since stopped expecting him to come inside. Even in the rain he would be out with the plants, although spring didn't have him harvesting much. He kept to his end of the store anyway, cleaning up the outer room and then going through the Greenhouse out into the true garden.

Cassandra owned the store and the building next to it, a squat, converted Victorian with apartments on the second floor that overlooked the gardens. The gardens were warded as well as fenced in, for very good reasons, but Miki liked being able to keep an eye on them in his off hours.

To some, he supposed, they looked uninviting, especially at the moment, when many of the plants had yet to flower. He huffed in delight at every green shoot and uncurling vine greedily soaking up the sunshine and then raised his head to consider the early evening sky. He listened to the hum of insects and smiled when a light breeze pushed away his loose strands of hair and tickled his cheek.

He tucked his overlong bangs behind his ear and tilted his face up toward the sun, inhaling dozens of different perfumes and earthy, metallic soil.

The sound of a small, startled exhale took him by surprise. Miki dropped his head, sending his hair down over his face once more, and then blinked rapidly at the tall figure in the garden with him.

He hadn't noticed someone slipping into the garden while he'd been cleaning. He frowned and darted his gaze toward the Greenhouse, where the visitor must have clearly been able to see Miki and yet hadn't asked for assistance as several signs told him to do.

Most people didn't *want* to visit the Dead Man's Garden without an escort. Miki's blood seemed to thrum at the thought, although he couldn't have said why. A newcomer meant more work for him, more questions, more staring, usually.

Perhaps not this time. That wasn't a human in the garden with him. Nor was it a fairy. That, unless Miki was mistaken, was a werewolf. Over six feet of barely disguised strength, solid shoulders, and that ineffable almost-glow that Miki associated with beings, although he had never heard anyone else refer to it. Miki wasn't special. He didn't have the sight. But he knew beings when he saw them, even before they took a long, deep breath and then stared at him with eyes of pure, lupine yellow.

Miki swallowed. He had only ever met one werewolf before, and that werewolf had behaved as most werewolves did around humans and acted human. Glowing, reflective eyes had never been turned on Miki. The almost-glow around that were had never shivered as he started to growl.

Miki took a step back and the growl stopped. The were reached up and rubbed at his nose, as if it itched. In his other hand, down at his side, was a violin case.

Miki stared for a moment, peeking through the dark hair that hid half his face. "Customers aren't allowed out here unescorted unless they know what they're doing." The words were clear, but he looked away before yellow eyes could meet his again.

"Randall told me to wait outside." The werewolf had a husky, pleasant voice. He scratched his nose again, significantly. Weres did not like magic. Miki had learned that not long after starting here, when the police had come around as they sometimes did after magical crimes happened. The werewolf detective never stayed in the shop for long, and rubbed his nose whenever he ventured inside. It seemed magic was itchy to a werewolf nose.

This were had come into the shop anyway to visit Randall. Randall worked at the candle and beeswax counter, but this werewolf wasn't here for an enchanted candle, not if he was the were Randall had spoken of. Miki risked another direct look and found the werewolf's eyes hadn't left him.

Werewolves didn't flock to cities or centers of human magic. They certainly wouldn't garden, which was Miki's only subject of conversation. Miki had no idea what to do with this one.

The were didn't seem upset, or at least, not angry or irritable. He was overdressed to be standing in a garden, although not by much. He had on jeans and a sport coat over a dark V-neck shirt. If he'd had a scarf, he would have looked like a professor, which he might have been. The university here and the one an hour away in Madera had been hiring more beings of late.

His hair was nearly black, with thick patches of silvery gray at the temples, although he didn't appear to be much beyond forty, if that, making the gray very unusual for a were. Unlike the last werewolf Miki had seen, this one had some stubble, the same dark shade as the rest of his hair. His skin was the color of cherry wood, a smooth medium brown. Miki eyed the patch of skin left exposed by his T-shirt and then sent his gaze down to the stone-lined path they were both standing on.

Miki was wearing stained and muddy boots and jeans a little too big for him because he hadn't bothered to try them on when he'd bought them. The size of his jeans didn't matter as long as he could get them dirty, which they certainly were. His T-shirt had once been plain white, before pollen and sweat and soil had stained it. Thorns had ripped a few holes in it, which Miki had forgotten about until now.

The shirt he wore over that was useless. It was much too late for Miki to tug down his sleeves, although even a werewolf shouldn't see anything amiss with the tattoo on Miki's left arm. Miki nervously swiped his hair from his face, then froze as he realized what he'd done. The dirt that was likely in his hair after a day of work barely crossed his mind.

He paused and then deliberately pulled his bangs in front of his face as a screen, although the were's sharp eyes would have seen his birthmark already. The port-wine stain covered most of Miki's left cheek and part of his neck. His parents had paid for treatments before giving up on him years ago, and the stain had lightened to a ruddy pink. He had been warned it might darken again as he aged. The mark on his arm was the original red-purple, although hidden by the tattoo.

All his words had dried up in his throat, so he tried to remember what Kaz had told him to do when confronted with an attractive stranger. Kaz would want him to keep his gaze up. But this were, painfully beautiful as so many beings tended to be, wasn't going to care if Miki spoke to him or not, or how he looked when he did. It was good to remember that.

Miki busied his unsteady hands with retying his hair, although his bangs immediately slipped free. The rest of his curls almost reached his shoulders. He'd have to coax Kaz to cut it again. Kaz wanted him to leave the waves free, and hated them tucked away or cut short, as it ruined Miki's "youthful, romantic appeal." Kazimir had many thoughts about Miki's appearance.

Perhaps the werewolf did as well. His eyebrows, thick and faintly arched, came together in a brief frown, which was slightly better than a charm to ward off the evil eye, which some older humans still aimed at Miki when they thought he couldn't see.

The werewolf studied him for a moment longer, then closed his eyes and inhaled. Miki took the chance to stare directly into the were's handsome face and realized, with a small start, that the werewolf's expression might have nothing to do with Miki's appearance. The werewolf looked *tired.*

Werewolves didn't get sick, and they generally didn't grow tired. That was one of the many things they were admired for. Spells involving werewolf blood and other werewolf bodily donations were supposed to aid in strength and healing. It took a lot to exhaust a were. Nonetheless, something about this were, the shadows under his eyes, his slightly gaunt cheeks, that unexpectedly gray hair, suggested weariness, like how a human would look when recovering from a long illness.

The werewolf opened his eyes, which were still yellow, still fierce, and let out the breath he'd been holding. He smiled before Miki could dart his gaze away.

It was a friendly smile, wide and soft. Miki might have described it as goofy if he hadn't been talking about a werewolf.

Miki licked sweat from his upper lip. "Did you need something?" Conversation was beyond him. Even the thought of trying made him cringe. He stepped from the path, which was lined with smaller stones, though he and Cassandra had plans to put in a flagstone path along the same lines. It would lead from the sales floor through the small exit and out through the fenced-in main garden. There it would split to lead toward the poison garden or the bigger herb garden, both of which were fenced in again as well as warded, to protect them from animals more than thieves. Then the path led through a small door to the cactus garden and pond behind another fence. The back garden got more sun, which made it ideal for desert plants, and the babbling of the tiny waterfall in the pond was audible to those in the main garden with Miki. The sound was clearest to those sitting on the white bench in the corner, under the bower formed by wisteria vines.

"Most people know what they want when they come out here," Miki tried again. His tone was stern this time, although he very much doubted it would intimidate Randall's werewolf visitor.

It didn't. The werewolf's smile remained in place. "I didn't want anything when I came out here." He watched Miki go over to the herb garden and unnecessarily check the gate on the waist-high white picket fence surrounding it. "I mean," the werewolf corrected himself before Miki could say anything, "I came here to wait. Don't let me bother you, if I am." His show of teeth was distracting.

Miki looked to the herb garden, checking for signs of animal visitors before he left for the day. There were none, not even a nibble at the Rapunzel lettuce he'd planted to amuse himself. He wasn't sure if the werewolf's comment invited an answer, though he could imagine Kazimir would have had something witty or flirtatious in response to it. Or, knowing Kaz's scandalous past, something cool and challenging. He'd probably tilt up his head and icily demand what about the werewolf could be expected to bother him.

And then the werewolf would have fallen over himself to prove himself to Kazimir, and Kazimir would have had one more story of conquest.

Miki wiped at his cheek. "No." It wasn't much of an answer, but Miki wasn't used to wolves in his garden. He made himself speak more, his voice shaking with the lie. "No, you aren't bothering me." He kept to the herb garden, kneeling to examine the sprinkler system, which worked exactly how he'd set it up to and always had.

The werewolf let out a short, loud breath. Miki furtively kept an eye on him, conscious of the heat in his skin when the werewolf's smile curved wider. People who ventured into his garden asked for his help and then left. They were usually human, sympathetic but distant. They didn't linger and say nothing. Miki couldn't tell if the knot in his stomach was anxiety or fear. His mouth felt dry, his tongue large and stuck behind his teeth.

He ran out of things to examine in the herb garden and got silently to his feet. He hesitated, so obvious he made himself blush, and then went along the outer fence, checking the ornamental plants and their sprinklers as well. Roses could be difficult but held special significance in the human mind.

Not just human. Once, long ago, Kazimir had insisted that suitors had brought him orchids or roses. Miki brought him clippings sometimes, mostly to lift his spirits, although, oddly, Kazimir seemed to prefer simpler flowers. No one had ever brought Miki anything, but he grew whatever he wanted. No plastic-wrapped bouquet from a florist could equal that.

"Incredible." The werewolf's remark made Miki stumble, displacing a rock lining the path. Miki bent to replace it before meeting the werewolf's gaze, which remained steady on Miki despite how the were must have been referring to the garden. His eyes were less yellow now, getting closer to brown, as though he was calming down.

Miki tucked his hair behind his ear. "Yes it is." The garden was part of the reason the shop had the reputation and the clientele it did.

"It's not what I was expecting. Not that I was expecting anything." The earnest tone was at odds with the light, lingering smile on that handsome face. Between that and the violin case, he could have been the most harmless werewolf in existence, yet Miki kept to the outer fence as he slowly made his way back to the were.

Those eyes tracked him, flashing yellow again briefly before mellowing into dark brown. "Did you design and grow all this? How old are you?" There was a trace of an accent in the wolf's speech, not European like Miki's parents or Kaz, but Miki didn't know enough to distinguish what kind of Spanish the werewolf originally spoke, if he did. Miki sometimes still pronounced his *r*'s like his parents or forgot his *th*'s. He took care unless he was distracted, or emotional.

He didn't trust himself now, so he nodded and ignored the age question. He ducked a bird feeder, useless as it turned out. The smaller birds wouldn't approach with Cassandra's familiar, Greedigut, an owl, around, not even when he was inside. Hummingbirds darted in once in a while, but the majority of the garden's pollination was done by insects, especially bees.

As he got closer, he judged the werewolf to be a good five inches taller than he was, and built along more solid lines. His violin, if it was his, must seem delicate in comparison. Miki imagined the werewolf played both savage, wild music and soft, lilting melodies with his yellow eyes closed and his large hands graceful and sure. Miki wanted to weave a crown of flowers as the fairies would have, and drop the morning glories over the werewolf's head—white ones, ipomoea, stark and fragile. He'd always liked night-blooming flowers. Someday when he got his own garden, he would plant moonflowers to ensure he'd see flowers no matter when he went outside.

It was the stupidest thing he could have thought. Miki wasn't going to have his own garden any time soon, he would never have someone like this for a lover, and he had nothing in common with any fairy. He turned away, cutting across the garden to check out the New World pitchers along the bottom of the glass. He could see inside the Greenhouse, but didn't want to imagine how he must have seemed in there, if the werewolf had watched him cluck and fuss over his babies.

Something was struggling, very faintly, inside Mary, his bloody queen. "You greedy thing," he tutted at her before checking on her larger sister, Elizabeth.

A shadow fell over him. Miki tensed, but the werewolf was keeping his distance for all that he was clearly curious. "Carnivorous plants?" he asked, roughly satisfied in a way that made Miki swallow. "Do you feed them yourself?"

Certain tourists wanted to watch Miki feed them, the kind disappointed when he didn't offer them mice or small frogs, or feed the plants on command. Miki turned, daring a glance up. "Crickets." Once again his short answer wouldn't do. "But rarely. The cactuses in the garden beyond attract spiders, which gives them plenty to eat."

Spiders and flesh-eating plants together usually sent most tourists hurrying back to the main room, where the eye of newt on display didn't seem to bother them in the slightest.

"Cactus?" the werewolf asked, as if that was the most surprising thing about what Miki had said. He angled his head to consider the small door at the rear of the garden but didn't move toward it.

Miki tried again. "The flytraps are inside. They've been known to snack on a stray mouse or two." This was another lie. The flytraps would have gobbled up any mouse foolish enough to wander near them, but the shop had no mice. Greedigut saw to that.

"You say that with pride," the werewolf observed, making Miki turn to give him a longer look. He stopped when the werewolf stared at him in return, eyebrows raised.

He had nothing to say to that, except to point out that usually talking about the carnivorous plants sent people running. Cunning folk might stay behind, chatting, determined to be friendly, but even witches with familiars like Greedigut found the plants unnerving. People expected plants to be passive.

Not so, Miki's—Randall's visitor. Miki should have known. Violin case or not, this was a predator at his back.

He twitched, so warm that the tips of his ears seemed to burn, and felt younger than he had leaving home at seventeen. He pushed his bangs away impatiently and heard a sigh from behind him.

"Should I…." Miki paused to lower his voice, staring determinedly at Elizabeth. "Do you want to see the Dead Man's Garden?"

Surrounded by a higher picket fence painted dramatically black, marked with several signs warning visitors to ask for assistance and to *never* touch the plants with their bare hands, the Dead Man's Garden was hard to miss. Cassandra had warded the garden herself to keep out scavengers of the animal or human varieties. Every plant in the garden was documented, and every clipping and purchase made from it was also recorded. Magical healers used the poisons more than the regular magical practitioners, but followers of traditional magic, African, Native American, Asian, and European alike, all had the occasional need for a little toxicity.

Miki skirted around the werewolf with a flutter in his stomach and put his hands over his heated face. The flush would make the mark stand out, draw attention to it instead of to his wondrous, frightening garden.

He didn't hear the wolf follow him, but there he was, standing outside the opposite side of the black fence. The were sniffed the air discreetly, then sneezed.

Miki raised his head in surprise and realized he was smiling a second later. The werewolf fixed him with a look that was almost hurt, as if Miki should have warned him this was magic too, or perhaps he was upset that Miki was laughing at him.

But magic, and poison, didn't send him away. Miki's smile faded. He frowned for a moment, considering his visitor, then drew his attention to the plants with a wave of his hand. "The Dead Man's Garden." There was enough poison in the small patch of ground to kill even a werewolf. Miki's stomach gave another flutter. "For magical and medicinal purposes," he heard himself adding, softening it. "Obviously."

The silence from the werewolf made him glance up. The werewolf lifted an eyebrow. "Oh obviously," he agreed, smiling again even as he rubbed his nose. "It's pretty too." Miki started. Brown eyes met his, and Miki couldn't think to duck his head. "Was the garden your idea?"

"Dried herbs aren't as potent," Miki blurted, not certain what the werewolf was asking. "Many magical practitioners have an interest in botany, and grow what they need. But we're in a city, and most of them don't have the space."

The pleased expression on the werewolf's face didn't tell Miki how the were felt about any part of his answers. "Are you a practitioner?" The were inclined his head. That, at least, seemed to indicate some care on the werewolf's part, as if he didn't know how to feel about Miki casting spells. He seemed more put off by magic than by the idea of Miki feeding living mice to the plants.

"Not really," Miki admitted at last, wondering how much time had passed, why the werewolf would stand and wait for his answer. "Some. Mostly I like making things grow." He could have blushed all over again at the childish-sounding response.

The exhale from the werewolf was almost relieved. "You seem good at it. This is the last thing I'd find in the back of a magic shop, even one called Bubble Bubble."

Cassandra's sense of humor included things like using people's expectations of magic to draw them in, then subtly move them in a different direction. She kept a poison garden for healing, which said everything about her Miki had ever needed to know.

He didn't know how to respond to the werewolf's comment, and once again thought of how Kaz would chide him for his lack of wiles. Kaz never understood the plight of the ordinary, or the ugly. "We're one of a kind," Miki offered when the silence had gone on, then quickly slipped away. He bent over the Beauty of Rosemawr by the fence and inspected it as though he hoped to find aphids on the soft rose petals.

"You're busy." He didn't understand anything of the disappointment in the wolf's tone, or why he would find Miki with his face near a rose so fascinating. "Can I help you, while I wait?"

Miki would trust absolutely nothing to an amateur, except something that didn't matter. He gave the werewolf a frowning, sideways study, then nodded toward the Greenhouse. "There's a hummingbird feeder in there I haven't hung yet. I want it over by the wisteria." The garden ought to have more birds than one cranky owl.

Nonetheless, he straightened in dizzy confusion when the werewolf nodded and turned to go into the shop. Miki watched him navigate the Greenhouse, stopping briefly to consider the plants or perhaps the steamy temperature, then finding the red bird feeder and returning with it. Miki hadn't put any sugar water in the feeder yet, but he was speechless as his visitor hung it up from a wisteria branch and twisted around to get his opinion.

Miki licked the edge of his mouth before he nodded. He didn't trust his voice again. The were's smile made his chest tight. Miki realized he was drifting forward and stopped at the black fence. The were's happy expression left him when Miki didn't speak, yet the werewolf remained. He came up to the edge of the fence too, exactly as they'd been before.

"You aren't dressed for gardening," Miki said, at the precise moment the werewolf scowled and asked, "Do the police visit you about this garden?"

"Yes. But if someone doesn't seem right"—if they glimmered strangely to Miki's eye was what he meant, although he couldn't have explained how or why—"we make them wait until a fairy can look them over before we sell to them." Fairies saw the truth. They'd notice something like murderous intentions. "Are you...." Miki paused. The were had said he was waiting for Randall, but Randall had told them all about his werewolf friend, asked them to take care. "Are you looking for a poison?" Miki didn't keep the frown from his face, no matter how the werewolf lifted his eyebrows.

The wolf didn't answer. He sniffed again, then dropped his gaze unerringly to a few purple flowers within the black fence.

Miki's heart seemed to beat harder. "Monkshood," he identified the flowers quietly. "Wolfsbane," he continued, when the first name rendered no reaction from his visitor. The werewolf glanced up in surprise. Miki wished his heart would slow. "Humans used to use it to kill wolves. It's toxic to humans as well. Don't touch it unless you've made your peace with the world."

It would take more wolfsbane than his garden possessed to kill a wolf of this size, yet he didn't share that information. He was too fixed on the stillness in the body across from him, the slow drag of breath, how the werewolf's gaze momentarily fell again to consider the pretty purple flowers that could spell his doom, if he chose.

Miki wished he hadn't seen it, or that he hadn't heard Randall say what he had about this wolf. He let out a shuddery breath and made himself keep his head up when the were looked at him. "As suicide methods go, it would be slow, inefficient, and messy." He could have stopped there. He shouldn't have spoken at all. But the werewolf parted his lips, so Miki lifted his chin higher, blushing hotly. "And of course, I could treat you." He wouldn't allow the werewolf to suffer that kind of pain in front of him. It hardly mattered if the were would hate him later.

But Miki's gaze landed on the flowers in question. His voice was a whisper. "I have always thought, if I were to... I have always thought, belladonna. There would be less of a mess." He had never shared that thought before and kept his attention on the plants, first the wolfsbane, then the nightshade. "Not that I will tell you which plant that is, or how to use it."

That one point he would make very clear. That was not what this garden was for.

"But it was such a pretty flower," the werewolf remarked after leaving Miki to shift uncertainly against the fence. He looked up and shivered to see the werewolf's eyes had gone yellow once again.

"People say that." Miki couldn't think, couldn't remember saying this much to someone other than Kaz in years. "People see flowers as serene and restful because they forget they are the products of vicious evolutionary battles too, that every day these flowers have to fight for survival, even with my help. Everything we admire about them is a weapon of defense or reproduction. Colors to warn away the wrong visitors, or to attract the right ones, toxins or a bitter taste to keep enemies away, but which also allow the plant to live because another creature finds the unique taste delicious, and takes some pollen with it when it goes. They develop scent to lure in the birds and the bees. All that scent and color and taste, it's all to keep them alive, to draw in what they need. They are more than just something pretty, although they are that too. Flowers are survivors."

Too late he heard himself, the vibrating emotion in his voice. The sun seemed too bright, as if the entire world was yellow.

The werewolf was quiet and slow, almost stunned. "What *are* you?"

Miki jerked backward and bent his head, leaving his unmarked cheek exposed. People with port-wine stains had used to be seen as cursed by some people, or touched by magic in some way. But Miki took a breath and glanced over. The werewolf had drawn his eyebrows together, his expression befuddled or worried. A werewolf was hardly going to accuse Miki of being a monster when some still thought of werewolves as monsters themselves.

Miki thought back to his question and shook his head. "A gardener. A human. No one." Asserting that he wasn't a being seemed offensive, so he tried again. "No one remarkable."

The lines slowly disappeared from the werewolf's brow. He heaved his shoulders as he inhaled, and then the goofy smile flickered across his face. "I think I have to disagree with that." He curled his hands tightly over the top of the black fence, then lowered his head. A moment after that, he raised it again and gave a firm nod. "Yes."

"No." Miki didn't know why he was arguing. "I *am* a gardener."

"A remarkable one." The werewolf seemed very pleased with his answer, or Miki's dumb silence. The werewolf took the opportunity to glance down, at Miki's body or perhaps just his arm. The tattoo was part of Miki's teenage attempt to draw attention away from his face, and the berries in the blackberry bramble made the large, dark birthmark on his arm all but invisible. Nonetheless, he had an urge to tug down his sleeves. There was nothing special about blackberries. They were weeds to a lot of people, tangled roots and prickly defenses that only wild things risked to get to the fruit.

Yet the werewolf was staring. Miki shivered, then jumped when Randall's voice cut through the air.

"Diego?"

Miki turned his head and saw Randall in the doorway to the sales floor, safely not setting foot in the garden itself. His attention was focused on his friend. "Diego, man, I'm off now. We can go. Let's get dinner." Miki glanced to the werewolf and felt his body seize with strange tension to know Diego's eyes hadn't left him. Behind him, at a distance, Randall finally looked at Miki, his eyebrows raised. Miki couldn't think of how to answer him and didn't want to take his attention from Diego for long anyway.

"Diego?" Randall's careful tone said more than anything else that he was surprised Diego wasn't bolting gratefully from the garden. He was probably shocked Diego had stayed as long as he had. Randall shot another glance Miki's way before clearing his throat and gentling his tone. "Diego, come on. Let's get some food in you."

Having to remind a werewolf to eat was another warning sign that something was wrong with this werewolf, but Diego didn't appear underfed. He must have been eating regularly for a while, at least, putting in the effort to live again. His friend was concerned all the same.

Miki tried a small smile, ignoring the startled breath from Randall to see it. "You should go," he prompted.

Diego blinked and angled his head up into the breeze, taking in the sunshine, or the evening air, for another few moments. He took a long breath and slowly let it shudder out of him. Then he met Miki's stare. "It was nice to meet you," he said politely. It was the strangest thing he had done yet. Miki hadn't been nice. He'd been rude and then pushy about the wolfsbane. He'd made him hang up a bird feeder. But the wolf seemed to mean it, so Miki swallowed and inclined his head.

"Man. You okay?" Randall's voice carried clearly across the garden despite how he lowered it. He curled an arm around Diego in a short, sideways hug when Diego reached him, and Diego relaxed his shoulders. "I can't believe you came out here. I meant for you to wait out front. No one stays around the Dead Man's Garden except for Miki. It's too creepy."

Miki pretended not to listen, his eyes down. Not that it mattered; he couldn't hear the werewolf's reply, only that he had one, low and rough. When they were gone, he tugged down his sleeves and went about seeing to the rest of the garden, making sure everything was as it should be before he left for the day too.

He was overheated in moments, but he left his sleeves down, and stayed until he was absolutely finished.

A LITTLE over a half an hour later, Miki left the shop and walked around the storefront to the alley that led to the side entrance to his apartment. He could go through the front door and use the back stairs, but he didn't like wandering through a witch's apartment unprotected, even if Cassandra promised him he'd be fine. The side staircase was narrow, but it worked for him, and Kazimir rarely left the building these days. When he did, he didn't have to walk if he didn't want to.

Miki's door led into his small kitchen, with windows overlooking the garden below. The living room, which with the open plan was really the other half of the kitchen, also had windows with a view of the garden, along with a small couch and TV. His bedroom was across from the bathroom and closet, down a tiny hall that ended with another door. That led to Kazimir's apartment, which was the mirror image of Miki's, only lacking an entrance of its own.

That was the reason Miki's rent was cheap, or so Cassandra said when she'd invited Miki to live with her; he had to put up with someone else going through his rooms if Kaz didn't want to use the stairs in his apartment that went to Cassandra's first floor apartment. Now, however,

Miki thought Cassandra knocked off large portions of his rent as payment for taking care of Kazimir, who certainly needed a caretaker.

Kaz wouldn't see it that way. The firebird had adopted Miki on Miki's first day in the building, pulling him firmly under his wing and nuzzling close as if the mark on Miki's face invited him to. Miki had been too stunned to protest.

Miki knocked on the door between their apartments before entering, although the only person he'd ever found in there with Kazimir, aside from Cassandra, was Rennet. The imp and Kaz didn't act like lovers, more like old friends. Very old, knowing how long firebirds and imps could live.

No one but Kaz was around when he stepped inside. Kazimir was lying on his sofa. He'd made himself tea, the antique, formal silver tea set on the coffee table at odds with his worn but comfortable blanket. It was not a cool day, but Kaz had the blanket up to his chin.

Miki tried not to notice the number of golden, gleaming feathers along the ground. There had been no feathers on the floor when he'd left for work that morning. They both knew what the feathers meant, but Miki was the only one who seemed bothered by it. He came forward, and Kazimir sat up, stretching luxuriously before pouring a cup for Miki. He handed it over on a saucer, one sugar cube already dissolving in the heat as Miki liked.

Kazimir's apartment got the morning sun. It was dim now, most of the light coming from Kaz himself. He was beautiful, with pale, unmarked skin, short hair of gold, and high, arching eyebrows. He had stopped aging—giving the appearance of aging—at about twenty-five, but he was closer to a century, Miki guessed, perhaps older than that. There was no telling how he'd ended up here, living in a back apartment above a witch, avoiding others. Miki had never asked, but he had looked him up once. Kazimir had been, maybe still was, a famous singer. How could he not be, looking like that, with the voice a firebird was reputed to have? This was like Maria Callas was Miki's roommate, although Cassandra called him Garbo when they were bickering.

The tea was strong. One of the few errands Kaz continued to do on his own was to head into the Russian shops for his tea and sugar cubes and dark bread. He took cabs. Miki was astounded every time he saw Kazimir stand on the corner and whistle for a cab with his fingers in his mouth.

"Zaichik," Kaz greeted him, with a few other words in his native Russian and then French that Miki didn't understand. Miki knew some Hungarian, but that was all. He remembered his mother telling him Russians couldn't be trusted. That was before she'd washed her hands of him at seventeen, for his face, for his attitude, for his disgusting interest in men that made him too like a being, for his interest in crawling in the dirt.

"English, Kaz," Miki reminded him, as he did almost every day, and took his tea into Kaz's small kitchen. He'd started keeping some of his food there when Kaz had begun showing less and less of an inclination to come into Miki's apartment to eat. Kaz didn't move much anymore. He was thinner than Miki now, and starting to look older.

But he'd made tea. Good tea. Miki scrubbed the dirt from his hands and then prepared some oatmeal and toast and eggs. He made some for himself too, not much caring what he ate, and returned to the living room. Kaz had thrown off the blanket and covered himself in a flimsy silk bathrobe. He tutted to see Miki hadn't bothered with more than one plate or fork per person, but accepted his food.

He ate two bites of egg and then sat back to nibble his toast. Miki eyed him as he cleaned his own plate. He ate some of Kaz's food, resolving to make him less tomorrow, then went into the kitchen to wash the dishes and leave them out to dry. "Did you watch anything good today?" he called out after a while. Kaz found soap operas ridiculous, but had a weak spot for daytime talk shows.

Kaz was shaking his head when Miki returned. He pulled his feet up onto the couch and smiled when Miki covered him with the blanket. "I was reading, little rabbit," Kaz informed him, as if the book weren't on the coffee table. Miki recognized the yellowed pages and missing cover. The volume of short stories was a rare book, hard to find, according to Rennet, unless you were an imp with a talent for chaos and random chance. "I am closer to my Yasha with every page."

"Kaz—" Miki couldn't keep the worry from his voice, and Kazimir opened his eyes wide before beckoning him over with graceful gestures. Miki fell onto the couch next to him, and Kazimir's long fingers swept through his hair, pulling it from the band at the back of his neck.

"We must find someone to take care of you, bunny, before I meet my Yasha again." He combed out Miki's tangles with his fingers and scratched his scalp and didn't react when Miki tensed and shook his head. "What a pretty boy you are." Kaz always ignored how Miki didn't want to hear his lies. He tapped a finger against Miki's lips to shush him, then gently traced Miki's nose, his cheekbones, his eyelashes. "Exquisite, when you aren't scowling and hiding behind your hair. If I weren't fond of you, I would have made you mine. But you do not deserve the tragedy."

Kaz's touch was meant as a comfort. He couldn't help that Miki flushed for it. No one ever touched him but Kaz, even if Kaz didn't mean it. Miki closed his eyes, pale hazel green, as Kaz liked to inform him, and allowed Kaz to pet the light olive skin of his unmarred cheek. "So young and so pretty," Kaz told him again, with a sad little sigh, and probably a pout. "Yet you waste it."

"You're welcome to it." Miki didn't blush for the offer. He knew Kaz would pat his cheek and call him a silly rabbit, which he did.

"You are not for me, though you make a lovely houseboy. You, silly rabbit, require attention and care I could never give you, even if I were young again."

Miki didn't require care, but Kaz never listened to that argument either. Miki curled up closer to him and kept his eyes closed. Kaz scratched his scalp soothingly, then paused and hummed under his breath. Miki was instantly suspicious. Kaz had recently taken to prodding Miki more obviously to join the rest of the world. "Rabbit, did you speak to anyone today?" He did not mean with customers.

Miki opened his eyes and knew Kaz could feel it when he stopped breathing for a moment. Kaz pulled Miki's hair from his face and leaned over to try to peer at him. Miki felt hot. "A were came into the shop," he explained reluctantly, trying to turn away and finding out Kazimir had strength left in him.

"A werewolf in a magic shop?" Kazimir pursed his lips. "Interesting."

"Yeah." That should have been it. Miki should have been quiet. He knew what Kaz was like. Instead the words burst out of him in a rush. "He came outside to avoid the itchy smell. He came outside to the garden."

"Your garden?" Kaz studied him intently. He was almost too bright to look at directly. He spread his fingers over Miki's marked cheek to keep Miki still. "Where he stayed?" He lifted one eyebrow. "With you? And you let him?"

"I hardly run everyone off," Miki scoffed, despite his memory of the surprise on Randall's face.

"Bunny, you do exactly that, and skillfully." Kaz nearly preened. "I could not do it better."

Miki sat up to give Kaz a knowing look. "You reeled them in first."

Kaz continued to gloat. "In my youth, I crushed many a man under my silken slippers." He smiled proudly. "Most of them deserved it. So many wanted the voice, or the feathers, the inspiration, not me. Only Yasha…." He trailed off without finishing, his smile fading. He shrugged, and his robe revealed one golden shoulder, the skin thinner than it should have been. "It's the nature of a firebird. They capture me, but I destroy them."

His expression was too solemn. Miki nudged him in encouragement, although he had heard most of the tales before. "Until Yasha."

Kazimir closed his eyes, momentarily rapt at the memory of his lost lover, Jacob. Miki put a hand to his chest, unable to imagine a longing that could last decades. Kaz spoke to Jacob in his sleep, reread Jacob's strange little book frequently, but it didn't ease the ache he lived with, every day. Even when Miki made him smile, the longing was there. Maybe that's why he said Miki was not meant to be his, despite his fondness for him.

"Yasha loved my voice but didn't want my inspiration. He didn't want to capture me, so I tried to capture him instead." Kaz was quiet, not sad exactly. "He was not afraid of me." When Kazimir focused on Miki again, the room seemed too dim. "He hid from his writing until me. He was not afraid, not enough to let himself be stopped."

"There's nothing frightening about me, Kaz." Miki got up quickly to stretch. He kept his gaze on anything but Kaz's face. If people were intimidated by a few plants, by a frown, by color splashed onto his face, Miki couldn't help that. He couldn't be anything but what he was. He took the tea tray into the kitchen, cleaning what he could. "People simply aren't that interested."

Perhaps if he weren't plain and boring, then his plants might not scare off any friends or suitors, but not even a fairy wanted to spend time with someone who had poisons as a hobby.

"Was the werewolf afraid of you?" Kaz called out as if he wasn't done with the conversation.

Miki stopped, aware Kaz could see him. He was warm again, breathing harder. The werewolf hadn't seemed bothered by anything but the possibility that Miki might use magic, and that was likely due to the itch in his nose more than a real fear.

Kaz was watching him expectantly, so Miki put down his dish towel. "He was Randall's friend. Randall told us he might stop by, and that if he did, to treat him carefully. He's the one… the one who lost his mate six years ago. She was human, I guess. She had cancer." Miki didn't know the specifics of what *mate* meant to a werewolf, but he knew it was serious. Diego had lost a spouse, and six years later he was still being handled carefully by his friends. He had seemed tired, unused to being outside, and that had been no casual look he'd given the wolfsbane. At some point, that werewolf had thought about giving up.

"He wasn't afraid because he was too distracted to be," Miki explained to the diva lounging in front of him. "He's essentially a widower, Kaz, and still missing her, clearly. Even if he were inclined to, I doubt he'd look at me anyway. His mate was a woman, and even if he were bisexual, I doubt he'd choose someone like me."

Kaz waved a hand to dismiss these points. "Male, female, otherwise and in between, werewolves don't see things as humans do. In fact, sight is almost an afterthought. But even if it wasn't, you are very pretty, rabbit, very unusual." Kaz smiled at that. Miki did not. Kaz didn't seem to notice, or care. "Did he smell you, this big, strapping werewolf?"

Strapping. Only Kaz could use an old-fashioned word and still embarrass Miki. But Diego was just that, big and strapping and handsome, and he had definitely sniffed the air around Miki before speaking. He had made a point of it. He'd wanted Miki to know he'd been smelling him. Imagining what he might do if he'd come closer, how he might inhale carefully at the back of Miki's neck, made Miki lick the corner of his mouth. He didn't want to acknowledge the triumphant narrowing of Kaz's eyes. "I've met a werewolf before. They sniff everyone." He was admitting everything, and shook his head firmly. "He's still in love, mated, however werewolves put it."

That was final and even Kaz would have to admit it. Miki dropped down next to him when Kaz went quiet. Kaz meant well, Miki knew that. He was worried about who Miki would talk to once he was gone. But he didn't understand what it was like to be plain or boring.

Kaz was effortlessly beautiful, with a lifetime of seductions behind him. Kaz had found his one, his mate, and lost him, decades ago, and he still talked about him.

It was a pain Miki wasn't sure he wanted to know, wanting someone that much. He didn't imagine himself wanted; that would have been foolish. Kaz, Cassandra, a few of the practitioners who came into the shop, they liked Miki, but they didn't *want* him. Kaz said Miki frightened them off, but that wasn't true. Want was want, even when it was impossible. It was staring at a handsome, troubled werewolf and wishing he would approach, knowing he wouldn't.

Miki patted Kaz's knee, then got to his feet. "I've got to go shower and do some laundry. I'll see you in the morning, all right, Kaz?"

"He's not dead." Kaz stopped him at the door.

"What?" Miki turned his head to consider him, noting too late that Kaz had stolen his hair band and would never return it. Waves of hair curled around Miki's face, tickling his chin.

"He's not dead, the wolf," Kaz elaborated, rolling one wrist impatiently. Miki thought he understood what Kaz meant and nodded slowly. Movies made it seem as if weres who lost a mate through death or desertion gave up, went off to die in the woods. This werewolf was still around, although he was clearly recovering from what Miki had first thought was an illness.

"It can feel like death. You want to die, knowing they are gone and will never return. For a while there is barely life in your blood, but it's still there, rabbit. It survives. He survived. He chose to. That tells you something of him, doesn't it?" Kaz startled him for the second time in less than an hour.

Miki took his hand from the door and spun the rest of the way around. Kaz had shifted to sit with his back against one arm of the sofa. He had his chin up and his glow was blinding. A tiara of diamonds wouldn't have been so bright.

Miki thought of the wolfsbane, wondering if the werewolf had known what it was the whole time and if he'd responded as he had because Miki had told him about the belladonna. He sucked in a breath. It was surprisingly painful to think Diego had seen Miki's small attempt to save him and been kind in return. It made him want Diego more.

Which was impossible and didn't matter.

Miki tossed his head to send his bangs out of his face. "He's not interested in me, Kaz. No one is, but especially not someone like him, for so many reasons." He didn't raise his voice, but it trembled, making him feel like the rabbit Kazimir had named him. "*You* think I'm unusual and pretty, but if anyone else is looking, they don't look for long once they find out what I do, what I like. And in his case…." There was no use arguing. Kaz regarded him like a stone-faced emperor. The debate was familiar. Kaz couldn't help himself. He thought Miki would be a fine catch for someone, and nothing in Miki's experience of being turned away, being turned away *from*, could convince Kaz otherwise.

Miki sighed. "Fine, muse." He gave in, but snatched one of Kaz's books from a shelf before turning to the door. The book he'd read and return and pretend it was punishment for Kaz, as though Kaz minded him borrowing any of his books. Kaz would try again tomorrow, tell Miki to be coy, as if there was anyone to be coy with. Kaz would insist he was pretty and a prize. But he would see; Diego would not be back.

MIKI WAS in the corner, pruning the roses and checking for cane borers, when a shadow fell over him. He stilled, shivering slightly at the sound from behind him, too rough for a polite cough to get his attention. The growl was low and unthreatening. It felt like a greeting, though Miki couldn't have said how.

It had been two days since the last time a werewolf had been in his garden. Miki didn't know what to make of this and took his time cutting the branch in front of him before he straightened and turned around.

Diego stood only a few feet away, once again in his sport coat and nice shoes, holding his violin case. His head was up, as if he was trying to catch a scent in the breeze. His eyes were yellow, yet nothing about him seemed wild.

Miki had thought werewolves went feral when in pain or overcome by emotion, and that when that happened they ran away to live in the woods. Yet Diego still looked like he didn't get enough sun. Perhaps that was normal, and weres preferred the moon to the sun even when feral.

"Have you ever seen a night-blooming garden?" Miki asked and then felt warm all over at his own stupidity.

"A night-blooming garden?" Diego echoed, apparently not put off by the strange question. "No, I've never heard of one." The yellow left his gaze as he spoke, and he angled his head down, leaving Miki no way to escape his intrigued stare. "I should like to see one. I have recently rediscovered that life's surprises aren't always bad. Sometimes they can be a shock, but not a terrible one. In fact, they can be an unexpected delight."

Miki swallowed and tried to tuck his hair behind his ear. His leather pruning gloves prevented him from making sure his bangs would stay. They trickled slowly back over his eyes when he ducked his warm face. "I've always wanted a night garden," he explained at last, then hurriedly changed the subject. "Are you here for Randall?"

Diego hesitated, then inclined his head in what Miki assumed was agreement. "I am sorry I didn't return sooner. I was… I had some thinking to do."

Miki wasn't certain what Diego was apologizing for, or why, or if he ought to ask. It was early afternoon, but Randall might have wanted to take his lunch break with a friend. Miki waved toward the bench. "The wisteria offers some shade." The seeds were poisonous, but Diego was hardly likely to eat them. But to be safe, Miki didn't offer the information.

"I'm allowed to stay?" The wide smile Diego offered him made Miki's silly heart beat faster. Diego was only teasing him.

Miki shrugged nervously. "It's safe to sit there. And you won't get in the way."

It didn't dim that smile. "I'll trust in your expertise." Diego walked along the path to the bench and then sat. He put his violin case in his lap then reached up toward one of the hanging wisteria blossoms. He didn't touch it, perhaps mindful of Miki's lesson in flower defenses the other day.

That wisteria required pruning as well to keep it from becoming invasive, but it made a lovely sight, curled around the white trellis above the bench. Diego studied the hanging blooms, then the twisted vines. "You ever sit here to admire your handiwork?" He looked out over the garden and then glanced at Miki with a satisfied sigh. "The garden is almost framed."

Diego was the one framed, a large, handsome gentleman surrounded by cascades of lavender flowers, a wolf on a white garden bench. He seemed content.

"I'm working when I'm out here." Miki chewed the inside of his lip. "I have no reason to rest there." If he were less rude, he'd move closer if Diego intended to continue this conversation.

"No one to sit with you?" Diego's expression was difficult to interpret. Like his voice, which was gentle and rough at the same time. Miki thought that might be how it always was with Diego, or perhaps any werewolf. Like a fairy fully dressed, werewolves used words to accommodate the humans around them. Another werewolf would probably have known exactly why Diego's tone was regretful but his grin was pleased.

"People don't like talking to me." Miki picked at the imprint of a thorn in the index finger of his leather glove. "But plants are good listeners, if you have something to say." He caught Diego's grin growing wider, as if he liked that answer.

Diego patted his violin case. "Music doesn't listen, but it doesn't judge either."

"Judge?" Miki questioned softly. It wasn't his fault that Diego hadn't run away yet, that he seemed to want to keep talking.

"Music doesn't care if you have an accent or forget words in English. It doesn't need English. Music speaks its own language." The way Diego spoke made Miki want to know all about what kind of music Diego played, what he preferred. He could teach, or he might be in an orchestra, which meant he likely played classical, the kind of music Kaz would know. But Miki didn't want to mention Kaz. A musician would probably have heard of Kaz, might even want to meet him, and no one who saw Kaz's beauty was going to want to keep spending time with Miki.

Already, Miki was running out of things to say that didn't feel pushy or inappropriate. Or maybe they weren't. Kaz would tell him that his big, strapping werewolf wanted Miki to ask about his music, that's why he'd mentioned it. Kaz would insist that Diego wanted Miki to step closer and say whatever he wanted.

Miki sucked in a breath. "Some people think music makes plants grow better," he blurted, much too loud, and flushed with embarrassed heat. "Excuse me," he threw out, and crossed the garden to head into the shop. He went to the Greenhouse and stripped off his gloves in order to splash cool water on his face.

He stumbled out into the shop moments later, feeling as young and stupid as he was, and found Diego watching him from the doorway to the garden. He'd left his violin case outside and had a startled expression on his face. "Your heart," he said, giving Miki the mortifying realization that Diego had been able to hear him panicking. Miki directed his attention to the glass terrariums on display, letting them calm him as much as they could, ferns and moss and orchids in different size jars and bowls, each of them offering unique, pretty landscapes to soothe the soul. They were nothing to the werewolf watching him, *concerned* for him.

"Have I embarrassed you?" The roughness seemed to be winning out in Diego's voice. The growl slipped into his words, attracting the attention of a customer wandering among the mossy birdcages.

Miki shook his head. He didn't feel any cooler, even with his cheeks damp. "Do you know everything I'm feeling?" he whispered, not quite in agony at the thought, but close. Beings must be used to people finding them attractive, and probably politely ignored it. Miki should never have brought up his emotions. "Never mind."

"How about these?" Diego went on after a pause. His tone was so fiercely resolute that the stray customer jerked to a halt, then quickly backpedaled out of the room. Evidently he had no interest in being in the same space as a determined werewolf.

Miki watched him go in total confusion, then blinked a few times before facing Diego again. "These?"

Diego gestured toward the various tables and the plant life on sale. "Do these plants listen too?"

"Listen?" Miki couldn't think with Diego staring at him like that. Diego had been worried about him. He didn't even know Miki.

"The past few days have given me much to think about, and I could use something to share my questions with. If you think I could handle one of these." Diego appeared serious, so Miki slowly turned to consider his creations.

The terrariums were essentially self-sustaining, requiring only occasional trimming. Each was its own world, protected by glass like something from a fairy tale. But Miki shook his head. "You can't talk through glass." The normal thing to do then was to convince Diego to buy some other plant, perhaps a clipping of a harmless herb if he cooked, or flowers if he had a window box. But those things required effort. "Do you want to care for something?" Miki wondered aloud. He hadn't thought a grieving werewolf would have much attention to spare.

"Something strong, but pretty." Diego gave a nod. "I think I would like that. Something living in my house with me."

"Oh." Miki let out a breath. "Then…." He hesitated, then went up to Diego, unsure how to feel when Diego paused before turning to the side to allow him to pass. They nearly touched, and Miki realized the muscles he had from working in the garden were nothing next to a werewolf's natural strength and presence. He stuttered out a word, an apology or explanation for his racing heart, and looked up in time to catch Diego bending his head to inhale Miki's scent as he passed.

Miki moved on quickly, his stomach cool and fluttering, his skin damp and warm. "Let me show you something else," he murmured, conscious of every physical reaction Diego could hear and scent and see. Diego followed a few feet behind him, stopping only to retrieve his violin. Then he was at Miki's back and trailing after him into the cactus garden.

When Miki turned, Diego stopped looking at him and considered the small pond and waterfall in the corner, built from stone and sheltered by the other side of the overhanging wisteria. A hummingbird dipped around him and then wildly veered away. Diego hardly seemed to notice. He looked out over the small patch of sun and rocks and cactus and gave a happy sigh.

"It's hard to kill a cactus," Miki pointed out, to which Diego nodded. He moved past Miki and began walking around the clay and earthen pots full of desert plants for sale.

"The beauties," Diego observed, sounding as if he meant it. Miki let his shoulders droop in relief. Not everyone understood the appeal of a spiky plant that couldn't be touched. Diego finally stopped in front of one in a low, round bowl and picked it up. Miki was a little surprised that he didn't choose a succulent, or a cactus with a flower, but something simple and green. He sniffed it. "Reminds me of my childhood," Diego offered, with a grin in Miki's direction.

"It's a hedgehog cactus, nothing fancy." Miki approved as Diego brought it to him. "It should flower with enough care. Give it air and light, lots of light," he instructed. "It's used to a harsh life, but treat it gently and it will thrive." He reached for it, then remembered it wasn't his anymore. "They can ring you up, up front."

Diego stayed put and held up the pot in one hand. It was tiny in his palm. "You don't want to say good-bye?"

It was one thing to mention talking to the plants and quite another to realize Diego had heard him do it and knew he wanted to do it again. Miki would have to remember the range of werewolf hearing from now on.

His lack of magical training was never as obvious as when he tried to ensure something came to pass for his plants. Nonetheless, he leaned in. "Do well," he whispered to the hedgehog about to leave his garden forever. "Bloom."

He darted his gaze up. Diego was watching him, his eyes shining and his lips parted. "What's your name, Remarkable?" Diego asked, too quiet for the question to be idle, although he must have heard Randall identify Miki when they'd met.

"Remarkable?" Miki repeated in amazement, then shook his head. "You could play your violin for it. It might like that."

"I will." Diego's smile somehow made that a promise. "Should I also talk to it like you do?"

"*Yes,*" Miki snapped, a cut off growl following the word. He reminded himself Diego wasn't mocking him. Diego had asked for a plant to talk to. Miki angled his head away. "I'm sorry. Sometimes the others tease me about that."

Diego straightened, glancing toward the shop as if searching for whoever would dare. Miki's mouth fell open right as Diego turned back to him. He tossed his head and then offered Miki a crooked, tender smile. "Don't be upset. I didn't mean it as a bad thing. You're sweet with your plants, even the carnivores."

In a dazed sort of slow motion, Miki could feel the blush traveling from his cheeks out to his ears, and then down his throat to his chest. "Just because something scares some people doesn't mean it doesn't deserve love. They're doing what they've evolved to do, and it's beautiful, and terrifying, like sharks." Like wolves, he wanted to say, but held it in. Wolves were not mindless killers, and neither were werewolves, but they frightened people anyway, merely by being what they were.

He felt as if Diego knew what he hadn't said. He took a step closer, and Miki raised his head in surprise. Diego spoke quietly. "Please. What's your name?"

Miki stared for a moment, then jerked into speech. "Miklós. But everyone calls me Miki."

"Miklós. *Miki*," Diego repeated slowly. "I'm Diego, if you didn't already know that. Diego Villalobos." His accent seemed to grow thicker, leaving Miki stunned and silent. "It is a pleasure to know your name at last, Miki."

"At last?" Miki echoed, his mouth so dry he barely heard himself.

"Diego? Are you out here again?" Randall stepped out into the garden and appeared bewildered to find Diego near Miki once more, and holding a plant this time. "You're getting a cactus?" Randall came a little closer, pushing his glasses up and frowning in concern. "Is that a good idea? I mean, you aren't exactly…." He trailed off, as if regretting his somewhat tactless words.

"Cactus are strong," Miki told Randall, but his gaze immediately returned to Diego. "I trust him with it."

Diego turned from his friend to fix Miki with a warm stare. His smile was slow, but as light as ever. It wasn't goofy as much as it was childlike, hopeful. "I think Miki will help me, if I have trouble."

Speechless, Miki nodded, and got an even sillier grin for a reply, careless and toothy. Randall made a surprised sound that he tried to switch to one of approval. But then he smiled too and bobbed his head gratefully in Miki's direction. It wasn't subtle.

Miki glanced down at Diego's hand, which was tight around the clay bowl holding the cactus. Profound grief, like any pain, changed people. Diego must be very different from the were he'd once been, the younger werewolf who had found his mate. Parts of him were the same, but he must have been unwell for a very long time for something as simple as buying a plant to rate that strong of a reaction. Miki thought he understood why Randall was so surprised, but pleased. People could go through the motions of living, working, eating, dressing themselves, but a plant was responsibility and a pleasure. Keeping a plant was something beyond simply keeping yourself alive.

He smiled in encouragement, even as he had to wonder about a bond so deep that six years had barely shaken it. Diego was kind, and beautiful, and most likely talented. His mate must have been exceptional.

Randall called Diego over, reminding him he only had an hour for lunch. Miki sighed as Diego thanked him again, by name this time, and then let his friend lead him away. He looked back before he left. So did Randall, shooting Miki a curious glance that made Miki hurry over to resume pruning the roses before he could embarrass himself anymore by wanting someone he couldn't have.

He forgot about his gloves until a thorn pricked his finger. It drew blood, so he stuck his thumb in his mouth, dirt and all, and went inside to get his gloves and bandage himself up.

HIS STEPS were heavy as he went up the stairs to his apartment that night, but when he opened the door, it was unlocked, and Kazimir was smirking at him from his living room. Miki's heart immediately sank.

Kazimir was wearing silk pajamas, a knitted scarf, Turkish slippers, and holding a feathered fan, which he swept across his face as naturally as breathing before snapping it closed. He tapped it against his arm thoughtfully. "Your wolf is very handsome," he observed, making it plain he'd seen everything. Knowing Kaz, he'd understood everything too, though he hadn't been able to hear a word.

Miki closed the door behind him and leaned against it. "He's not my wolf, Kaz."

"He could be." Kaz reopened the fan with a flick of his wrist and curled it behind him, almost as he would have done with his tail feathers, not that Miki had ever seen him as a bird.

Miki didn't want to say Kaz was getting delusional in his old age, but he was definitely viewing Miki through some rose-colored glasses. He sighed. "He's *grieving*," Miki reminded Kaz. "For his *wife*. Who was undoubtedly as good-looking as he is." His thumb was still stinging. Miki pushed himself from the door to remove his dirty bandage and wash his hands in the kitchen sink.

He could hear Kaz chiding him over the sound of running water. "I told you, my bunny, weres don't see things as humans do. Neither do fairies, which you would know if you didn't trot out your flesh-eating plants and poisons to drive the fairies off. A few thorns won't deter a werewolf."

Miki frowned down at his injured thumb, then at Kaz. "One predator to another," he remarked, raising his voice slightly.

Of course, Kazimir was unperturbed by his attitude. He sank gracefully onto Miki's sad couch. "If you want the wolf to leave, you will need to do something else."

He knew Miki didn't want Diego to leave. He had to know after witnessing Miki lead him around his garden and lose control so much he'd dashed inside to splash water on his face. Miki didn't want to think about it anymore. It had already been on his mind all day. Diego hadn't returned with Randall when his break was over, but Randall had eyed Miki curiously every time Miki had ventured into the shop to go to the storeroom.

"They aren't supposed to recover from the loss of a mate," Miki insisted. "A mate is supposed to be with them forever. The perfect match. Now it's gone." Soul mates, mates, however the werewolves explained it, it was magic Miki wasn't privy to. He didn't know much about how the process worked, or what it entailed, but he knew the stories.

"Is that why you're refusing?" Kaz clucked his tongue. "This idea in your head of being less than her?"

"I'm not refusing anything." Miki dried his hands roughly. "There is nothing to refuse. But I think I live with enough ghosts already." That, he hadn't meant to say. He closed his eyes and listened to Kazimir's heavy breathing.

"Ghosts are all I have, zaichik," Kazimir finally answered. "Ghosts and you, now that my imp is as thoroughly settled as an imp can be. That is why I need you to be happy before I go."

"So you spied on me?" He couldn't say if Kaz had spied on him the day before, but he might have. He had been strangely confident that Diego would return. At the thought, Miki opened his eyes and turned.

Evidently forgiving Miki for his small moment of temper, Kazimir waved his fan lazily and faced the window. He stretched out on the couch as if he expected someone to paint him. Considering the portraits of himself by various artists he had stacked in his room, it was a familiar pose for him. His native country might be trying to persecute and deny its own queer and magical people, but evidently it hadn't in the days of Kaz's youth.

Kaz arched an eyebrow and gave Miki a careful but knowing look. "If, however, you want the wolf to be yours, I could help you."

Miki snorted and gestured at himself, his boring, ill-fitting, dirty clothes, his uncontrollable hair, the stain on his face. He pointed at Kazimir, all gold and regal beauty.

Kazimir flicked his fan open and dragged it over his body as though it were a part of his arm. "Winning a man isn't about looks, my foolish rabbit, any more than conquering a country is about strength… at least, not entirely. You want the wolf, I will teach you the skills required. If you know your stories, you would know to listen to the freely given advice of my kind."

In the silence that followed, Miki realized he wasn't blinking and that his heart was pounding. If Diego had been there, he would have thought Miki was terrified, which would have been correct. Miki dragged in a breath, but it didn't do anything. If it wasn't about looks and he did this, and Diego rejected him, it would hurt. Any of the other rejections Miki had experienced were shallow compared to that, if he actually tried for what he wanted. Only the disinterest, the *relief* on his parents' faces when he'd left, would be worse, and that still haunted Miki when he looked in the mirror.

What Kaz said made sense; there had never been pity in how Diego treated him, or disgust or boredom. But for it to work, Miki would have to lure him in with only himself, and he had nothing for that, no perfume or feathered fan, no color. Diego hadn't only known great love, he'd known other lovers. Miki looked as young and inexperienced as he was, a scared twenty-two-year-old who had never been kissed. He should stick to the dirt where he belonged. "You're beautiful, Kaz. You don't understand. If Cassandra hadn't taken me in, I'd be nothing. On the street, forgotten," he choked out at last. "I should… I should go take a shower before I make dinner."

"Humans," Kazimir continued, as if Miki hadn't been silent for too long and then tried to change the subject in a fainter and fainter voice. He pursed his lips and tucked his fan away. "When he comes again, and he will, for advice with his cactus that he may or may not need, keep your chin up, feel his gaze on your bared neck, and then meet his eyes. Then you will know."

Miki was suddenly, tightly breathless.

Kazimir took advantage of the quiet to add to his instructions. "When he asks you something, no matter what the question is, do not answer right away. Let him wait. Let him come closer. And again, when he looks at you, when he's inhaling you, meet his gaze before angling your head away. He seemed to like it. He worked harder to make you look at him again."

"Kazimir." Miki gave a small shake of his head and watched Kazimir sweep a long, heavy glance over him that Miki had never seen before, not directed at him. It set a fire low in his stomach and made him tremble. "Kazimir, you…."

"How he stared at you is how you should be stared at, rabbit." There were plans in Kazimir's eyes, plans about what he could have done, wanted to do, with Miki. "How I would have, if I had been younger. As if he wants to devour you, or keep you safe, and cannot decide which."

"That is—" *Ridiculous*, Miki wanted to say. But Kazimir took that heated gaze off him and slapped the closed fan against his thigh.

"Now you see." Kazimir didn't seem too pleased about it, although he didn't stop talking. "Ask him to play his violin. Men love to be flattered. He might even be good. I'll wager he's dying to play for you. Werewolves are especially susceptible to the desire to show off for the one they are courting."

"Kazimir, stop." Miki finally got it out. "I can't do those things. Game playing would be ludicrous from someone like me."

"Chéri, do you want this one for your lover? Do you want to kiss him and see that he is watered and fed and cared for as much as your plants?" Kazimir closed his eyes and sagged against the couch as if he could no longer hide his exhaustion. "Don't you? Isn't that what you want?"

"I want…." *To tear Diego's clothes off*, Miki thought weakly. To deck him in flowers. And yes, to see that he was fed and content. But voicing that would make its impossibility too real.

Kaz tutted without opening his eyes. He dropped the fan to his lap. "If you do not want to lure him with scent and color, then win him directly by asking him to be yours."

"I can't do that either," Miki admitted, wishing to be beautiful as he hadn't since he was a teenager. "His answer would be no. Even if I were attractive enough for someone like that, he's still mated, whether or not she is there."

A thoughtful hum was a strange answer. For a few seconds, Miki thought Kaz was falling asleep, and then Kaz let his head loll onto a cushion and opened his eyes. "Do you imagine there is only one? That we each get one love, our whole life long? Once in a lifetime doesn't mean what you think when you live as long as I do." Kaz sounded like he was dreaming. "Each one is different. Some rare, some astonishing, but each is special. None more special than the first, perhaps, but every single chance is worth taking. Oh, rabbit." He grew even softer. "The bench under the wisteria," he whispered, with the light around him flickering. "It's a lovely spot, overlooking your poisons and your herbs." It felt like another directive about what to do when—if—Diego returned. And yet, though Miki waited, Kazimir didn't suggest what Miki ought to do about the bench. He hummed again, probably a song from one of his operas.

Miki was about to sneak quietly to the shower to be alone when Kaz sighed and finally finished his thought. "Jacob will always be a part of me. I miss him every day. Human lives are so short. Shorter when you—" He stopped there, the unfinished story for once unfamiliar to Miki. He went on after a heavy pause. "Don't waste the chance, not if you don't have to. Your wolf has already made his choice, and would likely tell you the same."

KAZIMIR HAD remained blessedly quiet on the subject for the next three days. He could have been feeling merciful, but Miki thought it more a combination of his increasing exhaustion and a way for Kazimir to force Miki to think about it on his own.

Miki tried. He gazed in the mirror and imagined baring his throat as Kazimir had suggested until his face was red and he couldn't look himself in the eye anymore. If it wasn't about looks, or wasn't completely about them, then something else about Miki was supposed to entrance Diego, and he stared hard at himself, trying to find it. Miki's looks were ordinary except for the wine stain on his cheek. He had dark hair that curled around his face, light eyes, and a slender but strong body. He blushed whenever he made eye contact with his reflection, and felt a fool. Yet he kept trying, wishing that just once he would see something beautiful reflected back at him.

Hope was a terrible thing now that he'd finally let himself want someone. It only grew worse as the days went by without any sign of Diego.

Perhaps that's why he wasn't prepared when he walked up to the front of the shop after a coffee run for his coworkers and saw Diego standing by the doors and staring inside. Miki had only been gone a few minutes. The coffee shop was two storefronts down, and the employees usually had their drinks waiting by the time Miki or whoever had been sent got to the front of the line. Miki had been gone ten minutes at most, but Diego had the confused, impatient posture of someone uncertain if they should stay or go.

"Diego." Surprise stopped Miki short and prevented him from running away when Diego turned toward him with impossible amounts of pleasure in his expression.

"Miki!" Diego bounded over to him. He took the tray of coffee drinks from Miki's stunned hands. Diego didn't have his violin with him, and as far as Miki knew, Randall wasn't working today. But he couldn't get the question out in time. "You weren't inside, and I thought maybe it was your day off. Oh…." Diego paused and frowned for a moment, probably because Miki was staring dumbly at him. "Are you on your break?" Diego growled and then stifled it before looking down at the pavement. "I… had a question. It can wait."

"About your cactus?" Miki wondered faintly.

Diego raised his head. A short complaint rumbled out of him, but he nodded. "Yes. The cactus." But when Miki pushed out an understanding noise, Diego stepped out of the way of a pedestrian and held the door open for Miki with one hand. The full tray of drinks was nothing to him. "I've put the cactus in my living room, in the window for all to see. Do you think I should name it?"

Miki felt tiny next to Diego, but stopped next to him outside the doorway. He didn't mean to smile, and hoped Diego took it kindly. "Yes, I think you should." He was warm from being so close, and they were blocking the door, so he continued inside, dodging displays to head to the main counter so he could deliver the coffee and give Cassandra her change.

Greedigut, who should have been sleeping, was watching him curiously from his perch over the register. So were Cassandra and Ngige, a PhD candidate and Cassandra's assistant. Miki glanced from them to Diego, who pushed the tray onto the counter before resuming his position at Miki's shoulder. Miki thought Diego would be smiling a friendly greeting, but his expression was serious. When his gaze met Cassandra's, he nodded respectfully before something made him sneeze.

"You shouldn't be in here," Miki scolded him softly. Kaz hadn't said he should scold him, yet he did, and Diego responded with a shrug and let himself be led outside. Miki was so distracted he forgot his iced hibiscus tea, and had to go back for it. He needed it. When Cassandra winked at him, his mouth went dry.

"Randall isn't here," Miki whispered as he walked, afraid of what he might see if he turned around. "You don't have your violin."

"No rehearsals today." Diego's answer reverberated through Miki, making him stop at last. Outside, the breeze tugged his hair free. It left Diego looking slightly wild as well.

"Is that why you're in the city?" It wasn't that weres didn't come into the city, it was that, except for that detective, most didn't stay. Too late, it occurred to Miki that Diego might not want to talk about his life before, or why he'd chosen to live in Los Cerros. "I've never heard the city orchestra," he offered, but didn't think it mitigated any accidental rudeness.

"I thought it might be good to get away, someplace new. And I never minded the city. We used to—" Diego made a sad sound and looked away. "As long as I leave for somewhere less populated a few times a year, see my family, I'm fine. The city has fewer memories, different scents. So far it's been good for me." He lifted his gaze to Miki.

Miki swallowed some more tea, hoping it would settle his stomach and cool his heated skin. "I thought you needed… trees." Angry werewolves howling at the moon in movies came to mind, usually in some dark European forest.

The comment made Diego's expression lighten a bit. "Not all wolves are from the woods," he chided Miki, but gently. "I grew up in mountains, near a forest but not far from the edge of a desert."

"Oh." Miki felt foolish. The condensation on his cup made his palms damp. If Diego grew up around cactuses, he probably knew enough about them to not need Miki's help with one. He couldn't ask. "Do you perform in events for the city?" His voice rasped.

"Yeah. If you ever want tickets, I could provide them." Diego gave a start, as if his own words surprised him. But then he took a moment and inclined his head. He met Miki's stare. "I can provide them," he said again, before angling his head to the side as if listening to something inside the building. Probably the shop employees gossiping about what a lonely, sad figure Miki was. But Diego crooked half a smile, then fixed his attention on Miki. "Are you still on your break? If I'm bothering you, I can go."

"No!" Miki shut his eyes. He swallowed before reopening them. "I work through my breaks, usually," he corrected himself in a calmer tone. He turned and thought he saw a flash of gold in his apartment window. He froze, his heart beating frantically for Diego to hear, and then turned abruptly in the opposite direction and walked over to the bench under the wisteria. He sat awkwardly at one end, hands tight around his cup of tea.

As if that was an invitation, Diego stared after him for a few moments before trotting over to join him. He sighed deeply as he sat down, and lifted his head to gaze out over the garden. "Do you have a garden of your own at home?"

After just embarrassing himself, Miki saw no point in making Diego wait for an answer. Nonetheless, he licked his lips first and watched Diego lean toward him. "No. I can't afford a home." That was another harsh truth. "I probably won't ever be able to, though I… I like to dream of it, sometimes. I'm good with plants, but I don't have the experience to build a business on providing magic supplies, not on my own. This will have to do. I do have some of my own," he confessed, refusing to glance up to where Kazimir was doubtless watching them. "Some basil and thyme in the kitchen window, and a moth orchid from the grocery store. There's a small hanging pitcher there too. She eats any flies that might wander in, though I fed her a spider once."

"You're not squeamish, are you?" The rough, growly note in Diego's voice was apparently pleasure. He didn't seem to be asking, although he exhaled and leaned against the bench a second later. "She wasn't squeamish either." Miki stilled, and Diego glanced at him, his frown becoming fierce. "I don't mean to upset you by mentioning her."

"No, I thought, *you*…." Miki cleared his throat. "You can talk about her. If you want. I… I have a roommate, a friend. He's a firebird." Diego was as taken aback by that as most people. That was rarer than meeting a dragon, and Miki had never met a dragon. "He's been around a very long time, and for decades of that time he's been missing his…." Jacob and Kaz had never married; it hadn't been allowed then. Neither were they werewolves. "His One," Miki finished at last. "He still talks about him. If you want to talk about her, I understand." He wanted to see the love in Diego's expression, but turned to face the garden at the last moment, not certain he wouldn't wind up haunted by being so close to real passion. It wasn't meant for him.

"*Decades.*" He could hear Diego's awe. "One? Only one?" Diego asked after a minute of quiet and the thrum of nearby hummingbirds. "It's not… it's not one. It's… friend and lover and… *mate*." Diego growled a little, sounding frustrated at the lack of a human, or English, word. "Has your firebird ever chosen another… one?"

"Kaz has had all kinds of lovers." Miki sighed. "He tells stories…. But I don't think any of them were like his Jacob." He darted a careful look over and found Diego's attention fast on him. He'd thought the very concept of *mate*, of *one*, meant there could never be another who would compare, yet Diego was listening intently to his every word. "He says he became much choosier after Jacob, that it would have to be someone Jacob would have approved of for it to be worth that much pain again, but that if he ever did meet someone who could stir those feelings in him, he'd grab ahold of them without hesitating. He says Jacob would have demanded it." Miki tried to dispel his unhappiness with a shrug. "Jacob must have had high standards. He was a writer. Brilliant, according to Kaz, but not famous."

Diego put his hand down between them. Miki kept his gaze on it. "Your friend's Jacob must have been very wise." Diego spoke seriously. "To feel that again after…. To feel that again is worth anything. If you do… you must embrace it. And yet your firebird hasn't chosen you?" Diego shook his head, as if that confused him. He pressed his hand flat to the bench. "That is his loss."

Miki turned toward him without taking his eyes off Diego's hand. "He says I don't deserve the tragedy. Anyway, he still loves Jacob, and I'm not… I'm not special, like that."

Diego's soft growl shook him, but it only lasted a moment. "Rena was my mate, although because she was human, it took her longer to see it. It taught me patience. I was not very patient before her. But she was stubborn, so stubborn. She played cello." Diego took a long breath. "She had some fairy blood, which could have made her flighty, but she was fierce. Her eyes changed color when she was mad or…." Miki thought Diego wasn't going to go on, but then he shook his head and cleared the rust from his voice. "Sometimes I'd provoke her over harmless things to see her in a fury. We were children, I think, but we liked to make each other smile. She wanted me to smile. I lived to make her happy."

"She was lovely," Miki offered when Diego didn't add anything else. Without knowing her, Miki was certain of that.

Diego leaned farther toward him. His shoulder was warm against Miki's for a moment. "No one else allows me to talk about her." Miki stared up in surprise. Diego quirked the corner of his mouth, so indescribably saddened Miki ached in his bones. "They think it will break me, or they sense I don't want to share her with them. Wolves who haven't lost a mate don't want to know how it feels, and can't understand. They liked her, but they don't know how she was special like I do. Only her family understands, but I think I remind them of her. It's painful for them."

"I'm afraid I don't understand mating," Miki offered delicately after a while, dropping his attention once again to Diego's hand. Diego turned it, palm up, as if he knew Miki was staring.

"We don't either." Diego seemed bothered by that. "We feel it. We know when it happens, but how or why… we don't know. It's supposed to be once. That's what they say. Once, and it doesn't happen for everyone. We fall in love all the time without it. But then there it is, and we have to decide."

Miki ducked his head. "You don't waste time," he echoed Kaz's words.

He felt Diego glance at him. "No. Not once we've made up our minds. But that doesn't mean we can't wait, that we don't woo."

"Woo?" That was an old-fashioned word Kazimir might have approved of. He had even implied werewolves courted each other.

"Take care," Diego amended. "We can take care. We aren't animals."

Miki frowned. "I didn't think that." Honesty made him direct his frown at his feet and go on. "I was startled when you first came here. I'm usually alone in the garden." And Diego's eyes had been yellow. "I've only ever met one werewolf. He wasn't like you."

Diego turned sharply to stare at him, his gaze as lupine as it had ever been. "That," Miki added softly. "You don't hide what you are."

"I was startled too," Diego told him, relaxing a fraction. "That's why. I didn't mean to scare you."

"You didn't hear me before you saw me?" Miki was confused. Diego should have been able to hear Miki long before he'd left the Greenhouse to enter the garden.

"Startled," Diego repeated. "Stunned. I heard you, but that was nothing to when you stepped out."

Miki couldn't keep his eyes up with his body growing so hot. His skin felt shivery, sensitive in the few places where the air touched it, but inside he was heavy and warm. He moved his hands, forgetting about his tea, and it crashed to the ground, though it somehow landed upright. Diego kept staring at him. Miki blinked. "My break is over. You can stay, if you like. If you want." His breathing seemed so loud. "Your cactus—"

"Miki." Diego said his name with a slow rumble beneath it.

Miki could not raise his head no matter how he tried. "Yes?" A whisper was all he could manage. He turned his face away and felt more than heard the catch in Diego's breathing.

"Your scent." Diego's words were in Miki's hair, brushing against the exposed skin of his throat. Miki took a deep breath. Diego did the same. The rough undercurrent in his voice grew stronger. "It's been a long time since anything smelled good to me. I'd like to stay around you, if you don't mind. If you would allow it, despite my age and how I do not know my footing here."

Miki wondered if Diego was watching the blush steal over his skin. It felt as if he was. Kaz would tell Miki to look up and find out. But he couldn't. To not see that look in Diego's eyes would hurt too much. He licked hibiscus from his lips. "Don't give the cactus too much water. Centuries of its ancestors have ensured that it will survive on very little. What it needs is sun." He was certain he'd said this all to Diego before, but he couldn't think.

"This morning I tried to make it comfortable," Diego assured him, tickling Miki's ear with his breath, making Miki struggle to hold in the strange feeling in his chest, as if he wanted to moan. Diego's tone was gentle. "I told it, do well. Bloom. But I don't know if it's listening. Maybe it's used to your voice. Maybe you're magic, Miki."

"I'm ordinary," Miki insisted. "I'm nicer to plants than to people. I grow poison and carnivorous plants. I'm… marked." He put a hand up to his cheek.

"*Marked.*" The harsher growl carried through the bench they shared. It made Miki tense, but not with fear. Kaz, he reminded himself. Kaz was watching. Kaz had to see that no matter how much Miki desperately wished, there was nothing holding Diego here but a desire for conversation.

On that thought, Miki took his hand away and swallowed before slowly lifting his chin. With his head angled to the side, his neck was bared. Only a few curls would hide Diego's view.

His heart was loud to his ears; he couldn't imagine how it would sound to Diego's. He waited, hoping for one moment longer, and then raised his eyes.

Diego wasn't looking at him. His eyes were closed, his breathing uneven.

Miki shoved himself to his feet, kicking over the tea. From the corner of his eye, he saw Diego rise, but Miki kept going, slipping into the shop and then into the limited shelter of the Greenhouse. People inside the shop might see him, but at least Kazimir wouldn't. Miki couldn't bear to think of Kazimir's disappointment, even if Kaz had to admit the truth now.

Diego liked Miki's smell, but not how Kaz thought. Diego simply wanted someone to talk to. Miki had so few friends, he would like another, even if he thought looking at Diego right now would leave him as sore as a day laying stones. He had wanted so much this time.

He blinked, but his eyes continued to sting. His eyelashes trapped stupid, useless tears.

"Miki?" Diego had followed him, concerned again. Miki reached for the distilled water without bothering with the watering can and began checking the dampness of the soil in each of his plants. It let him keep his back to Diego.

"Did your mate grow anything?" Miki asked with his eyes on his work.

The frustrated sound from Diego almost made him spin around. But Diego's voice was soft when he spoke. "Mold in the fridge. Neither of us was much for cooking. You're more tidy?"

"Things have their place," Miki explained, examining each plant without seeing it. The big bottle of distilled water was nearly empty.

Diego reached up to the shelf above the sink and handed Miki a new one before Miki could think of a way to ask without showing his face. Miki accepted the bottle, shivering for the presence at his shoulder.

"*Miki.*" He thought he was imagining the whine in Diego's voice, the plea. Perhaps Diego could smell the excess salt in the air.

Miki wiped at his eyes. "It's nothing that matters," he insisted, the lie probably excruciatingly glaring to someone like Diego. "It was something Kaz said. I thought of it when I shouldn't have," he explained, when Diego didn't seem satisfied. He searched for a new subject, but once again, all he had of interest to anyone were his plants. "Will you tell me when you decide what to name your cactus? I'd like to know."

Diego stared down at him for a few moments longer. "Would you like me to come back?"

He was so doubtful that Miki turned without meaning to, giving Diego a full view of his wet eyes, which Diego didn't like to see, judging from his short, angry exclamation in Spanish. "Yes," Miki told him anyway. "Yes, please."

But he went cold to hear how desperate he was and hurried away in the next second, slipping out through the Greenhouse door into the shop. He couldn't tell if the others saw him disappear into the storeroom, but Cassandra must have. Greedigut flew in after him and sat in the corner on a high shelf, his sharp eyes watchful and concerned.

ONCE AGAIN, Miki came home to find a firebird in his apartment. For a moment, he hoped Kazimir was asleep so he wouldn't have to answer any of his questions. But then Miki took in the amount of golden feathers surrounding his couch, the pile of downy gold underneath Kazimir's reclining body, and gasped in dismay.

"They won't bring fortune," Kaz informed him sleepily, without opening his eyes.

Miki's heart began to beat again. He came forward, only to collapse onto his knees in front of the couch. Feathers flew around him, then resettled. "I don't want a fortune," Miki whispered, watching a single quill land on his leg. "All I want is my own garden someday." He could scarcely voice that simple wish, knowing it would never come true. "Flowers, herbs, vegetables." His voice broke. "An orchard—a small one. I wouldn't ask for more. That's all I want, Kaz."

"Truly?" Kazimir dropped his hand to the top of Miki's head. "Is that truly all you want, my rabbit?"

Miki shook his hand away, refusing to answer the question. He was in no mood for sly insinuations or any more false hope. If Kazimir had seen them in the garden today, then he knew better than to tease Miki like this. "You aren't a jinn, Kaz." Miki brushed the feather from his leg and reached up to take hold of Kaz's hand. He pressed his fingertips against Kaz's wrist. "You don't grant wishes. I know you want to help. But please. Stop."

"Trapped creatures rarely grant the wishes their captors think they do." Kazimir allowed Miki to find his pulse, then pulled his hand away to resume his stroking of Miki's hair. "But do not doubt my power."

Miki turned his face toward the couch and pressed in. Some of the silk of Kaz's robe was cool against his raw cheeks. It felt like a wish granted, but Miki shook his head again. "You aren't a fairy godmother either."

Kazimir turned as if curling around him and petted down the back of Miki's neck. "No. No, I am not. But would you really not ask for beauty? A ball? A prince?"

Miki trembled and knew Kaz felt it. "Not anymore," he admitted quietly. Kazimir stopped breathing. Miki sighed without lifting his head. "I… I tried, Kaz." He didn't know his own voice. He never thought he'd have to say it. He'd assumed Kaz had watched again. "I tried and he didn't want me. Not like that."

He didn't realize how much he'd been waiting to hear that he was wrong, that Kaz still thought he had hope, until Kazimir stayed quiet. Miki's eyes burned with tears he should have been done with by now. There had never been anything for him to mourn. He was a fool.

But Kazimir continued to pet him, carefully, slowly, easing Miki's breathing back down to something less fraught before he spoke again. "I can't convince you of anything, Miklós, I cannot even grant wishes, though I have made many believe I can. What I do is inspire, for better or for worse. I am a muse for good, if I wish, and for destruction, if you trap me."

Miki had no idea what Kaz was trying to tell him. He looked up. "You snuck into my apartment. Not the other way around."

Kaz stared at him, then gently wiped the tears from Miki's eyes. "I thought we could sit together and watch that gardening and home repair channel you love, while you worked up the nerve to tell me about your wolf." So Kaz *had* been watching. Miki gave a start. Kaz clucked his tongue. "I don't see the truth, or the future, rabbit, but I know everything there is to know of romance. I had a better look at your werewolf today. If you knew them, you'd know how desperate he is to please you. If you want a garden, you will only have to ask and he will get you one, if he has the means. You've chosen well."

"Stop it." Miki frowned. "He's not mine. You know he's not. Don't be cruel. He is wonderful. He's understanding and kind, and I think he used to laugh more. I know he used to smile all the time, with her. He lived to make her happy, he said."

Kaz heaved a dramatic sigh that said Miki was missing the point. No doubt if Miki had been special, he would have been able to lure Diego in anyway.

"Have *you* made him smile?" Kazimir clucked his tongue once again, indicating he knew the answer already.

The memory of Diego's ridiculous smile made Miki drop his head to the couch. He couldn't look at Kaz while remembering how it felt to have that beaming expression directed at him. "He's mated." Miki spoke in a small voice. "He still loves her."

Kazimir patted the top of his head. "Love doesn't vanish after death, rabbit. You shouldn't expect it to. You humans have big hearts, with lots of room." Miki opened his mouth to question that, and Kazimir started to sing, shocking Miki into stillness. He couldn't even breathe at the clear, exquisite agony of Kaz's voice. He couldn't understand the words; he thought the piece was from an opera at first, then realized it was simpler than that. But the words didn't matter. The music, as Kaz sang it, filled his heart and then left him empty when Kaz went silent. He realized he was crying again and couldn't remember the last time he'd wept this much.

"You can contain everything. You can make room. You can experience it all, Miklós." Kazimir continued to smooth down his hair as if he hadn't left Miki shaking. "Your wolf has chosen this; you can also choose it. I don't claim to understand the feelings the wolves call mating, but if he is worth anything, if his mate was, she would love you too."

"Kazimir." Miki turned to breathe cooler air and allowed Kazimir to tilt up his face. "Mates are perfect for each other, and he is so different. No one else who comes into my garden has ever made me feel…. He wanted to talk. That's all he said, Kaz. He wants to talk about her, and I smell like someone who will listen."

He didn't understand Kazimir's saintly smile. "You could use another friend, for when I am gone."

"Kaz!" Miki exclaimed sharply. Alarm made his voice crack.

He got a hand waved languidly through the air in front of him. Kazimir spoke dreamily. "And when I am gone, bunny, take my feathers. Take every last feather you have swept up and set aside because you were unable to bring yourself to bin them, and sell them. Sell them and get your garden. If you choose not to invite the werewolf, then invite new friends and serve them tea as I have taught you. But I believe… I believe he will be there. He will be with you, if you allow it." Miki sat up to push his head against Kaz's chest and wrap his arms around him. Kaz curled tighter. "Don't be sad for me for too long. I am very old, rabbit, older than you think. The world has made me so. I am tired, and I miss him."

Miki sniffed. He was making a mess on Kazimir's robe, but Kazimir didn't seem to mind. "Would he like me?" The question was stupid and immature, but Miki asked it anyway, and let Kazimir draw him up onto the couch to sit against him. "I wish I could have met him."

"He was better with people than I was, for all that he was a beast to the powerful. He would have seen your gentleness and treated you so well. Oh, rabbit." Kazimir settled back into the cushions with Miki tucked under his arm. Kazimir could go on for a while about his Yasha, and Miki didn't mind listening as long as Kazimir was still with him. "He was rude and snored when he drank, which was often. He fought for my honor when I had none. He was onto my every trick, and fell for them anyway. I set out to win him, and he caught me—which he was insufferable about. He would have adored you. He would have fought for you. He would have challenged anyone who dared to hurt you. It was what he did. It was probably what he was doing the day…." Kazimir drew in a long, shaky breath. Miki held still, frozen for the one story Kazimir did not tell. "We should have left before then. Before they marched in. But he was stubborn, and there was work to be done. I don't even know why he went out that day."

Miki trembled, but Kazimir was strangely steady.

"He was missing for two days. The third.... The third day, Rennet, a child we were supposed to be hiding, sneaking from the country, snuck out instead to find him. For me. I didn't ask, but he was an impulsive boy." Kazimir took another long breath. "I think Jacob would have been happy for that, in a small way. He wouldn't have wanted it to be me. But I wouldn't have wished that for Rennet. To see what was left of him after two days in their hands."

Kazimir went silent while Miki buried his face. Kazimir began to pet him. "My Yasha," he said at last, on a sigh that made Miki ache. It seemed stupid, suddenly, to wish for a love like that, even if Miki didn't face the same dangers.

Miki held Kaz tight, trying to warm him as best he could, though he didn't radiate heat the way Diego did. Kazimir shivered despite his efforts. "That is why I share him with you. He would have wanted me to. He said the world was cruel—" Kazimir cut himself off and stopped petting Miki for a moment. "He said the world was cruel, so we should grab happiness when we find it. He would have done anything to protect you, rabbit. He would have been so pleased to watch you try for your wolf."

After a long time, when Miki thought he could speak in more than a hoarse whisper, he angled away. "What do you mean?"

Kaz blinked at him as if the answer was obvious. "He would have loved you. You aren't afraid of me either. You care for me, asking little in return. He would be pleased to see us here. Me, in my old age playing the gentle advisor. You, with your youth, stretching out toward your lover. He was right to take a chance on me, and without him I wouldn't have known what love was, and how to tell you to win your werewolf."

Miki ducked his head, although his blush was so hot he thought Kaz could feel it. Kaz stroked his cheek with the back of his hand.

"Diego doesn't see me as a lover." Miki tried to convince Kaz, but his voice was almost nothing. "I did what you said, but—"

"I saw him follow you, lost and hopeful." Kazimir breezed through Miki's protest, almost his usual difficult self again. "When he comes tomorrow, make sure you are alone with him. Leave some of your skin bare. Wear a shirt you have not washed, so your scent is stronger. Touch him, if you can. Wolves touch, all the time. You will have to get used to it if you accept him."

He seemed so sure. Miki put his head down, his chest tight, his stomach fluttering. "Accept?"

"He has a great deal of discretion, for a wolf." Kazimir made a thoughtful noise. "A wolf who is undoubtedly confused and guilty, as we all are when we try to love again. But then, his mate was human, yes? He must understand how you can be, the delicate encouragement often required with your kind. Humans do not come with instructions. Some of us were forced to learn them."

Miki sniffled, feeling childish even as he continued to speak. "I haven't forced him to do anything. I wouldn't."

"You don't have to," Kaz assured him. "Just ask, or—" Kaz hummed his opera piece for a few seconds. "—be what you are. He will follow. He *likes* what you are, rabbit. Let him show you how much, and he will never want to do anything else. Let him give you happiness."

Miki couldn't quite grasp what he was hearing. He couldn't ensnare anyone, even if he wanted to. "You're mistaken, Kaz. I'm cursed. I'm the one pushed away."

"Cursed?" Kaz said a few words in his mother tongue and then pulled Miki's head up by grabbing some of his hair. For the first time Miki wondered what Kaz had been like before he'd met his Jacob. He must have been so different, like Diego before Rena had taught him patience. Then he wondered what Kaz must have given Jacob in return, and thought of that strange book of little stories, and the other book, those secret pages in an old leather bag that Kazimir kept to himself, the stories Jacob had never wanted to create because he'd been terrified to write again.

Miki suddenly wanted to know, with a bone-deep need, what Diego had shared with his mate, and what he might share with Miki, if what Kaz was implying was true. It couldn't be true, but he knew he'd dream of it. "He wants me as a friend, Kaz. Only a friend." Diego had made Miki's heartbeat quicken for the first time in his life, but sooner or later even Miki's heart must accept the truth.

Kaz leaned in to whisper at his ear, repeating his instructions as if Miki hadn't spoken. "Leave some of your skin bare. Make sure your scent is strong, and he will be helpless before you. But treat him well, rabbit. He's brave to try again."

Miki shook his head breathlessly. "We're friends."

"Of course you are." Kazimir released him and sat up. He petted Miki's hair one last time in a distracted way, then flung himself back against the cushions and reached for the remote. He turned on Miki's TV, which was already set to the gardening and home channel, and regarded Miki with mild amusement, all the while glowing like the sun. "Now, what's for dinner? Oh don't look shocked, bunny. The first rule of life is, even if you see no hope, the world continues, so you might as well get on with the day to day."

Miki stared at him, then slowly wiped the tears from his face. He didn't move right away, but Kaz didn't seem to truly expect him to. His last lesson imparted, Kaz appeared content that the rest would work itself out. He focused intently on the gardening show he probably had no interest in.

After a while, Miki got up to prepare some soup. He didn't feel like eating, but Kaz was right, of course he was; the simple actions were calming. "I love you, Kaz," he whispered when he came back with the food.

Kazimir accepted that, and the food, like his due tribute. "You will do well, rabbit. You will make me proud." He exhaled happily, then scooted over to give Miki more room next to him.

He didn't say a word when Miki barely ate a bite, and he leaned back when they were done, letting Miki lie against him while Miki watched his garden show and dreamed about what could be.

MIKI WAS crouched low in the herb garden, snipping leaves and flower heads off the dandelions, when he sensed a familiar not-glow shimmering at the edge of his vision. For a moment his hands faltered and his heart kicked into a faster rhythm. He took a few more cuttings and dropped them into a mesh bag while he tried to get himself under control.

It was no use. He'd spent most of the night hot and restless on top of his covers, curled around a pillow, his head full of hopes he'd never let himself contemplate in detail before. He imagined teenagers felt this way and wanted to blush with shame. Diego wanted Miki as a friend. Miki wanted him as a friend too. He also wanted more, which was his own fault, not Diego's. He shouldn't be afraid to face him now.

He slipped his shears into his pocket, then stood up. Nestor was outside the garden fence, waiting on his dandelion cuttings, but Miki's attention went past him. He met Diego's gaze, then quickly looked down. Diego had on the sport coat again, as if he had come from rehearsal, but he didn't have his violin. In his hand was a plastic cup with a straw, filled with what looked like iced hibiscus tea.

Miki swallowed, his mouth completely dry, then finally turned to Nestor. He handed him the bag over the top of the fence, then made his way outside of the garden. He took his time locking the gate. It was almost closing time, he might as well. And it gave him something to do with his trembling hands.

"I thought dandelion was a weed," Diego remarked.

"It's a beneficial weed." Miki got the lock into place and bit his lip. A glance over revealed Diego was watching him, and Nestor was watching both of them. Nestor, an older man who wore sandals even on cold, wet days, wasn't exactly a witch, and Miki would guess his magic use was erratic at best. He came for herbs more than anything else.

"Dandelion is good for salads. And wine," Nestor explained to Diego, after tilting his head up to meet his eye. "Do your kind drink wine?" He didn't appear to notice that the question made Diego blink a few times in surprise and probably offense. Nestor turned to Miki and did something leering with his eyebrows while shaking his bag of cuttings. "I'll bring you two a bottle when it's ready. You have a good night, Miki," he added, as if he wanted to make sure he embarrassed Miki before he left. Then he nodded at Diego and turned to go back into the shop.

Miki put his hands over his hot face, recalling too late that his fingers were dirty. He yanked them down and wiped them on his shirt. It was an older shirt, thin and loose enough that it fell around his collarbone. It was the only shirt he owned that showed more skin. His plaid outer shirt was the same one he'd worn the day before.

"Diego." The last time he'd seen Diego, he'd cried and run away from him. Yet Diego had returned. He must be very lonely, even with his friends. He must truly need to talk about his mate. Miki choked but made himself speak. "I… I have to clean up before I go, if you wanted to talk about something."

"Miki." Diego stopped him and dragged in a long breath. The sound that escaped him afterward was almost a groan. He took a moment to reopen his eyes, and when he did, they were only half-open, as if he was drugged. "*Miki*," he said again, heavily.

Miki was too warm in his plaid shirt and plucked at it in indecision. After moments of hesitation, he stripped it off and draped it over the fence. It left both his arms bare, and he scratched at them awkwardly while Diego tossed his head and fixed the discarded shirt with a confused stare.

Explaining why he'd worn the shirt again was out of the question. Miki moved away from it, heading toward the shop, only to stop dead when Diego held out the plastic cup of iced tea. Miki closed his hands around it without thinking, but then glanced up. He didn't understand.

"You didn't get to finish yours yesterday, because of me." Diego ducked his head, giving Miki a second to imagine their roles had been reversed. "So I went to the coffee shop and asked for what looked like that. It smells the same. Is it all right?"

"It's perfect." Miki swallowed, then remembered to take a sip. The flavor burst into his mouth, exactly right. Diego was staring intently at him, as if more than tea was at stake, so Miki smiled. "Thank you. No one has ever…." He cut himself off, but couldn't hide the embarrassed pleasure to know Diego had thought of him. "Thank you."

Diego's beaming, careless smile was one of the most beautiful things Miki had ever seen, and hardly seemed equal to a simple "thank you." He took another sip under Diego's rapt attention.

"They said it was hibiscus. You even drink flowers," Diego commented, watching Miki as if Miki was performing magic.

Miki took his mouth off the straw and lowered the cup so he could stare down at something safe. The garden was empty of anyone else, as was the part of the shop he could see. Closing time on weekdays tended not to be busy. Nothing was left to do that couldn't be done in the morning. He'd already locked up the gardens. Diego couldn't have picked a better time to talk.

Miki raised his head and felt as if his ribs were squeezing his heart, which was pounding like it was trying to get free. Diego's eyes were dark and brown, and something in them made Miki burn under his skin. His thoughts stopped, fixated on one single idea. "You shouldn't look at me like that." Distress made his voice faint. "Not if you don't mean it. I don't know what to do."

Hearing himself admit that was humiliating. He turned his head so he wouldn't have to watch that internal light disappear from Diego's gaze.

"How am I looking at you, querido?" He couldn't tell if the rumble in Diego's voice meant he was puzzled or pleased, and he didn't know what Diego was trying to tell him in Spanish. It was like talking to Kaz, except Miki wasn't sure he wanted to know what nickname Diego had given him. He didn't want to be a rabbit, not to this wolf.

Miki clutched the plastic cup to his chest. "Like I'm beautiful. I'm not. I'm just me. I'm nothing like Kazimir. He tries to help, but his advice doesn't make sense for someone like me. He told me to use scent, to use that shirt." Miki took a breath. "I'm sorry."

"You wore that shirt for me?" Diego leaned toward him but stopped when Miki tensed. "Why?"

"You're beautiful." Miki addressed Diego's hands, his shoulders. "Of course you don't understand how it feels to be around someone like you and know they could never want…." Miki trailed off and put the cold drink to his warm face. "Thank you for this. I'm sorry I worried you yesterday. You can talk now, if you'd like. I want to be friends. I'd like that very much."

Yet his eyes were stinging again, and his face stayed flushed and hot, and he could feel Diego's gaze on him. Diego saw everything, and what he didn't see, he could hear and smell. Miki tucked his hair behind his ear and stayed still. "I talk a lot, around you," he finished, aware that it was almost a question.

"I like what you have to say." The heat from Diego's body was also in his voice. "But you are not a firebird, so why compare yourself to one? You are not anyone else but you, is that not good enough? You told me you were a gardener and you said it proudly."

"Yes, but then you said—" Miki glanced up sharply. Diego raised both eyebrows. Then Diego had said Miki was remarkable. "You like what I am?" Miki gave a slight frown. "I grow poisons."

"But would never allow me to harm myself." Diego sighed, a content sound.

Miki frowned harder. "I raise plants that consume living creatures."

Diego flashed teeth sharper than any thorn.

Miki paused and turned his face again. "I talk to plants because there is no one else to talk to."

"You asked me to come back. And here I am." Diego said it as though it was easy, as if Miki had no right to be surprised.

"Because of your cactus?" Miki wondered slowly, absolutely puzzled although he was holding the iced tea Diego had brought him.

"No." Diego came a little closer. Miki lifted his gaze and thought of Kazimir telling him that he made the wolf work harder for his attention. He met Diego's stare when Diego continued. "The cactus likes me, I hope. I think it will do well in my care."

Miki darted his attention away but then brought it back to Diego's face. "You keep looking at me like that." He licked the taste of perfumed tea from his mouth.

"I have always looked at you like this, Miki, querido, even when you had tears in your eyes and I didn't know what I'd done wrong." Diego wasn't smiling. "You've forgiven me?"

Miki shook his head and had to fight to speak above a whisper. "You didn't do anything. I was wishing that you might want me. And you didn't. It was me, not you."

Diego straightened as he pulled in a long, long breath. Then he released it. "Miki." He stopped as he seemed to realize something. He continued with slow, deliberate caution. "I didn't come here for advice on a plant."

"You came here to talk?" Miki didn't know what it meant that Diego showed his teeth before he nodded, agreeing almost ferociously. He also didn't understand why Diego would straighten up and visibly calm himself before inquiring if he could stay while Miki finished his closing duties.

He must want to talk afterward, but if that was so, he didn't keep his distance. When Miki whispered that Diego could stay and then slipped into the shop in confused silence, Diego followed him. Miki closed and locked the back door, then went into the Greenhouse without checking to see which employees were on the floor. The iced tea he left on the shelf with the watering can and distilled water, while he used the hand broom to sweep the tables free of spilled dirt and bits of landscaping fabric and moss. Diego observed all of it, and the look on his face remained the same, everything Kaz had told Miki it was.

Miki trembled but made himself work, knowing the look would fade, that surely when he met Diego's eyes next time, that heat would be gone.

When the tables were clean, he reached for the big broom. Sweeping had never made his heart race before.

“Am I that interesting?” he asked to break the heady silence. He pitched his voice low so the others wouldn’t hear. He got the impression the rest of the employees were pretending not to see his after-hours visitor, although Diego took the dustpan and knelt down to help Miki collect the day’s dirt.

“To me, you are.” Diego was trying to make Miki blush now. He had to be. He poured the collected dirt into the bin in the Greenhouse and nodded when Miki suggested he wash up in the sink.

Miki frowned without meeting his eyes. Perhaps Diego was used to an audience when he worked and thought Miki was the same. “This must be very different from your rehearsals.”

“Yes, and no. You have your own rhythm when you work.” Diego stood over him by the sink, exuding warmth. “Do you care for music? My music might not be anything compared to a firebird’s song.”

“But you aren’t a firebird, you shouldn’t—” Miki protested blindly, raising his head and half turning. Diego’s smile sent shivers through him. Diego would know that too. This time Miki did not think Diego’s silence meant he was politely ignoring them, any more than Diego was pretending not to hear the racing of Miki’s heart. Miki focused on getting his hands clean. “What do you like to play?” he asked after a few moments, and moved enough to find a towel.

“Anything with spirit. But mostly I play what the orchestra is performing.” Their hands didn’t touch when Diego took the towel from him. Miki looked up again. It was getting harder not to. Diego worked his jaw, but his voice was even when he spoke. “If you would like to come one night, I would be very happy.”

The words caught in his throat. Miki ducked his head. His heart was deafening. “I’m not—”

“Miki.” Diego brushed Miki’s cheek with his palm. Miki lifted his eyes. He felt his lips part. Diego was careful. He cupped the side of Miki’s face, sweeping his thumb against the very tip of Miki’s eyelashes, then slowly pulled his hand away. “Miki, won’t you leave your garden?”

Miki’s breathing was loud and fast, but he couldn’t slow it. He wasn’t prepared for the measuring study from Diego, and dropped his eyes again. Kaz would fret about that, call him a scared bunny and yank his head back for him if he wouldn’t, so Miki turned his face and angled his chin up.

His loose shirt meant more of his collarbone was exposed. He could feel his blood rushing through him and the heat of Diego standing so close to him. His birthmarks were clearly visible, highlighted by the red in his cheeks, but Diego traced them with the back of his hand and then his fingertips. Miki lifted his chin higher but still could not look.

"Miki." Diego's short growl made him tremble. Miki closed his eyes and turned into the touch. The growl grew pleased, louder and almost declarative. Miki breathed harder.

"You're mated." He fought back the rest as Diego ran his fingers down the side of his neck.

Diego stopped, although Miki didn't feel as if Diego looked away from him, not even for a second. "Yes."

"You still love her." Miki swallowed. "She was amazing, and I'm just—"

Diego leaned closer, cutting him off. "Do you know how you are to me?" The whisper carried across Miki's skin. "*What* you are to me?" Diego buried his nose in Miki's loose curls. "Miki." He inhaled and stroked Miki's throat until Miki's moan finally escaped. Diego's voice was a wolf's. "I want you to hear me play. Say you will come to hear me. Please."

Miki made a small, embarrassed noise to think of how he wasn't moving away. He couldn't tell if he should have, if Kaz would have said to tease or make his strapping wolf beg more, but he didn't want to. "I want to hear you play." The admission was a fraction of what he wanted, but it made Diego shimmer, even with Miki's eyes closed. Miki had no breath left in him. Kaz had told him to accept. He didn't understand, but he gave a slight nod. "I… yes."

Diego slid his hand up to cradle Miki's jaw. He spoke as though Miki had said no. "Then won't you open your eyes? Please?"

Miki swallowed and looked. He was twisted toward Diego, trembling in his hands, but also warm, so warm. The expression on Diego's face had not changed. His gaze was hot on Miki's mouth, on every inch of his bared skin, but he stood between Miki and the others, and his hold was gentle.

Miki turned the rest of the way around, bumping the edge of the sink. Diego carefully leaned in and bent down to breathe under Miki's ear. Miki let his head fall back and shuddered in shocked confusion at Diego's small, soft whine. He rested first one hand, then the other, against Diego's chest, and Diego made the sound again, close to a whimper. Miki blinked, then angled his head to give Diego access to more of his skin.

He moved and Diego followed. Diego inhaled along Miki's throat and whispered, his lips brushing the skin he'd just warmed with his breath. "I will live to make you happy. Let me, querido. Please."

The Greenhouse air was hot and damp for the bloodthirsty plants around them. Miki pushed a hand up, slowly wrapping an arm around Diego's neck. He curled his fingers into Diego's hair, and Diego made a noise, relieved and grateful. He didn't struggle until Miki leaned against the sink, taking his scent away.

Diego followed him again, the scent and heat of him, his skin, his hair, the quiet rhythm of his heart, and Miki twined his other arm around Diego's waist as he finally understood. He parted his lips and Diego growled. Miki knew what he was. And he knew what Diego was, and told him, moments before Diego pressed close and kissed him.

Diego was his, and Miki would live to care for him.

The Dragon's Egg

Present

IT WASN'T unexpected for Arthur to be up before Bertie, but this morning of all mornings, Bertie could admit to being miffed at finding himself alone in their bed. He took comfort in the warm sheets and the knowledge that Arthur had not been up for long. Perhaps Arthur had gone downstairs with the intention of bringing Bertie breakfast—a very small possibility, as his treasure disliked crumbs in the bedding. However, not even tea with toast and marmalade would have made up for not waking up next to Arthur after a month of not waking up next to Arthur.

Bertie was sick of not seeing Arthur when he first opened his eyes. For weeks now he had longed to wake next to his beloved as he had longed to fall asleep beside him. It had been a *month*, and he had dreamed of this almost as much as he had dreamed about using Arthur as a dragon's boy was meant to be used. Leaving Arthur for so long had not been his wish, but Arthur with his arms crossed and his eyes sad was more than Bertie could bear it seemed, so he had capitulated and agreed to go alone.

He had committed to the lecture tour months before Arthur had finalized his ideas for his dissertation, and could hardly have expected Arthur to drop everything to stay with him. Bertie had told himself that repeatedly over the past few weeks, every time his instincts had roared for him to kidnap Arthur from the university and keep him close at his side. In this modern, human-run world, one respected the wishes of one's human mate, and that included leaving them to finish their schooling in peace.

Bertie could not be more proud of Arthur's dissertation or of Arthur himself. Not too many would tell their husband to leave them when they would need the most support. But Arthur had firmly insisted that Bertie had to honor his contract with his publishers, and travel about visiting his fans and answering their questions. Bertie adored his fans, he truly did, but he adored Arthur more. He had left only because he knew the determined tilt to Arthur's chin had meant Arthur would not be dissuaded.

Bertie had chosen a determined, focused human for his boy.

Almost too determined, in fact. If left to himself, Arthur would work himself into an early grave. He wouldn't smile, he wouldn't eat, he would study and write and study some more. Despite Bertie's attempts to keep Arthur safe and cared for, he suspected that deep down, Arthur still thought it could all end at any moment, and that constant work was the answer.

Or perhaps the answer was more terrifying than that. Perhaps Arthur needed to keep busy, to have projects and plans and things to care for, and now that he was settled with Bertie and his education was all but complete, he was growing restless. Bertie read no trace of restlessness in Arthur's e-mails, no hint of boredom in his voice, but everything in Bertie ached to take care of whatever needs his pet might have.

Consequently Bertie had spent the last four weeks agonizing over Arthur from a distance. He had both hoped Arthur wasn't working too hard and had nightmares of Arthur taking a job at some faraway museum in order to keep busy. Arthur did so love to care for things.

Worry had made the separation even more painful, although Bertie would never tell Arthur how bad it had been. Dragons were not humans, and he could not expect Arthur to know the agonies of a treasure out of sight and unprotected. Instead, Bertie had spent a great deal of time in airports and hotel rooms trying to make sure Arthur knew how much Bertie missed him and their home.

But telephones were a cold technology that seemed to alter the sound of what he meant to say. Letters meant nothing if Bertie couldn't know Arthur's answers or see his face as he read them. After Bertie's complaints, Arthur had attempted some visual encounters on the computer, but Bertie had looked at the little window showing his smiling Arthur and lamented there was nothing for him to hold. What was his was too far away.

Now what was his was *still* too far away, and Bertie frowned as he tumbled out of bed on four legs. His movements were awkward and stiff even in his natural form. He was feeling the exertions that his human body had made a few hours ago.

To think last night Bertie had been pleased to know he would be sore this morning.

Yesterday, when Bertie walked in the front door, Arthur had scarcely been able to wait for Bertie to enter the house before he had dashed forward to enfold Bertie in his arms and exhale his name. Bertie had held and touched him in return, mindless with need for him before they had even kissed.

In fact, reflecting upon that moment now, Bertie realized that despite Arthur's brave face on the computer screen, his treasure had been overwhelmed with similar worries and an urgent wish for Bertie to come home.

Arthur's desire had been so strong that Bertie had responded immediately as Arthur had wanted him to. Arthur did not take charge as a rule, not in matters of sex, but Bertie did not dislike the desperate strength in the hands dragging him to the living room. Bertie could barely breathe at the memory of the sure way Arthur had held his gaze as he'd pushed him to the floor, the unexpected heat of Arthur pressing inside of him, and the fierce pressure of Arthur's teeth at his neck. Arthur had been full of longing, and anger at being left behind, and then an exquisite insistence upon pleasure that had made him shiver and shudder and kiss Bertie over and over once he was spent.

It might be rare for Arthur to want to take the lead in such matters, but when he did, he was as competent as Bertie had come to expect from him in all things. Once Arthur had researched and considered and made his plans, his hesitation was banished.

Last night he had been so sure and forceful that Bertie had been happy to promise to never leave him again. He meant it, although he had a suspicion, supported by the final scrape of teeth at his shoulder blade, that Arthur had more pent-up feelings to demonstrate.

He was not surprised Arthur felt that way after being neglected, if not outright rejected, by his extended family. Knowing that did not ease Bertie's anger, to think of Arthur practically alone and friendless, with Kate to watch out for, but no one to watch out for him until he'd knocked on Bertie's door.

But then, of course, he thought of meeting Arthur, and getting to know him, and falling in love with him, and he couldn't regret that part of Arthur's story, at least. He did not think Arthur did either.

Last night, Bertie had argued, sleepy and satisfied with his treasure sprawled out on top of him. He had gently reminded Arthur that Arthur had told him to go in the first place, but Arthur had banished that argument by whispering his name, shaky with longing, and Bertie had wisely gone silent. He did not always understand human emotions, but after a few years with Arthur he knew humans had odd notions of duty and how things were supposed to be.

Bertie had given in to duty this time, as Arthur had wanted him to, but the next time Bertie would make Arthur understand. Their love was magic, and it wouldn't be denied. *Bertie* would not be denied again, even if, of course, he found it difficult to refuse anything asked of him by his dear boy.

On that somewhat firm thought, Bertie shuffled out into the hallway, dragging his claws in the rug and shaking his limbs one at a time to help with the ache in his lower back. He paused near the top of the stairs, glancing around for a moment before returning to his human form. He still could not bring himself to walk down the stairs on four legs in front of Arthur, though he blushed at his own foolish vanity. Arthur would chide him, but on this Bertie would not relent. Some things required mystery and majesty and the appearance of strength, and Arthur's high opinion of him was one of those things.

They had seen each other sick. Bertie had witnessed Arthur with food poisoning. Arthur had once laughed himself silly at the realization that yes, even wondrous and powerful dragons experienced gas, but Bertie refused to let his beloved see him waddle down the stairs. A man had to be a man. Or a dragon, as it were.

Bertie felt the heat in the house grow around him as he skipped down the first few steps. But he stopped near the bottom. Arthur wasn't in the kitchen after all. Arthur was standing not far in front of him, staring down at the floor in front of the sofa.

"Did we leave a mark?" Bertie crept up next to him, first worrying that they must have added a new stain to the rug, and then that he must have left a book out too close to the fireplace. Arthur, with his librarian's heart and warrior's soul, hated it when Bertie left his books by the fire, and would fight to protect them with his last breath.

Bertie prepared to apologize before he remembered that he had been gone for a month and couldn't have left a book anywhere, much less near the fireplace. He did, however, vaguely recall wandering downstairs in the middle of the night, feeling as though he'd forgotten something and assuming that he must have been more jet-lagged than he thought, but he certainly hadn't been reading anything.

Besides, in addition to his school workload and his assistance with Bertie's current project, Arthur, the clever boy, had been scanning and uploading all the rare and old books in Bertie's collection to a digital library, in case Bertie got careless with his books again. No books were in danger today, so there was nothing for Arthur to be upset about.

In fact, perhaps there was nothing in danger because the house was *too* safe, too empty of things for Arthur to look after.

Bertie eyed the tense line of Arthur's slight shoulders with alarm—alarm that did not ease when Arthur barely glanced at him before pointing to the center of the room. Bertie looked in that direction and nearly tipped over his own sofa in a swoon.

"Exquisite," he exhaled, rapturous delight hot in his chest and stinging at his eyes. "Oh, Arthur." He reached out, his fingers brushing the back of Arthur's hand before he swept forward around the sofa so he could fall to his knees in front of the most precious thing he had ever seen.

The egg was lying on its side. It was not so big, not yet, but as jewel bright and healthy as it ought to be, and warm to the touch. Bertie ran his palm over the surface to make sure the shell was hard enough to protect the beautiful treasure inside and yet soft enough to give room for it to grow. The egg thrummed with life he could feel so deeply that it was as if his own heart's rhythm changed to match it.

"*Mine*." Bertie allowed his pleasure to shake through the house, but paused when Arthur stumbled.

Arthur was not afraid of Bertie's magic, yet he was clinging to the sofa to stay on his feet. Bertie frowned at him without turning his head from the egg. "*Ours*," he added loudly, so Arthur would not misunderstand his parental pride and feel excluded. "Oh, darling," he went on, his love rocking the foundations as he pushed his palm over the shell until he found the faint heartbeat. He leaned in to let the scent imprint on him, to share his scent with it.

He had thought, somewhat vaguely, of children, someday when things were settled and Arthur was out of school and ready. The logistics he had fully intended to leave to Arthur: adoption, a dragon surrogate, whatever Arthur wished. This was a surprise, to say the least.

"That's…." Arthur seemed to be having trouble focusing, which was most unlike him. "That's a dragon's egg." He wasn't coming any closer. Bertie blinked at him, starting to realize that something was seriously bothering his pearl.

"Yes, it is," Bertie told him slowly, and lifted his head to look over Arthur, who was shivering in his underwear and T-shirt despite the warmth fogging the windows.

"How did it get here?" Arthur met his gaze, very directly, his voice strained, and Bertie scrambled to his feet. He had an urge to laugh, which was probably not very helpful in the situation, but Bertie hadn't been a father last night and this morning he was, and he thought Arthur really ought to forgive him some small hysterics. The situation required *some* degree of hysteria. Especially when he considered how quiet Arthur had gotten, which was generally a sign that Arthur was fretting.

"Arthur, surely I don't need to explain the birds and the bees to you," Bertie purred, only to flinch at the betrayed look Arthur gave him. He hurried forward in the next second to wrap his arms around Arthur and pull him close. "I'm sorry, pet, I didn't mean to tease, but you see—"

"That's an *egg*." Arthur seemed to understand.

"*Our* egg, darling." Bertie drew in a long breath. It was so wonderful to say it that it was almost painful. He stroked a hand over Arthur's shoulder blades and turned his head to press his lips to Arthur's ever-so-faintly stubbled cheek. "Can't you see its colors?" The shell was black and shining at the base, like the colors of Bertie's scales when he was in his true form. It lightened to blue at the top, as blue as Arthur's eyes. It could have been made from onyx and sapphire and aquamarine, except for the licks of ruby red where the light hit the surface, red like the fire that was as much what Arthur was made of as Bertie was. Red that might not even be there as humans saw colors.

Bertie suddenly could not press further to find out if Arthur did not see the black and red and blue together. It would hurt both of them to know that Arthur saw only an ordinary, if large, egg. In the brief silence, Arthur trembled. Bertie slid his hands to Arthur's wrist and gave a tug, but Arthur refused to budge.

"I admit, it's rare in these, forgive me, male upon male, circumstances, but it's not unheard of." Bertie lowered his voice. Arthur responded to his coaxing tone with a frown, which was as adorable as it was confusing. Had Bertie been less than clear on the finer points of dragon magical biology? He supposed the cases of an egg in their situation were unusual enough that the casual dragon scholar, if there were such people, might not have heard of them. Bertie really ought to sit down with Arthur to discuss it.

There weren't any books on the subject, in fact, merely rumors and old stories. Bertie might have written them down somewhere, but that was a matter for another time. They had a much more pressing issue to discuss.

"Will it be a girl or a boy or something else, do you think?" Bertie wondered out loud, his head spinning as the thought of a real child actually took hold. "What language should be the primary one in the home? English would be convenient for you, but my mother would never forgive me if her grandchild couldn't respond to her in what she feels is a far superior tongue. Oh dear. Father is going to want the child to attend a private college, and you won't like that, will you?" Bertie gasped. "Do you think it will like sports? American football? What am I going to do in that case? I *can't* watch the Super Bowl, Arthur, please don't make me."

"*Bertie!*" Arthur shut him up with one word. Bertie recognized the tone; Arthur thought Bertie wasn't being reasonable. Possibly he was right; Bertie *was* rather excited. He tried to calm his spiraling thoughts about chemistry sets and paper dolls to listen, but Arthur's pallor was getting him worried. He was dreaming of the future, and Arthur was worrying about the banalities of the here and now. "That egg, Bertie. *How* did it get here?"

The specific nature of the question was almost reassuring. It meant Arthur was beginning to do more than react to the unexpected present Bertie had left him in the middle of the night. Bertie leaned in again, until he took up all of Arthur's vision, and Arthur had to stare at him. Sometimes it was a matter of human thinking getting in the way. Bertie could forgive the jealousy if Arthur had been abstractly asking him if Bertie had gone behind his back with some female to make an egg for them, but he could not allow this doubt. It would eat away at Arthur, who had been left behind by too many people already.

Bertie bent down and placed a kiss to the tip of Arthur's slightly snub nose. He had to brush Arthur's blond hair from his eyes. It had gotten too long in his absence, but he rather enjoyed the feel of it sliding between his fingers as he held it away to give Arthur another light peck of affection. The kiss was the merest fraction of what he wanted to do, but he was so hot with his many growing emotions that he knew Arthur could feel it even where they weren't touching. He watched Arthur's skin slowly turn pink at the warmth, watched Arthur's gaze stay on his until Arthur's eyes grew wide.

"I love you very much, you see," Bertie told him, as though he hadn't spent years making sure Arthur knew this. Arthur froze for a moment, as if this was not the answer he had expected, but he finally accepted it with a lick of his lips. Bertie suspected the action was also a hint that Arthur would have taken a real kiss had it been offered.

"But…." Arthur was whispering—keeping a secret from the egg, Bertie realized with hidden delight. "I don't understand. Did you make that while you were gone?"

"*We* did, foolish boy. We made it right here." Bertie kissed Arthur's nose once more, trying not to get distracted by Arthur's aroused blush and the catches in Arthur's breathing—it had been a very lonely month. He pulled at Arthur's wrist again, and this time Arthur followed, albeit very slowly.

"Arthur," Bertie explained as Arthur stumbled after him, "I don't shift like a were of any kind. As a dragon, I simply choose to be human. To *appear* human. In particular, I choose to look like a human male, because that is my preference. Biology and magic are a bit of a tangle when it comes to us." He lived with a fire in his belly, which Arthur knew. Surely this couldn't be that difficult of a concept after that.

His announcement got Arthur's attention. He could see the new idea enter Arthur's head, could see Arthur trying to calm himself down by considering the implications. Arthur's sharp mind was no doubt pulling the statement apart layer by layer and dividing it into lists of things to be studied at a later date. Bertie would let him do that if it would help Arthur see. "This situation is rare, as I said, but not unheard of," Bertie finished, although the more he thought about it, the more he realized it was very rare indeed.

In fact… in fact, this egg existing was a once in a lifetime sort of occurrence, and Arthur should know it. So he bent to put Arthur's hand against the egg.

For the barest second Arthur pushed out his fingers, spreading them wide over the warm, uneven surface, absorbing the heat and the sensation of life as Bertie had. Then… then Arthur pulled his hand away.

Bertie did not let go of him or stop his impulse to punctuate his words with the press of his lips to Arthur's skin. "You took me last night, Arthur. Do you not remember? I certainly do."

"Yes, but—" Arthur gave a small, choked moan. "Wait, last night? That fast?" He was breathless with discovery and confusion, but he allowed every kiss. His hands slid over Bertie's skin, one palm still warm from where it had rested over their egg.

Bertie closed his eyes and accepted his good fortune. "You must have missed me more than you could say," he murmured in satisfaction, and enjoyed Arthur's half-stifled squeak.

"Of course I did, I missed you more than… more than words. I had *dreams*." Arthur was probably scowling, attempting to remain unmoved despite how he was nearly swallowing his tongue. He was probably still confused, the poor lamb. "Bertie…." He pulled back a moment later, his furrowed brow very evident. "Are you saying I'm the father? I mean… you know what I mean."

Bertie should have mentioned this very, very slight, almost mythical possibility earlier, he could see that now. Human minds took some time to wrap around new concepts. He patted Arthur's cheek and gave Arthur's pert little nose another kiss before taking a step and kneeling down to give the egg a kiss as well. Then he got to his feet with a bounce and the urge to fly. If his wings hadn't been so small, he would have.

"You need a think, I can see that. I'll just make us some tea, shall I?" he offered merrily as he went toward the kitchen. He ignored Arthur's narrowed eyes. "Perhaps coffee for you, treasure, you might need it. I'll call my parents this afternoon. Do you want to tell your sister by yourself, or do you want to wait for her to come over and surprise her?" Arthur's sister might need to see it to believe it, much like her brother, but with Kate, surprises were not always a good thing. Bertie would have to leave the decision of how to tell her up to Arthur.

"*Bertie*," Arthur warned him, his hands gesturing furiously between him and their egg as if he needed more information when Bertie had no more to give him. All there was to say, Bertie had already said. He loved Arthur and Arthur loved him, with a love like fire itself. Bertie was a dragon of a powerful line. His treasure had a need, and Bertie had filled it. Arthur would understand if given more time. This was rare, this was exceptional, perhaps even unbelievable to a human, but this was real.

Only once the kitchen doors were closed behind him did Bertie stop and take a long, deep breath as the weight of what had happened—what they had created—hit him.

It was marvelous really, as well as terrifying beyond all measure. Bertie spun on his heel to return to the living room and gather his frozen, frightened Arthur into his arms. "I love you so much, darling. So much I will give you anything you ask for." He crooned the explanation into Arthur's shiny hair and curled his arms about him. "I will give it to you even when you don't know what you're asking yet."

Arthur pulled away to give him the most perplexed look. Bertie didn't understand it. He suspected it was a human thing, and resolved to deal with it as soon as he'd had his tea. Some issues could not be dealt with before his morning cup. And Arthur would need caffeine as well. This Bertie could also provide.

Bertie kissed Arthur on his wrinkled brow and patted his pink cheek. "All will be well, Arthur, you'll see," he chided gently and swept into the kitchen to make his Arthur breakfast. He chose to ignore Arthur's loudly voiced protest that he hadn't asked Bertie for anything.

The truth was right there in their living room, after all.

SOMETIMES IT was best to give Arthur the space to think things through. Arthur was a creature of preparedness and research, not given to rash decisions, or one to have much faith in magic, despite living with a dragon and occasionally having dreams that might or might not indicate a human gift for sight. It could be vexing, to tell the truth, but Bertie would not have it any other way. As he had been pleased to discover the first time Arthur had kissed him, once Arthur's mind was made up, there was nothing he would not do. Until then it was simply a matter of waiting for Arthur to believe.

That Arthur would cherish and protect the hatchling was not in doubt—not to Bertie anyway. He was not so sure about Arthur's thoughts on the matter. Bertie suspected much of Arthur's current state of confusion was due to his human mind failing to grasp how love could create an egg.

Arthur, as Bertie knew too well, believed that Bertie adored him, but somehow did not see himself or his own love as anything extraordinary. Therefore, to Arthur, no magic had been involved when he had lovingly ravished Bertie on the living room rug. To him it was a mere matter of anatomy.

Arthur wasn't rude. He wouldn't come out and say so, but the signs were small but obvious, if one was looking, and Bertie was more than willing to put aside his work to do just that. And as it happened, he had a few concerns of his own that he'd rather not think about yet. He would always rather focus on Arthur. As he had thought the very moment he had first laid eyes on Arthur, this human was worth watching. Who else but his Arthur could have brought this egg into being?

Arthur had a dissertation to finish and a digital library to curate, as well as notes on Bertie's latest work, which he did not hesitate to offer when Bertie needed help, even when Arthur was at his busiest. He kept an eye on Kate and made sure to return calls from Bertie's parents, even after confessing once to Bertie that he didn't think they approved of him. He managed the groceries and the bills and saw to the cleaning. Bertie would have been exhausted in his place. Arthur did these things because he was Arthur: he loved his sister, he loved the books, and he loved Bertie. Caring for others kept Arthur going. It made him content and satisfied and most of all, happy.

He was a wondrous jewel. He was the sort of creature that existed in fairy tales and legends, so of course he would have a dragon as a consort and something so rare as a dragon's egg to love.

Bertie was biased, he could admit, but facts were facts, and the egg they had made was proof. Arthur, for all his nerves and fears, was going to care for their child as he had never cared for anything, not even Bertie. He had already begun his research.

Bertie had found books on the biology of reptiles among Arthur's things.

Slightly insulting, that; a dragon was no ordinary reptile. But Bertie let his irritation go the way he pretended not to mind how Arthur had gotten home late because of checking out more than a few grimoire and notebooks from the university's library, texts unrelated to his dissertation. Bertie did this because he knew Arthur and because he also knew Arthur had been losing sleep to stay up to read those books, and other books besides. Hidden among Arthur's regular nightstand reading list, Bertie had discovered books about child development and the diary of a Regency-era dragon, which the two of them had found at a store for used books a long time ago. Bertie had been delighted, but unsurprised, to find that the pages Arthur had marked before passing out against Bertie's shoulder were the sections about the dragon's childhood, though he had privately wondered if they would be helpful at all when the child was hatched.

The surprise came when Bertie returned home from a lecture several days later to find fire extinguishers bolted to the wall at strategic locations throughout the house, and Arthur standing hesitantly over the egg, which was still on the rug before the fireplace, although now resting in a nest of pillows.

"I was thinking," Arthur began, his arms crossed tightly at his chest. "The bedroom at the start of the hall.... There should be a nursery." Color flared in his cheeks at the word. "There's plenty of space there, if I move the books."

As Arthur did not mention things casually, this was clearly a request. Bertie put down his bag and nodded as he considered that. The room wasn't far from theirs, and a growing hatchling would need space. "But you already have too much to do," Bertie offered up as his only argument, and stared as Arthur gave a long, relieved sigh, as though he had honestly thought Bertie would say no, as though Bertie had *ever* said no to Arthur. Bertie had lent some of his treasure to museums for Arthur. *Museums.* He almost shuddered to think of it, his beloved things in the hands of others.

"I think that's a marvelous idea," Bertie said after a moment, clearing his throat to make sure he could speak evenly. "I should have thought of a nursery." Then he very carefully picked up the egg. The egg had grown considerably in the past week, something that had sent Arthur back to the library for more answers. He probably hadn't found any, possibly because he was still expecting their child to be a dragon child, as though his own magic and love did not exist.

In all honesty, Arthur's blindness was a bit vexing. Arthur was capable of love as few other creatures were. He was the very definition of special. Bertie suspected their child would be the same, whatever waited behind the bright shell.

"I remembered you mentioned once that sometimes as a child you had set a few things on fire without meaning to," Arthur explained behind him as they went up the stairs and passed yet another fire extinguisher. "Are you taking it to the room now?"

Arthur moved from side to side, close on Bertie's heels, and Bertie turned in time to notice the way Arthur had his arms out to catch the egg in case Bertie tripped or lost his grip. Bertie had expected protectiveness from Arthur, but not hovering, and resolved to talk to Kate about it the next time she visited. Kate must have been very patient with Arthur, or had needed this level of attention after their parents' death, because Bertie had never heard her complain.

"Get the door, will you, darling?" Bertie was simply grateful that the egg had been so much smaller that first night. He'd never have managed it now, however it had happened, he was certain of that. Even a dragon was not built that way.

Arthur opened the door and then stepped to the side so Bertie could bring their egg into the room. Bertie considered locations before setting the egg down in front of the window. The window overlooked part of his yard and part of his neighbor's, which was why Bertie had only used this room for storage.

"It's dusty in here," Arthur commented, not at all casually, and Bertie could not contain his wide, relieved smile. Arthur must already have something in mind for the room, and Bertie was happy to indulge him, as he always was.

"And a trifle dark, don't you think?" Bertie tossed back, and loved Arthur even more—which should not have been possible—for how very seriously he nodded in reply.

A GREAT many of the books Bertie had stored in that room were gone the next day, banished to some other place until Arthur considered how to rearrange them. The egg sat in the light of the window on a new bed of pillows, untouched by Arthur's hands as Arthur fussed over the rows of books he'd decided to keep in the room. It pained Bertie to see Arthur avoid the egg itself, but he said nothing about it as he came in and sat on the floor with his laptop on his knees.

The laptop he left unopened as he stared at Arthur's handiwork.

Arthur glanced at him. "The education of a child is no laughing matter," he announced, although Bertie had not said a word, either about the state of the nursery or how Arthur had yet to touch the egg without Bertie insisting. He waved his hand over the books until Bertie obediently squinted at the titles, seeing *Mother Goose* and *Gulliver's Travels*, *Tom Sawyer*, *Huck Finn*, Perrault and The Grimms' largely incorrect fairy tales. Several books of Chinese fables were there next to Spenser and Lang and Bullfinch, as well as *The Reluctant Dragon*, which was side by side with *Journey to the West*, *Peter Rabbit*, *Aunt Nancy's Spider Stories*, *Little Women*, *The Black Cauldron*, *Coyote and Fire*, and *The Phantom Tollbooth*. *Peter Pan* and a new book called *Norse Tales of Magik and Gods* ended one shelf, *Anne of Green Gables* from start to finish took up another. There, at the top, next to a translation of the *Popol Vuh*, was a faded copy of *The Lost Ones*, an obscure title that Arthur loved, but which even a fairy would not have deemed appropriate for children. Most of the books were at least thirty years old. Some were practically ancient.

Arthur would never have let Bertie touch the ones that were falling apart. Bertie's chest actually hurt to realize that. If it had been possible, Bertie would have thought he was having a heart attack. As it was, he put a hand to his chest and made a wounded sound. He had to fight to keep from roaring. Only Arthur could wound him and make him so proud in the same moment. Each and every story on those shelves was a message, a lesson, from Arthur to their child. Arthur had not the spirit for magic, either human or being, if Bertie did not count his dreams, but these books were spells to give their child knowledge and power. For their child, Arthur practiced the strongest protective magic there was.

This was Arthur nesting. Bertie thought it magnificent even as he realized what it also meant. Arthur would never have let Bertie lay a hand on any of these books without supervision, but here they were in this new library Arthur was building, in a nursery for a child to read and dirty up and destroy. Arthur's loyalties were already changing, ever so slightly. Arthur's love had shifted not just from books and history but from Bertie as well. Arthur already loved their child more. The knowledge was equal parts pleasing and painful. He was a pearl, and Bertie would give him anything.

"We'll need more shelves," Bertie struggled to say, all the words he had ever learnt leaving him at once, and all his breath too. He wondered what he looked like. It could not have been good; Arthur stopped what he was doing and hurried over to sit in front of him. He had to sit nearer to their egg than he ever had before to do it, and that was enough for Bertie's moment of jealousy to pass, or to at least become manageable. He dropped his head to Arthur's shoulder and closed his eyes when Arthur stroked a hand through his hair.

"Am I doing okay?" Arthur worried after a moment, then made a noise of protest when Bertie snorted a laugh. Bertie petted him to apologize but didn't raise his head. "It's not funny," Arthur huffed. "Your mother and father already dislike me, and they are going to think—"

"*I* think you are doing a bloody good job," Bertie cut him off, still needing to laugh, or cry, or destroy a medieval village. "Considering that neither of us has the slightest idea what we're doing." Arthur gave a start of surprise, and Bertie shook his head against Arthur's shoulder. "Did you think I had all the answers, pet? I can only tell you about *my* childhood, if that is any help."

Arthur's hand tightened in his hair, then relaxed. "It might be, if your parents ever felt half this—" He swallowed. "—afraid." He was still trembling a little, probably with too much coffee and not enough sleep. Bertie put aside his laptop and drew Arthur forward. Arthur let himself be pulled, ending up half on the pillows with Bertie lying down alongside him. Arthur reached out, keeping his hand in the air, his fingers almost trailing over the bright eggshell, before he dropped it to his side.

"I should call Kate. I still haven't told her. She's going to be pissed at me." Arthur pushed out the words, exhausted from exertion, or lack of sleep, or nerves. "I just can't… I can't quite believe it."

"Neither can I, love," Bertie couldn't help but say, and wrapped a leg around Arthur in lieu of his tail. He understood the uncertainty about magic in general, but he did not see how Arthur could doubt this one thing, the one thing Bertie was most sure of. This egg had happened because Arthur loved him, and he loved Arthur, more than he could ever say. It was the manifestation of that love. It would change them in indefinable ways, yet it would make them stronger. It was not something to be doubted.

Yet Bertie looked at that bookcase full of rare books and felt a pang, somewhere deep inside where dragons should never feel cold. But it was Arthur he was worried about, so he said nothing that was not in answer to Arthur's many thoughts on the upbringing of young dragons.

Bertie had no proof that it was anything other than a dragon in the egg. All he had was legend, and tickling suspicions, and the absolute certainty that Arthur was forgetting his own contribution to this miracle.

Arthur was in his arms, close enough to touch their soon-to-hatch hatchling if he dared, asking frighteningly specific question after frighteningly specific question about Bertie's formative years, until Bertie was sure of at least one more thing.

Arthur might have doubts, but he didn't want to have them. Arthur wanted to see. It was only a matter of time now.

"YOU SEE, my little gem, the world was, if not hostile, then often unkind to Arthur before he came to my door. So although I doubt he would say so himself, he regards knowledge as something of a weapon, or perhaps a shield." Bertie patiently explained the situation to their child. Well, to the shell of the egg that surrounded their child. Sawing and hammering could be heard above them, distinctly audible even downstairs.

Bertie hummed distractedly at the bluest part of the shell. "One thing you will have to learn is that Arthur feels safest with information in his grasp. The unknown leaves him wobbly and a little lost."

Movement in his peripheral vision caught his attention, and Bertie raised his head. The new scent of disturbed drywall and sawdust did not take away from the warm taste of Arthur in his mouth; that luscious scent made him want to find Arthur and hold him. Arthur's scent always did. Sometimes Bertie did not resist the urge, but at the moment he looked over until he found Arthur in the study doorway. Arthur was regarding Bertie as though he'd done something unusual.

"Were you talking to it?" Arthur continued to refer to the egg as "it," more from a lack of knowing the correct preferred pronoun or form of address for an unborn hatchling than anything hurtful, at least as far as Bertie could tell. "Can it hear in there? They say human babies can."

"Sh—" Bertie bit his tongue, carefully not admitting to the inkling of a feeling in his gut that their baby had a feminine spirit. He could hardly explain it himself and kept meaning to ask his mother about it. "It's possible. I don't believe a study has been done, but the shell is not so thick as to keep out sound, and the egg has stopped growing. In fact the first crack should appear soon." Dragons lived too long and didn't reproduce enough to make a study of the eggs feasible, but naturally, Arthur focused on the more scientific sounding information before jerking his head up and loudly swallowing.

"The first crack? Really?" His voice was rough, his eyes wide. He looked at Bertie, a smile crossing his face, though it quickly vanished. He swallowed again and studied the egg with a haunted expression before turning away. "Then I should go back to watching the workmen to make sure they finish on time."

Arthur, the darling, would insist on staying upstairs to keep an eye on the builders while the nursery was being redone. The fact that the workers did not seem to know a dragon was in the house, much less that they were down the hall from piles of gold, did not deter Arthur from his self-appointed role of guardian. The magic in the house would never let the workmen take anything if they did try, which Arthur also knew, which was why Bertie did not think Arthur hovered over the workmen out of concern for the gold. It was the doorway of the nursery where Arthur spent his time, where he stood, strong and fierce and divinely little, with his arms crossed like an angry sentry. If smoke had begun to stream from his nostrils or wings had sprouted in his back, Bertie would not have been surprised.

"Arthur has the heart of a dragon," Bertie addressed the egg again, in a whisper as well as in his mother's tongue, since Arthur did not speak that or any other dialect of Mandarin, and he did not think Arthur would care for being embarrassed by praise. "But why did you come down?" Bertie changed the subject, and his language, quickly, and resolutely ignored his computer screen. With the noise and the egg, he hadn't been getting any work done as it was; he saw no point in trying today. The mysterious fairy, or fairies, named Poppy, the so-called Angel of the Ardennes, had already waited a hundred years to be told. They could wait a bit longer for him to collect and share with the world. There were many, many tales from the First World War about fairies meeting soldiers, possibly apocryphal, but they all had similar themes, and Bertie found them fascinating.

Or he had before he found their egg.

If Arthur hadn't been so distracted, he would have had something to say about Bertie's procrastination. Bertie wanted to shamelessly take advantage and keep Arthur down here with him, but his question seemed to distract Arthur even more.

"Oh." Arthur paused and gave him a hopeful look. "One of the contractors mentioned…." He was so carefully excited that Bertie simply could not wait for him to finish.

"Yes?" he pressed, as charmed as he had been the first time Arthur had shyly but eagerly asked something of him.

"We could expand that window," Arthur explained, enthusiasm lifting his voice. "Make the window itself wider, then give it more of a bench seat."

"That sounds lovely." Bertie could picture it instantly, the whole image and not only the small pieces Arthur was sharing. He knew Arthur. The shelves were for the books, and the bay window with the wide bench seat was for Arthur to read those books. That was where Arthur would curl up with their child and teach her to read. If the bench was wide enough, Bertie might sit there too, curled around his treasures. "It sounds lovely," he said again, his chest tight. Arthur was planning their future, and Bertie had no objections to it. "The better for reading to h—it," he agreed finally, and Arthur ducked his head, as if surprised that Bertie had guessed his intent.

Bertie clucked his tongue, then opened his mouth to taste the tart crush of Arthur's unsettled feelings. Arthur's face was flushed, and Bertie could not help how his voice lowered as he spoke, rumbling with unsettled feelings of his own.

"If our child is anything at all like you, it should enjoy that very much," he murmured to put his pearl at ease. He didn't miss how Arthur glanced at the egg, or how he then glanced to Bertie. Some part of Arthur was still startled that Bertie would want him, even after years together.

Bertie frowned imperiously at him for the doubt. Arthur turned a lovely shade of pink.

"I should get back," Arthur repeated himself, but followed through this time. "We'll have to get them to hurry to get something like that done…." He was out of sight before he finished his thought, likely something about the expense.

Bertie waited until he was gone before he turned back to their girl with a sigh. "If you think this is bad, you should have seen how long it took for him to admit that he cared for me," he told their egg, and rolled his eyes at the ceiling. "I do hope you didn't inherit much of his human stubbornness." He meant it. Not that it stopped him from turning around to stare at the chapters he wasn't writing and pretend to write some more to make Arthur and his publisher happy.

Fourteen different written direct accounts existed of the moment the fairies had left the forests and run toward the human soldiers destroying their homes. The writing was French and German, in several dialects. Countless diaries and telegraphs from the front reported similar stories. Ten confirmed accounts of the fairy named Pavot had survived. *Those* tales, of course, began to spread later in the war. Always with the same elements of the tragic and beautiful fairy rescuing an injured soldier or stealing away a soldier sentenced to death for his perceived cowardice, and not the shell shock the poor soul likely truly had. Pavot, or Poppy, was the most famous of the living, mythical creatures at the time and the one Bertie did not believe was truly real. Pavot was the symbol of hope for soldiers staring across every patch of no-man's-land the Great War had created. Perhaps the stories held some truth. Poppy was possibly an amalgamation of many fairies, but the accounts were too varied for them all to be real.

He was a creation too. A beautiful idea brought to life to save men sent to destroy the world. Bertie had first encountered him in that book Arthur loved so much, the one he'd cried over when he'd first read it. Arthur recognized true magic even in a story, but being human, love like that made him hesitate. He needed Pavot to be real almost as much as those soldiers had.

Perhaps Pavot was, or had been. Hope was sometimes rewarded. Even when the world least expected it.

Bertie made a notation to that effect, thinking of the conclusion of the book he'd barely begun. But that was all he wrote. His attention stayed split between the noises upstairs and the jewellike shell of the egg, and after another hour of staring at his unmoving cursor, he returned to worrying over Arthur.

HE FOUND the files Arthur had been keeping from him purely by accident, after the workmen had gone home later that afternoon. He'd been searching for Arthur's last chapter notes and found the lists instead. If information was Arthur's shield, lists were his sword, and Arthur had been obsessively preparing for battle.

In the file were lists upon lists that hinted at every anxiety under the sun—from common human childhood illnesses and the few dragon sicknesses, to good local schools, and articles about children being bullied for mixed parentage, and the low rates of adoption of being children. There were lists of names that Arthur seemed to like and lists of names he didn't like, lists of places that sold fireproof cribs, and a horrifying chart of medicines and potions every parent should keep around the house in addition to any protection spells they might desire. There was also a column of places Arthur had gone to that he had ominously titled "Was Not Welcome."

Bertie closed the file before he'd finished reading and immediately sought out Arthur. There was too much to say and no correct way to say it, but the clawing need to save his pet was too strong for a dragon to deny any longer. He found Arthur in the kitchen reheating dinner and said only, "Arthur."

"Arthur." And Arthur turned around, hesitant to meet Bertie's gaze because his eyelashes were damp and his skin was pale. Bertie kissed him, with his hands at Arthur's face and their bodies pressed close together. Arthur had kept his fears from him, to protect him. He shouldn't have. "Arthur, darling, please don't worry."

Arthur kissed him back, hard and almost furious, scraping his hands through Bertie's hair and bruising his shoulders. "Bertie, I can't do this," he started to confess, stopping when Bertie kissed him again. Bertie took Arthur's breath and his every sigh and crushed Arthur to his chest. Arthur's scent was melted gold, and the flush in his cheeks begged to be licked away. He was precious and scared, and he was all Bertie's, something he seemed to have forgotten.

Bertie was Dragon. He would care for what was his. He pulled back enough to growl it into Arthur's ear. Arthur shivered and tried to argue, tossing his head and shuddering, but when Bertie stepped between his legs, he allowed it and eased his head up so Bertie could flick his tongue against his throat and taste the very essence of him.

Arthur had not forgotten after all, but Bertie needed him to acknowledge it again, no matter how embarrassing humans might find it. "I am Dragon, and I will care for you." Bertie bit and sucked into Arthur's flesh until Arthur moaned. He pulled Arthur's clothes away to reach his skin and used kitchen oil to open Arthur up. He was not altogether man anymore, dwarfing the kitchen and Arthur, enveloping them both in heat and smoke, but Arthur growled back at him until Bertie picked him up, and he gave a pained groan when Bertie entered him. He strained beautifully, panting against Bertie's shoulder, then opened his mouth to slide kisses of acceptance along Bertie's skin.

Bertie gave him everything, all his might and magic. The strength Bertie rarely used kept Arthur up, would keep him up forever if Arthur needed it to. Arthur must not be allowed to forget again. Bertie braced himself against the counter, and Arthur wrapped his legs around his hips. He kept his head down and stifled his cries as though the hatchling was already there to hear them, but Bertie did not have it in him to share a laugh over it. He thrust into Arthur and murmured, "Louder, darling, louder," as he mouthed the sweat-matted line of his Arthur's hair and feasted on the hum of his pulse. He roared when Arthur tensed and curled against him, shaking their home for the world to feel.

He would see to Arthur, and he grunted in satisfaction when Arthur's gasps echoed through the room and jets of Arthur's seed hit his stomach. "Mine," he reminded a breathless Arthur. "My boy, always." It was enough to spur him on, make him lick at Arthur's soft, panting mouth and push Arthur down onto his cock.

Arthur whined sweetly as Bertie finished, but did not let go. His fingers were as close to claws as they would ever be, blunt nails digging into Bertie's shoulders when Bertie came and pushed deep inside of him for one long, divine moment, but the pain Bertie felt did not matter. Arthur, his luscious, one of a kind pearl, would understand now. Bertie held him too tight and kissed him too long, reluctant to let go now, though things were already returning to normal. Skin cooled, come dried, and Arthur's back would start to ache. Bertie would hold him until he was hard again if Arthur did not tell him no. Arthur was rare and precious, and everything built between them was the same. A library. Books. A child. "*Mine*," Bertie rumbled and rocked the house again with how much he meant it. "I am Dragon and you are mine. I will take care of you. Both of you."

Bertie was possessive, as all dragons were, and soon he would have to share Arthur. Already Arthur, *his* Arthur, was starting to love the child as he would love nothing else. It made Arthur more of a gift and served to make Bertie feel stupidly jealous, but he did not stop himself from petting Arthur until he could feel Arthur's young, human body start to respond again, or from lapping at Arthur's bruised, damp skin while Arthur trembled in his arms. He did not put Arthur down for a long, long time, long enough that he thought Arthur would complain, but even when Arthur's feet were on the floor, Arthur held on to him.

"Treasure," Arthur whispered, still shy about using that word, but gave Bertie a warm look as Bertie offered him a drink of water to ease his raw throat. For once Arthur's practical mind didn't have a thing to say about the mess, or Bertie's insistence upon pampering him. Perhaps he wanted to be pampered, to be the only thing Bertie had to worry about, one more time. Or perhaps, gratifyingly, he enjoyed leaning on Bertie's strength. It was not often Arthur would admit to weakness.

Bertie kissed him, and Arthur curved around him and shivered. "Soon we won't be able to do this," Arthur observed, voice still hoarse. So he had thought about what it would be like with an inquisitive hatchling running through the house, how quiet and careful they would need to be. Of course he had. Arthur had thought about everything.

"Do you mind?" Bertie honestly wondered.

Arthur shook his head. "Yes," he admitted, contrary and fantastically difficult, but laughed when Bertie did, with his face buried in Bertie's shoulder, until neither of them seemed so tense anymore. "I'm sorry I worried. I know… I know you will take care of me. I know you love me. I love you too. More than… more than I can say."

He was so delightfully shy about saying the words. But Arthur had no reason to apologize; Bertie's fears were the same. However, there was a time to confess, and it was not now, with Arthur so anxious. This was the time to remind his Arthur that he was not alone anymore. He was the chosen consort of a dragon, and Bertie loved him very much. Bertie would take on any burden, even if Bertie had to force Arthur to let him.

"Share your worries with me." Bertie spoke quietly, refusing to think that he was pleading. "My exceptional Arthur, it does not make you any less to tell me. My Arthur and our child." Merely saying the words made Bertie want to stretch his wings to the walls with pride.

"I want to protect you," Arthur confessed, and clung to him, his fingertips pushing into Bertie's skin. There was more he was not saying, but for now he still was not quite ready. "I *will* protect you. Both of you." He was quiet against Bertie's shoulder, but his grip tightened. "You are *mine*."

Bertie hissed with open pleasure. For now this was more than enough. His Arthur had the soul of a dragon. A soul of *fire*. "Fire begets fire," Bertie told him, knowing Arthur wouldn't yet understand that he had one less thing to worry about. Before Arthur could demand an explanation, Bertie urged him against the counter once more and stopped his mouth with a kiss.

THE SOUND of Arthur's melodious and steady voice drew Bertie up the stairs and down the hall, despite how a nap in front of the fire sounded brilliant. In an effort to be more helpful to Arthur, Bertie had offered to take on some of his errands. He hadn't realized that would mean choosing and ordering a crib, then venturing into one of those stores usually frequented by wealthy, pregnant, human women.

He had quite deliberately gone into one of the stores on Arthur's "Was Not Welcome" list. He didn't think Arthur had intended it as a vengeful hit list, but it had been thoughtful of him to prepare one for Bertie. It saved Bertie the trouble of sneaking around to determine the sources of Arthur's ever-growing concerns.

Once inside the boutique, he had rather enjoyed the stunned silence as his presence had been noticed, the very real fear that lingered at the back of every human's mind when they saw a dragon, competing with their hunger to do business with a dragon client. A dragon would have money, and Bertie was from an old line and carried himself as such.

They also weren't sure why he was there, not at first. They'd thought, perhaps, for a wife, or, quite possibly, a concubine or some other ridiculous, racist notion. Their reaction when he'd informed them he was shopping on instructions from his Arthur had been interesting. A moment of stillness, a nervous swallow, that strange, shifty glance to the side that some did when uncomfortable.

Bertie had paused too. It had been over a hundred years since the beings had revealed themselves to humans again. Long enough to learn their ways, or to remember the ways lost when the beings had hidden themselves in the first place. Certainly long enough for the humans, Western humans in particular, to lose this shyness about their own romantic hearts and sexual natures.

He'd grinned, showing teeth, knowing he had their attention, and then explained that to them. They should know their history. Of course, none of them were going to protest, not with the money he could spend in their shop. Even if it had been fifty years ago, and human attitudes and laws had been harsher, they wouldn't have interfered in a dragon's business, not openly.

But Arthur, anxious, uncertain, was another matter. Bertie had lashed his tail at the thought—somewhat close to losing his temper, he would admit now—and explained that too. Bertie was fortunate. A powerful dragon was sheltered from things that many others had not been, but the struggle of the beings was often similar to what it was for many humans. They lived in the same countries, fought the same wars, watched their human lovers die of age or illness, raised children if they wanted them, tried not to eat them if they did not. They struggled to find work, get an education, find a home, and acceptance, and love. All this in a world, in a country, where they, like many humans, were not welcomed into positions of authority and power.

It helped being an expert in the subject of the past. Bertie had been immersing himself in the First World War, the Western world both before and after beings had appeared to those bewildered, shell-shocked soldiers. He also knew the fairy tales of peasant women told for centuries before Perrault and the others had thought to write them down and change them. Bertie could, and did, tell these women what was real and what was not. By the time Bertie had gone from general history to more local history of neighboring Los Cerros, with its woods and fairy village, a small crowd had gathered. American schools, it seemed, glossed over these things or didn't bother to teach them. It made him wonder what was the point of loaning his precious things to museums if people didn't bother to go to them, or to use their minds once they were there.

Then he recalled the story that had inspired his newest book and reminded himself that even a little thing could change the world.

In the end, he'd sighed and returned to the subject of Arthur. He was hardly likely to get away with roasting and eating *all* of Arthur's enemies, so he had left the women in the shop alive, if properly shamed. Arthur was no less of a person for loving a man, no less deserving of respect than any of their other customers.

Of course, he hadn't known then that these women were not in the business of respecting every customer. He hadn't known that in addition to their prejudices, these were women who seemed to enjoy frightening every expectant parent they came across. He might have convinced them Arthur was worth cooing over, but then they had started in educating him on all the things it took to raise a child these days, all the things that could go wrong, especially with magical children, or so common "wisdom" went, and what to do then, and what he needed to buy to prevent or help with that.

It had been an exhausting nightmare. He was amazed Arthur had stopped at fire extinguishers and covers for the light sockets and a complete collection of fairy tales. The women told him he needed to childproof his home, and delightedly filled him with fears about steps they might not have taken.

He very much doubted Arthur had skipped any steps; Arthur was preparedness itself. Nonetheless, Bertie had found himself listening, wondering if humans knew these things, and if his dragon ignorance was going to get their child killed. Then he realized that Arthur had felt—been made to feel—the same insecurities.

They had insisted on recommending preschools and gym programs, and talked about early admissions. For all their cooing, they had sotto voce remarks to make about which schools unofficially kept beings off their enrollments lists and which others specialized in helping fairy and half-fairy students. There were also schools less accepting of perfectly natural nudity, different body types, and excess body hair. Werewolf children weren't adoptable, they had told him, all while hinting that they assumed he and Arthur had adopted. Pixy children were not considered adoptable either, in situations where their parents were gone, because they acted out when they were often forced by overworked teachers to choose a gender—and at a young age! Bertie had objected. Fairies might mostly feel their gender from birth, but everyone knew pixies didn't decide until they were older. But those were the facts, the simple, horrifying facts. And that was without taking into account how a child of mixed ancestry would be perceived and treated.

Then there were more schooling issues to consider. The private schools in this area that accepted beings, it seemed, were not the best. And public schools would damage the child's future career. The future career was everything, even for children.

Bertie had tried to protest—the child wasn't even hatched yet—but he had quickly been overruled. Bertie was a dragon of proud, noble lineage, and a powerful creature in his own right. One did not coo at or lecture to a being of his strength, or so he had thought, but if there had been fear in the hearts of those women in the store, it had been overridden by the desire to discuss the *business* of babies.

How the world had changed from what it must have been all those years ago.

Humans seemed to place much pressure on each other and in their future offspring. Things had to be done "right," although Bertie confessed to not understanding what exactly that meant. He had thought safety and health would be paramount, but he had been quickly informed that he should consider enrolling in schools now, if they would accept his child, and that he was lucky to live in the neighborhood he did, because that high school had a winning football team.

Football. *American* football. The "right" preschools. Child's future ruined.

Nonsense.

If Arthur had been dealing with that on a frequent basis, no wonder he had panicked and thought himself unequal to the task of raising and protecting their treasure. A baby, and a husband, and a dissertation, and a degree, were enough for any one person to worry about. Yet Arthur had likely had advice and expectations thrown at him from all directions. Bertie hadn't helped. He'd thought Arthur had only been worried about raising a dragon, and what an egg meant to their relationship. This was something else. This was fearmongering about failure and a malicious hatred of beings and their differences presenting itself as concern for them, and the one thing, the absolute one thing that Arthur feared most was failure, especially failing to protect those he cared about.

Of course Arthur had prepared such powerful magic with the books in the nursery, researched as he had. Those women had expected answers, and Arthur hadn't been ready. They had pounced and dug in their claws. They'd wanted him defeated. Their smug concern for every answer Bertie had given had almost been enough to have Bertie again considering what trouble he might get in for roasting and eating them. But visiting with Arthur and their baby while in a human prison had no appeal, and Bertie possessed knowledge they did not.

Arthur hadn't been prepared before, but he certainly was now, and determined too. Arthur was going to raise a child to change the world. Arthur had so much love to give he couldn't help but do anything else.

Knowing that, Bertie had controlled himself and left the store.

He was ready to rail about the humans in that shop the moment he walked in the house, but there was no sign of Arthur downstairs, or indeed, of any workmen, not even their truck outside. Bertie wondered if that meant they were done for good as he started a fire in the fireplace to replace the heat drained from the house by his absence. Then he heard the sounds from upstairs and forgot the very existence of the construction workers.

The sounds were coming from the child's room, which surprised him and yet didn't, because where else would Arthur be if the nursery was done? Bertie checked the study to be sure, but their egg was most certainly not where he'd left it. His face hurt with the force of his smile. Arthur must have carried it upstairs. Arthur, Bertie realized, must have wanted Bertie to be out so he could take the egg up on his own.

Bertie pictured Arthur longing to welcome the baby to the nursery yet too uncertain to want an audience, and dashed up the stairs as fast as he could without tripping over his own feet. He skidded to a silent stop in the doorway, holding his breath so as not to disturb the scene before him, but his mouth moved, shaping Arthur's name. If he had spoken, his voice would have rang out.

There was a pretty picture before him, so lovely his hands curled to hold on to it. The walls had been painted as brightly as scattered jewels—no pastels for a child of dragon and man. They'd left space for the specially ordered crib against one wall, which wouldn't match these colors now that Bertie thought of it, but he did not think Arthur would mind. Bookshelves lined the walls, many of them empty, though Bertie and Arthur and the rest of the family would remedy that soon. The curtains over the wide window were drawn back to reveal a splendid view of the yard. Arthur sat on the fat, padded bench amid far too many pillows, with his back to the wall and his legs crossed. The egg was on a purple cushion in front of him.

Arthur was bent over the book opened across his lap, and he was reading aloud. Bertie recognized both the words and the book after a few moments. It was Lang's *The Yellow Fairy Book* and the story was "Fairer-Than-a-Fairy," which seemed more a warning about ensuring their child had a name that would offend no fairies than anything else. Perhaps Arthur had been worrying about that too, or perhaps he had been here reading for hours and come to that story by chance.

"FAIRER-THAN-A-FAIRY" DEFIED the curse of the jealous fairy Lagree and married Prince Rainbow before Arthur took a moment to clear his throat and catch his breath. He angled his head toward the egg and dropped his voice to a whisper. "Enough for today?" he asked, and it took Bertie a stunned moment to comprehend that Arthur was asking that question of their near-born.

Bertie could hold still no longer. Arthur raised his head quickly when Bertie moved forward, but Bertie crossed the room without a word, kicked off his shoes, and climbed onto the bench seat, where he lay down with his body curled around the egg. He nestled his head into Arthur's lap, displacing the book. Arthur lifted it out of the way and stared at him. He blushed as bright as an apple.

Bertie's tone was warmer than he meant it to be. "Go on, pet." When he reached up, Arthur's face was burning hot to the touch, like he had fires inside, which he did, although not as Bertie did. "I have been waiting for this moment." Bertie thought it safe to confess now that it had happened.

"Have fun at the store?" Arthur pulled his bottom lip into his mouth for a moment but didn't bite it.

Bertie shrugged at him. "It seems other parents have all the answers, or like to pretend that they do." He didn't know what else to say. He had no doctorate in humans. Perhaps they drove each other to terror out of love. If he had known Arthur had faced this whenever he inquired about a baby, he might have stepped in sooner. "They might think they know about schools and tutoring programs, but we know other things, and surely that is useful too. Can they list all of Henry VIII's wives and several of his mistresses?" Bertie demanded archly. "I think not."

Arthur wrinkled his nose and sighed. The line of distress appeared between his eyes, then vanished. "I don't feel like I know enough. I feel like I should know everything. I feel like they all think—" He cut himself off with a look at the egg, and then he whispered, *whispered*, at Bertie as though he was considering the child's feelings and did not want her to hear. "I'm not the mom," Arthur blurted in a hushed voice, and Bertie spent a long, uncertain minute staring and blinking at him. Then he stared and blinked some more.

"I'm afraid you've lost me," Bertie admitted at last, and Arthur put the book down.

"People put pressures on parents, Bertie. Especially mothers. They… they think I'm the mother and I'm not. I'm a man. But even if I *was* the mother, I wouldn't know the things they expect me to know. But the thing is, I'm not, Bertie. All I can do is give it this room, these books, my voice." Arthur fretted with his clothes, then Bertie's hair. "You should have, I don't know, found that willing female you once talked about, someone who knows what they're doing if you want to raise a child. I… don't. I can't be what it deserves, what it needs with the world so—" For probably the second time in his life Arthur had admitted to failure, but Bertie felt himself grinning and relaxing against Arthur's thigh. Arthur did not seem to notice that, for all his denials, he'd stopped pulling at Bertie's hair in agitation and was now smoothing his hand over the shell, feeling the heat, seeking out the heartbeat. Bertie could tell when he found it because his mouth softened. "I'm not the mother," Arthur finished, seemingly unaware of the regret in his tone. "I don't know what I am. Nervous babysitter, I guess."

Bertie wriggled up to get a better angle to look at him. *Finally* Arthur had spoken, only to reveal that he was worried about being good enough. Ages ago, years ago, when they hadn't known each other well, Bertie had said a few words on the subject of children, and Arthur had been stewing over that sentence since then.

Bertie tried to remember his long-forgotten comment on how these things were usually done. But all he could think was how Arthur was still uncertain about his role in creating the egg and equally anxious that he wouldn't be prepared enough should something go wrong. He was, perhaps, also upset about people automatically thinking of him in the mother role. That was another human thing, the assumption that two partners had roles, and that one role was weaker, which was the one they deemed feminine. Bertie couldn't do much about Arthur's other concerns, seeing as he had them himself regarding his own parenting abilities, but he could take care of that last one.

"Not the mother?" Bertie echoed in disbelief. "Of course you are. A dragon mother rules the house, and you know as well as I do that what you say goes." He reassured Arthur in the firmest voice he could muster and gave him an upside-down pat for good measure. Arthur frowned at him, though his mouth stayed soft with revelation and his fingers were stroking circles against the egg's shell. Bertie continued, "I am not sure what your exact worry is here, my pearl, but even if you weren't the child's mother, you would still be the father. Surely that is obvious." Bertie shut his eyes, content. "Fire for fire. A pearl for a pearl."

Arthur made a noise that seemed frustrated, but he released a long breath. "Those women, Bertie." He paused, perhaps gathering his thoughts. Bertie paused as well, more for the subject change than for any concern about his Arthur's loyalty to their child. Their child was once in a lifetime magic, and Arthur was a once in a lifetime boy. But when the silence went on, Bertie made an encouraging noise so Arthur would continue. "You said, then, when you said you wanted children. You said hatchling*s*. As if you wanted many. More than one."

"Oh." Bertie hummed. "So I did. And I meant it. But I'm not certain this is a situation that will repeat itself. What happened wasn't under my conscious control. The circumstances were—"

"Rare," Arthur interrupted. "I remember what you said. But, those women… do you think it was true, what *they* said?"

Bertie wanted to say absolutely not. But with what he knew of humans, every horrible word was most likely true, or true enough. He patted Arthur for mutual comfort. "If it is, then we shall do something about it, won't we?"

"That's what I mean." He hadn't heard Arthur sound so tremulous in a long time. But then he was a knight again, a gloriously brave peasant boy in a suit of armor. His voice became steel. "I want to do something about it. Schools that mistreat their children, parents that abandon their own children, human or being, for being different. Those werewolves and pixies unadopted and misunderstood. You don't know, but, but it's terrible to be alone."

Bertie inhaled sharply as he understood what Arthur was not yet quite willing to say aloud. But he would. In time, with this child secure, Arthur was going to turn to Bertie and ask him to grow their family, to fill rooms that for now held books and dust, and put children, and perhaps teenagers in them. He was going to look over each and every one of those schools and denounce them. And the world would listen, because Arthur was truly exceptional, and because he had a dragon, and a dragon's fortune, behind him.

Change was coming, and perhaps trouble too, but Bertie could not make himself care. He took a long, long breath, drawing in air to feed the fire in his heart.

When he thought he could speak again, Bertie curled closer to his pet. "A houseful of hatchlings sounds wonderful," he agreed simply. He allowed none of his trepidation to show.

"A houseful?" Arthur let out a tiny, panicked laugh, but ran his fingers through Bertie's hair, as if Bertie needed the soothing. Bertie did, but after a few moments of being caressed he realized it was Arthur who needed it more. "You think I could… what if I… I'm a disappointment? Bertie, you—"

A trail of gray smoke coiled up into the air between them when Bertie cut him off with an angry huff. "You could never disappoint me." He would not allow this misconception to go on. "Never, Arthur. Do you understand? Even when you suggested I found a female dragon behind your back. Even in this room where I can feel you transferring your love from me, I am only proud of you. You are precisely the giving, loving boy I first met. How could I not be proud of you?"

A very strange sound left Arthur's mouth, something between a quiet roar of outrage and a confused squawk. He tightened his fingers in Bertie's hair and tugged until Bertie made eye contact.

"Transferring my love from you?" Arthur repeated, a warning in his tone Bertie had heard only a few times, and never once aimed at him. He opened his mouth although he had no argument at the ready. Arthur stared at him for another long moment, and then something in his posture eased. "I see," he added, in a much softer voice. "You have been worrying too, this whole time, and you never thought to tell me."

He smoothed Bertie's hair from his face and then heaved a breath. "You forgot some human biology, you know," he said, and gave Bertie a look so much like the one he had the first time he had pulled Bertie to him for a kiss that Bertie felt his fire grow hotter. Arthur's touch was impossibly cool on his skin, but it made him burn all the more. "My heart is only so big." Arthur paused to hold up his fist, then gave Bertie a smile. "But it's limitless. I love you so much it hurt when you weren't here. I knew you were coming back and I still ached. It was in my bones. Sometimes you sit with me like this, like any other night with a book or the TV on, and yet I think I won't be able to breathe with what I feel for you."

Arthur ducked his head and glanced away as if embarrassed, but he swept his fingers through Bertie's hair once and then again.

"I am sorry," Bertie answered him at last, when he had tamped down on the conflagration in his chest enough to speak as a man.

"You are both mine," Arthur insisted, fierce and lovely and hushed. "I will do anything for you."

"I am sorry," Bertie told him again, a touch breathlessly this time. "A dragon is allowed some insecurities."

"Hide how you walk down the stairs all you want, but don't think that, okay?" Arthur swept his fingertips over Bertie's lips and made a satisfied noise when Bertie wriggled closer to him. "Don't think I don't love you as much as I—" He dropped his voice. "—as I did from the first time I woke up on your couch and found you'd tucked me in."

Bertie shivered. "That was all it took?" It seemed such a simple thing until he remembered Arthur's life before they'd met. A kind, thoughtful act in a sometimes harsh world was all Arthur had needed to fall in love. He deserved so much more, and Bertie intended to keep giving it to him, and anyone else so deprived.

He turned to kiss Arthur's knee and slide his hand up Arthur's pant leg to feel the warm skin of his ankle. "My pearl," he praised him before settling back with his head in Arthur's lap and his gaze on Arthur's upside-down face. He pulled Arthur's hand from his hair, kissed his fingers, and placed them over their egg, which was enough to focus on for now. He prodded at the abandoned book. "Now go on, Arthur, please, so she can love the sound of your voice as much as I do."

There was another noise from Arthur, who then gave a jolt so strong that Bertie opened his eyes again. "She?" Arthur demanded and appeared highly displeased with him. Bertie stared back, but this time Arthur's faith in magic held, and he did not ask how Bertie knew. He merely repeated it. "*She*," Arthur murmured, shocked, and began a slow smile, the kind of smile that spoke of his dreams, the visions he would not admit were visions, where he must have also seen a beautiful, fiery hatchling with a feminine soul. Bertie wondered if he'd seen a dragon, or a human, or something else.

After a few moments, Arthur picked up the book again to tread lightly through "The Three Brothers," as though they didn't have a daughter, as though Arthur hadn't asked him for a hoard of children in their home.

The world seemed a brand-new place, dangerous and beautiful and rich with hope.

Bertie shut his eyes once more, happy to fall asleep next to Arthur in the nest Arthur had made, even happier to know that he would wake up next to Arthur with their child between them.

He was wide awake in the next second, fully conscious and terrified at the tiny but distinctly audible snap of a shell being broken from the inside.

Being a police detective is hard. Add the complication of being a werewolf subject to human prejudice, and you might say Ray Branigan has his work cut out for him. He's hot on the trail of a killer when he realizes he needs help.

Enter Cal Parker, the beautiful half-fairy Ray's secretly been in love with for years—secretly, because while werewolves mate for life, fairies… don't. Ray needs Cal's expertise, but it isn't easy to concentrate with his mate walking around half-naked trying to publicly seduce him. By the time Ray identifies the killer—and sorts out a few prejudices of his own—it may be too late for Cal.

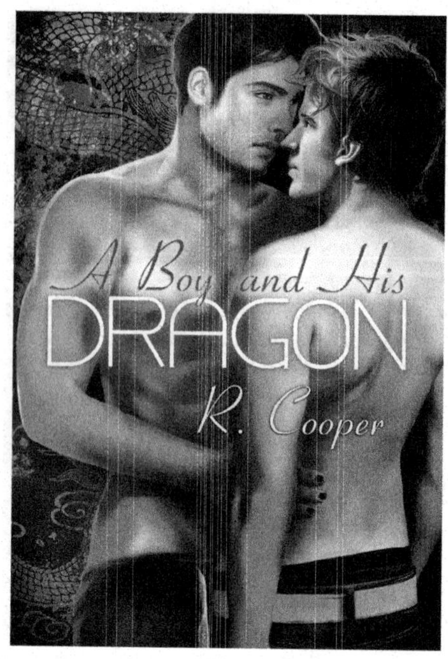

Arthur MacArthur needs a job, and not just for the money. Before he dropped out of school to support his younger sister, he loved being a research assistant at the university. But working for a dragon, one of the rarest and least understood magical beings, has unforeseen complications. While Arthur may be the only applicant who isn't afraid of Philbert Jones in his dragon form, the instant attraction he feels for his new employer is beyond disconcerting.

Bertie is a brilliant historian, but he can't find his own notes without help—his house is a hoard of books and antiques, hence the need for an assistant. Setting the mess to rights is a dream come true for Arthur, who once aspired to be an archivist. But making sense of Bertie's interest in him is another matter. After all, dragons collect treasure, and Arthur is anything but extraordinary.

Zeki Janowitz has returned to his hometown of Wolf's Paw to start his wizarding career. Unfortunately, Wolf's Paw, a werewolf refuge, follows centuries of tradition and shuns human magic and a very human Zeki. He knows he's in for a struggle, but a part of him has always belonged in the mountain town, or rather belonged to Theo Greenleaf. Years away at school haven't lessened Zeki's crush on the quiet werewolf. When town gossip informs him Theo still suffers from his mate's rejection and does not date, it does little to ease Zeki's embarrassing feelings. He decides now's the time to get the man he's always wanted.

Werewolves usually don't recover from losing their mates, and Theo barely pulled through by focusing on his love of baking. It's a daily struggle, and Zeki's return to Wolf's Paw shatters his peace. Theo doesn't know what to think when Zeki attempts to woo him, talking about his wizarding business and settling in town for good. It's like Zeki doesn't have a clue how his words years before left Theo a shell of a werewolf.

Beginners in love, Theo and Zeki must seduce each other with a bit of heavenly baking and magic.

On the run from his old-blood werewolf family, Tim Dirus finds himself in Wolf's Paw, one of the last surviving refuges from the days when werewolves were hunted by humans and one of the last places Tim wants to be. Kept away from other wolves by his uncle, Tim knows almost nothing about his own kind except that alpha werewolves only want to control and dominate a scrawny wolf like him.

Tim isn't in Wolf's Paw an hour before he draws the attention of Sheriff Nathaniel Neri, the alphaest alpha in a town full of alphas. Powerful, intimidating, and the most beautiful wolf Tim has ever seen, Nathaniel makes Tim feel safe for reasons Tim doesn't understand. For five years he's lived on the run, in fear of his family and other wolves. Everything about Wolf's Paw is contrary to what he thought he knew, and he is terrified. Fearing his mate will run, Sheriff Nathaniel must calm his little wolf and show him he's more than a match for this big, bad alpha.

R. COOPER has been making up stories since she was a wee R. Cooper. She has a weakness for strong-minded characters doing unspeakably hot things to each other and thinks margaritas are perfectly lovely. If she listed all of her turn-ons, it would take up this whole bio, but they include smart people, tailored suits with serious ties, shoulder holsters, funny people, sacrifices made for love, power struggles, the walking wounded, bravery, and good old-fashioned shameless sluts.

She also can be found frequently crying over pretty actors on her Tumblr. She'd question her life choices more, but every time she tries, she gets distracted by all the shiny love stories begging to be written. Mostly she just wants people to be happy. And pie. Pie is great.

E-mail: RisCoops@gmail.com

Website: r-cooper.livejournal.com

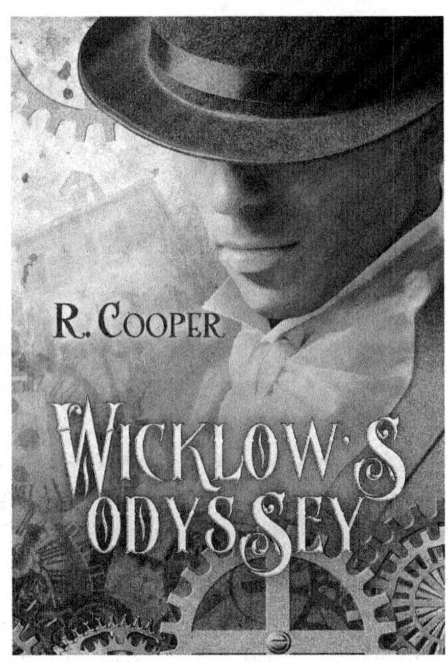

Union soldier Wicklow Doyle is infiltrating enemy lines to set up new radio communications technology in Confederate-held Charleston when his location is betrayed. After sacrificing himself to get his team to safety, he's on the lam, friendless in a hostile town. Determining who betrayed him without discovery by Confederate soldiers is dangerous, but Wicklow grew up in the slums of New York and knows how to handle himself. He isn't expecting anyone on his team to return to help him, much less Alexander Rhoades.

An effete dandy of great intelligence and conviction, Alexander Rhoades speaks through stories instead of giving orders, and he has earned the confidence of the rich and powerful. While Wicklow has come not to trust men with those traits, Rhoades has never once let him down. He looks at Wicklow in ways that make him burn beneath his skin and tells him stories of love and bravery Wicklow yearns to understand. Wicklow has absolute faith Rhoades's brilliant mind will uncover the traitor in their midst and find them a way out of the city. But when Rhoades tells him he's not alone, Wicklow isn't sure he can believe him. For the first time in his life, though, he wants to.

Let There
Be Light
R. COOPER

MEDIUM,
Sweet,
EXTRA SHOT OF
GEEK
R. COOPER

Play It
Again,
Charlie
R. COOPER

A
WEALTH OF
UNSAID WORDS
R. COOPER

CPSIA information can be obtained
at www.ICGtesting.com
Printed in the USA
FSOW03n1245051216
28186FS

9 781634 764025